This is a war novel. It is the story of an officer in the Brigade of Guards; his training; his affairs of the heart; his grim fighting and wounds in the Italian campaign; and his return to peace-time soldiering

# Noble Purpose

*by*

## Sacha Carnegie

London : Peter Davies

*First Published 1954*

*Made and printed in Great Britain for Peter Davies Ltd*
*by William Clowes and Sons, Limited, London and Beccles*

TO ALL THOSE, WHATEVER THEIR RANK,
WITH WHOM I HAD THE SIGNAL HONOUR
TO SERVE FROM 1940 TO 1952

*Countess :* ... Towards Florence, is he ?
*2nd Gentleman :* Ay, Madam.
*Countess :* And to be a soldier ?
*2nd Gentleman :* Such is his noble purpose ...

        *All's Well that Ends Well*

# Contents

|                          | PAGE |
|--------------------------|------|
| PROLOGUE : FRONT LINE    | 13   |
| PREPARATION              | 25   |
| INTO ACTION              | 95   |
| HOME AGAIN               | 215  |

# PROLOGUE: FRONT LINE

## Prologue : Front Line

THE man staggered against the force of the wind; a bitter wind filled with sleet that blew down from the mountains. Mountains which towered invisible about that miserable little hill and from among whose grey, rain-lashed rocks hostile eyes would look down when dawn came. He struggled slowly through the mud, shapeless and heavy in stiff sodden greatcoat beneath the iron-hard equipment. Twice he stopped to look into broken trenches, once he leant close and spoke to the pale blur of faces, then went on, swaying in the fierce gusts of wind, until at length he reached the shattered farm-house and came thankfully out of the wind. Some huddled shapes were crouched along the wall. The nearest one spoke.

"That you, sir?"

"Yes. Everything all right?"

"As right as it could be. Wasn't expecting anything quite like this."

"Nor was I, Sergeant Thomas. Uncomfortable, isn't it?"

The sergeant grunted.

"Makes all those schemes and exercises seem a bit stupid really. Attack, this, attack that. I mean where's it got us? Stuck in this stinking mud. What'll happen in the morning, that's what I'm wondering."

"I'm wondering a bit myself. Come on, we'll have a look round, then get down to s-some digging, better than shivering on our b-backsides."

Unwillingly the sergeant left the shelter and followed the officer into the howling darkness. As they went on their tour of inspection the officer thought back to the corporal from whom he had taken over those long hours before.

"'oo the flickin' 'ell are you? Ah, thank Christ you've arrived. I'll take you up the 'ill. Corporal Baker, 2nd — Thank 'eaven you're 'ere. It's bloody murder 'ere. Eight of

13

us left, nowhere to dig for dead 'uns. Shells, nothing but bastard shells all the time, can't put yer 'ead above ground in
day time." A little corporal, face deeply shadowed with
fatigue, speech bordering on hysteria, hands shaking. So this
is what war does to a man.

"Are there no officers?"

"There was one, from the Gordons, didn't 'ave time to
find out 'is name. 'E's in 'ere somewhere." He kicked at the
mud. The hand over had been quick and sketchy. "Jerry—
over there." He pointed into the northern twilight. "Mountains. Flickin' great mountains and 'e's on top—can see
everything, fifteen men killed, blown to bits." His voice was
crescendo to match the wind.

"No use digging—fill with water. Farm-'ouse 'ere—
you'll 'ave to dig, don't let 'im catch you in the open." They
were in shelter and round them crouched his eight men, close
packed like sheep, waiting apathetic for their impending
release. The officer could not see their faces for which he was
glad.

"Where are your sentries?"

"Sentries!" The corporal spat. "These men 'ave 'ad it!
I've 'ad it! You'll 'ave 'ad it after a week 'ere." His voice was
vicious. The other felt that he should object to the tone, but
somehow it seemed hardly the time nor place. For a moment
they stood silent, round them water dripped and splashed
from the jagged ruins, the smell of putrefaction was overpowering. In some strange fashion the officer felt secure
because he had beside him this little frightened man, who,
for all his fear and disgust, knew some of the answers; to
whom he could turn for guidance. But soon the corporal would
gather together his men and disappear into the valley below,
and then he would be alone.

You may sometimes have been left in sole charge of an
unfamiliar job.

'Sorry, old man, must be off now. Give me a ring if anything crops up—well, so long.'

But there, in that lonely storm-filled blackness there would
be no one to ask, no telephone to ring. He began to ask frantic
questions. What could one do if . . . ? Was there any wire?

The nearest German position? Did their patrols . . . ? The corporal no longer listened, for him that hell-hole would be but a memory and he did not want to tempt Fate by remaining a moment longer. Calling together his party he slopped away down the track with the tattered evil-smelling scarecrows, with never a word of farewell or good luck.

Thirty-two men waited for orders, and the officer did not even know the time. He stood irresolute and appalled while the water trickled down his back and his mind emptied itself of coherent thought. How to begin? What to do? For three long years he had been preparing for this moment, since that proud day when first he had glanced surreptitiously at the single star of newly commissioned rank. Preparing for war, for glory. But this surely was not real war? Where were the attacking battalions, the monstrous anger of the guns, liberated cities, flowers, wine? The wild excitement of a bayonet charge and droves of grey-clad figures with hands raised high in surrender, the gleaming cross upon his breast. That was war. Not the wind tearing at his clothes, the raging darkness of utter confusion, the all-pervading stench of wet death.

"What shall I get the men on to, sir?"

Sergeant Thomas, that magnificent man, his voice as steady and untroubled as if on his beloved parade-ground.

"Get them into s-some sort of shelter whilst I have a look round." So he had a look round, but saw nothing as he floundered about, tripping and sprawling in the icy morass, brain and body numbed, and so at last he had reached the shelter of the wall.

"One section here. Yours here, Corporal Hughes, and get them digging." Words shouted to overcome the wind. So many times had he said just those same words on so many of those fruitless, boring exercises on Salisbury Plain, on Exmoor, on the Yorkshire Wolds.

They dug and searched for any scrap of cover; as they dug so the water filled their feverish efforts and they dug again, cursing the storm which battered them. The officer plunged from trench to trench, encouraging men he could not see, stumbling on wood, metal and pulpy things. Appalled, exhausted and utterly amazed by the total lack of war-like sounds, for there was nothing save the occasional 'clink' of a shovel to show that men were abroad on such a night. Not a gun had fired. No flares had lit up the dismal scene. There was only the smell to remind him that they were at last in the front line. At length they gave up the search for perfection in their shelters and sank wearily into soaking clay coffins where they eked out the remainder of the night listening to the wind that rushed moaning above them. The officer, as befitted his exalted position, had a waterlogged hole to himself where he lay curled as though in a womb, legs cut off at the knees by icy water. His teeth, if once he unclamped his jaws, chattered loudly, and his body shook all over.

Then, slowly as if unwilling to uncover the horror of that hill, the dawn crept furtively over the mountains, a freezing mist-enshrouded dawn, dirty and grey-speckled with sleet. A stronger light filtered through the tangle of branches and groundsheets that made up the pathetic roof of his trench. In a few moments he would have to climb out and stumble round the position, look into the haggard faces. He felt ghastly ill with griping pains in his stomach that contracted and twisted his bowels. Inside him somewhere a small nagging voice urged him on. 'Go on, it's up to you. You are responsible for the lives of thirty-two men. Get up and take a grip on yourself! Make decisions!' Decisions! He stood, limp and useless, arms down-stretched, back bent, knees shuddering with the bitter chill that was in his bones, and as he stood thus gazing miserably at the mist which curled in the hollows and writhed as though imprisoned by the wire, feeling in his nostrils the honey-sweet smell of death, he wondered how anyone could expect decisions from him. He forced himself to go forward and to look about him with professional eye. Dig here. Wire there. Arcs of fire. Vague memories of old textbooks filtered into his mind. At Sandhurst a supercilious young instructor had once spoken reprovingly to him for digging a trench too shallow—or too deep.

"You've got to understand," he had drawled, "that I am not telling you these things for my own amusement. In the book it says clearly that the parapet must be . . ." He had

16

drawled on from beneath his toothbrush moustache, his beautiful service-dress fashionably waisted. In the book! Was this abattoir catered for in the book? This churned-up graveyard, waterlogged and decaying, did such a situation feature in the book?

Visibility was practically nil, and he could not see the mountains where the Germans lurked. Legendary robots conquering the world; tiny running figures balanced on the sights of a rifle. Close-quarter fighting, cold steel piercing the cringing belly. Attack! Attack! Learn to be aggressive. Hit him where it hurts and hit him again. Give the Boche a bloody nose! Pile on the stock phrases. Blood and guts. What after all was war without blood and white bandages and soothing hands? Those stinking bundles could never have contained blood nor felt the touch of soft sympathetic hands. That maggot-writhing lump of flesh could never surely have performed the ecstatic act of copulation.

He went round the platoon.

"Nice morning, Oliver."

"Eggs and bacon today, Corporal Nisbett. Crisp for me."

"Tidy little place you've got there, McLeod."

Dig. Improve the field of fire. Breakfast. Shaving. Plenty of water, eh? Guardsmen always shave.

"Use your bath-water, McRae." The black muck swirling round your knees. Ha! Ha! All around lay the dead who smiled with decaying lips to hear such foolishness. When the men had begun to stir and the air was alive with familiar invective and little fires were striving smokily against the wet, then he went to investigate the hill.

Monte Natale. The most western tip of a line which stretched from the sea on their left to the gates of Leningrad. A pimple of mud, shown on few maps, covered in torn, mangled tree-stumps cut low down as if by blunted axes, shell-holes lip-to-lip, abrim with rusty water. Broken weapons, rotting equipment, sodden clothing and everywhere the pulpy paper of a battlefield. Love-letters, newspapers, coloured comics. Socks, a ragged blue cardigan. Clinging to the surface of the mud. What soldier has not felt impelled to describe the mud of war? Knee-deep; thigh-deep and blackish grey. A

17

glutinous quagmire in which lies buried every type of debris.
Where scraps of human flesh lie undiscovered and unmourned
side-by-side with metal, wood and cloth. What he looked upon
was complete and utter desolation. Not of the lonely shore,
nor the darkening moor, but rather of the dung-heap. The
Lords of Creation had squabbled over that patch of suffering
earth and had left behind them, as pretty examples of their
handiwork, the rust, the filth and above all the dead which lay
unburied and partially buried. God alone knew how many
more lay deep in the mud. They lacked form or shape, they
lacked dignity. Some had died face down, some stared sightless at the sky, and drizzle fell softly down their gaping
throats. Some had been scattered piecemeal by the untidy
butchery of shell-fire; a single arm pointed stiffly from a
twisted tree—a signpost to eternity. A single head, green
and squashed like a burst melon, grinned at him from a shell-
hole. The weather in such circumstances is a great leveller,
and they all looked the same, yet among them were German,
American, British; khaki and field-grey sharing once more
the common grave. He felt, as he stood among so much
slaughter, no revulsion, no horror, no twinge of pity. He was
merely astonished that such disgusting objects could ever
have breathed and spoken and laughed, told funny stories,
made love. Look closely at death, learn his secrets, become
familiar with his finished products that you may gradually
replace awe by an armour of unconcern. So he forced himself
to peer at the German who hung in the wire, feigning insensi-
bility to the nauseous odour, making himself gaze deep into
the maggot-filled sockets where once his blue Nordic eyes
had smiled. He had come a long way that German soldier to
die hanging on the rusty tendrils of wire, his helmet lying
filled with brains and water. To die alone on a blood-soaked
Italian hill with no Last Post nor funeral volleys, no red-eyed
family. He, like thousands more, died alone in the midst of
muck and fear, to hang like a straw dummy till his bones were
white and rattling in the wind! For England! For the Reich!
For Mother Russia! For this flag, for that creed, for his
country, his family, himself? What did it matter to such as he,
the dead? The crawling things which make their money from

armaments had wished to wax fatter so he, that unknown German, and he the unknown British soldier half-buried close beside had died and in the moment of their dying had lost even their human dignity.

Daylight proper had come and the mist, paler now, less ghostly, brushed lightly over the hill. The officer stood at the spot from which he had watched the departure of the corporal. What had seemed in the darkness to be only a wall now stood revealed as the side of a building, bullet- and splinter-pitted, from which blackened beams pointed to the sky. A shutter swung loose in the breeze, and a torn curtain flapped dismally. He stepped through the doorway and saw the mist as it stirred in the corners and rose languorously through the gaping roof. A voice behind him exclaimed.

"Worse than the Gorbals, sir." McPhee wrinkled his long nose in disgust.

"Reminds me of that night we cleaned up the tube station. Looks much the same really, doesn't it? Useless, I'd call it." Pathetic remains of pathetic belongings, furniture, mattresses oozing straw, wine flasks, a headless image of the Virgin and a picture of Il Duce, mud-smeared across the jutting jaw. Clothes and a black felt hat floating in the oily water which covered the floor. A plywood cupboard yawned and inside there hung a gay flowered frock. Bully beef tins—ubiquitous relics of the British Army; a china cup untouched on the table; crude charcoal sketches of human mating on the one remaining patch of plaster; a Spandau charged with rusted bullets; squelchy sandbags. Then of course there were the central characters to that scene: the man, the woman, the child and the dog. McPhee, prying about for loot, trod heavily on the man who ejected a geyser-jet of water from his dough face, horrible gaseous murmurings from his swollen stomach. In the oven was crammed the dog, its tail dripping brown. There were many other things which some short days before had been useful and cheerful and alive, but then war came and created the still-life of a totally dead landscape, extinguishing life in the very beams and stones themselves. And the peasants who floated in the oily scum? It had not been their war, they did not care whether their killers wore khaki or grey,

19

spoke English or German. Doubtless they had protested to their God and asked to be left in peace to scrape the stony soil, but He had not listened and now their minute speck of earth had become a charnel house. In time the war would move on, scorching and destroying haphazardly, leaving one more monument to the childish stupidity of man. To smash to ruins other farms, to churn other fields into jelly, spreading across the land the ugly futile smear of destruction.

The officer and the guardsman turned away, and for once the latter seemed subdued.

"Do the people who—well, who arrange wars, do they see all this kind of thing, sir?"

"Probably not." He did not feel like embarking on conversation.

"Is this what we're put into the world for?" McPhee persisted. "What I mean is, sir, the whole thing's a waste of—"

"Quite, McPhee. Nip over and get Sergeant Thomas, would you?" It was no moment for theological musings.

All that day while the mist was thick, they tried to clean Natale. They covered the worst remains, gathered together the sopping fragments and cast them into a communal pit, repaired the wire, made small rough crosses, up-ended rifles with helmets on the butts. Buried the family. Drained their trenches and made roofs from gas-capes and debris. Many of the men were sickened by what they saw and handled, there was little talking, no laughter, and Sergeant Thomas swore continuously in an undertone. Towards evening the wind blew up from the sea and drove rain before it in lashing torrents. The mist was defeated and evaporated into wispy streamers, and for the first time they saw the mountains, rising grey and ominous, cutting through the racing clouds like the iron-clad bows of ships.

"Take a good look at the bastards, lads, we're goin' to hate their guts before we're through," advised Russell mournfully. It took exactly ten pints of beer to make Russell less mournful.

Just before sunset the wind dropped again and a watery sun appeared low over the rim of the sea. Cheered and knowing all about war they crawled out of the ground and stood in groups on the steaming earth looking across the farm-dotted valley to where their enemy lay. Nothing stirred, no sound save the drip of water and almost a faint sigh as the ground exhaled its wetness. Then laughter rang out. They felt veterans who had gazed upon unbelievable horror and had not quailed, who had been together for years and were friends. Besides, how warm the sun was, how pretty the tumbling sea, the backcloth mountains. Soon food would be on its way, and rum, and then sleep in renovated dwellings. The officer looked round the cheerful faces, listened to the ribald jokes and felt proud of his responsibility. In a moment he would wander down the track to Company Headquarters and chat with David. He stretched and yawned and rubbed his hand across a stubbly chin. There might be water there for a shave, to wash away a little of that stinking mud. . . . Far beyond the mountains there was the 'thud' of an explosion, then another and another, till they merged into a continuous rumble.

"Guns!" At last he was hearing the sound of the guns. Incidental music of war that tightens the muscles and turns the bowels to water. With a whine the first shells passed high overhead to burst on the village below. Wink! Wink! Wink! Puffs of black and brown among the remains of pink-walled houses. Now and again a stab of orange flame as the shell-bursts reverberated from the mountain-sides like huge drum rolls. The watchers grew excited and laid bets on the church tower; they were very ignorant and also there was a new feeling abroad. This was more what they expected.

"Christ, right on it. That's fifty lire you owe me, McAlpine."

"Och, away wi' yer, man. 'Twas luck, they'll no do it again."

But they did, twice, and the dust lifted slowly from a sawn-off ruin. Providence watched the sport for a while then grew weary of such foolery and gave the German gunners new ideas.

McLeod '08, not to be confused with McLeods '72 or '66 who were big, slow-speaking Lewis men, was a small dark man of lugubrious appearance. His mucker Reed was fat, fair and cherubic with ill-fitting false teeth. In the platoon they were known variously as Laurel and Hardy or Playmates. They were walking towards Platoon Headquarters where dance music was crackling from the wireless set, when a single gun fired. Hardy had made one of his jokes, and some of the men were laughing, if not at the joke, at his fat comical face. The approach of the shell rose to a vicious screech which brushed their necks as they flung themselves into the sheltering mud. It burst with a curiously muffled sound, debris pattered down, and as the cordite smoke drifted away they heard a sound that was unfamiliar to them; the strangled 'A . . . a . . . ah' of a mortally wounded man. The officer ran across to where Hardy lay on his back with, where his face had been, a shredded crimson mess, bubbling as he breathed. Close beside him tearing frantically at a field-dressing was his friend. "Jesus," he muttered, again and again.

Hardy died and lay feebly twitching; his teeth lying smashed in the blood-soaked ground. Laurel continued to kneel beside him talking softly in Gaelic, and from the wireless came the sound of a saxophone wailing. They had time to place a sandbag over the mutilated head and the gun fired again, this time with other guns. From that moment the hill became a mighty up-rushing fountain of mud and fragments. Among the shuddering crash of the explosions, the tall black plumes of mud—as the garbage heap flung high its contents —and the singing splinters, they crawled to the meagre safety of their trenches. For two hours the shells pounded that little hill from three directions, till the brains were numb and the ground was full of crouching, cringing animal creatures which winced and shook involuntarily, except for McPhee who slept, his knees pressed firmly into his officer's ribs. The latter huddled low and wondered, while outside the night was filled with rushing dervish sounds as great jagged lumps of steel hummed and whirred above the gas-cape roof. Counterattack? Germans approaching close under cover of bombardment to run in swiftly and finish off the stunned survivors? How many men were already casualties? A splinter buried itself with a 'thomp' in the wall of the trench, earth trickled down his neck. His legs were shaking. Surely commissioned legs should not shake? His mouth was as dry as dust. Two shells exploded on the very lip of the trench with a thunderclap of sound, he choked from the acrid fumes and shook his head which sang and throbbed. Sometimes he could make out the distant 'thud, thud' of the guns, time to count five and then the world went crazy. At the end of the first hour he found himself praying aloud for even a moment's respite. McPhee, a confirmed atheist, muttered drowsily: "I doubt that'll do no good, sir," and went to sleep again.

Then quite suddenly the storm abated, and from all around he could hear men stirring, calling to each other. Unwillingly he forced himself into the open where the reek of explosive was hanging heavy, and made his way round the position, scattering empty words of encouragement, striving to overcome the shaking of his limbs. There were no casualties except one Bren-gun which lay twisted and useless. Only Big Smith seemed perturbed. When addressed he answered in the high-pitched voice of hysteria, child-like he asked for comfort.

"Is it over, sir? There won't be any more, will there? We won't all be killed."

An officer's uniform and one is supposed to know the answers of God. His trench-mate, Laurie, with the squint, tried to soothe him.

"It's a' right, Davie boy. You're safe enough in here, besides Jerry's awa' hame to his bed."

One wasn't. He had stayed up to fire a last shell, and the officer, his mind occupied with many things, did not notice the approach until too late. He saw a vivid yellow flash and at the same moment felt himself lifted and thrown on his back by an irresistible force. There was no pain, but his right hand was numb, his legs were warm and wet, his mouth and eyes were filled with mud. He sat up and cursed, using language he was surprised to know and shouting for Sergeant Thomas.

"Look after things till I'm back—won't be long—just get patched up. McPhee! McPHEE! Where the devil's McPhee? Ah, there you are. Give me a hand down to the R.A.P."

David was asleep at Company Headquarters. He was sympathetic but sleepy.

"No idea all that stuff was falling on you; sounded like the village. I'll go up and see them, look in on your way back anyway." But he did not look in, for he did not come back, not for two months.

At the Aid Post the doctor rolled off his camp-bed and inspected the damage, using a regrettably sharp instrument.

"Lucky devil, it's hospital for you."

"Hospital! B-but . . ." A stab of pain ran up his thigh, the hand had begun to throb. Suddenly he felt incredibly tired. He said no more.

So he said good-bye to McPhee and felt the stretcher being lifted on to the jeep. As they drove across the Garigliano he could see shells bursting on Natale; twisting on the stretcher he could see the twinkling flashes of what was now a spectacle, then they turned a corner and he lay back on the jolting canvas. He was bitterly cold beneath the blankets, and the wounds hurt fiercely at every bump.

In the Clearing Station they put him down in the corner of a whitewashed room that might once have been a kitchen. He seemed to lie for hours until at length an orderly came and stuck a needle in his arm; another one gave him two monstrous sulpha pills and tied a label to his jacket. Gradually the morphia took effect, and though conscious he reached the glorious stage of not caring about pain, fear or in fact anything. In a wonderful dreamy haze he felt the stretcher rise into the air and float across the room, through the blanket-hung doorway, out from the smell of disinfectant and blood into the clear, cold, starlit night. Vaguely he heard the sounds of war but did not care. If he had not been so drowsy he would have liked to sing, for it was no longer his war. The ambulance drove slowly along the pot-holed road to Naples, and by the time he was lifted out the sky was lightening to dawn and the morphia fast wearing off. They put him into a bed with cold beautiful sheets, and a fair-haired nurse inspected his label. Her voice was soft and soothing as honey, her hands which undressed him and washed him were caressing and tender as a lover's. Another needle jabbed into his arm, and he slept.

So ended his first day of war; for which he had trained and trained and trained. To which he had looked forward so eagerly for three long years. In his case from a day in July 1940. . . .

# PREPARATION

# Chapter 1

In a way it all began for Gair Mainwaring even before that
date. In 1938, in Vienna, not long after the Anschluss, when
the frontier guards wore the black uniform of the SS and
Jews were on their knees, scrubbing pavements. He went to
Austria from the gay, carefree whirl of Budapest and found
that Vienna was an armed camp. The ghosts of Lehar and
Strauss had departed and in their place were the automaton
soldiers. For the first time he saw the Feldgrau of the
Wehrmacht, heard the tramp of ironshod boots. Tanks, guns;
over the city flew aircraft. From every other building hung
the swastika, in every other shop-window lurked a picture of
Adolf Hitler, the unbalanced little man from Munich. The
maid at the hotel burst into tears.

"Ah, no more is it Austria, to think I should live to see my
country stolen by these robbers with their guns and uniforms.
They will not stop here, ah no, mein herr, they have tasted
blood and many will die, many, many more."

At dinner in the gilded restaurant the orchestra played the
melodies of an older Vienna and the diners danced, whirling
beneath the chandeliers. Beautiful women, impeccable officers,
the haunting strains of the waltzes. Laughter and animated
talk, tinkle of glass and corks popping. An oldish officer with
one arm, stopped at the table and spoke to Gair.

"Englishman? Not since 1918 have I spoken to an Engländer. For how long are you in Wien? Only a few days, a pity,
such a beautiful city, not like the old days but beautiful still."
He spoke about friendship between their countries, and then
left to join his party. He was rather drunk.

Later that night Gair stood by the window and looked over
the rooftops of Vienna, at the lilac glow that hangs like an
aura above a city at night; below in the street was the sound
of many voices, the formless tumult of a crowd, and on the
ceiling of his room there appeared the flickering of flames, as

though a fire was burning in the grate. Across the window swept the hard glare of a searchlight. Somewhere a band was playing martial music. He went on to the balcony and from there had a grandstand view. He seemed to be suspended above an unbroken sea of flame, a river of flame that flowed along the narrow street, then, looking closer, he saw that between the flames were islands of blackness in which appeared the blur of upturned faces, for the street was packed with people carrying pitch-pine torches whose flames set the shadows dancing on the walls, glinted deep crimson in the window-panes. A roar of voices ascended with the smoke, and above it all there was the steady 'thomp', 'thomp', 'thomp' of the big drum. As dangerous as savage war-drums. He could see the faces, the black pits of open mouths from which came pouring songs and shouts and laughter. Glass was broken, there was a shrill scream, a wild roar of applause. The music grew fainter, the crowd paused irresolute, swayed first this way, then that. A woman's voice shouted.

"*Juden!*" The cry was taken up by a hundred voices, and with the excited baying of animals they began to surge towards the street-end, the torches gyrating wildly, faster, faster as they smelt the blood and the sport. In a moment the street was empty except for a couple who had stayed behind to kiss in the sudden darkness. All that night it went on as the brown-shirted mobs ran wild, and throughout his uneasy sleep he could hear the first ugly mutterings of the storm that would soon be as familiar in Europe as the rising of the sun.

Next day he stood on the pavements and watched the processions and parades. Soldiers on their feet, doll-like in their movements, colours flying, drums beating. Soldiers sitting stiffly upright in the cumbersome troop-carriers, rifles erect between their knees, faces identical as wooden dummies in the shadows of the grey helmets. Tanks rumbled over the cobbles, the tracks squeaking and the black overalled crews saluting a fat general who stood on a dais before a window on which was daubed a yellow cross and the word '*Juden*'. Guns rolled by, small vicious guns, larger guns, five enormous guns. Motor-bicyclists in grey leather coats. After them came rank upon rank of youths and blonde Rhine maidens in brown

28

shirts, black shirts, green shirts. In the rear behind these charmers were the SS, then the élite of the SS, the Black Guards. No spark of animation showed upon those plaster-cast faces. Booted, pistoled, betruncheoned. Big men, impressive men. But if the Austrians were impressed they did not show it and stood silent as mourners; no handclapping, no cheers, as they watched impassively their protectors.

Gair followed in the wake of the marching men till he reached a square and there for an hour listened to a man who spoke from a balcony. It was not Hitler, but whoever it was evoked hysterical response from the assembled Teutons who interspersed long respectful silences with tumultuous cheering. When the speaker had worked himself and his audience into a frenzy he withdrew. Then they sang. 'Deutschland über Alles.' The 'Horst Wessel' song, the anthem of a martyred pimp. Nazi marching songs filled with the heavy tread of the jack-boot. Evening had crept into the square, and the lamps lit up the singing crowds, and as darkness closed down so the frenzy grew. Louder blared the bands, above them searchlights criss-crossed in a silver maze, illuminating for brief moments the bombers as they lumbered through the beams. It was a great spectacle. Wagnerian. Dangerous in its effect on the spectator, devilish in its propaganda. It did not seem possible that only twenty years before those arrogant confident people had been grubbing for food in the muck-heaps of their defeated country. He listened, amazed and stupefied, to the songs that rose triumphant from ten thousand throats, the shouts of victory—of impending revenge.

"*Sieg Heil! Sieg Heil!*" A new challenge to Europe, to the world. Surging across that starlit sky, echoing in the ears of men in France and Poland and Britain causing them to pray silently.

'Not again, please, God, not again.'

Even Gair, who at the age of eighteen knew nothing about anything, felt faint prickles of uneasiness as he stood among that milling, jostling throng. Something was stirring around him that would wash away the security and fun in his life. Yet at the same time he was exhilarated, envious even of those young Germans. How fine it must be to march and to

29

sing in a foreign city! An insidious appeal to youth, to the adolescent lust for power which lurks somewhere in most of us, the urge to *be* someone. It is impossible to describe adequately the sense of physical and mental excitement that rose up from that multitude, almost like an odour. Drunk already with the power which they had not tasted but which they had been promised, with the blind faith that was to carry them through the holocaust of another defeat. But there were no thoughts of defeat as they celebrated the first bloodless victory in the streets of Vienna.

"*Sieg Heil!*" He heard the refrain, monotonous and infectious as a slow hand-clap, until he reached his hotel and passed between the sad-faced Austrians in the lounge. '*Sieg Heil!* We are coming back. You forgotten ghosts of the Great War, take heed and watch us as we try again.'

That was the start of their journey. For Gair Mainwaring it was also the start of a journey. For many millions of others it was the start—for many, of a journey that was to have no ending—but we are not concerned with their story.

\*　　\*　　\*

"Right, here's the King's Shilling."

The recruiting officer polished his glasses and shouted: "Sergeant Roberts, send the next chap in, please."

Gair stood outside fingering the bright silver shilling and wondering whether it would be wrong to spend it.

The King's Shilling. He thought of Tel-el-Kebir. Omdurman. Kipling. Mafeking. He didn't quite know why.

Swearing the oath had been difficult, he could still feel the sweat under his arms, for he suffered from what is politely and kindly termed an impediment of the speech.

'To stammer and stutter;
be unable to utter
a word.'

The little ditty went often through his mind. It was bad with strangers, in shops, asking for a third single to Woking or trying to say Paddington to an irascible, impatient taxi-driver; and now when signing on for the Citizen Armies. There's no doubt it was a bore—but not of course so bad as being blind or deaf or having polio—and so he wondered as he turned the silver coin slowly in his hand whether he would ever make the dizzy heights of second lieutenant. Because as he told himself for the hundredth time it would be more than awkward were he to hesitate or stick over some vital order. However, time enough to worry when the moment came.

Up till that day his only war-like activity had been a short spell in the Home Guard, or, as it was called in infancy, the Local Defence Volunteers, where, armed with an antiquated Webley revolver loaded with two verdigrised bullets and a ·22 rifle loaded with one ditto, he patrolled against possible parachutists. Throughout the small hours Gair and a companion prone to asthma, named Cyril, wandered in the dark woods or lay in wait beneath sopping hedgerows for the enemy to float earthwards from a fleet of Junkers. As nature rambles those moonlit or drizzle-filled expeditions were wonderful. One night he slew a cock pheasant that perched sharp-etched against the moon. Between them they plucked it on the spot and shoved the feathers down a rabbit hole, the warm naked corpse he carried home for future use. Sometimes the nightly routine was varied and they—still the same wheezing comrade—took up their posts on the bridge at Sonning to stop with the aid of a red lantern all traffic, pedestrian, and wheeled. At first Gair enjoyed it, it made him feel important as he stepped forward, the ·22 held menacingly, to question the occupants of a car. But then it grew dull and cold and almost unbearable to hear the revelry in the hotel so close. On the way off duty they would swagger to the hotel, park their weapons ostentatiously on the bar and daringly order beer.

An old Webley, a ·22 rifle and a hammer shot-gun, with those and some rusty strands of barbed wire they were to stop the victorious Panzers. All over the country it must have been the same; pathetic, glorious and, thank heavens, never put to the test.

"What do I do with this thing if a bloody great tank comes along?" asked Cyril, waving the shot-gun.

31

"Stick it up the exhaust pipe," suggested the barman. Now, if the large blond Germans who sat so close beyond the Channel had heard that remark they would not have known what to make of it; certainly they would not have laughed.

"But," they would have queried, wrinkles in their simple brows, "but, vot should be the reason for that, vy the exhaust pipe?" Those were the people we were up against.

Whilst Cyril and he stood guard at Sonning, the armada of little craft ferried to and fro across the waters of the Channel bringing back the remnants of the Armies which were to have hung washing on the Siegfried Line by Christmas, while the tanks, festooned with victorious dust-caked infantry paused to reorganise along the coast of France. During that breathless, merciful pause Gair Mainwaring received the King's Shilling and with it in his pocket went in trepidation to the headquarters of the regiment he had in mind to join. Just short of the iron railings across the road from Buckingham Palace he paused to straighten his tie and to still the racing agitation of his heart, then with a prayer on his lips he advanced towards the huge sentry at the gate.

"Yes?" bayed the guardsman in tones of brass.

"C-colonel B-baldwin, is he in, I mean—can I see him?" The huge man looked down and jerked his head.

"Inside, up the stairs and first on the right, orderly room, they'll tell you."

With a sudden twitching of Goliath limbs the sentry crashed to attention and into a rasping salute. A small man in a bowler hat hurried by like the White Rabbit, muttering from under his rectangular sandy moustache.

"Mornin'."

"Morning, sir. Better day today, sir."

Gair followed. So that was an officer. He heard from up the narrow stairs the sound of typewriters, a stentorian voice bellowed for Corporal McAlpine to hurry up with that blankety tea. He crept into a room that seemed filled with men at little tables, the typewriters clacked busily and in the close atmosphere was a faint smell of carbolic.

"Yes?" A kindly looking man in glasses and with an awesome coat of arms spread across his sleeve looked up from beyond tall piles of papers in wire trays. His fingers were ink-stained, but his buttons shone like tiny suns. Gair removed his hat before such magnificence.

"C-colonel B——" he began.

"Appointment?"

"Well—er, no."

"I see. Name?"

"Mainwaring."

"Colonel's very busy this morning, still I'll see him and ask. There's a chair. Corporal McAlpine, a mug of tea."

Gair sat and sipped his first hot sweet tea from a chipped mug. Ridiculous to suppose that he could ever give orders to such men! On the walls were coloured prints of guardsmen in every conceivable type of uniform, below the nearest he read 'Drummer Boy 1864'. Perhaps he would achieve that. A bell rang, and the magnificent man rose to his feet, swallowed a last mouthful of syrupy tea and moved ponderously towards a small green door. As it opened Gair got a glimpse of more men seated at desks, glass cases full of medals and the little man who had passed him at the gate, still in his bowler. The door closed.

"Still a drop o' tea left."

Gair proffered his mug but had no time to drink for the door opened again and the coat-of-arms man beckoned. He stumbled to his feet, dry of mouth, the butterflies playing leap-frog in his stomach, and entered the room.

"The War Office say it's just not on, even Tim Fanshawe said he couldn't help, he rang up the G2 whilst I was in the room. Think we'll have to send a letter to General Claude and suggest——" Bowler Hat broke off, and they all looked at Gair suspiciously as though expecting to see him change to Dr Goebbels before their eyes.

"Sit down," said a very grand person who sat behind the largest, most shiny desk that was covered with the most silver inkpots and trays. His face was brick-red, the blue eyes friendly and shrewd, the grey hair rumpled and rather long.

A beetle coming face to face with a group of blackbirds must feel the same as Gair did. He sat and twisted his hat and waited for someone to speak.

2                        33

"Well, I must be off. Don't forget about that business will you, Mike? See you tonight at the Club." He went out and everyone stood up, looking respectful.

"Now, what can we do for you?"

"It's—it's. I'd like to j-join up."

"The Regiment?"

"Yes, please, sir."

Colonel Baldwin leant back in his chair and tapped his teeth with a ruler. His chest seemed to be nothing but medal ribbons. There were food spots on his tunic.

"Don't see why not, d'you Guy?" A sallow-faced youth in a dark corner answered that he didn't see why not either.

"Got to ask you a few questions of course. You know, school, games and all that sort of rot." He drew a sheet of paper towards him and picked up a gleaming pen.

"This ink's no use, Guy."

"Nossir."

"Get some more."

"Yessir." He rang a bell. Coat-of-Arms appeared.

"Ah, this ink."

"Yessir."

"It's no good. Got any more?"

"I'll see, sir."

"Would you?"

"Yessir." He turned and thundered:

"Sergeant Innes." Another man joined the scene.

"Sir?"

"Ink! Get some more."

"Different ink," put in the colonel mildly.

"Different ink!" bellowed Coat-of-Arms.

"Yessir." Sergeant Innes disappeared. No one spoke. The third member sat at his desk and wrote furiously in pencil, looking up once or twice through his thick horn-rimmed glasses, lips working soundlessly as the muse possessed him. Tap, tap went the ruler on the colonel's teeth. Gair looked at the glass cases on the walls which were full of medals, row upon row of medals. Outside, cars passed up and down Bird-cage Walk, sparrows perched on the window-sill. A pretty girl pushed a pram slowly among the trees of St James's

Park. He wished he was anywhere else, even in the pram. Amidst a great stamping of feet the fresh ink appeared.

"Ah, excellent, Sergeant Innes."

Sergeant Innes, the gleam of impending promotion in his eye, made a ramrod exit.

"Now, Manners, where were we?"

"M-m—" Gair tried the correction but seized up over the 'm'.

"What?" asked the colonel, rubbing his face.

"Mmm—" Horn-Rim stopped his composition, Guy pretended to inspect his nails. The colonel stood up.

"Never mind, it doesn't matter, take your time."

"Mmm—" tried Gair and then gave it up and sat cheeks aflame.

"What games d'you play?" For the next quarter of an hour he struggled on whilst the colonel wrote down the answers.

"By the way, what did you say your name was?"

"I didn't m-manage to tell you, sir."

The colonel smiled.

"Spell it then." He wrote the letters one by one.

"Mainwaring. I knew a Mainwaring once. 'Fanny' we used to call him, killed at Gonnelieu, any relation of yours?"

"No."

"Fine chap, Fanny, put in for a V.C. at Neuve Chapelle. This—er—stutter of yours, do you always have it or does it come on if you're, well, nervous, y'know, with strangers and so on?"

"It's p-permanent, sir, but it has bad spells."

"I see. You're going to find it a devil of a nuisance in the Army, orders and what-not. Ever thought of having it cured? Tell you what, we may be able to take you in three months' time, it is July isn't it, Ian, when the next intake goes to Caterham—yes, I thought so. I suggest that you go off somewhere, I mean there must be people who—er—cure this sort of thing and try to get it better. Then report back here, to me personally, say at the end of June and we'll see then. All right?"

"Yes, sir, thank you." Gair got up wondering if he ought to shake hands, and as he did so the telephone shrilled.

"You'll find it a bit of a handicap, I'm afraid," repeated the colonel.

Horn-Rim lifted the receiver.

"Hello. Yes it's Ian s-s-speaking. Ah, it's you, old b-b-boy."

Gair looked, disbelieving his ears.

Colonel Baldwin suddenly began to talk rather loudly.

"These sparrows, Guy, ought to feed 'em, little brutes look hungry. Here cheep, cheep, cheep!"

" . . . b-but I t-told him it was impossible. N-n-no . . ."

"Well, Manners, I think that's all. End of June."

In a dream Gair went out of the room.

" . . . s-sorry, afraid I c-c-can't . . ."

In his heart hope was springing, for after all was not that room the Fountainhead, its occupants the gods who were to hold his fate in their hands, and if one of those gods suffered from an affliction of the vocal mechanism, well, then he felt himself already a brigadier and went upon his way humming blithely.

# Chapter 2

THERE has been much written about Caterham, where the Brigade of Guards has its depot, too much, and so we will skip lightly over the few months he spent being turned from a weedy civilian into a not quite so weedy guardsman. For Colonel Baldwin, true to his word, saw him again and gave him orders.

"You'll join the next potential officers' squad in ten days' time." So on a misty evening ten days later he laboured up Caterham Hill manhandling an enormous suitcase packed to the brim with spare underclothes and soap. In the guardroom he joined a forlorn group of young men in public-school ties, one looking more than out of place in a solicitor's suit and Anthony Eden hat plus spats and an umbrella.

"Christ!" A tall young sergeant in Coldstream uniform stood regarding them.

"Potential Officers?"

"Yes."

"Yes, SERGEANT!" thundered the soldier. He looked athletic and horribly tough.

"Look here," put in Anthony Eden peevishly, "I'm getting a bit tired of sitting here, I've been here since four o'clock and it's now almost six. I'm hungry too."

Let us draw a veil over the unhappy scene which ensued and join that band of officer material as they meet the man who was to be their tutor, guide, confidant and helpmate.

"You're a lovely looking lot, you are. Want to be officers, eh? Yessir, nossir, kick me arse, sir. I'm Russell. Guardsman Russell, Trained Soldier Russell to you *gentlemen*. I'm 'ere to 'old yore little 'ands and 'elp you to put on yore little nappies. One day you'll be lording it round the flickin' place and I'll 'ave to curtsey to you. But not now I don't, and so 'elp me Gawd you'd better learn to keep yore eyes down or you'll be up against Russell and Gawd 'elp . . . oh, my bleeding

37

'ead." Trained Soldier Russell disappeared unsteadily towards a doorway at the end of the hut, it slammed and from
beyond it came the sad, unmistakable sounds of a stomach
rebelling.

"On a starred night Prince Lucifer uprose . . ." began
Sheffield, then a bugle blew a melancholy call, a voice
screamed "Lights Out", and they went to bed in darkness.
Gair lay on the lumpy palliasse and wondered what the
morrow would bring. A low murmur of conversation rose
in the clammy darkness, someone took something out of
silver paper and munched it. He turned over and the straw
rustled, the blankets tickled his chin, below his head the
bolster was insufferably hard. A question floated in his mind.
Does discomfort make a better soldier? A question he was
to ask very many more times during the next twelve years.
Perhaps it does, for after all it is much easier to leave a straw
palliasse than a feather mattress. Yet at six next morning his
wooden bedstead—they make it of wood so it can be scrubbed
spotless twice a week—seemed like a little bit of paradise.
The wash-house definitely did not. Even at dawn, as the sun
peeped rosily over the flushed Surrey hills, and so on, there
was a smell of sweat in the wash-house and, horror upon
horrors, they had to share it with ordinary guardsmen who
were much bigger, much stronger and did not seem to mind
shaving in dirty cold water. Then they had breakfast, feeling
conspicuous in their check suits and suede shoes. Gair had to
fetch the porridge from the serving-hatch and could barely
carry the cauldron of glutinous grey mess.

"What's this stuff? England's revenge for Bannockburn?"

Colin pushed it away. Suddenly a roar rent the air, and an
incongruous-looking pair appeared at the end of the room.
One, a gigantic ginger-visaged sergeant, the other small and
insignificant but all powerful, for on his head was a gilt-
brimmed blue cap pulled low over his eyes, on his midget
shoulders the shining stars that raised him to the level of a
different being. An officer. Gair stared open-mouthed. He
says go, and they goeth, come and they cometh, verily he is
a king among men.

"Any complaints?" squeaked the man of power.

"Yes," answered Colin, his red hair ablaze. "This porridge it's—it's uneatable."

A low confused murmur swept round the dining-hall as the officer approached, stepping daintily, a stick held horizontal under his armpit.

"What's wrong with it?"

"It's disgusting. It's not porridge."

"Let's try it?" The officer took a mouthful, tried to hide a grimace and turned to the glowering sergeant.

"Er, it's not very good. Hardly porridge, I mean."

"Sir!"

"Better speak to the Master Cook."

"Sir!"

"Right you are then, Sergeant Stagg. Make a note of it."

"Sir!"

"I shouldn't bother to eat it if I were you."

"I won't," retorted Colin shortly.

The hall held its breath.

"Say, sir, when you address an officer." The N.C.O. looked close to a stroke.

"Yes."

"Yes—what?"

"Sir?" inquired Colin sweetly.

"SERGEANT!"

"Yes, sergeant."

The officer's lips began to tremble and wisely he turned away, the sergeant stalking behind, vast and outraged and fuming.

"Sir! Sergeant! What the hell is this? One of them with a blasted onion on his hat, the other a bloody dimwit with no more vocabulary than sir, sir. Ah, hell, roll on the Blitzkrieg." Colin stabbed viciously at a piece of salty bacon.

"England, we love thee better than we know," murmured Sheffield.

Gair would have liked to be like Colin, but he would have eaten the porridge, rather than complain. That first day of Army life was even less amusing than many, as from breakfast till late evening they were hounded in some semblance of military formation from place to place and back again to

39

place; to the accompaniment of the monotonous 'One-toop, three—one' shouted at them either by Sergeant Garner or Corporal Whiting or both. Without those magic little words life at Caterham was incomplete, sterile.

"It would be interesting to work out exactly how much breath is wasted by everyone here." Sheffield—he of the spats—was of an inquiring turn of mind. They were standing outside yet another store waiting to draw yet another item of equipment with which to increase the weight of the kitbags they had been lugging about for the last three hours. They looked a slapstick crew as they stood in creased suits and dusty shoes, with those shocking hats known as 'fore-and-afts' jammed on their closely shaven heads. "It puzzles me," continued Sheffield, "when I look round me and see such incredible smartness allied to such incredible stupidity, but then I suppose—"

"Stop talking!"

They drew a rifle, inches deep in grease, and one of the old-type bayonets, proper bayonets that would catch the sunlight and put the fear of God into the Boche, not those miserable skewer things they issued later, good for nothing but piercing tins. Then they drew a water-bottle and a sinister little package called a first field-dressing.

"What's the second one like, a m-miniature winding sheet I suppose." Gair crammed the latest additions on top of the battledress, denims, vests and pants woollen and the two colossal pairs of boots.

"Two sizes in here," said the comfortable-looking store-man. "One too big, the other too small." His fat face creased at the witticism.

"Squad! Squa-a-ad, 'Shun! By the left . . ." They were off again, staggering under their loads. Left! Right! Along tar-mac roads between rows of black huts and Nissen huts, past a church and a cricket field, among drab Victorian buildings festooned with iron fire escapes, till they reached the M.I. Room. Inside they joined a queue for inoculation. The doctor was tired, the needle was blunt, bending like a steel bow before plunging into the cringing flesh. One or two men fainted. Gair felt sick as the greyish liquid was forced into his

arm under considerable pressure from a muscular forearm.
That doctor had no bedside manner. At half past twelve they
hastened to dinner, then they hastened to another hut where
they found an officer who introduced himself as their company commander and spoke without conviction of the team
spirit. By then their arms were stiffening and the day seemed
to have continued for long enough. Gair sat on the hard bench
and remembered that the day before at that time he had been
sauntering slowly and lazily along Oxford Street. Would he
ever saunter anywhere again? It was unlikely.

"Room, room 'shun!" They shuffled to their feet as
the company commander made his exit followed closely by
a stout labrador which lifted its leg against the stove on the
way.

"Fall in on the road outside." They bustled off to their hut
where for a few unbelievable minutes they were allowed to
talk and smoke and sit down. But not for long. Corporal
Whiting raced them along for their next meal and back again
with the tea swilling about in jolting stomachs.

"Now we have what is known as Shining Parade. Normally each recruit sits on his bed and polishes and he goes on
polishing until I or Trained Soldier Russell or the company
officer tells him he can stop. Is that quite clear?" Sergeant
Garner looked round the hut.

"Yes."

"Yes—what?"

"Yes, sergeant." They answered in obedient chorus.

It was strange to think that among their number they had
two schoolmasters and a diplomat who owned a beautiful
wife, a Rolls Royce and who was a peer of the realm for good
measure.

"Right then. Sometimes during shining parade one of the
company officers or myself will instruct you in the regimental
histories of the five regiments of the Brigade which are—*you*,
half asleep there."

Gair came slowly to his senses. "Grenadier, Coldstreams—" "Aah, you miserable thing, you! Coldstream,
never Coldstreams. Well, go on."

"Scots, Irish and W-w . . ." It was no use.

41

"Help him, someone."

"Welsh."

"Don't worry lad, none of us mind except yourself, and we'll soon get you out of it. Now then, move yourselves and get your stuff unpacked and sorted out. I want this hut in good order within the hour then you can go to the NAAFI for tea and wads. Tomorrow we start work. Trained Soldier Russell, give 'em a hand with the equipment." Sergeant Garner stamped out. He was smart, he was strict, he was at times hard, but somewhere under all the shouting and cursing he had a sympathetic heart. What's more he was a thoroughly just man.

In the NAAFI Gair bought a pint of beer and a plate of sausages and chips from a girl with an hour-glass figure and a wide kind smile. He and Anthony sat at a beer-stained table and made the first tentative approaches to friendship. They found they had mutual acquaintances and had patronised when small the same kindergarten.

A piano beat out 'Run, rabbit, run', there was the thud of darts, snatches of conversation from adjoining tables, loud laughter.

"Don't they ever use any other word except that one?" asked Anthony.

"Incredible, isn't it. See that chap over there, I've been listening carefully and he's said it twenty-five times in about three sentences." Gair indicated a carroty-haired soldier with no back to his head.

". . . 'An I says to the flickin' bitch, look here, you may be a flickin' good-looker but if you flickin'-well think you can flickin'-well treat me in this flickin' way, you've got another flickin' thought flickin'-well coming. . . ." The guardsman belched.

"Edifying, really, that sort of conversation. Oh, my God," groaned Anthony into his beer, "to think that we have got to listen to that for years and years, perhaps for ever."

'Yes, and this is only our first day,' thought Gair, ruefully scratching a cropped head, that was already beginning to itch. He ordered another beer from the same vision and asked for pipe tobacco; her voice was coarse and rasping and went a long way towards cancelling out her looks. After three more pints of NAAFI beer both he and Anthony felt better.

"Not such a bad life really, I mean we are at least doing something."

"Yes. This sergeant d-doesn't seem a bad fellow."

"Damned good chap, I should think."

They reached the hut in darkness and bundled happily on to their beds of wood and straw. Gair lay staring into the darkness, listening to the well-earned snores of twenty-five men. Sometimes straw rustled as a body moved restlessly, an unknown voice muttered, "Hard enough to break your bloody wrist," as its owner strove to batter some semblance of softness into his bolster.

"Stop that talking in there," yelled Trained Soldier Russell from the foetid privacy of his bunk. Gair grinned smugly. The heavy footfalls of the patrolling sentry grew louder, then fainter; against the square of window Gair could see a rifle in a wall-rest, black and snub-nosed. That was one thing at least which he could do well, he could direct small lethal lumps of lead with great accuracy through the black mid-circle of a target. Whether or not he would be able to direct it with the same accuracy through the head, chest or belly of a fellow human remained to be seen. He slept and dreamt vividly of glory.

The days flashed by, for there were few dull moments. If it wasn't drill, it was musketry; if not musketry, it was bayonet-fighting, fixing the long-bladed knives with satisfying 'click' and squaring up to a row of sack dummies.

"Next!"

Adopt the position of aggression and start down the runway at a steady jog trot, trying self-consciously to utter ferocious cries. The battle-cry of the Turk is 'Allah il Allah Din Din Din', that of the Tommy should be the refrain of the bayonet-fighting course, 'In-out, on guard, pass through'. Then there was physical training under the guidance of a have-a-body-like-mine sergeant-major, who would have qualified for both Sodom and Gomorrah. When they returned limp and wet from vaulting over things or playing sweaty games in which Gair invariably found his nose pressed tightly into an armpit or a crutch, it was to change once more into second battledress for drill. Run a duster over the glossy boots and the highly polished rifle—a weapon whose any pretence of accuracy had been knocked endways by the incessant banging from the flats of hands.

"Strike the b——r, don't tickle it! Like this." Sergeant Garner slammed his rifle through the motions of the 'present', clouds of blanco—the guardsman's talcum powder, rising in the sunshine, the magazine leaping and rattling in its niche. Drill, fantastic, unbelievable drill. They raced from one end of the square to the other and then back again; strained their brains learning to salute—to the right, to the left, to the front, turning to the right by numbers and then to the left. They scurried in quick time, boots twinkling in the dust, not knowing whether to laugh or cry or do as some poor devil had once done—casting off his belt he had exclaimed: "Do with me what you will, I will soldier no more." Above them the sun of high summer spun in a brazen sky and drew the sweat from their bodies in gallons.

"Stand easy! Right, now Snowden, regimental motto of the Welsh Guards."

"Cymru am Byth."

"Yes, what's it mean?"

"I've no idea, sergeant, what does it mean, sergeant?"

"Next man, what's it mean?"

"To spring a leek, sergeant." Laughter. Garner snarled.

"That'll do; it doesn't take any of you to try and be funny with me. Last chance, what's it mean, anyone?"

He jabbed his rifle towards the squad.

"What *does* it mean, sergeant?" Snowden tried again.

"It means—Squa-a-d. Squad 'shun. Slope arms! Now, *gentlemen* we'll see who laughs last." Away they went at full gallop. Left-right, one-two-three-one. Left turn! Right turn! About turn! Mark time! Forward! Left turn! Sit down! Stand up! "Come on, come on, come on, move yourselves, we haven't started—get your feet going, Snowden, you aren't an officer yet." The words came at them like whipcracks from between the sergeant's foam-flecked lips, and all of them, schoolmasters, diplomat, undergraduates, gentlemen of leisure, span and stamped and suffered like puppets on a wire. Then, as they drew near to breaking-point they heard, as the faithful hear the call to prayer, the wailing sob of the sirens. For it was late August and the days and nights were filled with alarms and excursions. Day after day, night after night they ran for the trenches, festooned with gas-capes, eye-shields, gas-masks, steel helmets, weapons, including for some obscure reason the anti-tank rifle, where they sat on ridged duckboards and listened to the broken droning of the Heinkels. Sometimes they saw the bloody glow of the flames over London, heard all round the gunfire, the whoomph! whoomph! of the winking shells. One night a stricken bomber, limping for home, was caught in a searchlight cone, and tracer, like lazy red tennis balls, curved slowly into the silvery darkness. Two nights later the sirens tore them from their beds quite early, and after sitting, bored and sleepy, in the trenches for three hours the all-clear sounded and they went back to the hut. As Gair tumbled on to his bed he heard the sound of an aircraft engine. It grew louder, throbbing unevenly, and suddenly he heard another sound, an unfamiliar sound, a sort of whistle that rose to a screech like tearing silk and louder still. Someone shouted: "Christ!" and the earth beneath his bed heaved and danced. Explosions, one-two-three, and metal clanged on the tin roof. The night which had been so quiet was alive with a confusion of shouts and screams. In the morning they were marched not to the square, but to the Victorian buildings where they found and gathered up torn scraps of human flesh and placed them in sandbags. A bed, complete with mutilated occupant, lay twisted on the cricket field, and a head was found two hundred yards away. Gair did not see one body which could be recognisable as human save for the tattered shreds of clothing, and felt no shame at having to be sick three times.

Often they drilled as the Hurricanes took off from Kenley, three by three, and later watched as the survivors came limping back, pouring smoke, fabric ripped and torn; refuel, rearm and up again. No respite, no let-up for the exhausted pilots.

"God, what wouldn't I give to be one of those chaps instead of learning how to stamp my feet." O'Connor was killed two months later by a bomb in London. He did not have much of a war. A Hurricane came in low over the camp, breaking up as it came, the pilot jumped and landed by parachute near the guardroom; Gair and Drover were sharing a trench near where he landed. He was shockingly burnt, the bones of his hands laid bare and blackened, and he spoke through the crimson and yellow wreck of what had been his face and the words he spoke were these:

"Must get back, get back for another plane, must get back to K . . ." Mercifully he died. As they picked up the body the charred tunic came away and Gair could see the partially exposed ribs. It was not a pretty way to die, trapped in a broken, burning aeroplane, there was little glamour attached to being roasted alive.

Their last days of Caterham were a hectic maelstrom of trying to learn a bit of drill, a bit of musketry, of regimental customs and traditions, in between the raids. The intervals grew shorter, the raids worsened, the tempo increased and the peerless blue of the sky was aglint with tiny silver aircraft, streaked with vapour trails, smudged with the black woolly shell-bursts. They sat in the hot sunshine, helpless and amazed by what they saw above them, as the Luftwaffe stormed uninvited into the Surrey skies. Gair had a Bren-gun on a special mounting, and when three German aircraft flew low, without waiting for orders, he opened fire. The gun leapt against his cheek as, exultant and cheering, he watched the stream of tracer curving upwards. The bombers flew on, quite heedless of the bullets, and Gair narrowly escaped arrest and severe punishment. At the time it seemed unfair, for in war, if you had a weapon and the enemy appeared, was it not usual to use it? Instead of which he had to listen to one more endless peroration on the value of discipline. Later, some years later, he understood.

Near Caterham there is the town of Purley. As a town it is nondescript, but for Gair in his best battledress with the new regimental titles on the shoulders and the set-up guardsman's cap on his head it was the Promised Land, for in its ordinary streets there were luckless civilians who could gaze in admiration at the titles, the set-up cap and envy. On their last Saturday they marched to the guardroom and presented themselves for inspection, for no recruit could display himself to public view without first being minutely inspected. Hair, moustache, standard of shaving, crease in trousers, polish on boots and cap star, unsightly bulges in pockets, loose threads or traces of scurf on the collar. As they queued by the guardroom an aeroplane appeared at tree-top height and slammed over their heads.

"Ah," said Colin, who knew everything. "One of the new square-winged Hurricanes, wonderful machines."

Gair thought he had caught a glimpse of black crosses but did not like to query such confident knowledge. The queue edged forward. The aircraft hurtled over again, and this time the crackle of its machine-guns was vicious; pieces of branch fell on them as they lay face down in the dust.

"Square-winged Hurricanes, my bloody fanny!"

They picked themselves up and dusted down their crumpled uniforms.

Later, in the evening, they sat round in the bar of the Railway Hotel and listened as the sirens gave tongue. "There they are, six—eight—nine of the brutes!" A foolish rush for the window and then they heard it coming, like the approach of an express, and for the second time they were flat to the ground. "Mind my beer!" The bomb burst just beyond the bridge, plaster rained and the big window blew in with a delayed action cascade of glass.

"Better get to the cellar, ladies and gentlemen, bit more snug down there." They sat in a lamplit cellar among the barrels of beer and sang to a mouth-organ. Now and then the vaulted roof trembled but no one cared, for they were surrounded by unlimited beer. A stout woman with hennaed hair sang in a pleasing soprano that there would always be an England—doubtless at that very moment some stout *hausfrau* was singing that they marched against the very same England; confusing and contradictory. Two small gunners had a fight, and much beer was spilt. Naturally no one heard the all-clear till an angry customer put his head in and shouted through the pandemonium:

"'Ere, I say, the ruddy war's been over for the last 'arf

hour, an' there's a lot of us wanting beer upstairs." They picked their way back to the bus-stop over clutters of masonry and plaster; the streets seemed full of ambulances, and there was a pall of smoke hanging over Kenley. A woman lay groaning on the pavement surrounded by sympathisers, and a small boy with blood on his hair shuffled aimlessly through broken glass.

Next day they had their final parade and were congratulated by a senior officer with a black patch over one eye. They had, he informed them, done as well as could be expected owing to the continual interruptions.

"Never forget," he urged, "the supreme importance of this discipline which I dare say some of you consider to be so much waste of time. But it is not a waste of time, as has been proved on countless occasions and it will be proved again, and you gentlemen"—he called them gentlemen without the italics—"have a great and arduous task before you. It will not be easy, at times it will be damned difficult, but always remember this, that you will have under you some of the finest men in the world. I wish you the best of luck."

They passed round the hat for contributions towards a present for Sergeant Garner and met him and Trained Soldier Russell at the Railway Hotel. There was fraternisation between the ranks that night, and Trained Soldier Russell had to be carried most of the way back to camp, oblivious of the bombers which droned across the white face of the moon. Corporal Whiting would have been there if he had not been tied to the apron-strings of a large and possessive wife. The last night at Caterham was spent in the trenches while the fires of Croydon flickered pale in the moonlight and Sheffield was sick into his steel helmet.

Next day they girded themselves for travel, bade farewell to Garner, Russell and Whiting, kissed their hands to the NAAFI girls who crowded the windows to see them go and marched to the station in the midst of the raid, during which one hundred and eighty-five German bombers were supposed to have been destroyed.

## Chapter 3

GAIR associated Sandhurst in his mind with smart young gentlemen in pill-box hats. On arrival the illusion was dispelled, for those he saw were neither particularly smart nor particularly young. The first days were a nightmare. He had a room to himself but never found himself in it except for the brief frenzied moments when changing from drill order to singlet and shorts or from best battledress to marching order.

No one told them anything verbally; it was to be discovered on the 'Detail'. It was seldom possible to walk anywhere, and Gair found he required two more hands and four more feet. Existence was confusing. Sometimes he was called "sir" and then in the next breath "you 'orrible little man, you, get a move on". They were formed into platoons and worked throughout as such. In his platoon there were two Maoris named Pene and Toka who slept at every conceivable opportunity, drowning with their snores the voice of the platoon commander as he strove to initiate them into the mysteries of the compass, or how to get from point A to point B counting on the way all bushy-topped trees and churches with steeples.

He was a fanciful figure, Captain Lamming, in his tailored battledress and with his slow drawling tones and ebony cigarette-holder. From him they learnt about such things as parapets and parados, the composition of a battalion; magical words tumbled in a slow stream from his thin straight lips. Echelons, kapok bridging, traverses, double-apron fences. Northings, eastings, grids and bearings, magnetic and true. Point section. Arcs of fire.

Gair did not learn much at Sandhurst, what he did, had its origin in the mud of Inkerman, the squares of Waterloo. Bicycling the Army way. Prepare to mount! Mount! Right wheel!—or Wrong wheel, did it matter? Ride at ease, and away they went along the highways and byways until they

49

reached some hill or open field where they dismounted by numbers and gathered round Captain Lamming to hear how the day was to be spent. After some hours of digging or fill-ing-in what someone else had dug; or advancing in archaic formations over the daisies, stopping every so often to wave their rifles in various ways—enemy in sight, up and down; in large numbers round and round; no enemy, get down and doze among the daisies—or to crouch agog at the exciting report of one blank cartridge. Perhaps someone waved a flag, that meant a tank was coming, or two flags and they flattened themselves from imaginary aircraft.

"Get down, Mainwaring, you're UNDER FIRE from hostile aircraft, there are bullets all round you—you've been hit, Mainwaring! Fall down and wait for the stretcher-party."

"Ah, thank goodness." Gair subsided into the warm soft grass and smelt the rich earth beneath his face; after a moment he slept.

"Come on Mainwaring, do a bit to help, you're too bloody heavy to lift on a hot day."

"I'm full of b-bullets." They heaved him on to the stretcher and staggered across the field. What a delightful way of spending the day! He lay back on the canvas and revelled in the sunshine.

At the conclusion of every tactical exercise Captain Lamming would gather them round him in a democratic way and talk. Endlessly he would talk, and everything was either not too good or not too bad.

"Not too good today, not nearly enough life about it—oh, by the way, smoke if you want to—like a pack of old women. You've got to remember that the Hun is . . ." and once again they heard about the superman that one day they would meet. Pene and Toka snored in the evening sunlight, and Gair watched a kestrel as it hovered over some unsuspecting mouse. He loved those excursions for it gave him unlimited opportunity, while pretending to attack a copse or defend a ditch, to watch birds.

In the evenings there was freedom to sit in the canteen, play billiards on the bumpy cloth or cards on the coffee-stained tables, drink pints of cheap port and begin to talk like budding officers with an 'old boy' here, an 'old man' there. Then some hours of uninhibited healthy slumber to be roused by the disagreeable old man who made the bed and brought the tepid shaving water and invariably croaked, "We'll 'ave rain afore the day's out."

Every so often Gair did not sleep in the privacy of his room but went with other unfortunates to lie in the gym amid a welter of blankets, gas-capes, gas-masks and sand-buckets. In turn they were woken and solemnly dressed in anti-gas outfit and went out into the star-filled night where they stood being alert and watchful. Only owls and bats disturbed their vigil, an occasional car changed gear, and after one hour or two, some other pregnant figure shambled out and he retired to the mug of black tea, the blankets on the floor and the disgusting stench of unventilated human sleep. On other nights he was taken for guard with fellow cadets as sergeant and corporal. Gair stood outside the main entrance one night from twelve till two and watched and saluted as the officers came in from a party. Many were drunk, all were gay and noisy, festive in their evening blue; they lurched past him, arm-in-arm, happy and giving no thought to the morrow, no thought to the bitter cold. "Goo'-night, sentry." They disappeared within, a voice suggested beer. Gair shouldered his musket and strode his beat, envying. The gas-sentry rode slowly by on his bicycle, a great swollen balloon in the air-filled cape. Footsteps crunched on the gravel. Gair thrust forward his rifle and prepared to challenge but got no further than a brief expiration of misty breath. Damn! Try again. More mist. The steps grew nearer, a figure loomed large.

"Stop!" shouted Gair in desperation, the bayonet lunging wildly.

"Who is it? Advance one and be recognised." (Kindly remove your false moustache and wig).

"Captain Lamming. I say, not too good that, Halt, who goes there, you must have known that, sentry. Oh, it's you, Mainwaring."

"Yessir."

"Shouldn't have let me get so close. I mean, if I'd been up to no good or anything."

"Yessir."

"Well, good-night, Mainwaring."

"G-g-good-night, sir."

"I had an uncle who stuttered, did well in the last war, take a deep breath, I should." He went on his way. How kind people were, but how fatuous too.

There was an elderly man in civilian clothes who taught them about explosives, blowing enormous muddy craters among the Surrey bracken, spattering his audience with heavy showers of clods and stones. Later he was killed by a premature fuse.

A sergeant in oil-soaked denims spoke about the intricate mysteries of the internal-combustion engine, and they sat and took notes or copied the coloured diagrams that looked very much like coloured diagrams of lungs, bowels and blood-vessels. A corporal, equally oil-soaked, taught them how to ride motor-bicycles and for hours they rode slowly round-and-round a rutted paddock. After the fourth lesson he took them out and they streamed along at varying speeds, one-behind-the-other. At one peculiarly sharp bend on the King's Ride, Gair who had been dawdling, was making up leeway and inadvertently mistook the lever, accelerated violently straight into the wreck of a motor-bicycle which had also come to grief and was pitched high into the air to land on his head. Both machines were wrecked, Officer-Cadet Tadpole cracked a rib and Gair had a headache for two days.

There were dreadful night-patrols when the chaos was indescribable and Captain Lamming invariably lost his temper. Sheffield was appointed patrol commander on a night of blustering wind. The objective was the gas-chamber, but owing to the weather and a general lack of co-operation he went one way in the dark dripping woods and the patrol went another, ending in the hurly-burly of a pig farm. They were merry Boy Scout escapades those patrols which taught them nothing except how incredibly difficult it is to move silently in the dark. Some day they might have to, but no one thought of the future.

They took it in turn to be in positions of authority: company commander, platoon commander and so on. For the first time in his life Gair was faced with the prospect of giving orders and lectures to thirty other people, and for nights beforehand he hardly got a wink of sleep for dreading the prospect. He toyed with the idea of going sick, of desertion, of suicide. They were very kind, very helpful and they did not laugh at his temporary inability to give the orders, his moments of dumbness during lectures, and even the Maoris stayed awake. He got through the week, and the first tentative wisps of a new-born confidence began to enter his mind. No more was it 'I think I can', but 'I know I can', for he found during those lectures that people were inclined to laugh not at him but at what he said, and that is a great spur. As platoon commander he sat next to Captain Lamming at meals and found him to be an intelligent, sympathetic man who could talk of many things outside the narrow confines of military art. It was a good week, and at the end of it he held his head just that little bit higher.

"You're wanted at the Company Office, Mainwaring."

"I am? What have I done now?"

"No idea, but the sergeant-major's been bawling his guts out for you."

The other six candidates for the regiment were lined up as he arrived, polishing feverishly at his brasses with a handkerchief. Colonel Baldwin was inside and saw each one of them in turn. Gair went in last.

"Well, how's it been going?"

"Not too b-bad, sir."

"They tell me you've done well. Quite frankly, Mainwaring, I am surprised that you have managed as you have. You didn't find it a bad handicap?"

"At times, sir."

"You think you'll cope with being an officer?"

"I think so. I h-hope so, sir."

"Very well then, I'll take you, but on one condition, and that is, if it should ever for some reason or other become too bad for you to do your job properly, I don't say for one moment that it will, but if it does, then of course I should not be able to retain you as a regimental officer. Is that understood?"

"Yes, sir."

"Good luck, then." Colonel Baldwin took up his pen and began to write. Gair saluted and marched out in a daze of delight. In the seclusion of his room he looked at himself in the glass and imagined the stars, the Sam Browne richly polished and agleam, the braided cap, in his gloved hand an ash stick. Perhaps a moustache to go with the cap, he would see. So he had made it. In the short, inadequately short, space of six months he had become a man supposedly trained and competent to lead other men in battle. A raucous voice shattered his day-dreams.

"Come on, come on, outside for rifle inspection!"

A few days later the Regimental Adjutant saw the candidates.

"What's the name of your tailor?"

"Well, sir, I've always been to Joshua and P-peabody."

"They're not the Regimental Tailors."

"No, sir."

"The Regimental Tailors are Morton and Cadging."

"Yes, sir."

"They know exactly how to make the uniform."

"Yes, sir."

Conversation appeared to be heading for a cul-de-sac. The adjutant blew his nose loudly.

"That's settled then."

Gair saw no future in prolonged argument and murmured a discreet yessir but ordered his uniform from Messrs Joshua and Peabody, an old and reputable firm in Consort Street who though not lightning-quick were reliable and very pleasant old men. When finally it appeared it was roughly the right size and shape.

As a farewell to Sandhurst they put on a variety concert, and in a spirit of devilment someone suggested Gair as the compère. Make a legless man sprint a hundred yards! But with half a bottle of whisky inside him he forgot the serried ranks of faces peering palely from beyond the footlights. He announced each turn, he told stories that made the audience laugh—it was satisfying to hear the gusts of laughter sweeping through the hall and to realise that he was responsible.

He sang and had finally to be escorted from the stage, resisting wildly.

Next day he had such a hangover that he forgot the fact that he was now an officer of His Majesty's Brigade of Guards. He felt like nothing on earth and could take no pleasure even in the glory of the gold-braided cap, pressing as it did painfully on a tortured head.

They made for London and leave.

The streets of London were teeming with soldiers and at first he lost his nerve and dived repeatedly into shops to avoid the ordeal of answering salutes. With the coming of darkness and the bombers his thoughts turned to wine and women. Denise was away, driving an ambulance in Portsmouth. He felt at a loose end, all his finery wasted somehow with no female eyes to appraise, no female lips to murmur:

"But how very smart, darling."

A bomb commenced its descent, the sound grew to the crescendo which meant a near one and instinctively he nipped into a doorway. The blast propelled him through the swing doors into the palm-dotted hall of an opulent hotel. He sat at a little table and surveyed the highly coloured ladies who sat, many with pekinese dogs, as though waiting. None of them so much as glanced his way. Elderly men in City suits claimed acquaintance with some, a few went out into the glass-strewn street. Gair had dinner in the ornate restaurant surrounded by an entirely different set of painted ladies. He ordered wine as though he knew about it, port and a cigar that made him sweat. The constriction of the Sam Browne was comforting but he spilt gravy on his trousers. It was a lonely celebration and he wished that he had gone with the others to see the Crazy Gang. Having paid the bill he collected cap, stick and gloves and ventured into the blackout.

"Hello, darling, you come with me?" He felt the pressure of body against his in the sudden darkness, the smell of scent was heavy in his nostrils. "Come with me, it's not far." He hesitated, but the call of the flesh was too pressing to be denied. They were in a taxi, and he seemed suddenly to be immersed in the warm recesses of a voluminous fur coat. Invisible lips brushed butterfly light across his ear, an invisible hand wandered over the polished buttons, tugged at the Sam Browne. He paid the grinning driver and followed her with dignity into a little pitch-dark hall. The door closed behind him and the scent was overpowering, mingled with a smell of linoleum. "There are no lights, chérie, mind, the stairs are steep." Her voice was husky. Curtains were pulled back, and in the dim twilight glow of a distant fire he could see her undressing till she stood, a flame-tinged Venus rising from the sea of underclothes.

"Does a soldier practise love in full uniform? Perhaps you are shy, chérie, come, I will help you." She came close to him and he felt for the first time the naked body of a woman pressing close in the darkness. As his hand passed across her breasts so he kissed her and in that ecstatic moment he realised that she had false teeth. In a panic he broke and ran, remembering just in time his cap. Down the steep stairs and out into the street followed all the way by an unbelievable stream of vituperation. He had left his gloves and his ash stick but counted that a small price indeed to pay for his deliverance from the horror of intimacy with dirty dentures.

After ten days' leave he reported to Colony Camp, a Hore-Belisha camp with endless rows of wooden huts set amid Surrey pines. There they continued to do very much as they had done at Caterham and Sandhurst, but now a great number of people saluted them. No one, however, seemed to take newly fledged officers very seriously, and the mess was stiff with bad-tempered elderly subalterns with 1914–18 ribbons and port-stained faces who hardly ever left the deep leather armchairs except to eat or play bridge. Among them were more senior officers, heavily moustached, to whom it was rash to speak.

A story is told of one such.

"Good-morning," said a young officer brightly.

"Good-morning," answered the major, "and good-morning, good-morning, good-morning. Let that bloody-well last you till Friday." He dived behind his paper.

A massive warrant officer taught them drill; every day one of them had to come out and drill the remainder, shouting themselves hoarse.

"Mr Fothergill, sir, take the squad in rifle exercises."

"Mr Crichton-Seely, sir, some slow marching."

Gair never remembered on which foot to give halt and the squad would march interminably, up and down, wrath and boredom on their aristocratic faces.

"Lord Storey, sir, you're marching like a great smelly girl, swing your arms, sir! Halt them, Mr Mainwaring. Stand them at ease. Fall in, sir, please. Now gentlemen there's no life about you today, too much food in the Officer's Mess. Well, we'll have to have a chaser. Squad! As you were, Mr Chivers wake up, sir. Squad! By the left . . . left-right left-right, faster yet gentlemen." The sweat soaked into their service dress. Gair's puttees began to unroll. That happened at least twice a day.

Weapon training under Robert Craven-Bonsor, a purple edition of Robertson Hare who drank huge amounts of neat gin in which his little blue eyes floated and swam. They fired the mortar and the grenade-discharger and the already obsolete anti-tank rifle that kicked like an elephant. On one hideous morning they had to throw grenades.

"Serrated to assist in fragmentation." The fragments humming wickedly. Clubb, of course, let go of his too early— or too late—and it rose straight into the air to fall back among them; fortunately, as Clubb had also primed it, the grenade did not burst.

Tactics were taught by a man who knew, a man who had actually seen Germans, had in fact been chased by them among the mountains of Norway. A Norwegian of stout build whose English was quaint and flowery.

"And on our left were the marvellously big mountains of Narvik, from there the Germans came running at us across the snow, but I with my machine-guns stopped the and made them think with respect of Olafson." Under his

57

guidance they rushed among the Surrey pines or flung themselves panting into the coarse bracken.

"The German is not a gentleman in war, he does not expect to play it as the cricket, so you must learn to hit him, hit him marvellously hard." Gair secretly thought him rather bogus, and Maurice was convinced he was a spy.

One of the senior majors, a man of little breeding with a bristling moustache, delivered an embarrassing lecture on etiquette and codes of behaviour. How they had the privilege of wearing a cap at meals, playing bridge, or ensconced on the lavatory seat; they were never to speak of the Guards nor use the words mufti, Coldstreams or bagpipes. "It is not usual," he went on, "to use the following expression to describe a visit to London. Slip into flannel bags and rev up to the Big Smoke in the gutsy little bus. I see nothing to laugh at, Armstrong." Peas were more easily conveyed to the mouth by means of a fork, and no officer below the rank of lieutenant-colonel was to be addressed as sir. " . . . and never let me hear any of you speak of the Regiment as crush, mob or outfit." It was unbelievable, he must have had his tongue in his cheek, and yet did not appear to. For he took himself as seriously as God. On some nights, usually the wettest and darkest, another almighty creature, Herbert Finch, organised compass marches in the mire of Colony Bog. Major Herbert Finch was a soldier of the old school who believed in much leave and the very minimum of exercise, and when he did come into the open air it was in one of three cars, each larger and more opulent than the last.

He would arrive in his purring motor-car, and from then on they could follow his movements by the red glow of his cigar, the occasional gurgle of liquid leaving a flask. He knew nothing whatever about a compass and cared less, for three of his cronies were waiting to start a game of bridge. Later he would appear again, usually with one of the cronies and their voices were loud and petulant in the drizzle.

"I say, what a bloody awful night."

"Rotten, isn't it? Hullo there! Anyone there? Hullo."

"Come on, Herbert, they're all lost. Do 'em good a bit of rain, they need to learn how to rough it." Gair, floundering

58

uselessly from point X to point Y on a bearing of 269 degrees, shook the water from his cap and watched the head-lights scything the darkness as the Rolls turned for home.

They roughed it in the trenches as well. A system of earth-works complete with bays and saps and communication trenches dug in a wood and bearing no more resemblance to blitzkrieg warfare than a thin red line. For an hour at dusk they manned the sandy labyrinths of Finch's Folly and then, after dark, they repaired to a deep dug-out, where by the light of 'Journey's End' candles in bottles, they ate a four-course dinner and drank large quantities of wine. No wonder their German counterparts, already veterans of Poland and France, counted the war as won.

But soon the holiday was over and it was time to move on.

"Armstrong and Mainwaring will go to the Tower of London." Gair was bitterly disappointed. He had wanted to stay and train a platoon of his own or better still go to the desert.

"K-king's Guard and drill, what a ghastly prospect!"

"Oh, I don't know," said Anthony, who was more philoso-phical. "More fun to be had in London, anyway, it won't be for long, they're bound to send us to one of the battalions."

## Chapter 4

THE Tower of London. The Bloody Tower. The White
Tower. Grim, one-way processions through Traitor's Gate.
Ravens that hop and peck on the grass where stood the block
that was the last resting-place of many august heads. Beef-
eaters and great creaking gates; walls of such a thickness
that not even the improved explosives of the twentieth
century could so much as shake them, which was just as well
for a great deal of improved explosive cascaded from the
darkness and burst on Tower Hill.

Gair had a room in the chaplain's house which was not
very solid and shook crazily whenever a bomb went off. Lying
in bed he could see the reflection of fires and searchlights on
the walls of the White Tower and often, before the raid grew
too intense, he would wonder what other occupants of that
room had seen. Usually before long he wondered only
whether he would see another sunrise.

"Early bed tonight, I think, get a bit of sleep before the
fun begins." Leave the mess—where no one had spoken to
Anthony and him for the first three days, not even 'pass the
salt'—and walk across the moonlit square, hear behind
blacked-out casements the loud murmur of the barrack-rooms
and up the narrow staircase to the little old room with its iron
bedstead and three-footed chest of drawers and mice-riddled
wainscoting. Into bed and lie listening drowsily to footsteps
on the square, a bugle sounding some call, the hoot-hoot
of a tug on the river. Think of tomorrow with its drill parades
and its gas-mask practice in the moat and wonder if he would
ever go to war. To real war where it was possible to hit back
and not to lie helpless in a bed that danced on a bucketing
floor while plaster rained on an unprotected face. Ah! There
they go. The banshees wailing, their dismal note of fore-
boding and warning, as familiar a sound in the London skies
as that of trains crossing Hungerford Bridge. He snuggled

deeper into the narrow bed and suddenly thought of coffins; as apt accompaniment to the thought came the sound of the first bomber, flying broken-noted up the course of the moon-glazed Thames. The guns were firing from the Estuary to Tower Hill; searchlights hunted among the shell-bursts. He listened to the engines—nearer, louder—he was no longer drowsy. It was overhead, and its load went down on the City. More were coming, guided by the traitor Thames to the very heart of London. He heard a bomb begin to fall, then another, another, a stick of five were rushing earthwards, every one aimed at him personally, and from beneath the bed he listened to the gigantic noise of their exploding (one he was certain on the landing outside) and then the urgent call of a bugle sounding the Alarm. A few minutes later he was on top of the White Tower, in nominal command of a fire-spotting party.

"It's going to be a real bastard, this one," said one of the guardsman tersely.

"Aye, there'll be plenty of fires to spot the night."

"I got a brother drives an ambulance, 'e'll be busy, I reckon."

The river was burnished blood, and smoke drifted between the arches of Tower Bridge. Mingled with the infernal din of high explosive was the roar and crackle of flames from the burning warehouses on the opposite bank; now and then an accurately aimed bomb would fling high the blazing wreckage and showers of pretty sparks shot into the air. With a low rumble the side of a building collapsed hissing into the river and they could see the furnace within. Fire-bombs began to fall, raining in showers on to the stricken streets, flaring into brilliant flame simultaneously at a dozen points.

"Down!" yelled Gair. With a shrill whistle the incendiaries passed above them and clattered on the roof across the square. They heard muffled shouts and then saw figures scrambling among the spitting phosphorus, throwing sand.

"Look sir, look—over there by the bridge." Something swung lazily down on the end of the crimson-tinged parachute.

"A Jerry, boys, a flickin' Jerry."

"It's not a J-jerry, better duck again." The mine touched the water and even from where he stood, Gair felt the wave of blast; water and mud pattered on their helmets.

"Flickin' 'ell!" seemed to cover the incident. Still the bombers came, droning over the lake of flame till the Tower was ringed by fire and sweat broke out on their faces and in that sweat stuck ashes and dust.

Guns which must by then have been red-hot were firing without pause. Whoomph! Whoomph! A carpet of shells twinkled in the searchlight beams. Throughout those long relentless hours the White Tower built by the Conqueror never even quivered. When at length the bombers ceased to come, and the guns were silent, they could hear above the roar of the burning city the urgent clanging of ambulance bells.

"The lousy stinking flicking b——rs!" swore a guardsman.

"Blame the war, mate, not them bastards, on their way 'ome to a wife and kids, we'd do the same if we could."

"My brother drives an ambulance, 'ope 'e's all right. I mean, can't be much fun in that lot."

Most nights were noisy, but none so bad as that. Incidents stand out.

Tony appearing on the square, face blackened by soot, holding in his left hand a glass of whisky, in his right a heavy automatic which he brandished vaguely skywards shouting as he did so: "Come down here, you yellow-livered swine, come down and fight." The lights were on in some vaulted chamber filled with armour and history, no one could find the switch and so with unerring skill he shot out the bulbs, for which commendable act he received a reprimand.

Z Platoon. An emergency platoon that stood by each night in case of trouble in the streets, under the command of inexperienced youths who had to take the decision whether or not to open fire on their own people should the need arise. Often they were called out to spend the night in wrecked basements or burnt-out warehouses.

"On no account is anyone to pass west of such and such a street. Is that clear?"

"Yes, sir. But s-supposing, well—if there's p-panic or anything, what . . . ?"

"You'll see on the spot. Get out there as quick as you can, the police are a bit worried in case there's a rush. . . ." The telephone rang, and as Gair went out the adjutant said:

"Direct hit, danger of panic? Right, I'll send another platoon."

The big troop-carrier rushed them down Commercial Road crunching on the glass and debris, figures lay under blankets on the pavements, and an ambulance passed them at speed. Gair spent till dawn by a field telephone drinking sweet tea and listening to the guardsmen snoring. Sometimes a policeman came in, or a warden, once an old woman searching for her husband, her clothes limed with dust. They gave her tea, and she wandered away crying. No one tried to rush the flimsy barrier nor fling themselves against the bayonets, and as another smoke-grimed dawn appeared gingerly above fresh ruins they went home to shave and drill.

There was the time when they had to take sandbags and shovels to clean up the horror of a tube station which, packed with people, had received a direct hit. They worked by the flickering light of lanterns in a shambles impossible to describe, in a frenzied bedlam of shrieks and formless groans, amid the reeking odour of warm blood. The arch of the tunnel was coated thick with human remains, and even the toughest of the guardsmen had in turns to stagger above for air. To some who had never seen anything worse than a dead chicken, it was an unbelievable nightmare. An unborn child lay curled in a lacerated womb and with the rest of the bones and the flesh, they shovelled it into a sandbag. A short-cut to eternity. The pretty girl who lay fully conscious staring at her silk-stockinged legs, severed from her body by a yard of rubble. . . .

With their task completed they drove home again to shave and drill; there was no talk nor ribaldry in the trucks, and the faces of the soldiers were drawn and grey beneath the stubble.

Gair bought a dog off an impecunious comrade; a young Alsatian, black and gold, with twinkling intelligent eyes and steel-trap jaws. Her name was Tessa and she appeared to enjoy military life. Her exercise at the Tower consisted mainly of chasing the ravens, approaching with casual stealth and then leaping in for the kill, or harrying a poor little old terrier named Mickey Rooney whose owner, a yeoman warder, complained to the Governor.

She often joined parade and sat quietly beside Gair to the intense enjoyment of the guardsmen.

"Mr Mainwaring, get that animal off parade!"

"Yessir. Here, Tessa, come on—oh, for God's sake, get out of it." When the pipes played, Tessa would howl like a wolf ancestor.

Her pet abominations were pekinese dogs and strangers who attempted to enter her master's room; her pet amusements were finding hidden sticks or stones and barking at senior officers' field boots.

On spare afternoons he would take her for walks in Kensington Gardens where she would chase her old tennis ball and any pekinese within range and then lie grinning with delight in the smoky sunlight. As a companion Gair found her delightful as she did not require to be entertained with conversation.

The guardsmen loved her.


"Perhaps three extra picquets will help to make you smarter." The adjutant looked coldly from beyond the mass of papers on his desk. Gair went fuming to his room. Three days of confinement, of doing the boring routine chores, of commanding Z platoon, his evening with Denise ruined and all for a minute stain on his blancoed gas-mask pack. Was this how to win the war and free mankind? Every morning it was the same: the officers' parade for drill under the adjutant. Stand on the steps of the mess whilst he inspected them.

"Your puttees, Mr Carter."

"Hair-cut, Mr Mainwaring."

"Your turn-out's a disgrace, Mr Armstrong." There was fluff on his service-dress jacket.

"You must persuade your servant to polish your boots sometimes, Mr Cartwright, come and see me after parade."

The Afrika Korps had arrived in the desert, the Panzers were massed on the shores of France and this pompous, polished nitwit was fussing about specks of dust! In ordinary life the adjutant was a very pleasant fellow, but on the square, following their every sweating move with beady eyes, he was as popular as a skunk at a tea-party. They drilled each day while the ravens muttered hoarsely and hopped over the grass where the head of Anne Boleyn had fallen, severed by the sword.

Every so often Gair went on King's Guard. He was the junior boy, the Ensign, who in peace-time carried the colour. The Guard paraded in the morning, were inspected and then went via the tube to St James's Park, from there by march-route to Wellington Barracks. Part of the rigmarole was the fixing of bayonets, and on one fine morning Gair experienced trouble over 'bayonets'.

"Guard will fix b——" He tried again. Outside the railings the usual vacant-looking crowd was pressing close and gaping. 'Ullo, what's up with the officer? 'E's forgotten what comes next, look Ernie, 'e can't remember. The drill-sergeant was mouthing frantically, cursing these civilians masquerading as officers.

"Bayonets, sir, bayonets!"

"I know, you bloody fool," Gair mouthed in return. The guardsmen waited impassively. Faces were looking from the barrack-room windows. He longed for bombs to fall to blow away that appalling tension of his nerves. "Bayonets!" The word shot out, taking him by surprise.

"Well done, guvnor, got it at last!" called a bystander.

Then with drums beating and pipes skirling they marched to St James's Palace, clad not in the scarlet glory of peace but the brown sterile garb of war with revolver in place of sword, steel helmet in place of bearskin, where for two days of holiday they lounged in the Palace Guardroom and invited lovely girls to tea and drinks. At two in the morning Gair had to march round the sentries who stood each beside his little steel bee-hive shelter and question them on their orders. Breakfast on Guard was a gentleman's meal at half past nine, and then the day to idle away with sleep and a book till it was time for more lovely girls. Smoked salmon and Homard Americaine, soufflés and crême brûlé, sole meunière and the choicest wines. It was rugged on Guard.

"Excuse me, sir, might I have a word with you."

"Yes, Corporal Ferns, what's it about?" The mess corporal sidled closer, a sly gloating expression on his suety indoor face. "It's a little matter of a cheque, sir."

"A cheque. W-what cheque?"

"A cheque for two pounds seven and six made out to self and cashed through G. Bulstrode, one of the local tradesmen, sir—it's been returned marked R.D." His little eyes gleamed.

"Returned? R.D.? What d'you mean, returned?" To Gair it was all gibberish.

"No credit, sir, nothing to meet it in the bank." He breathed throatily.

"Good God, Corporal Ferns!"

"Sir."

"Well, I mean, can you pay him? You must p-pay him and apologise and all that sort of thing. I say, how awful, n-no credit."

The matter was hushed up. It was only surprising that nothing of that nature had occurred before, for the newly joined officers were living to a man riotously beyond their means. The mess was inhabited by many pre-war expensive officers who had always known the very best of everything and saw no reason to alter their mode of living. On pay of fifteen pounds a month it was difficult to meet a mess bill of eighteen pounds and the demands of the current girl-friend.

"It's as cheap to dine out really." That was the cry, and so they dined and wined in smart restaurants on non-existent money and went on to night-clubs where they felt very proud and conspicuous in their blue, often returning to the Tower between burning buildings and along blood-splashed pavements.

Then one day, like a bolt from the blue, came their posting orders. Armstrong to the desert. Mainwaring, Carter and Fitz-William to Headquarters Fighter Command.

"You lucky d-devil, Anthony."

"Ah, well, Mainwaring, we can't all be successful soldiers, and after all someone must stay to keep an eye on the women and children." Gair watched the draft parading, clumsy in their marching order, under the lowering evening sky. Six officers, and why, oh why, could he not have been among them? A few months later three were dead and three including Anthony herded into Italian prison camps, so perhaps he was better off at Bushey.

There cannot have been a more vital spot than Bushey during those months when the fate of Britain lay in the hands of a few young pilots and every fighter aeroplane was worth treble its weight in gold. At least, though not facing Rommel, Gair was more operational at Bushey.

"Our job is to defend this place against any and every form of armed attack, and defend it we will." Captain Maxton thumped the table, his thin face alight with determination.

Starting that very day they set about rendering the defences impregnable. They laid miles of wire, not in fences but in broad belts surrounding the underground Headquarters, and twined haphazard between the trees—until a senior Air Force wife complained she could not use her favourite short-cut through the woods. A path had to be left. (Unbelievable, isn't it?)

Pill-boxes, expertly camouflaged, were dotted at strategic intervals; however, owing to an oversight, their arcs of fire were in every case entirely masked by large trees.

"Cut them down!" ordered Captain Maxton briefly.

The merry ring-ding-ding of axes was heard, and the air was alive with whirring chips.

"What the devil's going on here?" The face beneath the oak-leafed brim was suffused.

67

"What's it look like, cock?" queried the guardsman without looking round.

"I am Air-Commodore Snatchpole, where's your officer?"

"Here, sir." Gair appeared providentially.

"Stop this cutting instantly. Who's responsible? Who ordered it? Why? Didn't he know the trees were essential for camouflage?" And much more.

"God help us if the pilots are as dim-witted as these men."

Camouflage won the day, the trees remained and the pill-boxes were useless except to Peter Rudd who utilised them as love-nests for a succession of attractive WAAFs. He and Gair shared a room, and on dance nights it was usual to wake towards dawn and hear the sound of amorous dalliance in Peter's bed, interspersed with the snores of his disgusting old spaniel and the unconscious yelps of Tessa. Maurice blotted an already stained copy-book by inquiring of a group captain who was holding forth to a crowd of goggle-eyed lady officers:

"When you say we, sir, do I take it you mean the royal we, the editorial we, or merely you and your tapeworm?"

What with that sort of thing, the precious trees, guardsmen molesting willing WAAFS, Tessa taken short in the ante-room and the incident of the steel cupola, there was not that spirit of close camaraderie between the khaki and sky-blue that one would have wished to see.

A steel cupola arrived fresh from the factory and ready for installation. Where to put it? Somewhere central, for with its steel mushroom top, revolving and slitted, it was clearly the pivot of the defence.

"Got it. Of course, we'll put it on top of the Headquarters, wonderful field of fire, covers all that wire." Captain Maxton was enthusiastic, Gair and Maurice less so.

"But how do we get it up there? The bloody thing weighs about two tons."

"Pull it up with ropes, relays of men, we'll manage." Donald Maxton was an enthusiast, but an intelligent enthusiast who knew what was possible and what was pure pipe-dream.

"Supposing we go through the roof?" No one paid any

attention to Peter, who was as usual rather drunk. It took an hour of solid heaving on the part of some thirty guardsmen to drag the inert mass of steel to the grass-covered top of the underground headquarters.

"And now the flicking thing's got to be dug in, aah, flick it!"

Gair cut the first turf with his little silver spade, and then the pickaxe gang set to, but no more than ten blows had been struck before a frantic message came from below to ask what was happening on the roof, the roof that was meant to withstand the largest of bombs.

In place of the daily expected parachute attack they had to arrange a mock raid by a neighbouring unit. From the enemy angle it was an unqualified success as a horde of men with burnt-cork faces and stocking-caps came pouring through the famous short-cut path that led them to the very door of Top Secret itself. They swarmed over the roof, hunting like rats for any opening, they stuffed tear-gas bombs down the air ventilators and caused a lot of confusion and choking angry men. Tessa barked wildly in the chaos and rushed about hysterically. Then they vanished, bearing with them a short-sighted aircraftsman whose glasses had been broken in the mêlée and who thought they were Germans. No one ever suggested another sham attack.

Maurice was the one who really enjoyed himself; he lay on the grass beneath a leafy oak-tree and read poetry or practised on his flute while the guardsmen stripped the Bren-guns or did bayonet drill all round him. Sometimes they stirred themselves and went for route marches through Watford, but mostly they manned the defences and waited tight-lipped, hawk-eyed, for the parachutists who never came. Donald Maxton painted and wrote articles on contemporary art; Maurice perfected 'L'Après-midi d'un Faune' on his flute; Gair watched birds, and Peter chased the WAAFs and drank quantities of gin. Not long afterwards the Regiment decided it could do without him, and, after a chequered career, he was torpedoed and drowned in the Merchant Navy. He had great personality but was what is termed a misfit. In action he might well have been an excellent leader, certainly a very brave one. He went, and then Donald went to Scotland on some hush-hush job connected with water-borne landings. The happy-go-lucky party was broken up.

Major Farrell who took over command had very different ideas on the efficient running of a detachment. He brought with him a whiff of the barrack-square and a strong smell of metal-polish.

"These men I see walking about here are not guardsmen," he said acidly. "They're—they're—" words failed him.

The officers clearly filled him with an even deeper horror, and one could imagine him complaining to his contemporaries at the Club: "It's fantastic what they're letting in these days, no smartness, no discipline, nothing. No conception of how to behave, why at the moment I've got a couple of real corkers, one of them moons round looking at birds all day, the other plays a bloody penny whistle thing,—ah, waiter, glass of port, please—no, it's perfectly true, their hair needs cutting most of the time too. What I can't understand is why don't they join a line regiment. God knows what effect it'll have on the men." The only effect which Major Farrell ever had on the men was to make them question even more than usual the necessity of a privileged class.

Fortunately the new régime did not last long, and amid the familiar atmosphere of order and counter-order the detachment packed its bags, handed over the thankless task to another unit and departed *in toto* for an area on the northern outskirts of London. They arrived to find another three hundred officers and men whom they joined to form the nucleus of a new battalion.

## Chapter 5

By the time they left Wanstead Common they did so as a completely equipped, up-to-strength battalion, but they were not trained. True they had practised section training and platoon training, they had more weapons to play with, more vehicles in which to travel—and they were possessed of great enthusiasm and eagerness 'to close with the Boche and destroy him'. They felt themselves turning from raw material into what they to a man considered to be a good battalion. In short, they had one of the greatest assets for war, *esprit de corps*. To lead them, they had probably the keenest soldier of all time, a man to whom champagne was so much dish water as compared to a mess-tin of tea drunk beneath a leaky canvas roof or better still watched by the cold eyes of the winter stars. He was indefatigable, he was energy plus, come rain come fine, his imagination was both vivid and usually unfettered, and above all Colonel Andy Gore was a very brave man for despite the loss of a leg in 1918 he was as active and mobile as anyone in his battalion. On the longest approach march over the roughest country on the darkest night he maintained his place in the van, surmounting every obstacle, leaping streams and ditches, scrambling over barbed wire fences, ploughing through acres of mud. Despite the pain he must frequently have felt he never once gave up nor lagged behind, and what is more, he expected that same standard from everyone else.

So, under Colonel Andy, they set out on a training tour which was to take them to many different corners of England and to keep them on the move for the best part of two years. By train, by lorry and on their aching feet. From camp to camp. Training, training, training, all the time, till even their dreams were peopled by devilish instructors who urged them on—and on.

71

Those of you who have lain on a camp bed tilted by the slope of a muddy hill-side and listened to the dervish scream of the wind as it rushed among the tents, slapping at the soaking canvas, plucking tent pegs from the slime, driving rain squalls with hideous tattoo against the flimsy shuddering shelter; who have lain and felt the drips upon your upturned face and have vainly sought warmth and oblivion in the recesses of a dampening sleeping-bag; have longed for and yet dreaded the coming of dawn, who have heard the sharp snap of guy-ropes and have emerged to greet the sodden daylight from under a heavy welter of poles and canvas, those who have experienced such things will understand and visualise only too clearly that first day-break in Morthoe Camp. Below them the sea, grey and angry, lashed the rocks. Above them the clouds disintegrated into steady rain, the wind blew and blew and blew away the officers' marquee writhing like a deflated zeppelin and carrying with it any hopes of breakfast. But McPhee was there, the cunning trusty little man from Glasgow, who brought Gair a mug of tepid tea and a boiled egg.

"W-well done, McPhee, how did you manage it?"

"The mess corporal laid the egg, sir, when the tent blew away. What'll it be today, battledress or denims?"

"Denims, oh, and by the way, I'll t-take you for the platoon route march."

"Me, sir? But there's all your kit to do and besides my feet are terrible, excused boots for two days, the M.O. said."

"There's nothing wrong with your feet, McPhee, and you know it, parade nine o'clock." McPhee went away grumbling. "Bring 'em tea an' eggs an' that's how they pay you back."

The platoon was surly. Its socks were damp and it had had nothing to eat but congealing beans and soggy bread. Roll on the flicking desert! Even Sergeant Thomas was bad-tempered and left out his usual cheerful: "Morning, sir, what's it to be today?" and merely rapped out: " Number Seven Platoon, ready for your inspection, sir."

Gair walked down the three short ranks, followed as

always by a gimlet-eyed Tessa, still not quite certain what he should be noticing, still apt to hear low growls from Sergeant Thomas behind him.

"Haircut, Smith."

"And you, Wakefield, you're like a bloody opera singer."

"Get yer equipment properly fitted, Smith '07, next time you'll be in the report, got it?" Gair hoped that in time he would develop an inspecting eye.

"Right, pay attention to the platoon commander, stand still, McAnespie!"

He explained how they were going to march for ten miles and at every halt there would be an observation test.

"We'll m-make it a competition between s-s—, between s— (oh, blast)—between sections." The use of a short sharp expletive was a certain release valve. Even the mention of a small prize brought no more response than a badly muffled belch from Brogan.

"Stop talking!" Brogan stared at Sergeant Thomas, his spotty face impassive. That's how it was some mornings when they were mulishly bored and showed it. Later in the day when the clouds had gone and the sun warmed their marching bodies they cheered up and sang.

" . . . she'll be wearing silk pyjamas when she comes . . ." Gair sang lustily. He was happy for they were a good lot and his first command.

"Coming round the mountain when she comes. . . ." The best platoon in the battalion. Kirk, Hinchcliffe, stocky men, miners from Fife. Lance-Corporal Hughes. Galbraith with his fund of dirty stories. McRae, big red-faced farm labourer, deadly with the Bren-gun. Oliver and Polson, the inseparables from the same West Highland village. McLeod and Reed, who was it they reminded him of? Laurel and Hardy, of course, one thin and lugubrious, the other fat and jolly.

"There were rats, rats, as big as flicking cats in the store, in the store. . . ." Lance-Sergeant Reilly accompanied on his mouth-organ, steel helmet on the back of his head. A born soldier who did not give a damn for anyone. No ties, no scruples, no religion. Gair twirled his stick and threw it for Tessa to retrieve. He liked them all and he hoped and thought

that they liked him. On the return to camp the piper played—
'Stabbing with practised melancholy this bright, uncomprehending world'—and bringing the deafest of Devon worthies
to their cottage doors to cheer and wave. McPhee limped
ostentatiously the whole way home.

Pleasant days among the bracken-covered coombs; lying
close to the murmuring sea, watching the gulls as they glided
down from the tall cliffs; digesting the haversack rations
while the midday sun rode high across the dark-blue sky and
the sounds of the guardsmen playing football with a tin or
throwing things for Tessa came to him muted by drowsiness.
Then, as always, it was time to work again, and Alec, the
company commander, mounted his Exmoor pony and rode
unsteadily among the platoons, his long legs trailing earthwards. Unorthodox in his methods, deceptively casual in his
manner, easy-going and placid until roused when he became
in a flash a different man with ice-chip eyes and acid in his
tones. Very unofficially he permitted his officers to carry
rifles on training for, as he put it: "They move quicker for a
bullet than for all the shouting in the world." Rarely were
the orders 'Get down' and 'Don't stand on the blasted skyline' heard, instead the slamming echo of a rifle, the whip-
crack of a closely aimed bullet and a startled guardsman would
spit the earth from his mouth and resolve never again to
dawdle in a gap. In the evening they marched back to camp,
tired but curiously content after their day of crawling and
hiding in the golden bracken. That's how it was every day, for
days, for weeks, for months. Learning to attack, to defend, to
patrol and to observe. It seemed to Gair that never in his life
had he done anything but teach men to kill and to save themselves from death. Every moment of every day was devoted
to practising better ways of killing. Camouflage and field-
craft, which came easy to the countrymen, but those whose
life had been within the close confines of a city, oh, how slow
and clumsy they were, placing their great feet on every twig,
unable to pick out men hidden on the hill-sides or to tell from
whence a bullet had come. In his platoon he had three game-
keepers, a stalker, and one, McDiarmid, who styled himself
professional poacher. It was those five who formed the back-

bone of the platoon, knowing as they did the meaning of keen eyesight, stealthy movement. They knew the ways of the countryside, and McDiarmid, with his home-made snares, provided rabbits for dinner.

Gair had the idea that they should be taught self-reliance, how to act on their own and not always to wait for orders from superiors who one day might well be dead.

"D-develop initiative, Sergeant Thomas, that's what we've g-got to do, make them think for themselves and not be a flock of d-damned sheep." Sergeant Thomas looked shocked, for these were ideas that went directly against the training of the barrack-square. The platoon was transported fifty miles away in a blacked-out lorry to an area where traffic was practically non-existent, split into pairs and sent off. The first pair home consisted of two men who not so long before had been a male nurse and a colliery banksman.

There was little time for relaxation, no way to relax except an evening of heavy drinking or a visit to the local sea-side resort that seemed to be nothing but deserted boarding houses and sad little bungalows with 'To Let' signs in the window.

They forgot the meaning and shape of a woman as they rumbled slowly through the West Country, moving from camp to camp until at length they settled for a month or so in tents pitched under beech trees which, however fine the weather, always dripped. On a hill named Cheese. Marston Pigott had one advantage over the previous places. It was near enough to London for an occasional hectic week-end from Saturday midday till 2359 hours Sunday. Finish work, run for the tents, quick rub beneath the arms, scramble into Service Dress.

"McPhee! McPHEE! Where's my forage cap? And stick, and gloves—and that infernal gas-mask? All right Peter, just coming." McPhee always chose that moment to present his wage slip.

"The sevenpence halfpenny's for blanco, sir."

"Hell, I won't have enough for the ticket, g-get it off the mess sergeant, sorry, can't stop." A rush for the station cramming with a thousand other soldiers into the one small stuffy train that chuffed them slowly to a few hours of freedom.


Dinner with Denise. The lovely, desirable Denise. Expensive drinks at the Berkeley, the Ritz, what matter? Expensive dinner at some smart gilded restaurant, dancing with the feel of her hair on his cheek, his lips. The dark oasis of the taxi and kisses that tasted so much sweeter after so much abstinence. Hot words in the pale darkness, ending in a moment of madness with:

"Darling, will you marry me?"

"Darling, if you mean will I go to bed with you, the answer is —"

"'Ere we are, number twenty-eight."

"Come in, we'll have some coffee."

Gair leapt from a bed which he had not left for fourteen hours.

"Hell's bells, I've only got ten minutes to get that train."

"Darling." He looked across the room at her. The gold of her hair shone in the light of the bedside lamp, her naked shoulders were whiter than the pillow itself, the twin mounds of her breasts pressed through the sheet.

"Darling," she said again in her lilting, rather husky voice. Later he woke and looked at the clock again.

"In for a penny." He drew her close.

Two hours on a bench at Paddington surrounded by people who snored, who were drunk, who were sick. His eyes smarted, his face was rough, the cap star needed a polish. There was spittle on the ground and an unused contraceptive; wagons banged into each other, and an engine let off ear-splitting steam. His head began to ache and he assuaged the dryness of his mouth with a cup of tea off a trolley.

"You do look tired, dearie," said the elderly woman serving. He dozed and wondered why he could not still be with Denise. It seemed so pointless to sit on a dirty bench as the first greyness of daylight showed dimly through the grimy glass roof and lovers fumbled deliriously on the next seat.

76

"Officer there, mate, can't sit near 'im." Two sailors went past, a sheen of alcoholic sweat on their faces.

"One o' the foxy-faced kind, cor blimey look at 'is comic-opera 'at." The speaker was violently and disgustingly sick all over the lovers.

Gair found himself a corner seat and set off to face cold reality.

"A fortnight's extra picquets," said the adjutant, and as Gair was going out : "Hope it was worth it."

He did not get another chance of a lost week-end for many months.

"All right, sergeant-major, let's get started."

Company Sergeant-Major Mooney strode to the flimsy hut door and flung it wide.

"By the left, quick march, left-right, left-right—maark ti-ime. Orders, Halt! Right turn! Right dress! Eyes front! There are two guardsmen in the report, sir."

Alec pulled at his moustache and said quietly :

"Guardsman Oliver." The man stepped forward with a crash of huge boots, saluting as he did so.

"Guardsman Nisbett." Nothing happened.

"Come on Nisbett, you've been in here often enough, wake up, man!" Mooney glared ferociously.

"Both same case," murmured Alec and read from the charge sheet.

"Whilst on active service at Long Deverill Camp on the 22nd November, 1942, they did absent themselves from 2359 hours leave until they returned to camp at 0530 hours. Absent 5 hours 30 minutes. Lance-Sergeant Barker." A figure that had been lurking in the background, leapt into view. Tessa let out a warning growl.

"Sir, on the 22nd November, 1942, I was sergeant in charge of the camp quarter guard when these two guardsmen reported to me at 0530 hours, knowing them to be absentees I placed them in close arrest and reported the case in the usual manner, they were clean, sober and properly dressed.

Sir!" He leapt back again. There was silence save for the stertorous breathing of the accused. Alec scribbled on the blotter and Gair standing close behind him could read, 'Why not clean, bright and slightly oiled?' With considerable difficulty he suppressed a muffled laugh.

"Well, what have you got to say, Nisbett?"

"The fact is, sir, Ted—that is, Guardsman Oliver and myself left ourselves too little time to catch the eleven o'clock train from Salisbury seeing as we had been visiting friends the other side of the town. Old friends, sir, we hadn't seen for, oh, since before the war, and —"

"I see, and you, Oliver?"

"Same case, sir." Dumb insolence on his hatchet face.

"Sergeant-major, what time is the last train from Salisbury?"

"One-twenty in the morning, sir. Gets into Long Deverill at one-forty-eight."

"I see. And how did you while away the time from eleven o'clock until half past five?"

"Walking back, sir."

"Over six hours, Nisbett?" Alec added a halo to his angel on the blotter.

"We lost our way, sir—it was foggy." His face the picture of injured innocence.

"Take a map next time, and a compass. You'll both be confined to camp for three days. March out." With a flurry of stamping, saluting and twinkling of legs the pair were expelled from the room. The sergeant-major reappeared carrying an enormous leather-bound ledger.

"There are fourteen men in the deficiency book, sir."

"Good God!" Alec unwound himself from the chair.

"Mr Mainwaring'll settle them." Gair's heart sank. He hated taking company orders above anything else, he could never summon up righteous anger over dirty boots and besides reading the charges took him an age. Sullenly he sat down in the chair of office, before him a flock of Alec's little pencilled sheep scampered across the blotter. He took a deep breath.

"Right, sergeant-m-major, m-march in."

78

"Deficiencies! Deficiencies 'shun. . . ." In they came, piling one against the other like badly shunted trucks, till the small room was jam-packed and shuddering beneath the impact of twenty-eight boots striking simultaneously and more men, witnesses, were still fighting to get in.

"'A-a-alt! Right turn! Right dress! As you way-er! Stand still the right-hand man. Right dress! As you way-er! Parkes, *will* you stand still. Right dress!" Once more and the ink would upset. Dust rose in clouds.

"Deficiencies, sir." Sergeant-Major Mooney planted the book in front of Gair. "Those marked with a cross, sir."

Gair's eye roved down the names. Nisbett again and Oliver. Polson three times in a week. The crimes were shocking. Dirty cap star, dirty brasses, dirty boots. Haircut, unshaved for parade, late for fatigue parade. Two had had dirty flesh—momentary vision of dark-grey tripe—and one had been in bed two minutes after reveille. He blurted through the charges, what have you got to say, and you, and you—as if I bloody well care—extra drills, extra fatigues, admonished, one after the other till his ear-drums were bruised by the banging and shouting, his mind awhirl with the excuses, some feeble some clever, some too clever. He initialled the last punishment, and with a further frenzied scramble they got out through the narrow doorway and departed grumbling or rejoicing to the NAAFI.

"Phew!" He threw his cap on the table. Judgment was over, court was adjourned, justice had packed her scales and gone home.

He must speak to Nisbett privately, probably trouble at home, that was usually the answer when a steady man started to go wrong. Gair went to check the platoon kit.

It was then that they joined an armoured division and a new sound came into their lives; the high whine of the big troop-carriers in which they were now to travel, glorying in the title of lorried infantry.

"Yes," emphasised Colonel Andy. "This is a great step

forward, from now on our mobility will be doubled. Gentlemen, we ride into battle, but it is going to mean a lot of hard work from everyone, learning entirely new methods, working with the tanks. . . ." For half an hour he painted a glowing picture of the immediate future.

"I've got to go over to Brigade and find out about Exercise Touchdown; starts on Friday evening." Maurice sighed loudly. "Primarily it is to practise the rapid deployment of a lorried infantry brigade, but I do happen to know that the divisional commander is red-hot on road movement. There'll be a conference for company commanders this afternoon, and a warning order for the Battalion by evening." He limped away, shouting for his orderly who rejoiced in the appropriate name of Foote.

So that was the end of the interesting, intimate training of platoons and companies. From then on it was a steady succession of large-scale schemes, brigade and divisional level, each one more excruciatingly boring than the last, which invariably began at dusk; it was invariably drizzling as they embussed and sat gloomily waiting their turn to pull out into the convoy and move slowly on to the gloomy wet expanses of Salisbury Plain. There cannot be a soldier worthy of the name who does not know the Plain, who has not dug trenches in the chalky soil and crouched in them till at the witching hour of first-light he has gone forward through the dark mist to attack Tinker's Furze or Fox Covert or some infernal neolithic earthwork. Gair lost count of how many nights he spent in the little hot cabin of the troop-carrier, staring ahead through watering eyes at the tiny splash of light of the next vehicle, desperately fighting off sleep in the heat of the cab, jerking the driver awake as they ground slowly along the narrow roads, stopping, starting, stopping again. Through hamlets where fortunate folk were sleeping accustomed and impervious to the ceaseless low roar of traffic that passed along their streets day and night, the continual smell of exhaust. Winterbourne Stoke; Stapleford; Wylye; Tilshead; Chitterne. How well he knew the names, as he searched for them on a rain-spotted map by the intermittent glow of a dying torch. In the back the guardsmen swayed and lolled asleep, with a bored and bad-tempered Tessa curled among their feet. The convoy would stop. He shut his eyes, only for a second, opened them. No light in front. Kick the driver. Hell! Next map reference, road and track junction Maddington Farm, and the night as black as coal and rain streaming on the windows.

"Left here, driver." Or should it have been straight on? Too late. Road worsening, narrowing, finally petering out in a derelict farm-yard with fifty vehicles piling up behind and nowhere to turn. At the conference for all officers held in a local cinema beneath the fixed gaze of the stars, the general, a fiery man, had biting things to say about map reading.

"An officer who cannot read a map should not be an officer. In war he will be useless, I repeat useless, gentlemen." Gair sank lower into his British warm.

There was the occasion when, at the conclusion of a particularly sleepless three days, Roger took what he had worked out to be a short-cut home. The long line of vehicles bowled merrily over an excellent tarmac road, Roger rejoicing at his cleverness.

"Christ almighty!" swore the adjutant as a vast black shape roared just above the command car. "What the blazes was that?"

"Looked like an aeroplane, sir." The driver was unruffled.

Colonel Andy woke up and said, "Every officer must have an aeroplane two and a half inches long," and dropped off again.

Another shape hurtled over the wildly swerving convoy, and another. Later, the Air Force was interested to know why a column of lorries drove across the airfield when heavy bombers were taking off for the Ruhr.

Roger ordered a trayful of pink gins.

"Although I'm useless I might as well be happy."

Another craze of Higher Authority was the formation of boxes, both armoured and soft. For days on end they bumped over the Plain and formed themselves into squares, diamonds or lozenges; sometimes the tanks were inside the square, D or L, sometimes vice versa, very few people cared. That was known as laagering up, or down. Once in the chosen formation they would remain static for hours while the guardsmen chased hares or put the ferrets, which they always seemed to carry, into rabbit holes. Colonel Andy drove round, standing in his jeep, waving coloured flags denoting various activities round the box. Spitfires dived at them, enemy tanks rumbled and squeaked to the crests of neighbouring tumuli and fired blank at the laager. The ferreters continued regardless. Tessa ran riot, her nose caked in earth. They ate stale cheese sandwiches and spam every day. Sometimes, with a clatter, the general's carrier would arrive among them and he would leap out, a bizarre figure in black beret, khaki knickerbockers and a brown golfing jacket.

"Where are your air sentries?" he barked. "Your ground sentries, your latrines; arcs of fire, what are they? Are you in touch with the next platoon? What are those men doing? Stop them. What's your name? How long have you been commissioned? Well, don't you know better than to site your slit trenches in a line? It's what the Hun wants, just what he wants." Away he went, to spread alarm and despondency among other complacent officers. Glaring with his beady little eyes, chewing at his Hitler moustache. He was devilish in traffic jams, his language as he strode from vehicle to vehicle undiluted barrack-room. His was what is known politely as a forceful personality.

Then there were demonstrations, of battalion attacks with tanks, without tanks, tanks by themselves. From behind the white tape the spectators watched and listened to the harsh crackling voice of the loudspeakers. Guns fired hundreds of shells, and it was exhilarating to watch the plumes of black earth and smoke spraying among the cardboard pill-boxes, to hear the swish-swish of the projectiles and see the pseudo-Germans running for safety and waving white flags. Smoke-screens swirled in the still air, explosives of every description went off, aircraft strafed with cannon and machine-gun, and flame-throwers squirted through the smoke.

" . . . once the defences are softened up by the guns the infantry go in covered in close support by the tanks—there they go, gentlemen, into the final assault." Gair watched the little brown dots surge into the smoke, none of them fell, small-arms crackled and he could hear a faint piping cheer.

"Notice the consolidation once the position has been over-run. . . ." It all seemed so simple.

"I s-suppose we are becoming better soldiers," said Gair doubtfully one evening as he and Maurice sat playing back-gammon.

"Well, in the sense that we know how to lay anti-tank mines and can successfully wipe out a non-existent enemy I suppose we are—that's ten and six you owe me—but tem-peramentally I know for an absolute certainty that the military mind and I will never, come what may, see eye-to-eye." Maurice sat back and drank some beer.

"I say, anyone know anything about this new Sherman tank?" Tony Dewar looked up from some training pamphlet, puffing out his cheeks, his head on one side. One of our keener soldiers, he was a walking mine of military misinformation which he imparted with a wealth of erroneous detail.

"I tell you what." Colonel Andy jerked out of his fireside doze. Any who saw his face felt the flutters of apprehension, for they had seen that look before.

"We'll turn night into day."

"My dear colonel, what *will* God say?" drawled Alec from behind his paper.

"Yes, you see, it'll give us practice in night work. We'll simply reverse the time-table, dinner at breakfast-time, sleep all day and then reveille at dusk."

"By jove!" put in Tony. "What a splendid idea, sir."

"Holy smoke!" muttered Maurice weakly.

For two days he worked on his idea and then, challenging the gods, they turned night into day. It was ghastly.

However tired Gair was at the completion of a full night's work he could not sleep, and it was a relief to dress and eat his porridge and sally into the darkness, where he crawled or marched or dug or inspected weapons with a torch until it was time to return at dawn and drink his port. Everyone grew more and more tired, more and more bad-tempered. The idea, like certain others born of that enthusiastic brain, was not a hundred per cent successful. However, it was all part of that toughening process, hardening to the uncomfortable, the difficult, the fantastic, which one day was to stand them in such good stead. Another part of that process was the boxing. It was competitive, with prizes and free beer. Gair, returning one night from Salisbury, not quite himself, put his name on the list. Next morning. Enter McPhee with shaving water and the usual tuneless whistle escaping from between his stained teeth.

"The boys in the company think it's very plucky of you, sir."

"What are you t-talking about, McPhee?"

"Boxing, sir."

"Boxing, b-bloody sport, should be abolished." He felt shocking, his head throbbed, his teeth and tongue were furred.

"The boys of the platoon'll all be there tonight, sir, to give encouragement." Often during the day he toyed with the idea of reporting sick, he could eat no lunch, his fellows were heartless.

"Got a gum-shield, Gair?"

"Don't forget to wipe your nose with your glove."

"And snort loudly, while you shuffle your feet and wave your arms about."

"I believe there's a very pretty nurse in the Salisbury hospital, officers' ward." Nothing seemed amusing, and that evening as he approached the NAAFI and heard the thunder of voices, his knees began to buckle and he had to swallow repeatedly.

"In the green corner Lance-Corporal Tyson of W Company (prolonged and exaggerated cheering), and in the red corner Second Lieutenant Mainwaring of X Company (cheers mingled with cat-calls). Gair sat facing a company storeman, a muscular young man with a complacent look on his large square face, and felt very skinny; there was goose-flesh on his arms. Someone hit a bell, and in a blur of hangover and fright Gair advanced to touch gloves, and almost at once leather connected sharply with his nose, which began to bleed, his eyes watered, and unbidden a murderous rage took hold of him.

"Go on Tyson, go on, boy, give it to 'im, lad. Tell yon officer to get his hair cut! Black his eye, corp!" The glove shot out again and hit the suffering nose. Beyond the glove Gair could see a mocking smile. Tyson bobbed and weaved and snuffled, now and then he smoothed his crinkly hair, grinned at the crowd. A piece o' cake, boys, just watch me. It was pleasant to have a chance to settle an officer good and proper. He came bobbing in, his left flicking at the red splodge of nose.

"Come on, sir." Little Kirk was near the ring, cap on the back of his head. Suddenly Gair knew what he had to do, he felt better, his head was clear and he was very angry. He waded in. Once, twice he connected, wiping away the smile, and again, his blows were not scientific but they seemed to hurt. Pandemonium broke loose. Tessa howled.

"Cummon the officer, give it to him, sir"—"Good old Gair," yelled Kirk, waving a beer bottle. "Go for the body! Hit him—hit him again!" Gair lashed out steadily, there was blood on his gloves, already the breath was panting through a crimson foam, his legs were weakening and he knew it was this round or never.

"The body, hit him in the stummick." Kirk was dancing up and down. Gair summoned the last ounce of flagging strength and aimed a vicious right-hander at Tyson's heart. The storeman stopped in his tracks, went chalk white, his eyes glazed and slowly he fell over. The cheering raised the roof, Kirk and Hinchcliffe invaded the ring and clapped him on the back. Two or three fights broke out in the audience. He felt quite the hero. But never, never again.


The weeks went slowly by, and the occasions on which they had proper nights in camp grew fewer and fewer.

"The Battalion will prepare to move. . . ."

"The Battalion will move . . .", and away they went on

another figment of High Level imagination, at the end of which it must be supposed that someone had learnt something. Certainly not any of them. Except perhaps the art of going without sleep for longer and longer periods.

They crossed imaginary rivers in imaginary assault-boats, once even they sailed across a Channel marked out by white tapes and Alec was violently sea-sick. Umpires came among them.

"You are being heavily dive-bombed." Pause. "Well, what are you going to do about it?" Pause. "Well . . ."

"Why not put on your water-wings and float away?" Alec was tired, bored and bad-tempered, there was rain beginning and two more days to go.

Oh, those umpires! So earnest, so lacking in humour. Appearing always when least required, painting the picture, creating the chaos of war. You're dead, you're dead. But I fired first, sir. You're a casualty, abdominal wound, and you, G.S.W. in chest.

"This bridge is blown, no one can get across, I say, stop, you there. . . ." It was night. The guardsmen rushed the umpire and threw him into the river, pelted over on to the enemy shore. Gair, who saw the incident, had to sit down, he was so weak from laughter, while the sodden umpire dragged himself from the cold water reflecting perhaps on how flimsy was the barrier of rank. So it went on. In North Africa the Germans were cleared from the mountains of Tunisia and trapped at Cape Bon. Great events were astir, but to those who sat in the swaying troop-carriers or dug their hundredth trench in which to greet their hundredth open-air dawn these happenings meant little. Most of them had ceased to hope for foreign service, it was like hoping for the moon or more pay.

"And what did you do in the Second Armageddon, grandpa?"

"Ah, my child, I fought in the imaginary wars on Salisbury Plain. I was in many fights, ah, yes, I remember well the

86

battle of Breakheart Bottom and the day we attacked Robin
Hood Ball. Yes, yes, great days, my child."

The platoon theme song had as its chorus the simple yet
pithy words.

> 'We're going to be b——d about,
> We *are* being b——d about,
> But we *won't* be b——d about!'

Words that rose triumphant through the stillness of many a
night and rang many a welkin and which seemed to sum up
the situation very adequately.

Then during the course of another hectic week-end he met
Helen. A blind date for a party, and at once he knew that he
would fall in love with her. They danced and stood smiling
with their eyes long moments after the music had stopped.
She was lively and quick and her long-shaped eyes were full
of greenish laughter. Her auburn hair which trapped the light
and turned it to gold and copper was rich and glorious. She
had the most beautiful skin and the most beautiful body he
had ever seen.

In the dawn they walked together across St James's Park,
and when they parted he did not kiss her.

A few hours later he took her out to lunch. As the evening
turned to blacked-out night they sat in the little flat, on the
floor against a sofa before a purring gas-fire, drinking cocoa
and saying little.

"Helen."

"Yes." Slowly their heads turned towards each other and
in the flickering light of the fire he could see her lips were
smiling, her eyes shadowy.

"Helen, I—I . . ."

"Don't say anything." He leant across and kissed her on
the smiling lips. The fire purred and sputtered and beyond the
curtained windows sirens began to wail. Later when the
bombers had gone home and the gas was lowering to extinction she whispered.

"You must go, darling."

"When shall I see you again?" She was in the ATS, and
like a million other cogs her soul was not her own.

"Often—very often."

A month later they were married amid much pomp and ceremony and ostrich-feather hats in a large church, and he returned after a short ecstatic week, to the Battalion in its new location in Yorkshire, Helen to some camp near London. For the first time in their short lives they learnt the meaning of a parting.

But after a few months Helen obtained her release from the Army and came with her unborn child to Yorkshire, where a Mrs Organ—a garrulous woman with a liking for Bakewell tart and a hatred of McPhee—rented them two rooms of her amazingly ugly house. And to those rooms he returned at the conclusion of the day's work to a Helen who, as she grew larger, grew ever more lovely.

Sometimes they had people to dinner or for drinks, but not often, for they had no money save his pay of which a large proportion found its way into the red chapped hands of Mrs Organ. Those were halcyon days, and nights of a great and wonderful contentment; and, though she knew that the sands of time were running low, Helen only once gave way before the blackness of the future.

"I don't know if I shall be able to bear it when you've gone. Oh, darling, what shall I do alone and having the baby—and—don't leave me, Gair, you mustn't leave me." She clung to him in the darkness. But always, as she sat and sewed and prepared for her child, she smiled and was gay. McPhee would have thrown himself under a bus for her, which was high praise indeed.

Upon Gair devolved, as sniper officer, the congenial task of providing enemy for the remainder of the battalion and with his eight marksmen, festooned in camouflage veils and with straw in their hair, he would set out for the training area, a desolate place on the Wolds where fences lay broken and tank tracks were impressed deep upon the rich agricultural land. Often the weather was fine, and Gair, after siting his men, would spend happy times bird-watching or merely lying on his back staring at the little lambs'-wool clouds and thinking of his wife. Then the attackers appeared, and when they were within a few hundred yards, advancing well spaced-out, here and there a twinkle from a bayonet or an over-polished piece of equipment, he rolled over, rammed a round into the breech and fired a warning bullet low above their heads. The little dots went to ground, and there was nothing to show that perhaps seventy or eighty men were out in front. He was the only one who fired live, his snipers used blank and they should all have had telescopic sights, but they also were imaginary. So, whenever he saw a man get up and run forward, Gair looked through his imaginary sight and fired as close to the little figure as he dared. Sometimes the fear of another bullet prevented the man from rising, and Gair would spend a hideous moment wondering if he had gone just that much too close. But it taught them to move.

There was a day on a large-scale demonstration watched by three hundred spectators when two guardsmen fell and did not get up again.

"Now, gentlemen, if you look closely you will see how the assault groups are crawling forward into position under cover of the fire platoon, which itself is continually edging forward—there's the first of the smoke going down now—yes, and there's the signal for the assault." His words were drowned by the storm of fire which deluged the hill-side; tack-tack-tack of the Bren-guns and the staccato ripple of rifle fire, the sharp 'crump' of the mortar bombs.

"There they go—keeping well up—firing together on a sign from the assault commander—watch the covering fire switch. . . ." The lines of tracer swung away from the pill-box target and from the row of brown figures which swept forward. A man fell, acting realistically, another man crumpled, clutching at his stomach and as the assault groups rushed upon the pill-box two more men stopped in their tracks and slowly sank down.

The assault was complete, the firing died away, the spectators discussed the demonstration.

"Close!" shouted the assault commander and the casualties got to their feet and went to join the remainder.

"Close!" he shouted again. But the two who lay huddled among the grey rocks did not move. A white-faced sergeant came running to Colonel Andy.

"Major Weatherall's compliments, sir, and could you send for an ambulance, two of the men've been hit. I—I think Guardsman McIntosh is dead, sir. The other man got it in the chest, but he's still alive."

"Oh, my God," said Colonel Andy. "Mr Mainwaring!"

"Sir."

"Take my jeep and get to the nearest telephone. The doctor and an ambulance." He turned to the spectators.

"Gentlemen, I am afraid there has been . . ." Gair heard no more.

Later he sat in the jolting ambulance, striving to staunch the hole in McLeod's side with his hand, where the field-dressing had slipped, at every jolt feeling the rush of hot blood against his skin, wiping away the scarlet thread which appeared at the corner of the half-open mouth. On the other stretcher lay the blanket-covered body of the dead guardsman, his boots clinking together with the sway of the vehicle. Gair had never been with a dying man, had never before seen the awful greyness of approaching extinction as it slowly drowns the colour of life. He looked closely at a face he knew so well, McLeod, a quiet rather shy man, one of the best in the company, and saw how already it was changing, as though decay was at work before the breath had left the lungs. It took on the look of the skull, the lips drew back from the teeth, and over the bony framework of the face the parchment skin began to tighten, the blue eyes were glazing, but moving still, and the air bubbled in his throat. He did not cry out nor speak. A shaft of sunlight slanted through the little window, and with his glazing blue eyes he watched the dust dancing in the beam. That was the last thing he saw in his life, for the punctured lungs could do no more and he died.

At the hospital they wheeled the bodies away on white trolleys; the equipment and the boots they removed and gave to Gair. The last he saw of McLeod was the grey army socks protruding beyond the blanket. A sad, unnecessary way to die. In the evening he got very drunk.

A month later he got very drunk again, they all did, but for a happier reason. The days of pretence were over, those long years of seeming to get nowhere whilst others had the adventure, the excitement, the glory. But it was not wholly a case of rejoicing for they were not to face the foe as a battalion, although they had trained together, knew each other, had confidence in each other. No, for reasons very obscure the battalion was to be broken up. Gair was fortunate, his company was to go intact, but not with Alec, who was posted elsewhere. In his place was David Hardy. Twenty-seven, very intelligent, very amusing, very talented. Sometimes the guardsmen were mystified by his remarks for he was too clever for them, he did not mean to be but his brain and his humour were quicksilver. Often his thoughts seemed miles away. Colonel Andy stumped into the mess one day, worry splashed all over his face.

"I say, it's a great bore, my orderly Foote, has had to go on compassionate leave and I can't find anyone else suitable."

"What's happened to him, sir?"

"You see, his father's died."

"Rather a case of one Foote in the grave, sir," remarked David from behind his paper. Gair thought then that he was going to like him.

Their party was one of rejoicing and one of farewell, the break-up of friendships, the disintegration of what had taken two full years to create, and for those reasons no one was abstemious. Towards midnight Gair awoke on the dew-soaked grass of a local field, under his head as pillow was his gold-braided cap, and he had no clear idea of why he should be there; he attempted to rise, but his legs were curiously weak, and he lay back on the solid ground. Cows came to inspect him and butted gently with their velvet noses, the sky was ablaze with stars and he heard dull explosions that were gun-cotton slabs being let off by high-spirited officers.

91

Many windows were broken, many civilians complained, but by then they were beyond the range of complaints. The company was entrained and bound for Colony Camp, after a departure of pure fantasy. Early in the morning they had staggered into full marching order, feeling like the wrath of God, and marched to the station behind the pipe band. Not an officer was completely sober, very few of the men, even Tessa seemed unsteady on her legs. At the rear of the company there drove an ambulance and in it was Company Sergeant-Major Mooney with a badly sprained ankle caused by jumping off a cupboard some hours before. The shrill tones of the pipes hurt horribly; a few early risers waved as they marched down the hill, but most of the inhabitants were lying fuming behind shattered windows. At the station Colonel Andy, with sorrow in his voice, bade them farewell. He had a bitter pill to swallow, first, to see his battalion broken up and, secondly, to be left behind, graded unfit. There can never have been a man so genuinely eager for battle and he had to be left behind to eat his heart out on the Staff, while the men he had trained unsparingly went away to war.

"Good luck to all of you." He finished abruptly and turned away.

"Give him a cheer, lads," called out Reed, and nobody told him to keep quiet. They gave an even bigger cheer to Alec, whom they had known more intimately and of whom they had been very fond. Everyone cheered and laughed away the tiresome lumps in their throats, the company sergeant-major was lifted into the train amid great applause, the station-master looked at his watch, a whistle blew. The pipes burst into the company march, and the train began to move, guardsmen cramming the windows, shouting, waving, singing. Gair could see the figures of Colonel Andy and Alec as they stood side-by-side on the platform, now and again they waved; the figures grew smaller, and the sound of the pipes faded into the rumble of the train.

They discarded their kit and composed themselves to the hard seats, their hangovers and the prospect of many hours' travel. In the next carriage men were 'Rolling out the Barrel'. They were starting for the war.

But before they set forth to battle there were the days of parting, the days which though he tried to spin them out flashed away with sickening speed, remorseless and irretrievable.

For a week the company remained at Colony Camp and every evening Gair drove in an overflowing bus to spend the night with Helen at her parents' house, with Tessa dozing in the corner, the corner where she would have to doze without him for no one knew how long. Gair had not thought it would be possible to feel so deeply the parting from a dog. But her lively brown eyes were entirely human in their knowledge that only a few more hours remained.

"A whole glorious week, darling."

Yet in a moment the days were gone, the nights, like the flare of a match, had blazed and died, and now it was time to go. "Look after her till I get back, Tessa." Somehow he got himself back to camp in a bus filled with silent soldiers who stared as he did out of the windows and saw nothing.

David met him with beaming face. "Departure postponed twenty-four hours."

Gair caught the next bus home and thought how beautiful was the suburban countryside. Twenty-four happy hours are but the single drip of water from a tap.

"I don't think I could stand saying good-bye again, Gair." She looked up from the pillow, and her eyes were dry and darkened with sadness.

It was raining as they drove back, the water dribbling hopelessly down the windows.

"Put off another twenty-four hours, but no more leave. Sorry." Hanging about the soaking camp checking for the hundredth time that the kitbags were correctly marked, the titles removed from shoulders—yet the cap stars remained—and delivering one more lecture on security to restless men.

"Parade 0200 hours, full marching order." At midnight he rang up Helen. He could say no more than:

"I shan't be able to c-come home—" and then it was useless. Her voice reached him, small and tight and then unable to bear it she rang off. Scribbled on the wall by the telephone was a picture of baby elephants—part of a sentence . . . ring

Mayfair 4683, telephone numbers, a German steel helmet. He remained staring at a jumble of pencilled lines which blurred and cleared, blurred and cleared.

"Time to be getting ready, Christmas-tree order." Tommy was leaving no one in particular and his round baby face was excited.

"At last," he added.

"Yes," agreed Gair flatly. "At last."

In the train he sat opposite Rex. 'God', he thought, 'I wonder if my face is so utterly miserable'. David slept, his skin paler even than usual in the sickly gloom of the compartment. Tommy tried to read for a while and then munched at bits of chocolate, as beneath the musty seats wheels ground out their secret refrain.

'Going to war, going to war.'

They rumbled through the drizzling darkness.

\*　　\*　　\*

How is it that each successive generation is fooled by war and men are ready, no, eager to throw their lives away for usually so very little reason? They must have read the literature about the one before, have heard their fathers and grandfathers speak of its filth and destruction; but then that is not what they do describe, they remember only the comradeship, the dangers shared, the free wine and the freedom of active war. The horrors are forgotten, and, to youth that hears the trumpets sounding yet again, the approaching holocaust has glamour and exciting hazard. Besides, each one has the certain knowledge that nothing will happen to him, to Tom-or-Dick-or-Harry-but-not-to-me, he unfortunately cannot visualise himself lying alone bleeding and in pain. Unfortunately, for it is possible that should men be able so to imagine there would be no wars, certainly fewer armies. But that is neither here nor there, for another batch of innocents is waiting to set sail and it would not do to hold them back from that which lies beyond the corner.

# INTO ACTION

## Chapter 6

THE men were filing slowly up the gangway, slipping and pushing, heavily laden with equipment, every face tired and pinched by the bitter January cold. Everything was grey. The ship, the quay, the drizzling mist, the faces unshaven after a night listening to the wheels which took them ever farther from home. For many, probably for most, it was the first trip abroad, the first time they had climbed on board a ship. An impersonal ship that had carried thousands to distant lands and would return for more and which cared little for whether this man had but lately married, if that one had left a pregnant wife or if the sergeant with the sad, worried expression had said farewell to a dying mother. At the appointed hour her engines would start and she would nose out into the Atlantic storms to join her convoy. She was a good ship, old and not over-comfortable, but solid and sea-worthy, and by nightfall some three thousand men would be packed inside her with only the thin dingy plates between them and the sea, the U-boats.

Gair leant against the rail and watched the bulky figures disappearing one by one within the steel side, he relit his pipe and the dead match spiralled down into the water. Two yards of scummy water, filled with old bread and orange peel, rainbowed with oil, milk-tins bobbing, two yards and yet it might have been the whole broad Atlantic. A sudden spurt of bilge shot like vomit into the water, tins came flying from a port-hole far below. On the quay, two officials came out of their office, pulled up their coat collars and hurried away into the soaking dusk. Lucky bastards, thought a thousand men who lined the rails in silence, they were not going anywhere except to catch a tram or a train that would take them across a few miles of English soil to a waiting wife and fireside. Gair bit hard on his pipe and thought with hot, sick longing of his wife. A voice on the deck below began a song, a few joined in and then it petered out like a match in a storm. He went below to the evening meal served by Indians, quiet as cats. His next-door neighbour was a Canadian nurse, fat and ugly and showing unmistakable signs of being jolly. He escaped on deck. It was dark; the glistening quay was lit furtively by shaded, flickering gas-lamps, and rain fell with remorseless permanency on to a ship that seemed coated in silver dust. Down below, the troop decks were packed, a piano thumped out 'Till we meet again'. On shore the town lay black save for the occasional bright flash of a tram, the glowing tips of cigarettes showed where people were standing on the dock-side. He crossed the deck and looked across the Mersey; beyond the swirling mist a foghorn boomed, a huge animal in pain, and quite close a winking red light showed a sunken ship. He paced up and down, up and down till the loud-speakers sounded to clear decks.

"All troops below. All troops below." The crackling voice which was to enter their very dreams. After a laborious journey along endless steel companionways, down little steep ladders, plunging ever deeper into the foetid clanging bowels, stumbling over piles of kit, pushing between swollen hammocks, through solid walls of noise, he reached the corner where his platoon were ensconced.

"Everything all right?"

"Get properly sorted out in the morning, sir," said Sergeant Thomas, who, in his shirt sleeves, was rigging a hammock.

"Cor, what a carry on, ain't it?" yelled Reed above the shindy of boots on steel, the throwing about of equipment in a confined space.

"What's that roaring n-noise?"

"Ventilators, sir. By God, we're goin' to need them before this trip's over."

"Heh, that's my flickin' 'ammick!"

"Ah, flick off, Polson."

"Life on the ocean wave, life on the rolling deep—heh, steady on Hinch, that's my rifle ye're using." Kirk broke off his song.

"Got to wedge this flicking bunk," said Hinchcliffe.

"Any chance of gettin' the port-holes open, sir?" asked Oliver.

"I d-doubt it, you're below the water-line." Gair wondered whether he should have told them. Some were trying on the bulging life-belts, boxing each other—"'it 'im in the tits, Jacko!" He looked at the narrow ladders and thought of the sea outside above the level of their ceiling and mentally he shuddered.

"Well, if there's n-nothing else." Sergeant Thomas turned his sweating grinning face.

"No, sir, if anything hits us there's nothing you nor nobody can do." He too had been thinking of the narrow ladders.

Gair fought his way back, and by now many of the recumbent figures were snoring and already the blue-lit troop decks were heavy with stale air. When he reached the little cabin, which though stuffy was like a mountain-top compared with the inferno below, the other two were in their bunks, asleep or pretending to be, and as he had no wish to talk he undressed quickly and climbed into the narrow bunk, cramped as a coffin and smelling damp. Above, not two feet from his face, the deck rang with footsteps, booted and soft-soled, once the slip-slap of bare soles. For a long time the normal sounds of a ship in port continued, the squeak of the ship against the fenders, bilge pouring, voices shouting and people hurrying along the passage-ways, the rattle of china and cutlery as the stewards laid for breakfast, and, muted, the sound of a train whistle, mournful as curlew on a lonely moor. Normal, everyday sounds. Against the light slanting through the door, hooked ajar in case of a torpedo in the night, he could see the fat life-belt hanging by his head, little red signal lamp clipped on. Rex began to snore, gently like a girl. Tommy was lying on his back, arms behind his head, knees up, staring at the springs of the bunk above. Gair turned his face to the riveted wall beyond which was the night and the sea and tried to sleep. Then the engines started. No one who has never heard the sound can imagine the feeling of excitement, the unreasonable agitation caused by the first slow strokes of a ship's engines. A slight shudder caused his bunk to vibrate, a new ventilation system began to thrum. He slept, and when he woke they were just moving. Far beneath him the screw bit into the muddy waters and sent them lapping against the quay. Throb! Throb! Throb! He unclamped the scuttle and peered out to watch the gas-lamps gradually fall away, the wet roofs of the warehouses flowing out of sight like ebony rivers, and then the ship began to turn, a faint breeze filled the cabin with the smell of the sea and the rush of water quickened along the side. Throb! Throb! Throb! Going away! Going away! Never come back! Throughout the ship men lay awake listening to the engines that were carrying them to the open sea and the unknown, with no soul to mourn their passing through the mist, save a few gulls. No bands, no flags, no cheering throng, nothing but the sad, lonely note of a ship's siren.

The convoy gathered in the Mersey estuary and then, shepherded by the attendant escorts, they headed north. Once round the shelter of Ireland they plunged into the January Atlantic, the clumsy troopships dancing heavily in the big seas. Immediately men began to be sick, where they stood, where they lay and soon no one had the strength of will to clear it up. By afternoon they were in the storm. Gair clung to the rail for hours, until the spray was invisible in the darkness; he watched the monstrous grey waves as they bore down upon the ship, trailing their long plumes of spray. The old ship leapt and twisted and plunged, down into the black valleys and rose up again, slowly, sluggishly, and always she shuddered. She shuddered when the seas struck her and flung her momentarily off-course; she shuddered when a wave passed below her and the racing screw seized on air alone. She rolled, over and over till the boats were scraping the seething water, and then she rolled back again; she jarred and stood still as the wind rushed along the decks, screamed with wicked frenzy in the rigging. The air was filled with blinding icy spray which lashed the helpless half-conscious bundles of humanity rolling in the scuppers. As the last futile remnants of daylight faded nothing could be seen, no horizon,

no sky, no other ships. They were alone and feeble in the
wastes of angry sea.

Down below on the troop decks the shambles was unbelievable, the stench of sickness unbearable. Only three of the
platoon were unaffected.

"Wakefield looks bad, sir," said McFarlane. But they all
did. How any of them retained the spark of life in that hell
of moaning, retching misery, amazed him. He felt his face go
green, the sweat was cold upon his skin and he staggered
weakly to the cabin, slipping everywhere in the contents of
innumerable stomachs. Lying on his bunk he lost count of
time. The ship was alive, panting and groaning as she fought
her way westward, and there was nothing but the horrid
sounds of straining steel and timber, the ugly crash of smash-
ing crockery, the pounding of the engines. Seas struck beside
his head with savage impact, the cabin stood on end as a
welter of shoes, books and equipment slithered up and down
the floor, the lifebelt with its little red light swung this way
and that. Sometimes Tommy lurched to the basin. Rex slept.
Gair woke later and it felt as though the ship was breaking
up, but amid the confusion of sound he noticed a difference.
The engines had stopped. They'd been torpedoed! She was
on her way down, and they were trapped, forgotten. He
looked at the door half expecting the mighty rush of boiling
sea. Tommy collapsed over the basin.

"Oh, my God, oh, oh——" His empty stomach turned
itself inside out. Rex slept.


For a day and a night the engines remained silent whilst
exhausted oil-soaked engineers worked frantically as the
cripple wallowed, a sitting duck. A corvette stayed for a little
but then bounced away into the greyness, winking 'Good
luck' with her lamp.

"Too rough for U-boats," said one.

"Don't you believe it, old boy, I was speaking to the
second officer and he said they fired torpedoes from away
down."

"Lifebelts will be worn!" rasped the loudspeakers. No

one took their clothes off for bed. What a farce! Lifeboats for a fraction of the numbers. Gair looked at the seas, tried his little red light; why not die in pyjamas? Most of the haggard, unshaven soldiers longed for death. The engines awoke to life again, and they set off to catch the convoy. The storm abated. They began to eat again, to shave and tidy up.

The days passed slowly. Lectures, if a corner could be found. The unpleasant task of censoring letters, prying into strange and unaccountable secrets; the pages of illiterate passion where a spade was most certainly a spade. Sentences filled with abuse or love written with a stump of pencil. 'Sealed with a loving kiss.' ''Oping this finds you . . .' 'You're no better than a bloody tart, go on, go out with Reg, see if I care.' 'Look after yourself, May darling.' 'There was a terrible storm, most of the lads were sick, but yours truly ate double (Ha! Ha!) every day.' 'The officers are a queer lot.' 'Today we saw porpoises and tomorrow we're having a concert.' Sometimes the blue pencil had to score heavily through some carefully composed descriptive gem.

They sat in the pale sunshine of the Azores and checked through piles of flimsy air-mail letters, whilst the unattached officers flirted with the Canadian nurses and the great fleet of ships crept across an oily sea towards Gibraltar. Boat drill. Gair was in charge of a raft for thirty men. He looked at them, standing happy, apathetic, sullen and imagined them fighting like animals in panic for the raft as the ship went down, blaring steam and flame into the hissing sea. In the evenings he played chess with Tommy or drank gin from David's cache, for it was a dry ship, a dry convoy.

The ship moved slowly on the Atlantic swell over a sea that was grey and silver. A bar of gold lay across the water, and round the sun the clouds were thin and transparent like wispy, wind-blown smoke, and as the afternoon lengthened to evening, the colours grew softer, the silver turned to pearl, the grey grew paler and the sun waned from glaring yellow to orange and so to copper. For an instant it hovered on the western rim of the world and then dropped from view, leaving a sooty wall of cloud, jagged-edged and topped with crimson glow. Gair lay back in one of the few deck-chairs and puffed contentedly at his pipe. Two energetic officers strode up and down the deck talking loudly of hunt-balls, laughter rang out from one of the gun crews, and, showing they must be close to land, some gulls glided above the masts. It was very peaceful, very still.

'Whoop! Whoop!' The destroyer tore a furrow in the placid sea as she steamed at speed back towards the rear of the convoy, a black flag flying taut from the halyard. Corvettes began to rush about, impetuously like terriers questing for scent. People crowded to the rails, and no one noticed the spectacular sunset. Astern, the destroyer was heeling over as she turned hard to port, little splashes appeared behind her and a moment later the sea rose into the beginnings of huge white mole-hills which swelled and then burst high into the air with a great explosion of water. Seconds elapsed, and then they could feel the curious muffled double thud against the ship's side. Field-glasses were brought into play, various imaginative souls saw stains of oil appearing on the surface. A bell rang for tea, and, as they trooped below, the sapper major who had survived three torpedoes spoke about a U-boat pack.

"Trailing us like they always do, catch up at dark, you'll see." Gair ate an extra large tea. The ugly nurse found it all too thrilling.

That night the sea was silvered by the full moon and the other ships showed by the bow waves. It was a strange thought that some sixty thousand men were crossing that broad path of moonlight beyond which lay Africa. Soon they would pass Gibraltar. A group of officers clattered on to the boat deck.

"Any sign of the Rock, yet?"

"You won't bloody-well be able to see anything, old boy."

"Hoh, Charlie, bring me my flickin' hoperah glass." The

sentence floated up from the men's deck, followed by a great gust of laughter. Gair grinned, they were happy now.

"Cor, chase me up a gum tree, look at all them lights, my missus wouldn't arf like to see that." Tangier glowed like a thousand fireflies, and on board the creeping ships there was not even the furtive spark of a hidden cigarette. They were quiet, bewitched by the incredible sight of a lighted town. 'Whoop! Whoop!' The strident call came across the water urgent and peremptory, stabbed their mood with its warning, and the night became alive with alarm, depth-charges exploded uprooting cataclysms of moon-lit water plainly visible through field-glasses. A blinding orange flash, a pause, and then the booming crash of the explosion.

"Must be that tanker." For a sheet of flame was spreading over the sea, and through his glasses he thought he could see dots which might have been boats, moving in the ring of fire, manned by men already scorched and blackened; others would be forced to jump by the appalling touch of white-hot steel as below the burning sea other men waited for death, rocked by the hammer-blows of the depth-charges. The tanker had been falling behind throughout the day, old and played out, but ploughing stubbornly on, striving to keep up, her engines pounding like a breaking heart. Gair watched until the flames no longer challenged the moonlight then turned to go below. There was no beauty in the night any more, and the gentle breeze brought with it the reek of burnt oil.

"I'm extremely glad to be spending the war on my own two feet on dry land, first that God-awful storm and then—that." Tommy rinsed out his mouth. "What a fearful way to die."

Next day they were hugging the coast of Africa, covered towards evening by destroyer-laid smokescreens to blind aircraft which might attack from the South of France, but nothing happened, and they sailed on towards Italy, the land of song and sunshine and romance.

They berthed against the upturned bottom of a ship and filed ashore at dawn. Surprisingly enough it was raining, and the low-hung clouds blotted out Vesuvius. They sat on their kitbags and waited. Not far away was a pile of cheap coffins, sometimes carts or ambulances appeared and unloaded more.

"Typhus, much dying, you see my sister, vairy pretty, very hygienic." The small boy whined it all in the same breath. David returned.

"We're going to catch a train, and don't ask me where to." They marched through streets full of garbage and mutilated beggars. Children ran beside them with the swollen bellies of hunger and offered their sisters, their brothers, their mothers, themselves for bully beef. Much of the dock area was wrecked, and starving cats staggered among the rubble.

The station was partially destroyed and packed with shouting, struggling people who wanted to catch the non-existent trains. Again they sat on their kitbags, and David went off to inquire; other troops arrived from the ship; the Italians went on shouting and struggling. There was a strong smell of urine. The train when it clanked in four hours later was made up of cattle trucks into which they piled; after another three hours the train moved unsteadily out into the country with a string of Italians running frantically after it, some were bleeding from the police truncheons and one by one they collapsed exhausted and lay like rag dolls by the rails.

At midnight they detrained on to a narrow track, and a man loomed out of the wet night.

"That the Guards? Right, follow me."

"And where," asked David icily, "are we going? Or aren't you allowed to tell us?"

"The I.R.T.D., sir, fourteen miles up the road."

"Only f-fourteen?" They had had neither food nor water for close on eighteen hours, and what on earth was an I.R.T.D.? Slowly the company fell in and marched off. They slogged those fourteen miles, uphill practically all the way, in a haze of uncomprehending exhaustion.

"But we must expect this sort of thing, we're the bloody Guards." Rex cursed fluently, barely beneath his breath.

"That'll do, Mr Segrave." David's voice was curt.

They marched among mountains, but no one cared, and as musical accompaniment they had the rumbling complaints of empty insides. Then exactly twenty-four hours after leaving the ship they reached a tented camp that lay clustered round a small smelly village.

After a week of training and route marches to get them into trim for death after the sea voyage, they moved north to another even smellier village, passing much devastation and signs of recent fighting. This next little village still had a few houses standing and a few roofs to keep out the sleet and rain, the razor winds. The battalion was resting after coming out of the line; after particularly gruelling weeks during which they had lost many officers and many men.

Twice they had been sent to attack Monte Mino, twice they had held the bare shell-swept crest against incessant counter-attack and against incessant wind-lashed rain; twice they had handed over and come wearily down the winding track and twice they had been ordered back to recapture the lost mountain. When they came down for the last time they left a lot of dead among the rocks, but the Germans had gone for good.

The newcomers sat open-mouthed listening to the stories that passed with the straw-covered vino flasks.

"Some ridiculous general said 'throw in the Guards'— well, throw them in again, and again, hah! that'll knock a bit of the blanco off 'em. Another bar to my D.S.O.? I don't mind if I do. A C.B.E.? No, not yet, wait till I've thrown 'em in again." Derek tilted the empty flask.

"Sergeant James, any more of this poisonous stuff left?"

"Oh, yes," he continued. "The graves commission had better put up a sign over the Mino cemetery; 'these crosses are planted here by kind permission of General —' whatever his damned name is; you look a bit shocked, Rex, you don't have to be, we're only fooling, we love it really." He splashed his glass full again.

"They told us we were going home after Alamein, then

after Tunis was taken, then it was 'be good little boys and do Salerno and then you can go home.' Now it's when we get to Rome, I suppose. God rot them all!"

Gair had never seen guardsmen who did not salute an officer, who were dirty, unshaven and often drunk, who put their hands in their pockets and slouched along the little streets in filthy boots. He compared them with his own platoon, clean and smart and fresh, and wondered if they too would disintegrate after years of battle, for many of those ragged unkempt veterans were five-year men who had done little else but fight since September 1939. In popular parlance they 'had had war'. But nevertheless it was a shock to see them.

Late-afternoon threatening dusk, rain teeming from a decaying sky and a sleepless night before them: the point of lowest ebb. The lorries, mud-spattered and with torn canopies stood lined along the village street while the men, sullen and unwilling, climbed aboard, only the ignorant new company showing signs of life. Gair hitched his equipment over his greatcoat and sheepskin jacket and clipped the belt with a sound of finality, then checked his impedimenta. Automatic, tommy-gun loaded with the heavy copper bullets, compass, map-case, torch, water-bottle, sterilising outfit, grenade, spare magazine, morphine tablets, a little phial of Horlicks tablets, a bar of plain chocolate and the over-tight steel helmet. Gas-cape, leather jerkin, groundsheet, field-dressing, lavatory paper and *The Diary of a Nobody*. Mess-tins, spare socks, tobacco and a picture of his wife. He hoped there would be no question of attacking anything, he could barely move.

"You'd better come with me in the jeep and help to guide them at the debussing point, your platoon's all right on their own for the journey up." He climbed in beside the adjutant. They drove out of the village and on to a pot-holed road which stretched ahead across the lonely darkening plain. There were farms, gaping to the weather like grey skeletons in the gloom. A few figures moved among the wrecked houses, once they passed a flock of sodden goats unattended. They drove into the bitter shafts of rain, into a landscape which grew ever more desolate as the greyness turned to black, and Gair crouched low behind the starred windscreen and felt the first insidious barbs of cold creeping through the huge amount of clothes. His feet were already numb within the three pairs of socks and the rain streamed down his face; the jeep plunged from pot-hole to pot-hole. There was an air of unreality about the whole situation, it was what one might see upon the screen of some warm and comfortable cinema and shiver with delicious contrast. He was driving, in that miserable uncovered jeep, out of everything he had ever known and into . . . well, he was cold and wet and saw no prospect of ever being warm and dry, he was tired and saw no prospect of sleep. There would be no bed, no light, no . . .

"Not much of a night for playing soldiers. What I should like more than anything at this moment is a comfortable armchair in front of a blazing fire with a good book and up-stairs a bed with white sheets where I should be able to lie until half past nine the next morning, hell! Sorry." The jeep lurched out of the hole, Gair wiped the mud-splashes from his face. Cold water was trickling down his back, and a chill penetrated into his very vitals. There had been no past, there would be no future, there was only this dismal drive to the line, a drive which might easily continue for ever.

A pin-point light bobbed about in front, they stopped and a disembodied voice said:

"Side-lights out, please, no more lights of any kind. 'E's been busy at the bridge again this evening." Behind them the lorries grumbled to a halt. "Put that cigarette out! Come on, lad, put it out, we don't want Jerry joining the ruddy party." Slowly in low gear they snailed through rain which was turn-ing to sleet; the jeep rumbled across a slatted bridge, below him Gair caught a glimpse of a broad white-flecked torrent.

"Garigliano, bad spot this bridge." The adjutant acceler-ated slightly. Gair had seen the name on maps, had read with detached interest about the crossing. Buildings loomed on each side, and suddenly the jeep swerved, began to slide and tipped sideways into a ditch, Gair banged his knee against metal, the pain made him blink.

"Blasted mules! Well, we're here." They climbed out; above their heads a rising wind moaned through the gaps in the walls. The darkness was full of movement, feet splashed and squelched in the mud, mules went by, heavy-laden and clattering on stones.

"The flicking Guards are here, now we can clear out of this flicking place."

"'Bout flicking time, I'd say."

Gradually the companies got sorted out.

"Number Seven Platoon?"

"Yes, over here."

"This way, sir." They filed behind the guide, threading their way through chaos.

"I say, anyone seen Battalion Headquarters?"

"Other end of the village, sir, cellars on the left-hand side."

"Yes, but which end of the village? Oh, hell!"

"G Company, all G Company over here!"

"Sergeant-major, have you seen my platoon anywhere?"

"Where the bloody hell's the guide for Headquarter Company. Heh, you, get those mules out of the way."

"Make less noise there!" The rain continued to pour down on to men who stood apathetic and invisible, many of them broke wind mutinously. Gair stumbled behind the guide, his platoon bulky like pregnant women, sloshed slowly up the slimy mud of a track which became steeper at every step. They clawed their way upwards, sliding back like spiders in a bath, pouring with sweat, knee deep sometimes; if a man fell he had to be hauled to his feet. The weapons got choked, the skirts of the greatcoats turned to flapping lead. Their hands, their faces plastered in cold filthy slime, their bodies awash with sweat and rain.

So cursing and panting and exhausted they came to Monte Natale.

## Chapter 7

UNDER Benito Mussolini the ugly red building at Pompeii had been a school where the Sons of the Wolf were crammed with fable and myth. When the Allies captured Naples it became a hospital; as a winter hospital it seemed unsuitable, the wards, classrooms once, with Fascist slogans on the yellow walls, were huge and high, none of the windows pretended to fit, none of the plumbing pretended to work, yet it was preferable to lie in the narrow iron bed rather than in the nightmare of Natale. For the whole of the first day Gair lay in a semi-conscious daze, his eyes when they focused saw nothing but a pattern of cracks on the ceiling. Now they were snakes, now they formed the outline of two horses and a tree, a diabolical profile. Strange sounds got through to his brain, voices spoke from far, far away, once he felt a hand on his arm, the prick of a needle, faces hovered wraith-like above him. He slipped into the limbo that is an integral part of pain, he swam hazily into consciousness and the pain was always there. In the evening he was slid on to a stretcher and carried along endless echoing corridors and down hollow-sounding stairs to the glaring brightness of the operating-theatre. The swaying stretcher had woken him sufficiently to see the skull-capped man as he tied clammy rubber tubing tightly round a bare arm. From close by came the sound of sawing. A lingering needle prick in the swollen vein, strong fingers on his wrist.

"Count slowly, please." The eyes looking at him from above the gauze were bloodshot, the mask billowed like a tiny sail.

"Five, six, seven."

"Slowly, please."

"Eight—nine—ten."

None of the frenzied choking struggle associated with chloroform, no roaring, swirling darkness but sudden candle extinction to wake and see the ceiling patterns writhing, to taste in his mouth the dregs of the night before, gloriously drunk, singing quietly to himself, grinning fatuously as his eyes unclouded.

"How d'you feel, Lieutenant Mainwaring?" The voice was soft and kind.

"Absolutely shplendid. Hey diddle diddle, the cat and the fiddle—what's your name? Shister Perry. That's a beautiful name. Shister Perry, she was very . . . oh." She held his head.

"Better now?" He felt more sober and looked about him up and down the large draughty ward. Many faces were turned towards him, smiling, some lay supine, staring as he had done at the ceiling. There were screens hiding a few of the beds.

"Give us another song, old boy, what about the Ball of—"

"That's quite enough from you, Major Tucker." Sister Perry turned to Gair.

"It's their only entertainment, watching people coming out of the anaesthetic, try to sleep, now." Her face was pale and oval, her eyes the darkest of blue and very tired, the fingers that soothed his forehead were long and slender.

"Sister!" Gair listened to the click-clack of her shoes as she hurried to the far end of the ward.

"That's mate, I think." Two men were playing chess on the next bed. He slept. Later he woke to the dim blue hospital light and to the pain, stabbing into his hand, lancing in red-hot splinters up his thigh; the gland in his groin was swollen and it throbbed with poison. He tried to move, and the nerves shot an instant message of protest to his brain, which in turn forced it between his lips as a muffled squeak. He bit the coarse sheet until the night-sister padded to his bed, felt his pulse, fetched a hypodermic and the waves of pain fell back defeated.


"But I've got a telegram for him, sister, very urgent they told me at the battalion, oh, come on, sister, just for a moment."

"Very well, then." The despatch rider waddled along the ward, unwieldy in his voluminous raincoat. At the bed he saluted.

"Morning, sir. How's it doing? Major Hardy's compliments, sir, and he hopes it's not too bad, he'll be along himself when they get out of the line." His huge hand, clumsy and red as a boiled lobster, fumbled in his pocket.

"Telegram, sir. Bit of bad news, I'm afraid, your company copped it bad, eight killed, they say, and a good many wounded, shelling. Mr Lewis got a splinter in the head." He fished out a crumpled envelope. "Can't move by day, sir. If a mouse blinks, Jerry let's fly with everything but the kitchen stove, 'ere you are, sir." He clumped out.

" . . . boy, stop, both doing well, stop, writing . . ." So he was now a father. Hardly unique, but he felt as though what he had achieved was as new and fabulous as the first emergence of life from the slime.

"Good lord, I'm a f-father."

"That's great, chum," said the Australian in the next bed.

The news flashed round the room. Congratulations were shouted, an unaccustomed buzz of conversation rose between the hideous yellow walls. Into their drab existence had shone a gleam of something beyond the narrow confines of their pain and boredom, and they let themselves go. The Australian sang lustily and the nurses' tinny gramophone played its only record, a scratchy rendering of 'Chiribiri Bin' by the Andrews Sisters. People hobbled across to wish him well and sat on his bed talking almost at once about themselves, and for tea he had an extra little cake. The matron, on her round, stopped and spoke about the excellence of modern gynaecology, her lined austere face expressionless as always. Someone must have told the Italian girls who swept under the beds and carried trays, for they gathered by his bed, leaning on their brooms, smiling and laughing, their lush breasts quivering beneath the overalls. One of them patted her stomach and made what must have been a coarse joke.

After tea they sang 'For he's a jolly good fellow' until the senior ward-sister reminded them brutally that men were dying. But the dying man in their ward did not mind, his lips moved silently over the words of the song, his eyes were happy. It was a birth that brought a brief moment of joy to a number of strangers, that helped one of them to die perhaps not quite so lonely. Gair lay and basked in the warmth of their well wishes until the lights went out, and then the pain began again and he dropped with a sickening jolt into reality. In forty beds men composed themselves for sleep, and soon from every direction there rose into the cold blue light the snores, the sniffs, the sudden bursts of wild talk, the cries and the delirious mutterings of sick human beings. Pad, pad, pad of the night-sister's soft-soled shoes, the faint wash of her torch by some bed where she wiped sweat from a sleepless face or felt an uncertain pulse. Every so often the man with no legs would shriek in his tortured sleep and call upon God to save him from the ceaseless hail of shells. "Ah-ah-ah -aaah! . . ." "No, Mary, I tell you, no . . ." "You lousy yellow coward . . ." Every sentence tailing into a formless mumble. The platoon commander in bed number ten, shot through the chest and unable to lie down, propped against his pillows coughing, coughing.

Rain pattered in flurries on the window-pane near Gair's head. He remembered Natale, strange really, he had only been in the line for a few hours and now here he was lying in a dry, warm bed while David and Tommy and Rex and the rest of them still crouched in the waterlogged mud. A party of four came quietly past his bed, carrying stretchers. They stopped at two screened beds, then they returned bearing loaded stretchers; behind them came the sister carrying a bundle of sheets and blankets. That happened often in the hours of darkness, the macabre procession of white-clad mutes was a familiar sight in the twilight wards, and by next morning the beds were neatly made and ready for other occupants. Gair was awake to see the stretcher-party come to collect on six occasions, and it never failed to fill his dreams with dismal spectres who glided silently in dim caverns and woke him soaked in sweat long before the dawn.

There were long fretful hours when he could not sleep, the stitches in his leg pulled viciously, his hand within the plaster cast itched unbearably, and he had perforce to lie and endure the zoological noises from all around. The mealy-mouthed padre in No. 26 who shouted unspeakable things at a woman named Bridget; the Australian who snored with a delicate 'click-clur', a sound so maddening in the small hours that sanity strains at the leash. He tried to conjure up the face of his wife and was horrified to find he could not see it save as though through frosted glass. The butcher, the baker, the dead German on the wire, rows of unwanted faces but never the one he longed to see. He tried to visualise her body, but that made him sick and hot.

From somewhere in the ward there rose every night without fail the plaintive, often agonised cry for a bedpan. Screens were brought by an orderly, they clattered and sometimes fell down, the voice telling him to hurry, in the low tones a tinge of hysteria. The orderly disappeared and returned bearing the precious object held like a frying-pan straight before him, named whimsically by the Americans Rose Bowl or Flying Fortress or even Headless Duck. Quaint names, but then they were in many ways a quaint people. Take for instance the American outfit which arrived rarin' to go at a particularly nasty position, led by a group of hard-swearing, hard-chewing, pistol-packing officers. As a unit they were new to war, to Europe, to everything.

"Where," they barked, "are these Goddamned Heinies? Let's get at 'em, fellers, then they won't know what hit 'em." Twirling the big ugly 'forty-five' their colonel, a Colonel Schwarz, demanded to know why there was not a little more offence round here. Why wasn't Jerry cleaned out of those little old mountains? That's what the folks back home in Wisconsin and Iowa wanted to know. Why was the war bogged down? Maybe it was because the Krauts hadn't met up with a first-rate outfit yet. Maybe that was it. Colonel 'Tiger' Schwarz took over the position with his quick-shooting hombres, and the goddamned Krauts hit them with all they'd got—not once, not twice, but day after day, night after night. The colonel understood why the war was bogged down.

The only American in the ward lay silent all the time, a bandage over his eyes. He was blind. His friends came to visit him, and the sound of their broad drawling voices seemed to comfort him for he smiled with his lips. Often at night he would call for Sadie or Mom, whom he would never see again.

Nights were bad. The mornings too, but in a different way, with all the hustle and bustle, the clattering, the dreadful cheery voices of those who liked to greet the dawns. Vesuvius still smouldered crimson in the dark sky when the lights flicked on, disturbing with its cruel glare.

"Lieutenant Mainwaring, it's half past six, come along, time to wake up and wash." He grunted irritably. Water splashed in a tin basin close beside his head as he buried it in the pillow.

"Come on, you've had an extra ten minutes as it is, and I've got better things to do than wake a lot of lazy officers." She was a Tartar, that small night-sister, snip-snap went her tongue in rhythm with her efficient little hands and feet.

"I'm always the first, s-sister, why not pick on s-someone else to bully."

"There's Major Snowdrop, he's already shaved."

"The man must be a raving l-lunatic."

"Here's your soap."

"Oh, all right s-sister, you win." Gair emerged into the light. A quick lick with the tepid water and lie back with a contented sigh. Ten minutes flashed by as he lay amid a babel of gargling, splashing, spitting.

"Breakfast." The orderly with adenoids handed over the tray. On the lonely expanse of white plate there huddled two diminutive sausages and five or six baked beans, and on the surface of the tea floated a curious grey scum. While breakfast passed slowly along the normal channels he dozed.

"Wake up, Lieutenant Mainwaring, temperature time."

He did not mind being woken by Sister Perry and lay watching her pale lovely face.

"Bowels open yet?" How could such peerless lips utter such a question?

"G-give them a chance, they've only just w-woken up."

She smiled and that would last him for the day. Sister Perry went on to the Australian who always tried to hold her hand,

115

but that was not a Hollywood ward, there was neither time nor opportunity for lurve. Gair shut his eyes. The bed shuddered violently.

"*Buon giorno.*" The Italian girl banged busily with her broom, her dark eyes made for a Hollywood ward.

"Oh, *b-buon giorno.*" Go away, you great creature, can't you?

"*Bambino?*" She leant on the handle which dug deep into her well-formed bosom and leered down at him.

"*Si.*" He turned over. Unabashed she commenced her noisy sweeping, whistling between her teeth.

"Heh, sister, can't you tell Elephant Girl to fall out?"

Captain Haseltine was always crusty in the mornings.

Then the procession filed into the ward. Doctors, surgeons, sisters, orderlies pushing rubber-tyred trolleys, covered in kidney bowls, rubber-tubing, gauze and gleaming instruments. The surgeon, a burly Irishman with sensitive, sympathetic hands, stood at the foot of the bed and uttered one word.

"Dressings." Screens were erected, and within the privacy of the little green cubicle there ensued an unpleasant five minutes as sharp instruments were lifted with a clatter from the tray and used to probe and snip and gouge. At length the surgeon would step back, lower the mask.

"And how's it feel now?" Then the trolley was wheeled away bearing with it its own particular smell of pus and ether; over for twenty-four hours.

The afternoons and evenings were the best times, for then it was possible to read or write or do very old and chipped jigsaw puzzles. Gair usually was left in peace. The Australian was allowed out and hobbled away to feast his bored eyes on the hidden exhibitions of Pompeii; on his other side the bed was occupied by a body which lay half-conscious within a cocoon of bandages, sometimes it moaned—oh, oh, oh, pitched high, but never moved.

Occasionally the happy hours were marred by visits from the hospital padre, a very caricature of a hearty beef-eating Churchman who sat heavily on open wounds and talked of himself, or the good-hearted Red Cross female suffering from far-reaching halitosis who brought round books and knit-yourself mats. She was very kind, very well meaning but she was a hundred-per-cent bore, and the sexual adventures for which her poor flat body was plainly yearning had patently never come her way.

"There's a most awfully good one here, by P. G. Wode-house, one of his best, I think, just the thing for bed, at least I think so. Oh, you've read it? Well, let's see, what else is there? Ah, one of the early Dorothy Sayers, a fascinating writer I think, so clever and yet so sort of unblood-thirsty. . . ." She prattled on. Gair tried vainly to dodge the halitosis.

With the lights in the evening there was brought to selected patients a glass of whisky or thick black stout, and for an hour or so the atmosphere became convivial. Major Snowdrop came and played backgammon or a strange card game of his own invention, changing the rules to suit his own hands. A nice man, Major Snowdrop.

"Used to be an architect in Civvy Street, now I'm a gunner. Put 'em up and then knock 'em down—sorry, old boy, spades are higher than hearts—prefer knocking 'em down, much easier, think I'll stay on after this show's over. Bound to be another one somewhere—that's my game, isn't it? Of course, me old bit of Ming'll have something to say, I mean she doesn't go much on the Service and—"

"Old bit of Ming?" Gair forgot to shuffle.

"Me wife, like to see her? Hang on a jiffy, I'll nip over and get me wallet." A fair porcelain creature standing by a rose-bush. Major Snowdrop was tubby, red-faced and balding almost as you watched. Me old bit of Ming! Gair said the words to himself many times, relishing the phrase.

"Hell, old boy, here's night-sister, well, thanks for the game—oh, square up any time—bye-bye." He waddled off.

That was how life went slowly by. The ambulances drove into the yard below his window, and Gair could hear the bang of doors, then later the stretchers were brought up to lie in a row between the beds. And from many of them there rose the unforgettable odour of the battlefield, of mud and blood and cordite. Men left the ward, some walking on their own two feet, some on stretchers as they had entered, cheerful and waving for they were going home. They were the ones for whom nothing more could be done in Italy; the broken wreckage was going home; they were supposedly the lucky ones. Others left the ward but they did not travel far, no farther than the narrow hole in the cemetery. Maybe they were the lucky ones.

There was however excitement; excitement of a novel kind. On a day not long before Gair was due to leave the hospital, Vesuvius, that tourist Mecca, that blurred background to so many snapshots of Naples, decided once more to rebel.

In the year of Our Lord 79 the volcano Vesuvius erupted, totally burying the little Roman town of Pompeii beneath a rain of choking, pink-tinged ash. In the year of Our Lord 1944 the volcano Vesuvius erupted again. . . .

Above the lucid blue bay the mountain smoked lazily, a white plume of smoke rising unblown into the clear spring sky. The sun turned the water to copper between Ischia and Capri, and in the streets of the towns along the shore of the bay people felt hot and lazy even though it was but early spring; they relaxed in the peaceful sunshine, for the war had gone beyond the mountains.

In the west a purple cloud hung low over the world, slowly growing and spreading like some malignant growth; thunder muttered in the cloud, and the air grew heavy and oppressive. Gaily-coloured fishing-boats, their bright sails flapping useless, made painfully for shelter in Sorrento and Castellammare, oars splashing white in the shimmering sea. Man and beast ashore were panting in the dusty heat, and on the slopes of the volcano the peasants collected their flocks and their belongings and prayed to the Virgin that she might calm the restive forces they knew to be stirring beneath their fields.

Gair knew nothing of these things as he wandered, lost in the mists of time, among the villas and the temples, along the roadways rutted deeply by the chariot wheels, and gazed fascinated at the mummified bodies pale grey and curled like embryos in a womb, striving to escape the hot ash which had filled their eyes, their mouths, their lungs. It was hot and he sat upon a low stone wall where perhaps the citizens had rested on balmy summer evenings and looked up at the mountain rising sullen above them. He mopped his face and slapped at a pertinacious fly. The curl of smoke was whiter still against the blackness of clouds which now hovered over the summit of Vesuvius. From those clouds darted forked lightning, stabbing viciously at the open crater. Briefly he remembered a trip to the crater before the war. Pie-crust lava between his thin-soled shoes and the molten furnace which bubbled and seethed and escaped as steam or white-hot lava through inky cracks. A broad stream of lava flowing slow and glowing, the air above it dancing in the brazen heat, and a man who sat, dipping coins in the searing flood, looking with his long-handled tongs like some medieval torturer.

The fly buzzed close to his ear, his leg began to hurt. It was time to go back to the hospital. A large fat raindrop fell with a minute splash on the dusty stone, then another. It grew suddenly very dark, the lightning sizzled round the summit which was now invisible except for, now and then, brief flashes and streaks of a deeper red. The rain came down in long unbroken threads of steel, splashing from the roadway where the chariots had driven. Gair swore to himself. At least half an hour to the hospital and already he was soaked to the skin. He limped slowly through the torrent between the wheel ruts where brown water foamed. People were shouting somewhere not far away, and a guide appeared, water dripping from his cap brim, running, pointing towards Vesuvius. He broke into a spate of words. Gair shook his head.

"Go! Go! Danger!" the man yelled. And then his mouth fell open, his eyes began to bulge, the gesticulating arms fell limply to his sides, he tried to speak but no words came, sweat mingled with the rain on his face, suddenly he began to wail; he fell on his knees and crossed himself "Jesu, oh Jesu." Gair looked up at the mountain and could not fully comprehend what he saw. As if pierced at last by the lightning the crest

119

split and began to open wide, a mighty roaring filled the air, below his feet he could feel the first trembling of the earth, darkness closed low upon Pompeii and he could barely see the face of the kneeling Italian at his side. The roar grew to a higher note, the crown of the volcano heaved momentarily like a living thing, expanded, seemed to hover for a second bathed in an awful light and then with a monstrous sound of splitting, shattered stone a great column of flame exploded from the mountain hurling hundreds of feet into the darkness a mass of molten rock and gigantic debris. Gair was stunned and deafened by the noise; faced by such a spectacle there was little room for fear, for any emotion save that of awe. Round them the buildings were soaked blood-red, the tongues of flame, like some stupendous blowlamp, bored into the bellies of the swirling clouds and filled them with smoke and dust while thunder, puny in comparison with the din, rolled and boomed across the bay and lightning flared continuously. How is it possible to portray even a fractional part of that moment when the hidden fires broke forth into the black skies above Pompeii? Gair limped frantically for the cover of a Roman villa while the contents of the mountain were whistling round him in the darkness, rock and earth and lava. The Italian had vanished, and so alone he crouched within the doubtful shelter of the villa, amid the ghosts of those who had died some nineteen hundred years before, and felt the building shiver frequently from the impact of larger debris; flakes of priceless fresco floated from the walls, the flagstones on which he stood rose and fell in unsteady breathing.

The devil's tattoo upon the roof grew less, and taking advantage of the lull he groped his way along the streets through a swirling fog of smoke and dust. The rain poured down again and washed him clean. He had lost all sense of time, of direction, in a world that had gone crazy; sudden blinding flashes of unearthly crimson brilliance, sudden moments of utter darkness; flurries of cold rain; clouds of choking particles and always the terrifying roar of the eruption. In the midst of a Stygian dust cloud he found a woman and a child who stood huddled mesmerised, waiting for death, and with them he struggled on and came by God's grace to the main gate. A fresh rush of falling lava drove them to shelter, and in the ensuing confusion they too vanished. By slow and devious ways he groped his way back to the hospital, stumbling on the rock and lava, hearing as he sheltered in doorways the prayers and lamentations of those within. Thankfully he reached the large solid hospital to find it was only three o'clock and it could have been midnight. Dim lanterns moved about the corridors and between the beds where men lay helpless, and felt the soft fall of plaster on their faces. The lights were out, and pandemonium held court in a building which shuddered and swayed. Glass tinkled, and many people seemed to be shouting at once. Doctors and sisters ran among the beds tying labels on badly wounded men, administering morphia, soothing, comforting, preparing for possible evacuation, but how and where to? There were always answers to whatever war might bring, but this—this was something different. This was angry Nature, and against her the answers are few and far between. They did not know when night had come. The hospital staff were magnificent, meals were brought and even in the midst of that Last Trump Captain Haseltine voiced a complaint about the tea.

"By God, I'm glad I'm seeing this. By God, what an experience, I must write it down, what a sight, what a God awful sight." The Australian scribbled by the light of a candle.

"My eyes, oh, my eyes. What's going on fellers? Someone tell me what's going on," the American pleaded. In that turmoil new patients were brought to the ward. Some died from the shock.

From the window by his quaking bed Gair could see the lava spilling down the mountain-side, an ever-widening, lengthening glow of destruction creeping ruthlessly on. For three days it crept, thrusting out thin tentacles of luminous liquid rock. An almost permanent darkness lay over the land, lit every so often by the bursts of flame. The building ceased to shudder, the lights came on, pandemonium changed to uneasiness and so to relief. Men shaved again, and the doctors got some sleep.

On the third day the ash began to fall, that same fine pink

ash beneath which Pompeii had suffocated, soft and fine as talcum powder, penetrating the closed windows and lying everywhere in a film of dust. Sounds outside were muted, footsteps padded, vehicles stole along in a pale-pink fog, their drivers masked. It choked, it filled the nostrils, the eyes; visibility was a few yards. Off-shore it lay lightly on the water, the wind blew it hundreds of miles and a soft rain of ash fell on the armies to the north. Vesuvius was hidden. She rumbled menacingly, and no one knew what further mischief she planned.

Major Tucker advanced the theory that the upheaval had been caused by bombing the crater.

"Stands to reason, I mean, after all, one bomb and look at the mischief it's caused."

Rolt, with the punctured stomach, described the ash as looking just like pink snow. Someone had to.

The ash ceased to fall, the sky was blue again and the warm sun smiled upon a volcano which smoked quietly and showed only by the ugly black smear of lava that she had ever woken. That night they heard the guns again.

## Chapter 8

SORRENTO is a beautiful little town, perched on the cliffs looking across to Naples; happy and carefree in its pinks and
whites and yellows. After the battered villages of inland it
was another world to men from the mud and mists who came
across the Bay for brief respite among the little cafés and
brothels of the tourist paradise. The inhabitants were different and did not wear the perpetual harassed look of people
who exist among bombardment and hunger, the girls who
flocked the narrow cobbled streets were gay and desirable
in their coloured frocks and wooden sandals, their bodies
were ripe and plump, their legs satin smooth, and they were
not thin and frightened and bitter like their sisters where war
had been. The eyes they turned upon the uniforms were
provocative and not filled with hatred.

Strolling along the pavements were British, Americans,
Poles and Frenchmen, Australians, New Zealanders, Sikhs
and Punjabis and Gurkhas. The vino shops in the back streets
were dirty and verminous and filled with soldiers who jostled
and fought over wine which was cheap and sour. The last
remaining storms of winter howled over the mountains, but
there, in Sorrento, the sun seemed always to shine.

Restaurants did a spectacular trade. Steaks and eggs and
thick-twined spaghetti doused in pasta rich and brown as
transfusion blood, every little table complaining beneath its
load—and yet in other towns not so far away whole families
lived on crumbs and dust. Today we enjoy, tomorrow we are
blown to reeking shreds.

Gair stayed at the convalescent home for three halcyon
weeks. He slept, he read, he wandered through the orange
groves behind the town and often he sat against a tree and
wrote long letters to his wife, stopping to listen to the cicadas
and the hum of life that rose from the red roofs below him.
Fishing-boats slept on a quiet sea, and puff-ball clouds dotted

the sky over Ischia. He wrote of his life 'which though so full was so empty without her. . . . I've got another week or so here. It is very beautiful, perhaps after the war we will come here, just the two of us. . . . We live in a pink hotel on the cliffs, called romantically the Torquato Tasso, so much better than Seaview or The Grand—and I share a room with a mad-man who throws books at imaginary rats. The leg is better, and the plaster is off the hand. Sometimes one feels bad sitting here in comfort while David and Rex and the others are still in the line; however, it is certainly most enjoyable. Last night, for instance, the San Carlo company came over from Naples to entertain the so-brave soldiers with "Madame Butterfly", pure Marx Brothers—as the stage was too small, the heroine too big—the floor-boards creaked, scenery fell down and the soldiers all stamped and whistled; bedlam and most diverting. Then dinner in the open air, ravioli, octopus and too much vino, accompanied by a sly-looking man playing an accordion. *Italie à la guide bleu.*

'Got back to my room (double room, very ornate with cherubs doing vulgar things on the ceiling. Edward VII slept in it but not apparently the virgin queen!) to find Fawcett (room-mate) throwing books as hard as he could go. . . .'

"Ah, there you are, Mainwaring, just in time—look out, there he goes, under the bed." Captain Fawcett was sitting up in the large gilded bed, thick sensible pyjamas draping his thin concave chest, wild-eyed and hair like a grizzled lavatory brush. Normally he gave the impression of kindly lunacy. An army doctor of nondescript age with cadaverous face pow-dered always with iron-grey stubble. He did not appear to drink much, and yet his boot-button eyes were always blood-shot and his scrawny hands shook perceptibly; his hair was unbrushed, his tunic stained with egg, and, with his grimy neck, his down-at-heel shoes, his nicotined fingers he gave out an aura of dissolution. He coughed unceasingly. Some-times Gair saw blood on his handkerchief. Throughout the day he wandered through Sorrento ogling the signorinas and with most of his vital buttons undone. Yet for all his air of decrepitude and decay he had a brain, for he was engaged in writing a treatise for the Royal College of Surgeons, and the room was strewn with huge unreadable tomes full of disgusting pictures of diseases. He read a passage once, as he spoke, twittering and fast, but it was unintelligible. The nights were Dante-esque, as those great volumes went hurtling about the darkness propelled with remarkable strength by matchstick arms. Light switched on and there he was, bleary and wheezing, every corner piled with literature.

"Brutes! Only just missed that one, must be on the balcony, I'll get him." Gair tried to humour the strange fellow by throwing an occasional library book at the wall, but the major was not taken in.

"Look here, Mainwaring, do you or do you not want to destroy these rats? Well, then show some enthusiasm. Watch me get this one."

He threw an enormous volume on the *Treatment of Boils*.

"Heh, up there, we want to sleep!" yelled a voice.

"Spoilsports! Well, good-night, Marling."

He was interested and helpful over Gair's speech.

"What started it?"

"Illness."

"Happy childhood?"

"Yes, v-very." Not a settled one, but extremely happy nevertheless.

"H'mm. Suppose a lot of fool doctors said leave it, it'll sort itself, tchah! Breathe slowly, speak slowly. Nonsense, no time to speak slowly these days, people have gone before you've finished." He relapsed into a torpor from which he suddenly leapt.

"Say 'the ladders to Heaven are long and laborious'."

"The l-l . . ."

"Sing it man, sing it." Gair had a momentary vision of breaking into song in the Forecourt of Buckingham Palace while mounting guard.

One day the kindly, eccentric Captain Fawcett packed his books into a battered wooden crate, his washing and shaving kit into a greasy little holdall and departed for England. He wrote a letter from another hospital near Bognor Regis. His treatise had been accepted, ' . . . but I shall probably die before publication. Don't forget to sing when you stick. Did you get any more rats after I'd left?' On the paper were some tiny spots of blood.

For a few days Gair had the lascivious great room to himself and then a newcomer arrived, straight from Cassino where he had been buried under rubble for a week with, as companions, four dead bodies. At first he rarely spoke, in the night he called repeatedly for help in his high precious voice, and once in the small hours Gair woke to feel a hand moving over his body in a slow caress.

"Darling," lisped the hidden voice. "You know I've fallen madly in love with you. I'm so lonely, so frightened at night, you will be good to me just this once, please darling." Sweating with fright and horror Gair scrambled out of bed. There was a hideous scene. The creature broke down and cried unashamedly into the pillow.

"You're so beastly to me, so cruel, oh, why does nobody understand me? After what I've been through."

"G-get out of that bed!" The pale ethereal tear-stained face pleaded with its brimming eyes. Gair, who had never come into such close contact with that particular side of life, stood, sickened and appalled and yet in some ways deeply sorry for the man. He wondered vaguely how you indented for a chastity belt, through Ordnance or the Quartermaster? He had finally to haul him from the bed, a horrid limp bundle of unrequited passion. Next day Gair applied to change his room.

"If it's anything to do with Captain Carfax, he is going back to hospital. He's in a terrible state, his nerves are shot to pieces." The commandant, a brisk no-nonsense woman with the O.B.E. glanced shrewdly at Gair.

"Don't judge him too harshly. With treatment and rest he will recover." It was many a long day before Gair had obliterated from his mind the unpleasantness of that night. He was pleased when the doctor at length pronounced him fit. Sorrento and its sweet delights had begun to cloy.

He went across the Bay to Naples on a perfect morning of sun and green-hued sea, spent some hours in the battered

126

station amid the same swarm of civilians who still waited hopelessly for trains and finally found an army truck which was going to somewhere near his destination. The driver was garrulous, and Gair was exceedingly glad when at the end of an all-night drive over execrable roads they reached the remains of a village.

"Well, sir, this is as far as I go, sorry I can't take you the 'ole way." Gair stood by his kit in the ruined village. What next? Where to and how? A battery of heavy guns was firing from beyond the crumbling houses, the muzzles jerking backwards under the camouflage netting, moulting hens scuffled in the dirt and a few thin children played listlessly among a scrap-heap.

An untidy little gunner came down the street.

"The Guards, sir? No 'fraid I dunno. Why not ask Major Turnbull over there in the Command Post."

"Have some cherry brandy," urged the hospitable Turnbull. A telephone buzzed.

"Same target? Right, will do." He spoke into another telephone. The rate of fire stepped up, and the tin mugs of cherry brandy danced on the three-legged table.

"Have some more." It was an hour or so after dawn.

"The Guards you want, eh? Hang on a moment. Sergeant-major, have we anything going anywhere near Castel di Sano?"

"Perhaps 1 c-could get a lift on one of your s-shells."

Ha ha, all round.

He sat in the back of a tattered, battered jeep, the cherry brandy swilling in an empty stomach as they drove below the noisy curve of those large shells. Ahead of them rose the mountains. They dipped down towards a large derelict barn.

"'Ere you are, sir." He got out and saw David coming towards him. He was home.


It was a quiet sector beneath the shadow of the Gran Sasso and, except for the patrolling, a holiday area. He climbed a grassy hill and found his platoon encamped among scrubby trees, each slit trench had beside it a small house of

stones and logs, it was like a Hebridean village. From a larger
house labelled 'Sheriff's House' emerged Johnnie Cairns on
all fours, his round face beaming. They lay on the grass and
Johnnie told him the news.

"You'll notice a few new faces, I'm afraid, but they're a
pretty good lot really, the reinforcements. Sergeant Thomas
is still with us and all the rest of the N.C.O.s—oh, except for
Corporal Phillips, he went away bomb-happy, crowing like a
pheasant."

"What's your future, Johnnie?"

"Leave, glorious leave and after that I suppose another
platoon, I don't know exactly. I've kept an eye on them for
you and I think you'll find them in pretty good heart. Hello,
Rex."

"Nice to see you back, Gair." Rex knocked his stinking
pipe against his heel and sat down. They talked in the sunshine; the guardsmen were playing cricket, and a long way
away shells burst. Vapour trails pin-pointed high-flying
aircraft.

"We're here for quite a bit, or so McPhee told me—"

"How is he? S-cruffy as ever?"

"McPhee is an admirable man, a delightful companion
but, let's face it, he's less idea of being a soldier—"

"Mr Segrave. Company commander's compliments, sir,
and would you go down and see him?" Rex shambled away,
his steel helmet perched on the crown of his head, string
from the camouflage net hanging over his face, a cloud of
pungent smoke billowing out of his pipe.

"How's he been?" Gair nodded towards the broad back.

"Rex? Much as usual, thinking of Alice all the time."
Alice was his wife and he never thought of anything else,
every day whatever the circumstances he wrote her a letter,
scrawled with a chewed stump of pencil.

"We've tried to make him play cards or read a book or
something but it's no use, he just sits and thinks and worries
about her the whole time. By the way, what news of Helen?
How is she—and the baby?" They talked of home. With a
shush-shush-crrumph three mortar bombs burst on the next
hill; the smoke hung for a long time in the still air.

"Do they often d-do that?"

"Hardly ever, some ass in Rex's platoon must have hung his washing out again, seems to drive the Germans mad. No, touch wood, it's very quiet here. There's talk of some offensive or other coming off soon but with any luck they'll forget us." Johnny had been wounded twice, and though the faded purple-and-white ribbon on his jacket testified to his bravery he had no false illusions about possible glory.

Gair took over the Sheriff's House and spoke to the platoon. There were a lot of new faces. Afterwards he had a talk with Sergeant Thomas.

"We lost seven of the boys at Natale, sir. McRae trod on a mine, that was after Natale, near Tufo, a nasty spot, sir. Polter and Thomas, they were killed the next day, direct hit on the trench, mortar bomb. McDiarmid set off a mine too, lost both feet, wanted me to shoot him, but I couldn't, sir, not in cold blood like that." Ten little nigger boys all round a mine, one of them trod on it then there were nine; the silly little jingle ran round his head. Christie and Easton, Munro and Smith, the steady reliable Brogan, they'd all gone and their places were filled by unknown, untried men. Gair sighed and went down to the derelict barn. David was gay as always but thinner and paler.

"You've just got back in time, we're at twelve hours' notice to move."

By the next day it had been cut to four, and a fleet of troop-carriers were concealed among the thin trees. Orders for the approaching move were issued, the guardsmen slept in their little stone houses emerging only to eat or play cricket with a pick helve and a milk-tin.

Offensive. Offensive. Break-through to Rome. Over to the west great events were afoot, and in their quiet backwater they sat and waited and wondered. And in their waiting there was a tenseness not improved by the stream of order, counter-order, which flowed round them.

"Move within the hour!" Gird my loins and mount my steed.

"No move before first-light." Ungird them, get off.

"Six hours' notice, two hours, one hour, back again to

eight. Rumours, those handmaidens of the cookhouse, the latrine, were legion. They were going to be pulled out and sent home. They were being kept for Cassino—and Monastery Hill. A hush-hush landing in Albania. McLeod had got it from Corporal Sturgeon who had heard Captain Draycott on the telephone to Brigade that it was Rome for them. 'Nothing less than the Eternal City for the flicking Guards.'

Three days went by and the troop-carriers still lurked under the trees. Then, at dusk on the third evening, a still May evening, a thousand guns opened fire and the flashes of the bombardment made a continuous crimson flicker from coast to coast and the warm darkness was alive with the screaming steel. In the mountains men moved forward and upwards; everywhere the Germans, dazed by the avalanche of shells, prepared to meet them. There was little sleep that night. Towards dawn the guns ceased their din and Gair, lying awake in the Sheriff's House, heard the wonderful song of a nightingale. Shush-shush! An unexpected batch of mortar bombs arrived through the paling sky, splinters sang a nastier song than the nightingale, the echoes rolled over the hills. And that was all. Their particular slice of the war was quiet. Cocks crowed in the little farms. He fell asleep.

"Cassino has fallen. The Poles have got the Monastery, sir!" McPhee was as near excited as he could be.

"The Monastery's been captured, the Poles have done it." "Hear that, boys, Jerry's been flung out of the Monastery." Hooray! Hooray! They sang and whistled and passed the magic words from man to man, from platoon to platoon.

"Thank the Lord for that, well done the Poles." David breathed a sigh. He breathed it for every man in the battalion. For days it had been hanging over them, the thought that they might be called upon to claw their way up those blood-soaked crags. No one had spoken of the thought, but it had been there, a spectre over every one of them. And now at last after all these months it had finally fallen, that grim pile of ruins above Cassino, and the way to Rome was open.

The next order to move was not countermanded, and they drove westward to an olive-grove some miles from Cassino, where they remained for a week, and when the wind was blowing from the town they could smell the unburied dead.

To celebrate joining another division—an armoured division—the officers of the battalion gave a party, a cocktail party with drinks in little glasses and sausages on sticks. Fortunately that night the wind blew towards Cassino. Not far away among the olive-trees was a villa, the summer retreat of some Neapolitan nobleman, and on the terrace, trellised, vine-covered and hung with pretty Chinese lanterns, the party took place. A Negro band from an American transport column played frenzied jazz, faces shiny black, and from somewhere women had appeared, great bus-loads of them, and couples danced in the heady glow of the lanterns. The drink was potent, the surrounding hills were visible in the soft starlight, the cicadas shouted unceasingly from the olive-trees. At that very moment, in that same velvet darkness made for serenades and lovers, the gun lines were aflame and men were fighting savagely to complete the breakthrough and dying on the rock-strewn slopes.

Gair sat at a table with Miles, the South African who had come to take the place of Tommy, and together they drank the rot-gut whisky—Miles seemed always to have whisky—and grew maudlin as they watched the dancing couples, locked close in the preambles of love, eyes closed, in many cases the dishevelled look of brief encounters, lipstick-smeared. He emptied another glass. Everything was magnified, distorted, the sex-laden saxophone wailing and cater-wauling, the laughter exaggerated, unhumorous; shrill squeals of delight, excitement, anticipation. Smash of a thrown glass and what might have been a slap or a pistol shot. During the pauses when the band were mopping their black faces he could hear the rumble of the guns, sometimes the long-drawn whistle of the big shells going over high, curving through the warm sky. Tomorrow we go to war, to drive the German armies over the mountains into shattered defeat, to get another crack at Jerry. Tonight we drink to forget and we lie with an unknown woman so as to have something to remember. He was becoming fairly drunk.

Miles sat silently staring at the spilt whisky on the table, the thin brown face sharp with shadow, dark pools for his eyes; then he began to speak, slurring some words and speaking to his clenched hands, drinking often to cover his embarrassment. He knew nothing of women, he said, the only one he had ever known was his mother and she was dead, he knew nothing of love.

"You can understand, you're married, what it's like to sit here and see these people necking and kissing all over the place and—well, damn it, I've never even kissed a girl and now I'm too bloody scared to go and ask one of these women for what she wants, I'm twenty-one and I only know a woman's body from dirty postcards. Tomorrow we'll be playing games again and—I don't want to die a blasted virgin," he burst out.

"Why not ask one? That one, with the r-red hair, go on, she'll give it t-to you, she's p-praying for it. Ah, go on, her partner's p-passed out."

"Yes, but—I mean, supposing she—I'm no use with . . ." Abruptly he got up and went across to the girl where he stood awkward and defiant. She smiled and they danced, she kissed his ear, they disappeared beyond the circle of light into the kind, protective darkness of the trees. Even for Miles, the shy lonely boy from another continent, it was that sort of party. He never got any letters, nor did he write them, and when he talked it was never of home or family but always of the war, the war, the war. Lonely, bitter beyond his years, intelligent and sensitive, nice-looking, but he had never kissed a girl. Gair swirled the whisky in his glass. Insects clustered round the lanterns, a table upset with a great clatter. He, sitting alone, did not envy those who had the women. He felt smug, he had his own woman. He had Helen.

"Gair. This is Giannina." She smiled with her large mouth. Miles was flushed, his mouth a scarlet mess of lipstick.

"Hello." Then they'd gone. For hours or so it seemed he sat and drank till the bottle was empty, his head reeling.

Vague figures seated themselves at the table, but he hardly noticed.

Miles came back without his red-haired mistress. A bottle of wine appeared. Their glasses were glowing red and filled with glorious fancies, with wings to carry them beyond the immediate future, with dreams to dull the reality of dawn, but that night was immortal, the saxophone was immortal, Giannina was immortal.

"Come on Miles, let's go to bed." Arm-in-arm they rolled towards their tent. The night was paling, in a few hours' time the tank engines would start up, the whine of the lorries rise as they pulled out one by one on to the road which led north. There should have been a woman's voice singing haunting melodies, but instead a hundred wine-filled guardsmen roared out 'Tipperary', the song of Ypres and Cambrai, Loos and the charnel house of Passchendaele. Of Alamein, Salerno and Cassino.

"God help us, if they're as t-tight as I am. Hullo, p-padre, off to bed? Late hours for a holy m-man surely—heh, look out Miles, that's my arm—enjoy the party, you lecherous b-beast? Goo'-night, don't forget the crosses, a c-cartload of bloody wooden crosses."

"What shall we do with the drunken padre . . . Put him in the vestry till he's sober . . ." Miles sang loudly. They sang in the tent, and from under Miles's bed there emerged a bottle of rum. As the candle slowly dripped away, outside there came the dawn of another day; Gair got to know his companion who opened his heart and brought out strange and unexpected things. The stars went out, an engine started up. They fell back on their camp beds fully clothed.

"Goo'-night Gair, you're a bloody goo' fellow."

"You're a goo' fellow too."

"Gair?"

"Mmm."

"We'll kill a lot of Germans."

"Hundreds, go to sleep."

The big shells whistled monotonously.

"Excuse me, sir, it's seven o'clock and Mr Bayerlein doesn't seem very well."

"Nor am I, McPhee, g-go away."

But McPhee was right, for when Gair had staggered from his bed and looked down unbelieving at the suffused face half-smothered in the pillow he knew that Miles was dead.

"Suffocation," diagnosed the doctor. He pulled the blanket over the damp curly hair. It was a dreadful, senseless way to die, but who knows what further pain and suffering he was spared, and at least he had been happy.

They buried him in the olive-grove under a wooden cross, the little rosy-cheeked padre said a few words to the group of silent men and then they left him, shafts of sunlight striking down upon the grave. Gair did not know where to write or send the few belongings.

## Chapter 9

As they drove through Cassino, the smell of decay, seeping from the rubble, was overpowering. Above on the misty skyline stood the ragged outline of the Monastery, and over the ruins fluttered the red and white flag of Poland; strewn on the slopes lay the bodies of soldiers who had followed a long road from Warsaw, lying in the tunnels and dugouts were Germans who also had seen Warsaw. There have been those who suggested that Cassino should be left untouched as a monument to the thousands who died, as a permanent reminder to generations of gaping sightseers of the futility of war, but then for maximum effect you would need to retain the smell. Take away the smell and there was nothing but an obliterated town, and obliterated towns in someone else's country mean little to twentieth-century man.

Gair sat in the lorry with a handkerchief over his nose and beside him the driver sweated green. At every yard little boards stuck up. '*Achtung Minen*'. 'Movement means Mutilation'. 'The Rose and Crown'. There were many craters filled with black water; a swollen body floated face up. North of the town the column halted. Ahead there was a battle and they sat for hours, no one bothering to get out except to relieve themselves against the dust-caked wheels. Gair started a letter to Helen, the driver tilted his helmet over his eyes and slept. One single shell came droning by, but otherwise the day for them was quiet. Just as they were preparing a brew, the battle moved on or stopped and the lorries ground slowly over a hill, along a poplar-lined road and then turned off up a narrow winding track to a village where they stopped again, this time for the night. His platoon was installed cosily in a cemetery where cypress flourished and the skeletons exhumed by shell-fire lay broken among the shattered gravestones. For three days they remained, pleasant days of rustic charm; ox-carts creaked, the peasants were friendly and a flourishing black market blossomed in bully beef and soap. Eggs for every meal, and the guardsmen comatose under the cypress trees. The graves were used as trenches, and Sergeant Thomas shaved from half a skull. A few parachutists were said to be lurking in the olive-groves and in the hills around them, but otherwise the tumult and the confusion had vanished towards Rome. Gair read his Penguin Conrads, Maughams and Waughs, wrote long passionate letters to Helen or lay dozing in the grave that McPhee had so cunningly fashioned into a sun-drenched bed. Sometimes he walked alone in the hills, setting off through the olive-trees and on to the grassy slopes above. A stupid habit, but he was prepared to risk the wrath of authority or an alien bullet to obtain a few hours' solitude. George Dundas had wandered alone and never been seen again. He loved to be alone, always had done since his early youth; alone he found he saw more, heard more, could go where he pleased, how he pleased with no need to listen, no need to talk. From the hill above the cemetery he looked across a land of silent hills, deep ravines with rivers winding and in the violet distance a little fairy-tale village perched high upon a rocky mass; beyond it the hazy outlines of mountains. A few farms, vineyard terraces, but mostly the faded green of windswept grass, the greyness of rock. He visited some of the farms, the inhabitants were surly and seemed ill-disposed towards the Allies; one aged crone mistaking him for a German, gave him eggs.

"*Inglese,*" he explained and smiled. She shrank away and spat, an incredibly hideous old witch, fear in the filmy eyes.

One day, during his solitary wanderings, he came upon a German bandolier and a trail of blood not yet turned to rust and followed it along the stones of a dried-up stream. For a long way he followed the crimson splashes, as at home in Scotland he had traced the path of a wounded stag; then he became hot and rested in the shade of a scrubby tree. He dozed in the silence. A fly investigated the blood spots, from the farm down the valley a woman's shrill voice shouted at a donkey. It did not seem strange that in the midst of this peaceful silence he should be stalking a wounded man as one would track a beast. From whence had he come, that stricken man? By whom had he been shot? Where was he perhaps dying? Within a few yards of an enemy who slept in a sun whose heat turned his own pain to a torture of fever and thirst. Gair woke and looked at his watch, started down again, and the German who lay, stifling his pain, would have a chance to reach a friendly farm, a chance of life.

On the way back along the twisting dust-white road between the steep scrub-covered slopes he found two dead Germans crumpled in the ditch, and as he passed, a blue column of swollen flies rose with hideous murmuring and settled quickly back again. Birds had feasted on the eyes, a rifle lay in the road. Next day Gair returned with the padre and a tin of petrol.

"Phew! Petrol's about the only answer. Well, we'd better get it over, you pour the stuff over them and light it and then I'll read a few passages for them." He was a conscientious little man the padre and he stood back in the middle of the road, his cap laid in the dust, his Bible open. Gair dropped the lighted match into the ditch and as with a 'whoosh' the flames shot high from the pyre he thought irreverently of holy spirit. The padre read loudly from the cloth-bound Bible. " . . . I am the resurrection and the life. . . . Man that is born of woman hath but a short time to live and is full of misery. . . ." Through the flames Gair watched the blackened objects crumble and fall apart. ". . . forasmuch as it has pleased Almighty God . . . to take unto Himself the souls of our dear brothers here departed we therefore commit. . . . dust to dust . . ." The fire died and sizzled. He closed the book. The flies, baulked of their meal, buzzed angrily above the oily smoke, ammunition popped in the smouldering remains and a steel helmet glowed white.

"That's the best we can do for the poor fellows." They walked without speaking along the glare-bright road.


On the horizon lay Rome, within grasping distance at last. To the right were the soft contours of the Alban Hills, and to the left, stretching down to the sea, was the flat bloody

plain of Anzio. Some, looking ahead to the Eternal City, said
that the Germans would pull out, others, like Guardsman
Finch, looking no farther than his hot smelly feet as they
basked in the morning sun, opined loudly that they would
fight.

"The bastards always do." Finch, a disillusioned veteran of
five long years, picked between his toes. McAnespie stirred
the tinned bacon in his mess-tin so that it spat and crisped,
making a delicious smell which wafted lazily to eager nostrils.

The platoon roused itself at the hint of food and left their
cocoons of greatcoats and strolled yawning and stretching to
where the fire crackled pale in the sunshine. It had been a
quiet comfortable night of sleep. A haze hung among the
vines and promised another scorching day. The men who
mooched about or shaved in little pieces of mirror were
tanned brown and their hair had a bleached and dusty look.

"Mr Mainwaring said it's been declared an open city,"
McAnespie poked moodily at the bacon.

"Mr Mainwaring said! 'E doesn't know everything."
Higgins, a small sawn-off Cockney, a weedy streak of bitter-
ness, threw himself down by the fire.

"What's bitin' ye, Hig?"

"Flicking officers, la-di-dah an' no better'n you nor I. Ach!"
Citizen Higgins was a great revolutionist, equality was to
him no mere catchphrase. *A bas les aristos.* To the wall with
privilege and success, down with all officers. His narrow rat-
face was screwed up against the sun, he blew his sharp nose
into a filthy handkerchief. He signed for his pay with a cross.

"Open city, eh? What's that mean, lads? Bags of women,
dipping the flicking wick every night, aye and vino too."

"Get awa' wi' ye man, the Jerries'll fight for every flicking street." Finch farted loudly.

"They say the second front's due any time now," put in
Robertson, the draper's assistant, a most superior young man.

"Just about takes it, takes a few of those flickers sitting on
their arses in England to have a bit of go and leave Finchie
and me in peace." Forsythe rubbed his cheek where a bullet
had passed through three years before.

"C'm on wi' the scoff, McAnespie."

"Maybe they'll forget about us now."

"Let's get to Rome, then they can forget, aye, for good. Women!" Oliver licked his thick lips.

"A ruddy countess for Mr Flickin' Mainwaring, an' for us nothing but a dose."

"Can ye no shut yer great mouth, ye miserable wee man?"

"Scoff up!" The battle-cry of Britain's men-at-arms. Messtins rattled, feet thudded. Gair listened to the familiar welcome sounds as he shaved leisurely with a blunt blade. It was good to hear them so happy. The face in the scrap of cracked mirror looked back at him in two halves, above the crack the eyes, blue-grey and slanting down at the corners, were looking with tolerant anger at yet another crimson nick on the chin. A disembodied, unattached chin on the other piece of mirror hung below a wide mouth, what is termed a mobile mouth. He wiped away the pink lather and dabbed the cut with cold water. McPhee brought his breakfast: hunks of greasy fried bread and bacon, a myriad tea leaves floated across the dark-brown mess-tin sea, flies gathered from nowhere on to the syrupy jam. McPhee hovered. Clearly he had something important to say.

"The boys hope that Mrs Mainwaring'll be all right, living in London as she does, sir." That was all. He marched away. On top of their own anxieties and fears and hopes they had time to think of his wife and to wish her well. He was deeply touched and wondered how best to thank them.

"Heh!" shouted Robertson, the superior young signaller. "Over here, news on the set." A faint voice, punctuated by crackles and sudden snatches of local communications, informed them that at such and such an hour Allied forces had landed on the beaches of France and were even then struggling to enlarge their foothold. The voice faded and another one, much closer, said:

"Say again all after Rome . . ." Robertson switched off.

"Well, that's it, won't be long now, September at the very latest, I reckon." He saw himself once again helping garrulous women to choose curtain material at Messrs Faulconer's Store.

Once at school when a sudden epidemic of measles or

mumps had broken out and the word had gone round that everyone was going home, Gair had felt exactly the same surge of light-hearted anticipation and joy as he felt in that shady dappled vineyard. Not so long now, all over bar the shouting. This time the washing really would hang on the Line. Dawn, so desperately slow in coming, was just about to break and the lights would soon go on. Davidson led a conga, snaking between the neglected vines to the reedy music of a mouth-organ. Gair sat and tried to take in the full import of those faraway words. Soon I shall be with Helen, I shall take her in my arms, I shall kiss her lips, her eyes, the little hollow of her neck and then . . .

"Mr Mainwaring, sir, you're wanted at Company Headquarters."

He gathered together his maps and his pencils and his message pad and went towards the farm-house. A cloud had gathered from nowhere, and from behind it shafts of sunlight fanned downwards to twinkle on the distant roof-tops of Rome. Neither he nor any of those men who laughed and played like truant children could see what lay beyond the golden horizon.

As the sun lowered over the plain of Anzio the battalion moved cautiously along the road to Rome. The streets were deserted, and the sound of the vehicles recoiled loudly from the houses. Those in front went warily, suspecting a trap but saw only faces peering between half-closed shutters, children lurking in doorway shadows; they felt the scrutiny of many eyes, expected sudden bursts of Spandau to rip apart the uncanny hush, shells to blast them as they drove. Gair sat rigid in the front of the truck, sweating from the engine heat and wondering if it was a gigantic ruse.

And then, from ahead where the leading company had reached, there came a murmur, faint at first, which grew louder from a murmur to the sound of cheering and louder still, till it was a gusty roar which broke upon them like a storm as they drove at snail's pace into a great Piazza crammed as far as the eye could see with faces and wildly waving arms, little flags, the amazing flash of countless smiling teeth, voices thundering like the sea upon a rocky shore.

"*Viva! Viva! Viva!*" Tumultuous, ecstatic, wonderful. A surging press of bodies, milling, pushing; climbing on vehicles at a standstill, urging upon the soldiers gifts of wine and flowers and kisses.

The nun, tears streaming down her pale face, who gave her crucifix to Corporal Fuller; the blonde girl who clambered to the roof of the truck cab and sat beside Gair, throwing her soft brown arms round his neck, smothering him in kisses, so that, spurred on by encouraging shouts from the platoon, he returned her kisses to the uproarious delight of many and to his own intense satisfaction. Her lips were honey-sweet, her favours fickle, for, after one last lingering kiss, she was away to the arms of stolid respectable McIntosh. Mingled with the continuous cheering was the joyous clangour of bells.

"Never seen the like o' this back in Kettering," shouted Garton, the driver.

Gair was infected, he laughed and waved and shouted. Hands reached up to touch him; an excessively ugly man kissed his boots. "*Grazie, grazie!*" they cried out. A woman with one eye was screaming in English. "Kill Germans! Kill Germans!" The grinning, tear-blotched face of an old man peered over the truck door and planted a slobbering kiss on the leather countenance of the startled driver.

"Christ! Eh, 'op it, you ugly old devil."

So it went on, that tumultuous welcome, acclaim and farewell until they had passed beyond the Piazza into narrow quiet streets, and as dusk thickened, they rolled across the Tiber, carrying with them the wine and the flowers, in their ears the gratitude of a multitude, on their skin the memory of warm willing lips, and came at length to a cliff honeycombed with caves, where they slept the sleep of conquerors, all unmindful of a battle flaring not far ahead.

The German rearguards fell back slowly and skilfully, and every night the skies were lit by the fires and demolitions. Sometimes the battalion was in reserve and slept comfortably in bivouacs on which the rare summer rain pattered ineffectually; sometimes the battalion was leading, the company leading, the platoon leading, and Gair spent watchful uneasy nights staring frequently into the dangerous darkness. They slept in little ruined houses, among the rocks on some hillside; under the stars; beneath silent trees, they dug innumerable little trenches in the hard dry earth and then moved on, often before they were completed. Nothing dramatic took place, they lost no men, except for Smiley who broke his leg leaping from a truck. A pleasant sunny war, a few shells disturbing the lazy murmuring days, a few bullets crackling over them or kicking up the dust. In France the German was brought to bay, in Russia he was struck by hammer blows, in Italy he was always out of range.

Until Sartano.

"Tomorrow I am going to be very frightened." That is how Gair Mainwaring, subaltern in His Majesty's Brigade of Guards, would have answered any query about the morning. He lay beside a stone wall and stared up at the stars as so often he had done at home while waiting for the duck to flight or the grey geese to fly inland by the light of the winter moon within his ears the cry of the curlew, the distant rustle of the sea, not the rasping cicadas, the pounding of his own craven heart. Tomorrow they were to attack. To him the ordeal was unfamiliar, and already he had died a hundred sweating deaths. Not for fear of mutilation or extinction, but that he might not be able to speak. In times of peace he feared the mockery, but now he feared that men might die through that failure. " . . . but if it does, then of course I should not be able to retain you as a regimental officer. Is that understood?" Yes, yes, of course it's understood; it had not mattered then, you could not say some word, you laughed and swore and no one minded, but now you were responsible not for laughs but for lives. He looked at his watch, four hours to dawn. When cruel daylight came he would have to smile and disguise the sick vacuum in his stomach.

The long hours passed, the sentries changed, the stars

curved across the velvet vault of sky. He got up and sat on the wall, he spoke to Brigham and Toler on sentry, he lay down again among the unexcited snores but he did not sleep. Strange really, the geese would fly, the wind would sigh in the tall firs by the house he loved, the stars would continue to sparkle and whether or not he lived or died on the morrow would make remarkably little difference to anything.

"Shaving water, sir." McPhee held out a mess-tin of rusty water.

Gair shivered, his shirt was damp with dew, his mouth dry. Seven o'clock, one more hour. He shaved, and around him the platoon prepared themselves for battle, not with prayers nor exhortations but clipped terse phrases.

"Gie us a hand wi' this pack, Jock."

"How d'ye feel, Hig?"

"Dinna point yon thing at me, keep it for they lads." McIntosh nodded towards Sartano. Gair could eat no breakfast, drank some tea and was sick behind his stone wall.

Final orders. David, gay and cool as if on an exercise. Back to the platoon, struggle into the sun-bleached equipment, check the tommy-gun, grenades, morphine tablets, field-dressing. Look at Helen's letter, postmark Perth. It was comforting to remember that there was such a place. The minutes ticked by. Already it was hot. In a few moments the guns would begin to fire. He went round the platoon, spoke to the section commanders. Were the orders clear? Sergeant Reilly wanted to know about casualties, Corporal Fraser wasn't sure of the objective. Nor was Gair. Nor David. Once beyond the shelter of the ridge it was Sartano, a small village with the added attraction of a fifteenth-century church, and no one seemed any too clear about what lay between. He wished them good luck as they sat on the lips of the slit trenches girded for battle, whiling away that last horrid quarter of an hour with greasy cards or crumpled letters. Some said good luck, sir, to him, some grinned, those familiar to attack said nothing and showed nothing on their faces, a few like Higgins found relief in ceaseless chatter. McIntyre found it in wine. He looked up at the officer, a thin dribble of red wine on his chin, and offered the straw-covered bottle.

"Have a drop, sir, it's a bit of a help."

"No, thanks, McIntyre, m-mustn't lose the way." The guardsman laughed politely, took another swig at the up-ended bottle, belched and put it tenderly into his pack.

"Keep the rest for the other end." He spat on his hands.

"Let's get going, sir."

With a series of dull thuds the guns opened fire, sending the shells high over them, whispering loudly as they headed for the village.

Gair looked at his watch. Five to eight. . . . Stoke the boiler. Helen calling that breakfast was ready.

'Do hurry, darling, the eggs'll be cold.' German shells screeched briefly before they burst beyond the ridge and jerked him into the sickening present. He remembered a picture in a book of grimy faces looking at watches. One minute till zero hour, and then over the top into a tornado of lethal steel. He could hear the whirring of fragments as two shells, heavy shells, burst on the ridge-top in fountains of earth and black smoke, remembered Natale and the feel of jagged metal and found his hands were shaking. He put them in his pockets, how unmilitary, how slovenly, Guards officers do not put their hands in their pockets for usually they do not shake. A few of the platoon were staring at him, he tried to look nonchalant.

'For God's sake!' he wanted to yell. 'Why do you trust me? What do you expect from me? Can't you see, you poor blind idiots, I'm so frightened my stomach's in bloody knots. This is not the sweat of heat, but of fear, naked horrible fear. Jesus Christ, I'm only a bundle of flesh and bone like you.' But instead he shouted: "Get ready to move!" On the ridge over which they must pass the earth was mushrooming. One minute to go. He was sick again and hoped that no one had noticed. They were fixing their bayonets and the sunlight darted from the skewer blades. Shells landed close in front and a man was hit and another; together they groaned and died. Half a minute still to go and two men dead.

'God, God, make me climb out of this trench.' The big shells were like express trains and his ears sang from the awful clangour of their bursting. Twenty seconds, twenty seconds of life in which to smell the earth, to feel the heat of the sun, to see the fly perching on his arm and to spare it, to hear the ticking of a watch.

"Time!" The whistle-blast was shrill and at its command men staggered out of the sheltering ground and plodded forward, faces expressionless, hoping for luck, for life. As though in sympathy with their hopes the German guns stopped firing and the platoon topped the ridge in an uncanny silence. In front of them stretched a long broad valley filled with rippling yellow corn, vineyards and here and there a farm, on the left the ground rose steeply into high ground thickly wooded, on the right was a lower rock-strewn ridge. Beyond the corn and the vineyards they could see the pretty little town of Sartano. The plodding figures spaced out into textbook formation and advanced into the corn that was breast high. Who could have planned this piece of madness? Advancing in slow waves into the sinister opening of a funnel, the high ground menacing on their left, uncleared, unshelled. Watch the high ground! It was hot in the corn, and they moved through it with a loud swishing sound. Gair had lost his fear and felt only a fierce anger against those who could plan such a travesty of attack. Nothing happened. No bullet, no shell as they ambled forward into the eye of the sun. Robertson was talking on the set, relaying in his sing-song signaller's voice the orders from behind.

"Go no farther than white farm-house immediately to your front."

For God's sake, was nothing to be done about the high ground?

"You've to report when you reach Bound Jupiter, sir." Gair nodded. Men paid not to think wondered with him at the treacherous calm and their eyes sought to right and left for possible solid cover.

Some six hundred yards away Parachutist Wehnke listened contentedly to the British shells that howled through the summer sky and blasted the pretty little town away below him. He nudged Parachutist Adler who was dozing.

"The Hauptmann said to hold our fire till they reach the edge of the corn, must be about four hundred." He adjusted the sights on Ledi, the Spandau he had carried at Kharkov and Smolensk. Adler replaced his helmet and dropped into the trench. They waited and watched the shells bursting uselessly in the valley.

"It amazes me," said Wehnke, who was a student of war, "how stupid the British can be, look at 'em attacking over the flat, still, let 'em waste shells on Italians, don't worry me."

"*Achtung!*" roared Hauptmann von Reichenau.

"There they are, moving in the corn, see 'em, Wehnke?"

"*Ja*, I can see them." He settled behind the gun. "Now me beauty, let's shoot straight today, shall we?" The gleaming cartridges stretched serpentine in the grass. He peered through the sights at little dots moving in the corn.

Von Reichenau watched through his field-glasses. How could they attack cluttered with all that equipment? Very brave or very stupid, being British, perhaps both.

"*Feuer!*" The tearing silk speed of the Spandaus was music to his ears. Wehnke clung tightly to the bucketing gun, and Adler laughed to see the dots running helter-skelter. War can be fun when you hold the cards.

The bullets from ten Spandaus crackled in the air. Eighteen hundred rounds a minute the estimated rate of fire. For a minute they crouched in the corn and eighteen thousand bullets searched for them. Heads of corn fell, invisibly cut by invisible reapers; a sewing-machine line of spurting dust moved at monstrous speed between Gair and McPhee. He wormed his way to the forward edge and from behind a pile of logs tried to locate the fire. Location of fire lesson one, listen for the crack, then the thump of the gun, but that was Yorkshire, one bullet, one rifle. Bullets hit the logs and whined off course, tiny chips of wood fell on his head.

"Robertson! McPhee! Sergeant Thomas!" They joined him. "They're on the high ground, among those trees, we've got to go left, once in the t-trees we'll be out of sight, no

146

time for orders here, pass the word we're going for the trees. First rush to that building, then the trees. Understood? Right, m-move on whistle."

Robertson, ash grey, repeated a message in a curious squeaky voice.

"Spandaus, sir, firing from high ground, you're to use all cover and push on." With a shrill 'twang' the top of the aerial fell, severed as by a knife. Push on! The war-cry of the planners. Issue out another row of medals and push on! Gair leant across and switched off.

"It's broken, Robertson, understand? Until I tell you, it's dead." Better silence than such orders. And they had not come from David, he had too much sanity. Going left to the trees. Disobeying orders? Using initiative? What the Hell!

"McIntyre! Nip across and tell Sergeant Reilly to get his section to that b-building." McIntyre ran crouching and was hit at once, for a moment he writhed and then he died, cut almost in half, the wine from the shattered bottle mingling with his blood.

"Good shooting, Wehnke."

"The bastards are making for the trees, won't be so funny now, come on with that other belt."

A mad rush carried them into the quiet seclusion of the trees, and on the way they lost Bromfield, shot through both hips, and cheerful little Urquhart, who fell over with such a surprised look on his chubby face. They settled, panting, behind the solid trunks, and suddenly Robertson broke into a storm of crying; he stood and shook, tears streaming down his face. Faulkner took the wireless, and they left him, sobbing wordlessly, mouth slack and open, his eyes opaque, and set out along the side of the hill towards the chatter of the Spandaus. Nothing stirred in the mottled sunlight; it was cool; sometimes careless boots clattered on rocks. With no warning the hill came to an end and fell away into a steep ravine

through which there ran a road. They crouched in the under-
growth on the tip of the spur and listened, Gair thought he
heard voices on the other side, the clink of metal. Not fifty
yards away Wehnke and Adler stared down the valley where
nothing stirred. Someone sneezed, and at once a shower of
branches was cut down over them. The ravine was uncross-
able in daylight.

"Dig!" Gair mouthed the word. They scraped shallow
hollows and at every sound the bullets scored the tree trunks.
Gair called for the guns, and fifty shells arrived, dissolving
the opposite hill-side into an inferno of smoke and flying rock.
After that the Spandau was quiet.

Parachutist Wehnke dragged himself away from the twisted
gun. He heard nothing, for he was deaf; he saw nothing, for
he was blind.

"Karl! Where are you Karl?" he croaked from the terrifying darkness. Adler, his friend, lay headless in the crumbling smoking trench.

Throughout the short star-lit night the big German guns
pounded the valley where two companies sought shelter
among corn stalks and low stone walls.

Robertson, suffering terribly in his mind, sat against a tree
and contemplated suicide, for he was a sensitive man.

Hauptmann von Reichenau withdrew his men silently;
their task fulfilled, leaving one machine-gun which fired
intermittently and killed Faulkner and Simpson the confidence
man, thus avenging Adler and Wehnke, who groped his
blind way through Sartano. Sergeant Thomas sat and whispered to Gair. No one slept, for the woods were alive with
changing shadows and twigs that snapped.

From Sartano rose the crackling tongues of flame, the
explosion of demolitions.

Next day at dawn the advance, no longer contested, swept
forward majestically to the town; the reserve battalion look-

ing clean and fresh, occupying the broken village. The platoon was left, depleted and forgotten in the woods.

Gair stood over the headless trunk of Adler and felt unbearably tired as the reaction flowed along his twitching nerves. A few more yards had been won, a few more lives snuffed out, their only crime the stupidity which made them go on—and on; that had made this mutilated thing go on.

"Bury him." Gair walked slowly down to report to David, and then before he slept, to make out the returns, of ammunition spent, of the wounded, the dead, the useless, like Robertson. Six letters to write. 'Dear Mrs ——, your husband, your son . . . Dear Miss —— your lover, your brother . . .'

For two whole days the battalion rested in the valley, friendly now. They cut the corn and played cricket, slept and drank warm wine from straw-covered flasks. Gair slept for fifteen hours and woke refreshed to reorganise the platoon for the next stumble forward.

## Chapter 10

DAY by day the sun grew hotter, the roads grew whiter with
dust and the vines, the silvery olive-trees and the grass were
covered ever thicker in what could have been whitewash. It
settled on the weary men as they slogged northwards yard by
yard against a stubborn enemy. The troop-carriers were no
more than memories, sometimes they rode for a short
distance on the tanks but the steel was too hot for comfort.
And always there were hills. On every hill were Germans,
then another hill with more Germans. They forgot the
meaning of sleep, their eyes ached from the continual effort
of looking into the glaring distance. To eat there was nothing
but tinned stew, tinned stew, tinned stew till it got that the
greediest guardsmen were emptying half-filled mess-tins,
marmalade pudding in that heat and the dusty tea, two bitter-
tasting mepacrine tablets to ward off the malaria that would
have been a welcome change. It was rumoured that some of
the German units overrun were found to be living off mouldy
potatoes, but it made the stew taste no better. There were
few prisoners, those they did see claimed always in monotonous tones to be Poles or Austrians. A small bearded man
with upslanting eyes was all they found on one hill position
sitting amid the debris and wreckage of shell-fire, against a
splintered rock, gazing dully at the mangled stump of his leg.

"Ukraine. *Kaput, kaput.* Ukraine." His beard was crawling
with lice, and he stank. Another one loomed out of the darkness. Smith '08, who was on sentry, shot him and smashed
his knee-cap. He screamed like a wounded horse until Gair
jabbed him full of morphia. He also had the high cheek-bones
of the Slav.

Although no genuine Germans had come in, it was good
to hear the bleating cry of '*Kaput, alles kaput,*' and to see the
hands held high and harmless above the head. The platitudin-
ous might have called it the thin end of the wedge, the crack

in the edifice. Those who gave themselves up were filthy, exhausted, hungry and verminous. There remained, however, very many more, no doubt equally filthy, exhausted and hungry, who did not give themselves up.

The urge for a day of solitude came upon Gair as he lay listening to the dawn noises, men stirring, weapons being cleaned, the clatter of mess-tins. Miles away the first gun of the new day thudded against the distant silence, hens lurking in the ruined farm clucked feebly and a donkey brayed. He lit his early morning pipe and lay contented in his shallow shelter looking up at the few nebulous clouds roaming lazily across the pale blue of the sky. A hen peered in, and flies, great bloated fellows fat from the delicacies of a battlefield, buzzed near his ears. After breakfast he went over to David.

"You d-don't need me this morning, do you?"

David paused in his shaving, the thin face very brown against the lather.

"No, we're not likely to move before tomorrow."

"Mind if I go for a stroll?"

"Not on your own." Gair pretended not to hear. . . . The road stretched rippling under the heat haze which put out of focus the untended vineyards, with the neglected shrivelled grapes, the distant mountains and the battered farm-houses bordering the road. He looked through a gaping hole in the side of a house; dirt and smell and flies, where war had been there was never anything else, they follow in its wake with disease and starvation as grisly companions. He stopped to light his pipe by the distended white corpse of an ox, its legs stuck stiff like those of a table. A rifle with broken stock lay in the ditch, and two German helmets, one empty jack-boot; farther on a bundle of erotic postcards, the naked contorted bodies on their glossy couch quite out of place on that empty white road; a fragment of a letter . . . 'Liebchen.' . . . that was all. It was all meaningless. What had happened by the dead ox?

Up to the corner where it disappeared the road was friendly

and safe. An aeroplane dived through the brazen heat, the sound of its engine a crescendo that all but drowned the stutter of its guns. Gair hitched the tommy-gun on to his shoulder and was round the corner, almost before he knew it. . . .

Ahead at a distance of about half-a-mile a sugar-icing town sat perched on its hill, as yet untouched, complete in the sunlight, pink and yellow and white, russet-tile roofs, cypress-trees grew on the hill and along the road which climbed winding to the first houses. He drew back into shadow.

A thought took his fancy. Hot perspiring tourists in a bus bowling down this same road listening to the guide who spoke in the universal language: . . . *et voilà, mesdames et messieurs,* you see before you Montepulciano, a beautiful example of an early sixteenth-century Italian town, famous for its churches and its wine. . . .

Seen close through his glasses it appeared to be dead, he wiped the mist from the lenses and looked again, house by house, window by window, every shutter was closed, not a figure moved except one that walked up the hill. Peaked cap, slung Schmeisser, jack-boots. So they were still there. He wished he hadn't come. Better go on, might find out something useful. He sidled into the cover. After pushing and plunging through thick spiky bushes he came upon the first warning: the familiar honey-sweet smell and a pair of crumpled legs, Charlie Chaplin legs, sticking from a bush, some distance away a black and crimson bundle lay beneath a blue blanket of flies and the smell was heavy among the grapes. The day was suddenly very horrible. A half-exposed mine was visible at the lip of a crater, and he made his way to the road, across twenty yards of deadly earth, feet stepping like a ballet dancer's, hairs prickling on his neck, his loins shrinking as he imagined the shattering blast which might come at any second. He reached the road edge and sighed aloud with relief, and at the same moment decided on bluff. Walk down the road as bold as brass and trust to luck, try to be casual, to be German. To help the gay deception he tried to hum but the sound was frightening, he had never felt more naked, more alone.

152

Two burnt-out lorries lay tipped like so much rubbish into the ditch, and charred bodies sprawled in the brilliant white dust; Herrenvolk, the Master Race in retreat, finishing their dreams of conquest on a modest country road. As he paused to look at the wreckage the ground trembled and the explosion knocked him off his feet, a pall of fumes and dust settled over the new crater in the road. His legs felt weak, and he yearned for the security of the company position. 'It's your own bloody fault for swanning about like this.' But a senseless stiff-necked pride kept him from turning back.

He continued on his way along the road until it began to climb towards the village, and then he dropped down into a field of ragged wheat and sat hidden wondering what to do next.

A man coughed gently, the wheat shook and a swarthy face below a black hat appeared through the stalks. The figure remained half-concealed, and Gair could see the little black hole of a weapon pointing at him; something in the eyes told him that a finger was tightening on a trigger.

"*Inglese*! Me *inglese!*" he whispered, hoping the tommy-gun was cocked. The man began to spit, thought better of it and edged closer. Across a blue shirt was a bandolier, two stick grenades were stuck into the Wehrmacht belt, the chest that showed through the shirt was hairy. This must be a partisan.

"*Si*, me *Inglese*, er—*dove Tedeschi*?"

"You spik English?"

"Of course I s-speak English."

"Where then you come from?"

"Back there." Gair thumbed over his shoulder.

"There are much soldier there?"

"Quite a f-few."

"How I know you not German?"

"My uniform, I suppose, this g-gun, I don't know."

"Wait, I get others." He squirmed away. Gair took the opportunity to cock the gun.

The wheat seemed suddenly to be alive with people. Blue-shirt appeared and beckoned.

"Come!" Gair crawled behind him. Two enormous men

153

with red handkerchiefs round their necks followed in rear. They crawled for a long time over ground stony and rough until Blueshirt came to a stone wall beyond which Gair could see olive-trees, vague glimpses of a house.

"Psst!" hissed Blueshirt. A woman's head popped above the wall. She was fair and very thin. They spoke rapidly in Italian. Then she looked at Gair and her eyes filled with tears, her lips quivered.

"Oh, thank God, you've arrived," she said in English. "It's been so long, so terribly long, you are the first Englishman I have seen for nearly five years." Gair talked to her across the wall.

"Yes, I am English, my husband is Italian, he is ill in the house, and I have been doing my best to help Tonetti and his companions. But you, how did you get here, where are your men?" When he said he was alone, her face clouded.

"D-don't worry, we'll all be here by t-tomorrow."

"I can't believe it. That the Germans are preparing to leave and that tomorrow we shall be hearing English voices, looking at English faces and—and the nightmare will be over." Her voice broke slightly.

"Please excuse me, it's—it's, well, I'm so incredibly happy, that's all."

"Can you t-tell me anything about the German units which are still here?"

"Hermann Goering, but they have only just arrived, before it was infantry, artillery, once we had tanks. They were always changing though." The dull echoes of an explosion rustled the olive-leaves, glass tinkled somewhere.

"That will be the bridge, they've been preparing it all day."

"Is there any chance of having a l-look at what's going on?"

"From our house, yes, but you won't start anything will you? I mean on your own. It'll be the town which'll suffer. You know what they did in Chiusi."

Peering through the slats of shutters from the darkened room out into the fierce sunlight, he watched the comings and goings of the Germans. Hermann Goering Division, large and sunburnt like posters of Strength through Joy. A dumpy Volkswagen drove past filled with officers, opposite his window it slowed, a magnificent target for a tommy-gun. She clutched his arm, but she need not have, for suicide was not in his plans.

A file of men tramped by, talking.

"They say that they have orders to be clear of the town by evening," she translated.

"I m-must get back." She gave him a flask of wine and came as far as the wall. The partisans were everywhere, among the trees, in the wheat, armed to the teeth and looking aggressive.

"God be with you," she said. "And come back tomorrow, all of you."

He went back to the company positions, walking as before, down the middle of the road, pausing every so often to drink from the straw-covered flask, and arriving in high good humour.

"Where the devil have you been?" asked David irritably.

"Shopping in M-montepulciano." He secreted the wine in his trench and went to see the commanding officer.

"What the blazes d'you mean by going off on your own like that?"

"I—I —" The adjutant broke in:

"They're going to shell the town from 1230 hours, sir."

"Oh, but they n-needn't do that."

"They needn't, needn't they? And exactly why needn't they?"

He told them. About the Germans and how they were pulling out, about the fair-haired English woman, and about the partisans, the bridge being blown, the mines on the road and among the thick bushes.

"They were Hermann Goering Division, sir, that's all I was able t-to find out." Gair saluted and disappeared. 'Do something to help and you get a rocket.'

The guns did not fire on the sugar-icing town, and the commanding officer confided to the adjutant.

"That's the best information we've had for a long time·

Bloody foolish but very useful, remind me to speak to David about him."

That night Gair lay in his shallow grave and finished the wine, and it was only then it struck him what a day of fantasy it had been. Strolling down the open road, Englishwomen looking over walls, wine in the sunshine, he tilted the empty bottle and felt terrific.

He had liberated a town, and the kindness of the gods had been infinite.


They advanced into Montepulciano the next day, skirted along the cratered road and up the twisting hill, past the wheat field. It was quiet and no one was there to welcome them. The leading section halted and the word came back.

"An Eyetie up front, wants to see an officer." Gair went forward to find the blue-shirted Tonetti crouching by the corner of the first house, his finger at his lips.

"*Tedeschi!*" he whispered, jerking beyond the house with his thumb, and into the easy-going warmth of the afternoon there stole a chill wind. Muttered on-the-spot arrangements, and then, guided by the partisan, Gair went with two sections over a succession of low stone walls through olive-trees buzzing with flies until they reached a higher wall. He could see the sweat spreading in a dark patch on the blue shirt, Tonetti was fumbling with his Schmeisser. Very slowly Gair inched up the wall until he could see over the top. A house, bright and gay and sun-splashed stood by itself, in front of the green door was an area of hard dusty ground and on that hard dust stood a platoon of German soldiers. An officer walked up and down, glancing impatiently from his watch to the house.

"*Schnell!*" he shouted angrily and two more men clattered down unseen stairs, out blinking into the sunshine and fell in with their companions. Every man seemed to be carrying a suitcase, bottles protruded from packs and a little fellow in the rear rank had draped over his arm a length of green material, most of them were laughing and talking.

"Bit of useful loot there," murmured Bridges, pushing forward the safety catch of his Bren-gun.

Gair waited till he saw the officer's body beyond the tommy-gun sight.

"*Stille halten!*" rapped out the German officer.

"Fire!" rapped out the British officer. The clatter of the automatic weapons was continuous, the hot cases jumped on the hot stones, and the noise slammed among the pink and yellow houses of the town. For an instant the Germans stood utterly immovable and then as one they broke and ran, away down the road towards the town, scattering behind them their loot, leaving their officer and five others in the dust. An arm beat feebly at the ground, and a voice cried again and again. "*Kaput! Kaput! Kaput!*" Nothing stirred in any of the shuttered houses. Bridges emptied the magazine down the street, the bullets cracked and sang about the silent town.

The little fellow was still alive but hideously wounded, twisted beneath the green material. Gair uncovered him. The Thomson sub-machine gun was truly a gangster weapon. The big bullets had carried away his lower stomach and almost severed the leg from his body in the mashed-up groin, his hands clawed spasmodically at the sickening wounds, he was fully conscious. Flies were gathering.

They searched the house and found it empty except for a young girl tied down upon a bedstead, a rag in her mouth, her gay summer frock pulled up over her head, bruises on her legs.

"That's one of the bastards who'll never do that to a girl again, even if he lives." Sergeant Reilly stood over the dying man.

"*Kaput, Engländer, kaput!*" He began to scream in a thin wavering tone. Sergeant Reilly shot him in the head, but the scream continued for quite a few seconds.

Calling up the rest of the platoon they went forward into the town itself. Shutters opened, heads craned out.

"*Viva! Viva!*" In the main square people appeared running. It was Rome on a minute scale, but here many were armed, festooned in bandoliers, grenades and knives. Italian flags fluttered over the window-sills, a priest, unshaven and pasty-skinned, shook Gair by the hand, pumping up and down with a feeble wet paw.

"Tank you, *signor*, many, many time tank you." The crowd closed round the leading sections and the soldiers could move no farther; vino was pressed upon them.

"N-no drinking," ordered Gair.

"Ah, roll on!" muttered Citizen Higgins spitting through the crimson paste round his lips. A bell began to ring, a large echoing bell, as inch by inch they made their way through the shouting, crying, laughing people, Tonetti like a snow-plough in front. A sudden fusillade of shots rang out but it was only a partisan *feu de joie*, two pigeons fell limp from the cathedral tower. Shutters opened again.

"Out of the way! Make way!" The guardsman panted up to Gair.

"Major Hardy's compliments, sir, and if you can spare a moment from the celebrations you're to make for the far edge of the town and then stop."

On the northern side of Montepulciano there was a superb view across a broad valley to where more mountains stood massive in the shimmering distance. As they stood leaning on their rifles in poses of unconscious grace, the first mortar bomb, fired from somewhere in that picture-postcard valley, fell on the festive town and before the dust had settled another ten arrived in quick succession.

"Get into the buildings!" Gair and Platoon Headquarters dashed for the nearest house. The heavy iron-studded doors were locked.

"Round the corner, sir, come on, before the next lot arrives." The next lot, augmented by shells, arrived as they made the dash for the corner, and Grimley, skidding round last, welcomed a splinter in what he primly called the fleshy part of his back.

A little house stood on its own separated from its neighbours by two narrow alley-ways. There were bars over the windows, a glass-covered lamp hung above the stout oak door. It was locked. Gair heard the next shells coming and shot away the lock; they tumbled in through the door, the hot blast of an explosion snuffing the flames of four candles that had been burning at the corners of a broad trestle table.

Between the candles lay the sheeted shapes of three bodies.

"Christ, they've been 'ung." Lauder dropped the sheet.

The ropes were thin and practically invisible in the swollen necks, the three tongues thrust huge and black from their mouths; the eyes did not bear looking at. Gair replaced the cover.

"N-not much of a spot to spend the night, I'm afraid."

"Walls pretty thick, sir, snug as bugs we'll be."

Later he went back through the littered streets, deserted now, beneath the shuttered windows, across an empty square to where the bell that had sounded such a joyous welcome lay cracked and dust-covered in front of the beautiful cathedral. There was a dead donkey with a torn Union Jack in its harness.

"We'll be here all night," said David. "Get them concentrated into a couple of strong buildings, put out some trip flares, there's a curfew so anyone walking around can't grumble if they're shot. Come along at seven tomorrow morning and I'll let you know what's going on. Good Lor', hanged are they? Pitch them outside for the night, you can put them back again in the morning and light the candles."

"Oh, I don't know, I mean they're probably heroes, m-martyrs, better leave them alone."

"Whatever you like, happy dreams."

Sergeant Thomas had gathered the platoon into three stout houses centred on what was presumably the morgue and in every house the Italians had descended to the cellars and were being unsociable.

"Not such popular boys as we were a few hours ago, ah, well, c'est le gware, I suppose." Grimley craned round to search for the splinter. Platoon Headquarters began to make itself comfortable.

"Any chance of proper scoff tonight, sir?"

"No, none at all, what have we got?"

"Two tins of M. & V., some chocolate and a couple of brews of tea, to do for the six of us. Don't suppose the Marx Brothers want any?" Lauder nodded at the sheet.

"Shall I make your bed down in this corner, sir?"

"Yes, McPhee, that'll do n-nicely. Call me with tea would you at eight-thirty?" McPhee began to remove the sheet.

Gair went round the platoon, a few stray shells were falling on the town, but nothing close. The night was very clear, and a deep mutter of gun-fire from farther east showed that somebody was passing a more hectic night. He saw three shooting stars and believed it to be good luck. When he returned the three terrible faces were covered by a camouflage smock, and in his corner were a mug of tea, a bar of chocolate, two of the four candles and the sheet.

"Wake me at two, whoever's on s-sentry." He rolled himself into the sheet and slept at once. Towards dawn the moon rose and lit with its cold light the three dead men, leaving the rest of the gloomy little chamber in shadow.

But no one noticed that macabre effect for all of them slept save McPhee the sentry and he was watching down the silver street to where a darker shadow moved and moved and then at the very moment his finger was curving on the trigger became a prowling cat.

Not a cloud passed between the stars and the new ruins of the fairy-tale town, and everywhere the night stood still and held its breath before the dawn; no one woke the officer, they let him sleep for they were understanding, kindly men.


Next evening the company was withdrawn, and before they went David and Gair had tea with the Englishwoman and her husband, an Italian count. They sat among the ruins of his charming terrace and sipped tea from little cups and dusted the crumbs off their fingers into the shell-craters.

On the following day the battalion was moving forward into the Chianti country.

# Chapter 11

"It's always us that has the dirt showered on us. Fourteen flicking days we've been mucking about in these flicking hills and what do we get for it but bastard heat, bastard flies and bastard patrols." Guardsman Forsythe, having voiced his grievance, lay back in the sun to snooze. Beside him Corporal Rowley composed a letter to Beryl, his steady; he sucked the pencil but no ideas came, it was too hot. Probably take him for patrol tonight. He hated the dark, always had, the wind sweeping through invisible branches, shadows playing all manner of tricks in the moonlight, the whisperings and the rustlings. Bad enough at home, crossing the Heath, but here where every bush could be a man. . . . He wrote, 'Last night I dreamt of you . . .' and ran out of ideas again.

"Corporal Rowley!" A stentorian bark cut across the lazy heat of the afternoon; wearily he folded the crumpled paper.

"Forsythe!" The guardsman did not move, but stuffed his mouth with the small shrivelled grapes.

"Guardsman Forsythe!"

"Ah, flog it." He moved in slow time, spitting out the pips.

"Right, sit down and wait for the platoon commander, do yer buttons up, Smith, no need to go about half-dressed just because you're in a war. You, Forsythe, shave yerself properly, no excuse for an old soldier, Bryan hair-cut, Louden'll do it. Scruffiest bunch I've seen for . . . Party! Party 'shun! All present, sir."

"All right, sit down. N-now the plan is . . ." Half an hour later;

"Any questions?"

"Supposin' anyone's hit?" queried Corporal Rowley.

"If it's on the way in he'll have to be l-left and picked up on the way back. Anything else? Good, final briefing at eight tonight."

Sergeant Thomas stumped off to see about ammunition. Gair sat tracing patterns in the dust with his finger. It had been a revelation to watch the enthusiasm on the faces of those two new men—what were their names? Bryam—Bryan, yes, Bryan and—oh, well, he'd ask—as though already they could visualise the ribbons on their chests. Forsythe on the other hand had become progressively more gloomy as he listened to how he was to spend his night. Gair suddenly remembered it was his birthday, a real festive treat, to go crawling over two miles of rocks and mines to see whether a bloody medieval castle was occupied.

"Just take a few men and see if the Germans have cleared out. I rather think they have, a fellow came in this morning who said if a sheet was hung from a top window they'd pulled out, well, there was a sheet. Still you'd better go and have a look round. Bring back some wine if you can, they make a very palatable brew of Chianti, and any of the daughters if they happen to be hanging about, the Baron's got three. Have some whisky. Yes, what is it, John?" Colonel Robert turned to the adjutant. Gair swallowed the large whisky. 'Just take a few men . . .'

He rummaged in the dust and wrote Helen, then he looked at his watch and lay down where he was and fell instantly asleep.

It had been a busy week. Point 835. The deaths of Colonel Iain and Tony, killed by the same shell, and Sergeant Faulkner. who left no next-of-kin; the little German sergeant-major running alone against the tanks. David wounded but away for one night only, taken away cursing like a navvy. Snipers and wild bayonetings among the rocks and caves of that sweltering hill.

Carter the undertaker's assistant lying footless in the minefield, and McLaughlin raving with a shattered skull.

Day after day, hour after hour they had edged forward in the heat, every moment of respite disturbed by alarms and excursions, until they came to Brolio and could go no farther without assistance, and sat out of view behind a low ridge for three days while the battle drew level on their flanks.

The Castle of Brolio crouched huge and stubborn and multi-eyed at the head of the valley, its walls of brick-red Siena stone lightly pitted by shell-fire, for they were many feet thick and could withstand the batterings of modern weapons, standing guard as it had done for centuries, barring the road to Florence and affording a welcome pause.

He woke for a moment and thought over his plan, it seemed to cover most contingencies, but as with mice the plans of soldiers go often astray. If the Germans had gone, well and good, only the darkness and the mines; should they still be there—time would show. He pulled the beret over his eyes and slept again, and everywhere his men slept the sleep of complete exhaustion.

In the castle Parachutist Wehnke lay on a sofa in the magnificent tapestried library and dozed fitfully, the wound above his eyes throbbed fiercely. Things were not so cushy any longer, what with retreat, retreat every day, the heat and the dust and this God-awful pain in his head.

"Better than Russia, you're a lucky sod, Wehnke, to be here instead of Russia." He spoke aloud. "Rather anyone else but me, I've had my bellyful of Russia." He shivered on the comfortable sofa. The Hauptmann said they'd be getting out and heading north again in a few days, pity really, secure, comfortable, plenty of wine, and those daughters, get any of them on a bed, poor old Adler would have gone crazy over the daughters. Sentry tonight, worst time, two to four and on with that lunatic Bergdorf. My eyes aren't up to it yet, perhaps they never will be. 'Sorry, Wehnke, got to take your turn with the rest.' The Hauptmann, he was all right, but that doctor, Christ, what wouldn't I enjoy doing to that little runt of a doctor.

"Return to your unit, Private Wehnke, every man is needed. *Heil Hitler.*" Heil flicking Hitler!

"For Germany, Private Wehnke." Oh, *ja, Herr Doktor,* for Germany. I piss in your eye for Germany, *Herr Doktor.*

Shells burst somewhere against the walls, the sound muffled and puny, clouds of red dust floated away on the light breeze, like blowing peas against a brick, thought Wehnke and slid from pain into sleep.

It was dark when the patrol paraded. There were four of them and Luchino the guide, a stocky figure in a straw hat. Gair made them jump up and down, Forsythe rattled like a dust-cart.

"Empty your pockets." He had to peer close in order to recognise the blackened faces.

"Tinker, your n-nose is shiny." Tinker dabbed with the burnt cork. Their berets they wore pulled over the forehead like old Frenchmen.

As the first faint milky radiance behind the sky-lined trees showed where the moon would rise, they set off, padding quietly in their rubber-soled boots. Until they reached Tin Hat bridge the little file of men kept to the white road and then they struck into the trees and rocks; the air by the bridge was sinister with the smell of decay and explosive. A moment after Corporal Rowley had left the road a gun fired, and as they stumbled among the dark trees climbing laboriously on to the ridge the shell burst, glaring orange, in the dried-up river bed, rocks and dirt pattered through the leaves. Corporal Rowley, glancing back, saw the whitish cloud and thanked Christ he had not lingered; Forsythe swore nastily; Smith and Bryan, the excited newcomers, quivered and clutched their sticky weapons ever tighter, Luchino, the Italian guide, felt sick, and Gair resolved to avoid the ugly spot on the way in.

By the time they were half-way the moon was above the trees and hung like a luminous cream cheese, lighting with awful clarity the sprawling mass of the castle that lay, a slumbering beast of prey, on the far side of a small valley. With Luchino at his side Gair crawled to the forward edge of the wood and lay in the meagre shadows of straggler trees to check on the route. Just below at the end of the open slope lay a farm-house starkly shining in the pitiless wash of the moon, no cover save a few scattered boulders on the slope, black oases on the silver ground. It was warm and very still.

Gair whistled silently for wind, for rain, for clouds to move across that cruel face. Corporal Rowley lay watching the rear, his heart thumping furiously, he was not enjoying himself.

"Farm—crawl—from rock to rock—keep closed up." The whispered words passed back to his unwilling ears. Smith and Bryan like pointers on the leash, gave off a current of suppressed excitement, the remainder of the patrol were anonymous shapes keeping close to the ground. Luchino felt the fear that accumulated in his stomach and turned to wind that sought escape from his stirring bowels. Only the Virgin herself knew what the Germans would do to him if he should fall alive into their hands. He was finding that, like so many, he preferred to wage his war vicariously.

They edged their way, inch by inch, from boulder to boulder and lay sweating and panting in the sanctuary of the shadows, then on again, across the next patch of brilliance; when a weapon clinked on stone they froze to breathless statues. Nerves taut, bodies and legs and elbows cruelly treated by the sharp rocks, they wormed their way to the farm-house which might itself be enemy held. The windows were squares of utter blackness, and crouching beneath one Gair could hear nothing but the sound of mosquitoes. Once within the house it was as though they moved in thick black hoods. Someone stumbled on the cellar door, and there, huddled below, was the family with its goats, its hens, its pig, in a lamplit hell of stench and heat. A wall-eyed man spoke rapidly to Luchino.

"He say *Tedeschi* are gone, today they are going to Firenze, this morning he say."

"Ask him how many there were." Wall-Eye asked the old crone who asked the simple looking girl, they all talked at once, the pig adding his word.

"He say forty—fifty maybe, very tough mens."

"We'll g-go on, now we've come so far. Smith and you, Bryan, stay here. This'll be the r- the r- Hell!— the meeting-place, in case we get split up, if we're not back in three hours make your own way to the c-company." He posted them at the corner of the building facing along the track that led down a gloomy vault of trees to the castle.

"Right, here we go, Corporal Rowley at the rear, and for

God's sake move quietly, n-no sneezing from you, Forsythe. *Avanti*, Luchino."

It was easy to imagine things on this black and silver night. Those bushes, were they moving? Had they moved? Wehnke peered from where he stood beneath the oak-tree, and his eyes not yet fit for the darkness watered and ached. Beside him Bergdorf had a cold and sniffed unceasingly; sometimes he blew his nose with trumpet blast. Another hour of this. Still, tomorrow they were leaving for Florence, rest and girls for all.

"Stop that blasted sniffing, can't you."

Thirty yards away five men lay flat to the earth and heard the angry whisper. Two hours it had taken them to reach that point below the towering walls; hours of serpentine movement, feeling gingerly for trip wires, praying for noise to cover their snail approach. They now lay sweating and bruised, hearts swollen to suffocating size, within spitting distance of the walls and there had been no challenge, no sign nor sound of life. The whole of Tuscany held its breath, the British guns stood ready for the signal, muzzles raised to the silent sky. Gair was puzzled. If the Germans had indeed gone, then surely there would be some indication from the Italians, voices, the bang of a door, something; if they had not pulled out it would have been hardly possible to get so close without discovery for it seemed to him that the noise of their progress had been extraordinarily loud. And now this whisper suddenly out of the deeper gloom ahead. Italian? German? He had not been able to distinguish. Against the sky Gair could make out the tangled shape of branches, foliage. At the base of that tree people were standing. What to do? If only this was Salisbury Plain with cars on the road and where it would not matter overmuch who was standing so still in the shadows. A cricket chirruped but ceased as though frightened of the silence.

At his heels, Luchino was enjoying the war less and less.

Gair edged forward through the grass. Forsythe wondered if he had a round up the spout. Corporal Rowley felt the insidious approach of a sneeze.

Yes, there was something out there in front, something that clinked and kicked a stone. Parachutist Wehnke unhitched the Schmeisser and nudged his dozing companion.

"Willi! Look out, there's . . ." He leant forward, his eyes filling with water from the intensity of his efforts to see and challenged softly :

*"Wer da?"* A faint click. He challenged again, kicking Bergdorf into watchfulness. Willi yawned and sniffed and shook himself free of sleep, his last conscious movement. The tommy-gun clattered, echoing from the wall and the squat copper bullets tore into his chest and some went whack-whack-whack into the branches above. Wehnke flung himself down firing with dead fingers, his sunburnt face a jellied hole.

Gair was seized by a terrible excitement as he fired and felt the heavy leap of the gun in his hands, while the Schmeisser bullets tore the air close to his head like angry bees, a grenade thrown by an invisible arm burst with a searing crack on his left and one of the singing splinters found a soft warm billet in Luchino.

"Get back! To the farm! Run, you b——s, run!" All hell was breaking loose. Spandaus opened up from various points in the darkness, and tore apart the night hysterically; multi-coloured tracer whined and ricochetted to the stars in dazzling spurts. Another grenade went off behind them, and, looking up, Forsythe could see figures on the wall, above, short stabs of flame when they fired.

"You crumby bastards!" he yelled and stopped to fire. Gair turned and loosed another magazine to discourage pursuit.

German mortars landed fifty bombs in the area of the farm-house, scaring Smith and Bryan out of their wits as they waited for what might come down the path, and to Sergeant Thomas the firing was a series of little pops, but he could see the tracer soaring above the trees.

"Aaah," sobbed Luchino as they dragged him to the shelter of the farm. His fear had gone but Jesu, how his leg hurt. No more could Maria sneer at him for a good-for-nothing. Luchino Frascati wounded on patrol, a good guide, a brave man.

"'E's fainted, sir." Forsythe was breathing heavily. What a carry-on, Jerry kicking up a fair shindy now, someone'd get a bollocking for sure, sentries caught out good and proper. He hoped Knocker hadn't swiped the last of the vino.

"P-pay attention, Corporal Rowley you and Smith get back to the company and warn, about a casualty, no, don't go by the woods, stick to the r-road, we'll be in as soon as we can."

After half a mile of laborious progress, carrying the helpless guide and pausing on frequent occasions to avoid the effects of various missiles arriving haphazard in the trees by the road, they halted among bushes and Gair sent up the signal. Red over green, hovering like railway signals then falling, dying as they fell.

Twelve guns went off as one, and Hauptmann von Reichenau investigating the circumstances in which two of his sentries had died received a sliver of steel between his ribs, and parties of Germans searching the immediate area of the castle were scattered and flung into confusion.


The moon was fading into the dawn when Gair returned from Battalion Headquarters. He, having just killed two men, was quite the hero. With his own hands he had done it, unaided except for a sub-machine gun, a personal affair. He felt no elation, no remorse, only a numbing weariness. He flung himself down on the dew-soaked grass, rolled into a greatcoat and slept.

On the operating-table Luchino slept; Von Reichenau slept. And beneath the castle walls Wehnke and Bergdorf with the cold slept the deepest sleep of all.

Two hours later Gair was woken and required to listen to more orders. On they must go. On and on.

"Oh, and by the way, Gair, you're to be my second-in-command so get another star on your shoulder, promotion back-dated to last month. You'd better hand over your platoon to Sergeant Thomas, one day perhaps we may get another officer." Gair went to break the news to the platoon. It was easier to leave them now for there were only six of the original members with whom he had begun to train three years before.

"Congratulations, sir," said those six.

"Another star to polish, still Mrs Mainwaring'll be pleased," said McPhee. An even untidier, dirtier McPhee but faithful and cheerful as always.

The Brigade of Guards possesses many great qualities, the greatest being the standard of discipline it maintains. In peace-time there is discipline of an even stricter variety but that is the discipline of robots, automatons who strut and stamp in the public eye. It is iron, it is rigid, it is absolute.

At times during the endless grind of war there must be some relaxation of this systematic obedience, the iron must bend or it will break.

Such times of breaking were the neglect of duty on the part of Smith and Tolmie, the Higgins trouble. The pace was beginning to tell. Beyond Castel di Brolio the land was furrowed as by a giant plough into countless hills and ridges, and they came one evening to the fifth ridge—or the fifteenth, fiftieth, and wearily dug in for the night. There had been desultory fighting, and now the company was stuck out at the sharp end of a narrow salient projecting into hostile darkness. All speech was whispered, movement cut to the relief of sentries, and in the deeper gloom of the small hours Gair went round the positions. When he came to Smith and Tolmie they gave no sign of having heard his approach, for they were asleep, standing up against the tree trunk, their heads lolling useless, weapons on the ground. He got close and then hit them in the ribs, savagely. Winded and very frightened they woke and grabbed for their weapons while he cursed them with all the blazing anger of fatigue and strain, viciously and obscenely, then he left them, relief dawning on their broad ordinary faces.

By rights and the book of rules they should have been arrested, court martialled for a crime that not so long ago was punishable by death, but he took no action, did not even tell David. Sleeping at their posts, endangering the lives of their comrades, for that there is but one answer. Yet they were good men, Smith '24 and Tolmie the plumber's mate, good men pushed beyond their limit.

"In the Brigade of Guards there is a tradition, an unbroken tradition of unquestioning obedience. For any infringement of that discipline, however petty, there can be no possible excuse, d'you understand, Mr Mainwaring? You, I think, are inclined to be a little on the easy side with the men, but with experience . . ." Yes, colonel, with experience. Here was the experience, raw and unpolished, and he had failed the unbroken tradition by ignoring a deadly sin. How blind! How weak! Now they'll go to pieces, the rot will spread and there will be no one but myself to blame. But the moment of blindness paid. Smith and Tolmie apologised, shamefaced.

"I hope I hurt you—I m-meant to." They grinned ruefully and went back to their trench.

The Higgins trouble was worse for it was the action, premeditated and mischievous, of a troublemaker, an attempt at open revolt, mutiny they call it.

For some days the tempo of the advance had been in uneasy fits and starts against an enemy who fell back, hit back and fell back again through the swirling dust, the dazzling heat, and used his guns with devastating accuracy, and at every halt whether voluntary or brought about by the German rearguards they had to dig. On that David insisted relentlessly. No food. No sleep. Dig in! Prepare to move. Stop within two hundred yards. Dig in! Forward again, firing breaks out from ahead. The men say need they dig this time, sir? Yes, dig! The dispirited clink of entrenching tools or picks scratching at the stony earth, the muttered curses of exhausted sullen men. It was on yet another thorn-covered slope that Higgins threw down his shovel and told Corporal Rowley:

"I'm not digging another bastard trench, not for any flicking officer. Dig he says, oh yes, sergeant-major, the men must dig. What's the b——r playing at? Trying to drive us nuts?" The disagreeable little man spat out the words.

Corporal Rowley gave an order.

"Ah, stuff it!"

Sergeant Thomas was called and he gave an order. Higgins spat. Some of the others were digging even more slowly.

"Seen the company commander?" asked Corporal Rowley.

"Gone to Battalion Headquarters, corporal, Captain Mainwaring's in charge, over there with eight platoon."

Gair went across to Sergeant Thomas.

"What's the trouble?"

"It's Guardsman Higgins, sir, gone bolshie and won't dig, he's a bad lot, wants rifting out of it in my opinion."

"P-probably just what he's after, a court martial, a nice cushy cell and remission of s-sentence." Under the curious but not yet hostile gaze of many men Gair went over to Higgins, who was reclining against a rock. He wished he felt more certain of himself and of what he was going to say.

"Get up!" The guardsman hesitated then slowly shambled to his feet, insolence in his pig eyes, humming tunelessly.

"I b-believe you think that this company would be run better b-by you, Higgins." The man did not answer. All pretence of digging had ceased, ears were pricked, sharp eyes noted every expression on the faces of the two actors in the little scene. Sergeant Thomas hovered in the background, clenching and unclenching his huge hands.

"I'd be more than willing to change places with you, any time you like. That's what you want, isn't it? Your officers are useless, b-brainless and cowardly, they get special food, hours of sleep, all the f-fun that's going, while you do all the dirty work, that's it, isn't it, Higgins? You're as good as I am, aren't you? I'm sure you are." Gair felt as he had done that night in the ring, the same murderous rage had hold of him, willingly and without a qualm he would have shot the man. Higgins scowled at the ground.

"All right, while you're Guardsman Higgins, you'll bloody well do what your useless officers tell you, understand? When

171

this b-blasted war's over you can spit in my face, but right now you'll dig. Go on pick up that shovel and d-dig!'' Supposing he didn't. Gair waited, scarlet in the face, breathing quickly.

"I'm tired, I'm too tired,'' muttered Higgins.

"Tired! Christ alive, we're all tired, bloody tired and sick of it all. In the German Army you'd very likely be shot for this, but if you think you're going to be sent away to lie about in a safe prison cell you're very wrong and if you're not at least a foot down by the t-time I come back there'll be trouble.''

Gair walked away having very little idea of what form the trouble would take.

"Watch him, Sergeant Thomas.''

"Don't worry, sir, I will.'' The big fists clenched again.

Fortunately within half an hour they were on the move again, so face was saved all round.

By the evening Higgins was dead.

Another attack went in. The company sat and watched in reserve and saw the shell-bursts blossoming on yet another hill, saw the midget figures scrambling and falling on the steep slope, heard the Spandaus, the grinding squeak of tank tracks and then moved forward across the newly won ground, their equipment coated in dust and stiff with sweat, faces caked in white masks through which the eyes stared, blood-shot and infinitely weary and gummed with fine grit kicked up by the man in front. With them travelled an overpowering smell of unwashed bodies. Picks and shovels swung in ragged unison and sun-faded berets sat like pancakes on dry unkempt hair.

Not for them the dizzy rush through a rejoicing country-side; champagne, flowers, spinning wheels. Just the slog-slog-slog of blistered feet, raw and lame and swollen like the feet which had slogged through the Peninsula, the Crimea, Flanders. The glare was molten and skewered the pricking eyeballs.

"Keep going, Taylor. The first ten miles are the w-worst.'' Ha! Ha!

"Cheer up Fowlis, there'll be beer in Florence.'' Ha! Ha!

Splash of tepid water in the hip-slung bottles, men spat out the choking dirt.

They passed over the newly taken position, won from the parachutists, remnants from Cassino who lay where they had fallen among the shell-craters. One, a fair young man, sat in the ditch, arms folded, eyes open, the sunlight glistened on the golden stubble of his chin, flies settled on the open eyes. Two of his companions lay upon the road, pasted by the churning tank tracks. Bryan turned aside to vomit. The living victors were digging in. Shouts in the still afternoon air.

"See you in Florence, mate!"

"Aye, Jock, maybe."

"'Ere, you in the rear, pick up the step. Call yourselves guardsmen, cor lumme, wot a shower."

They left the hill behind them and passed into the virgin land, an arid land of parched browns and dried-up greens. Somewhere ahead as always the Germans waited. No gun-fire. No sudden machine-gun bursts. Nothing. And no cover save for patches of shrivelled grass between the rocks where lizards basked. With his eyes screwed up against the glare, Gair looked right and left at the summer landscape and did not like what he saw. He was commanding the company while David had two days' rest. In front he saw Rex's platoon disappearing into a dip in the road.

"Keep well spaced out!" How many countless times had he used that phrase? But always they concertinaed, huddled instinctively into dangerous proximity.

"See if you c-can c-contact Battalion, tell them we're pushing on." Something in his tone made a few of them smile.

And so they too dropped down the sudden dip towards the crossroads running through a little copse of stunted olive trees.

A German officer lay on his stomach and watched the crossroads through powerful glasses. Not far away were four long-barrelled guns, their black muzzles horizontal, the crews standing ready.

For months they'd done nothing but retreat, and now at

last he had his four 'eighty-eights' and an observed target. The first platoon passed across the powerful lenses, enveloped in its own dust cloud. He made no move. More figures appeared, starting down the slope.

"*Achtung!*" He could see a wireless set, what appeared to be the commander.

"*Feuer!*" Four lanyards jerked, four muzzles leapt back and almost immediately four shells burst on the crossroads. Clang of the breech blocks, slam of the guns firing as fast as the crews could load the long gleaming shells. The target area was obscured, once or twice he saw a flash, brilliant even in that sunlight. He was happy.

The company fought its way to the Arno and sat for many days in Florence looking across at the Germans on the north bank, there was a lot of sniping among the old houses, but no one knew whether or not Florence was to be like Rome, an open city.

Gair was not with them. He lay in the same ward in the same hospital at Pompeii and wondered, when he was not asleep or drugged, how and why he was still alive. Remembering with awful clarity the shambles of the crossroads. . . . The first shells, shrieking into the quiet afternoon had blasted him flat on his back, torn a gaping hole in his thigh; they had killed three men instantaneously and reduced a fourth to something which screamed to be shot. Deafened and stunned he had stood up, again to be flung down. Yelling and cursing he staggered to his feet.

"Get off the road! Oh, you bloody crazy bastards, get off the road!" An explosion threw him against a tree where he lay vaguely seeing the crawling figures that ostrich-like strove to bury their heads from that inferno of splintering rock and steel. A man hurled himself down by Gair and then another on his other side. The three of them lay close below the tree. First one was killed and Gair could feel the murdering splinters as they struck the man, smell the phosphorus grenade in his pouch that began to splutter and burn. Then on his left Higgins was blown against him by the blast of the

174

second shell, showering him with hot blood. Gair knew at that moment he was going to die, in a second when the third shell burst he would die, and knowing it he experienced a wonderful sense of peace, a moment of absolute and complete happiness. No more being tired, being frightened, hungry, no more effort required. It would all be finished. In spirit he was already dead, and only the body clung on stubbornly. He did not think of his wife, his unseen child, nor did his past flash before his eyes as he lay between two dead men and waited for the shell that would give him release, but the German did not pull the string and then came fear instead.

He clawed at the pitiless earth, ground his face in the dust and prayed aloud for Christ, oh, Jesus Christ, help to get me out of this. Panic, uncontrollable and degrading entered his soul, and he squirmed helplessly, anywhere to escape the deluge of steel and rock that whined in the reeking clouds of dust and cordite smoke. Please, God, please, God, save me from mutilation. Pain stabbed at his neck, he felt a heavy blow on his hip, then the shells ceased, and from all round he could hear the feeble cries for stretcher-bearers. Weak and dazed he shook off the foul panic and tried to stand and as he did so an apparition staggered out of the settling dust, blackened and crimson-spattered, face shining in a sheen of blood, one arm hanging by tattered ribbons of flesh, with the other it saluted.

"You got it bad, sir?" His voice a croak. It was Corporal Rowley, the quiet man from Dumfries who was frightened of the dark, and he saluted as though on parade. There must be something fine in a tradition which makes a man salute at a time like that with his other arm blown practically off. Crazy perhaps but magnificent. In that corporal was the spirit of Hougoumont, the Alma, Passchendaele, Tobruk, Anzio. The spirit which has made those men fight just that little bit harder on a hundred battlefields, made them go on just that little bit longer, those men who strut like dummies in peacetime and earn from the ignorant the title of play-boy soldiers, but who often die just that little bit better. Corporal Rowley who saluted as he was dying was one of those men. He was a Guardsman.

When the dust had subsided and the afternoon had resumed its brightness, Gair went round, crawling and dragging his right leg, the open wound packed tight with dirt and the pain beginning. Twelve men were dead, Smith the good soldier who had slept on sentry gazed with grey face at his neatly amputated legs.

"Been better to have had a court martial, sir." His eyes usually so placid were glazing. Most of the wounded who lived would have been better dead; rock splinters make terrible wounds. The one remaining stretcher-bearer ran among them giving what little succour he could, and the sunshine was full of frightened groans and cries. By then Gair could hardly see, nor hear, his whole body felt sticky with blood and he sank forward on his face unconscious. What followed was hazy and disjointed.

A journey on a jeep-stretcher past rows of big lorries filled with reinforcements who looked unhappily at the bloody bandages, the drained dirty faces. The cattle on the way to the abattoir smelt blood and did not like it.

A dressing station, the old familiar needlepricks, the large white sulpha pills, the old familiar smell, the blankets rough against his neck, the blood-specked walls. He knew not whether it was night or day, faces swam into brief focus, lips moved soundlessly. There were women in battledress, who spoke softly and raised his head to drink. Sometimes he lay in a bed, sometimes on a stretcher; sometimes he was carried to lamp-lit tents for spells of searing pain as white-coated shapes bent over the wound. Then an ambulance over jolting roads, an aeroplane in the jolting, sickening sky.

And quite suddenly he was back at Pompeii, in the same ward, and Sister Perry was saying:

"Hello, you've not been long." To Gair it seemed like centuries.

## Chapter 12

WAITING in a stone corridor, helpless on a stretcher in a long queue that edged slowly towards the wide white doors of the theatre. Beside him lay a Gurkha, grey like the shirts the Indian soldiers wore, whimpering to himself in soft bird-like tones, far from the mountains of Nepal; through the big windows at the end of the passage Gair could see a picture-frame view of Vesuvius; she blew little cotton-wool puffs of smoke into the unbelievable blue of the sky.

The Italians stopped picking their teeth and combing their scented hair and carried him through the white doors and laid him none too gently on the table.

"Haven't I seen your face here before?" He looked up into the haggard face of the surgeon and nodded.

"They haven't left you alone for long this time, have they?"

He stepped over to the wash-place and scrubbed his arms. Two tables were in use, and on the other one Gair, by turning his head, could see the final phase of an operation. Two surgeons were busy on a bundle of flesh, sewing busily with long curved needles which flashed in and out, in and out, all the length of the iodine-yellow arm, turning a yawning furrow into a narrow red line. The other needle rounded off the stump of a leg. He expected to see the final approving pat. 'Well, there we are, dear, all finished, I think.' Snip, snip went the scissors to finish a devilish sewing bee, and fragments of skin floated to the floor and were swept away with the rest of the human debris by a skinny fellow in white rubber boots.

The patient snored through the foam in his nostrils. There was a slaughterhouse smell in the white room.

"You mustn't look over there, it's not good for you." Nanny to small boy. A theatre-sister blocked his view with her two enormous breasts, he had never seen such colossal mammary glands, and his last remembrance as he rushed into

177

unconsciousness under the pentothal was of those twin mountains of sex and sustenance as they strained at the flimsy
barrier of the white gown and of the surgeon's voice as it
said:

"I'll incise deep." There was little time to waste as the
queue in the passage lengthened.



It all seemed much the same. The ward was just as full,
the nights were as bad, worse even because of the heat. The
orderlies were just as slow and grumbled as much; the pretty
sister from Head Wounds doubtless still managed a night or
two with the radiologist from Physiotherapy.

No longer, however, did the nights throb with gun-fire;
men were still busily blowing each other to bits but on different ground, north of Florence in the Apennine foothills.
Mars had moved on to plough new pastures, leaving the
summer sun to blaze upon the dreary task of clearing up the
mess, but now there was a different feeling abroad, songs
were heard, in the fields peasants pottered unafraid. War was
no longer any business of the Neapolitans, but in its back
areas they waxed fat. Some of them did. Others lay starving
in the gutters exhibiting their fearful mutilations, sent their
daughters of eight and ten to walk the streets, heavily made-
up, their thin little bodies the price of a cake of soap, a tin
of bully, miniature whores already riddled with disease and
the miniature pimps their brothers, in greasy rags.

"Heh, mister *capitano*, my sister love you? Very much
clever at love, very clean, very soft." In the slums the rats
were still as bold, the typhus still erupted spasmodically.

And still the broken bodies arrived at the hospitals. Nothing altered that steady flow.

Sister Perry was very tired, very strained, her disposition
not quite so angelic. The regal matron had suffered a nervous
breakdown and her replacement, round and dumpy with
currant eyes, was a more talkative woman. Gair was in a
corner bed and on his right was an oldish captain, blinded
at some romantic little village near Rome. On his return

home Gair wrote a short story about that man. Here is an extract.

'". . . one for you Captain Farquhar, no two, and one for you Captain Jameson, a nice fat one, too." The blind man did not open it but lay quietly, just fingering the bulky envelope. I read one of mine, the other from my wife I hoarded as an evening treat.

'"I say," said Jameson, "I wonder if I could ask you to read my letter to me, of course if you'd rather not I'll get Sister Perry." Reading aloud was not my forte, but I told him I'd have a try.

'"Don't worry if you get stuck, after all there's no hurry is there?" He smiled, but his smile deprived of the eyes was somehow dead.

'The letter was written in a spindly, nondescript hand on thin scented paper, covering four sides in all, and matching perfectly the woman whose picture he had shown me. A small fair person, pretty in an ordinary sort of way, very made-up. Joan was her name, and evidently he worshipped her.

'"Bit younger than I am"—and possessing apparently every human virtue.

'"She doesn't know about my eyes yet, and I don't quite know how to tell her, keep putting it off."

'I unfolded the letter as he lay smiling, staring sightless into the hot blackness of the bandages. It began "My dear Harry".

'"My dear Harry, is that how she starts?" I began to invent.

'"W-well, no, as a m-matter of fact . . ." He smiled again.

'"Ah, I see. Don't bother to read out the—the personal bits if—well, you know, yes, go on." How could I go on when the first sentence was —

'"This letter may come as rather a shock to you, Harry, but it's the only answer. God knows I've been over it all in my mind till I am almost crazy with unhappiness. It's no use, Harry, this pretending is no use, I have to tell you this. I don't love you any more and surely it is best to be honest. After all we are both grown-up people . . ."

'"If it's difficult for you, I can easily ask Sister Perry."

179

'"N-no, no, I can manage."

'". . . and can face this thing . . . it's nobody's fault, Harry, no one's to blame for my feelings towards you. You have been away for so very long and I've been so dreadfully lonely, oh you can't imagine what it's been like all these months . . ."

'Jameson was becoming impatient.

'"There's nothing wrong, is there? For God's sake, man, is everything all right with her?"

'"Yes, everything's fine. She's v-very well and is m-missing you as much as always."

'". . . after all, there are no children and people get over things in time . . ."

'"She wants to know if there's anything you want, clothes, books."

'"The garden, doesn't she say anything about the garden? Joan is so good in the garden." I rustled the paper and then sweating and unhappy I struggled through a series of outrageous lies. Why had he not written for so long? He was to hurry and come home to her. For the first time in my life I thanked the fates for the hesitation in my speech. And all the time I saw the cruel words staring from that flimsy scented paper.

'". . . and, of course, Harry, when you come home I shall give you grounds for divorce . . ." How selfless. How magnanimous. The bitch! The bloody, unspeakable bitch, who had not the guts to be patient for a few short months out of her life.

'"Is that all? Nothing about what she's been doing? Nothing about Foxy? That's a little terrier I gave her when I went abroad."

'"She s-says she'll write a proper letter very soon."

'"Ah." I handed him the abominable letter and fumbling he put it under his pillow.

'"Thanks very much. It means a lot to get a letter at this sort of time." For many minutes he spoke of his beloved wife, Joan, and I do not know now I kept from shouting out aloud.

"Of course I'll never see again, I have come to realise that, but after all they're pretty clever over blindness nowadays and—well, we'll manage somehow, the two of us."

'If only Jameson could have died in ignorance, but he did not for that would have been altogether too painless an ending. Whatever power or influence that controls our destinies would wish to see the pathetic little story dragged to its ultimate conclusion.

'Perhaps I should have read him the truth there and then. 'Should I?'

Summer is a good time to be on the coast of Southern Italy for then you can bathe and sail and sit at the little wine-shops by the sea drinking the Lachryma Christi drawn from huge wooden casks: then you can bathe again in the moonlight and see the phosphorescent droplets melting off your fingers. Sleep the afternoons away, sunlight in muted strips between the slatted blinds, a wonderful time for love.

Gair did not return to the Torquato Tasso for his convalescence but went instead to the Villa Angela, and on his balcony he could sit and gaze across to Capri. It was a glorious month at the Angela, well repaying the discomfort and unpleasantness of a wound. He shared a room with Paddy, a crazy little Irishman who claimed in his cups to be an unfrocked Jesuit priest.

"'Twas too hot a pace for even the Holy Jesuits to stomach." Paddy with his one twinkling brown eye. On Paddy's birthday Gair went with him on a tour of the wine-shops, and at daybreak they were somehow asleep in a general's car and Paddy with his boots off. There was high-level trouble.

Serenades beneath the window of Mrs Duval, the attractive honey-coloured Red Cross widow who ran the villa, and more high-level trouble, but Paddy in common with most of his countrymen was born to trouble.

"Where can I be getting a boat to sail?" he asked a fellow patient.

"Dunno, go and ask that old chap over there." An old man with a broad brimmed straw hat and untidy white moustache was walking slowly down the road towards the sea.

"Heh!" Paddy sprinted after him.

"Heh, you—y'old devil, can't you stop to answer a civil question?"

A minute later he returned, worried incredulity in his eye. "Holy mother o' Jasus!" he gasped. "D'ye know who that was?"

"No."

"'Twas no less than Croce—Benedetto Croce himself, and there was I swearin' like a drunken fishwife—oh, Mother of every saint alive and dead, 'tis a real clanger I've dropped."

There was a gang of cripples at the Angela, who though in many cases limbless, all of them be-crutched and plaster-of-Parised, spread the maximum amount of alarm and despondency in their wake.

A night out in Naples. Dinner at the officers' club and oranges thrown at the hideous chandeliers and a bunch of grapes bursting on the bosom of the Italian soprano who sang among the potted palms staining a deep purple her massive womanhood.

"Gentlemen, gentlemen, please." The rabbit-faced officer in charge of the club close to tears. Jeep-ride to the Tarantella, a sordid, boring night-club out of bounds to British personnel, where bottles exploded against the flamboyant painted nudes who adorned the dingy walls. Two prostitutes who fought savagely over a handful of occupation lire notes, long nail-marks gouged crimson down their faces and near-naked flanks. Shouts and cheers and wild laughter until the advent of the 'Snowdrops', automatics heavy in their large hands. White helmets crammed over ears by crutches used as cudgels, and then in the street bullets loosed off to whine above the slumbering city. Very fast down the broad deserted Via Roma with none but furtive couples in doorways to see their mad passage over the cobbles. Various cripples dropped off the vehicles like sprayed flies, no one noticed, no one stopped, sirens wailed behind them, military law was very excited. And then somehow the incident closing with everyone calling everyone else a mighty swell guy.

Capri. Small mountainous island of goats. Of tourists and beggars, the home of Gracie Fields. To that little island of magical name went Paddy and Gair and two friends; not as tourists on pleasure bent but as the uninvited and unwelcome guests of the U.S.A.A.F., for that most cosmopolitan of playgrounds was reserved for the American airmen.

So they hired a boat with a wall-eyed attendant and rowed across the pearly sea disguised in fishermen's clothes, their pockets filled with shaving brushes and tins of bully. Tidier clothes in a kitbag. Wall-Eye landed them in a secluded cove, and from there by devious ways they came to the Albergo Quisisane and forgetting their ruffianly appearance they moved through a collection of high-ranking U.S.A.A.F. officers and demanded rooms. Eyebrows were raised, shoulders expressively shrugged, a few of the officers began to take note of the English voices. Later, after dodging officious-looking military policemen they reached their haven and refuge, a convent run by German nuns.

"The Virgin be cautioned, the man said 'twas a monastery and here we are surrounded by Jerry nuns." The Villa Helios was spotlessly clean.

"For us," said the Mother Superior, "the war has no significance, you are English, we are German, it does not matter. I hope you will be comfortable here with us." They shared a whitewashed cell overlooking the Marina Grande, there was one little white bed and blankets on the floor for the rest. The nuns they hardly saw, but heard the soft sound of their singing from the chapel, and they passed a young novice scrubbing the bleached stairway. Her smile was secret and unembarrassed. She was very beautiful.

They roamed the fabulous island, swam in the pellucid glimmer of the Blue Grotto, wandered among the pine-trees of San Michele and trudged up the five hundred steps to Anacapri. They halted frequently for refreshment, and Paddy never once stopped talking. They took a rickety taxi to the rock from which the Emperor Tiberius, feeling in need of relaxation, is reputed to have thrown a large quantity of slaves. In the evening they ate prodigiously in a restaurant by the harbour. A preposterous side-whiskered man in a tartan shirt strummed a guitar and sang Lili Marlene. His name it appeared was Signor Macgregor and he knew Piccadilly. Some hours later they found themselves at an opulent villa, involved with a party of hospitable friendly Italians, where they drank much sweet iced champagne and a Wagnerian woman sang. Toasts were drunk to some Entente, to the downfall of some other. Gair sat on a leopard-skin sofa and heard from a tearful little man in a hazy sort of way, how the Germans had destroyed every one of his six villas in Calabria. He cried into his sweet champagne. Then everyone in turn made a speech. Signor Macgregor strummed on his guitar until Brunhilde slapped his face. She wished to sing. When dawn was but a memory they crept with exaggerated caution into the convent. The nuns were filing into chapel with downcast heads, one of the younger ones uttered a stifled giggle as the unkempt, unshaven quartet climbed unsteadily up the stairs.

Next day a storm blew up and prevented their departure, and they sat penniless in the white cell playing poker for matches while the rain speared across the window-panes and with the soft sound of singing rose a delicious smell of food.

In the evening they could stand the pangs of hunger no longer and borrowed money from the Mother Superior to pay for a meal. She, I suppose, would be termed a good German.

As they waited on the quay for the Sorrento boat they were spotted by American police and escorted on board in disgrace by four gum-chewing hirsute creatures.

"So we finally caught up on you guys." With dignity they boarded the smelly little boat.

On the quayside of Sorrento harbour there is a place you will be unlikely to find in the guide-books. A high-arched cave burrowed from the cliff, the rough-hewn walls limewashed. At the back in the dim recesses lurked great barrels guarded by iron gates and blessed by a statuette of the Virgin holding in her hand an ever-illuminated torch bulb. From those barrels there came to the small uneven tables a coarse white wine, potent as arrack, to be drunk from thick tumblers beneath oil-lamps encrusted with cremated insects, that hung among the onions and the jars of pasta. Looking through the vaulted entrance you saw the harbour and a thin line of open sea. On the walls were clever charcoal drawings of German officers, proud Teutonic faces under the set-up caps, drawn with bold sweeping strokes.

Smoky Joe was the man who owned the place. Signora Smoky Joe it was who attracted by the excellence of her cooking the soldiers who came nightly to join the old Italian fishermen, choosing her menus from the succulent piles of eggs, octopus, lobster and whitebait that lay on the shining stone slab. A sow-like woman sat by the door and knitted, mumbling to herself.

On Gair's last evening a party went from the Angela to find the cave already crowded. Fishermen, Frenchmen, a group of magnificent Sikhs. Wine was brought, cloudy as rough cider and reminding of vinegar; the noise increased.

"Who's for a song?" Paddy leapt on the table, his perky red face split in a huge grin of good fellowship. Desmond the New Zealander broke into 'Carmen', the Frenchmen started a rival song, the Sikhs sat impassive, the fishermen sullen, and from the walls the faces stared down at their conquerors. Glasses were raised to them.

"To you, gentlemen, and I wish you were with us." They'd taken his eye, but Paddy would have stood them a drink. Glasses were banged on the table, a bottle fell to the floor with the sound of a grenade. An instant of stunned silence then the food arrived, eggs and chips and whitebait clasped lovingly by the crispy brown tendrils of octopus. Smoky Joe their host, joined them in his filthy singlet. An ex-lieutenant of the fast-moving Italian fleet he was never sober, never shaved, never clean, and soon his head fell on his arm and he snored. The heat grew unbearable. Gair went to the entrance, past Grandma who knitted steadily with her dumpy twisted fingers. Bumping gently against the stone-work of the harbour, the gaily painted fishing-boats lay at ease on the silver ripples, sails neatly furled, enjoying the soft slap of water against their sides, nodding their masts across the stars. From inside the noise was deafening, snatches of Italian, French and English, sudden bursts of song, loud raucous merriment. All were friends and no doubt if Fritz or Karl or Ludwig had walked in they too would have sung and laughed and together for a brief moment they would have made a mockery of the artificial hate of war. Angels passed overhead and a comparative silence fell. Smoky Joe had woken and was telling a story.

" . . . so you see, vous comprenez Kapitan, my wife she vair gut tart, mit him she essaye for my help when I come home from the sea, comprare Kapitan? For practice . . ." A huge flurry of laughter. He loved to amuse the simple *Inglesi*. Paddy began on his repertoire, brothels from Buenos Aires to Belfast. Gair moved away, he had heard them all. It was like the night when Miles had died; tomorrow he was going back.

The darkness was thin and troubled only by a slight breeze, Naples danced like a cluster of fire-flies on the water and sparks sprayed from Vesuvius. He wandered to the water's edge. Somewhere an accordion played a czardas, wild, tempestuous and passionate. It would be better to return to the mountains where it was not so easy to yearn for the impossible things, the round white arms of Helen, the smell of pine needles, the sparkle of frost on the grass, the rush of a northerly gale, a log fire after dark. And Helen: Helen: Helen. In the lamplight of an open window two heads were outlined and slowly they came together, one broke away to blow out the lamp, leaving a black square behind which there was paradise. In one of the boats a girl laughed as the moon rode out from behind her veil of cloud, she laughed again, for love in the moonlight has a quality of madness. Men would be lying revealed to their enemies and cursing the bland white orb. The girl in the boat began to sing a Neapolitan love song.

Gair walked up the hill to the town, in the grip of a savage ache of desire. It would be quick, it would mean nothing and some day he would tell Helen. Conscience, that furtive wrecker of so many lives, pricked timorously and repeated over and over the sterile little words he knew so well. Faithless. Weak. Animal. Then he saw the woman, in shadow and

walking slowly away as he came closer; he increased his
pace, it was hot and the wine fumes writhed in his brain. She
stopped and glanced over her shoulder, like all dim-lit
women at a distance she looked mysterious, alluring. He
could see that her hair was shoulder length, her body was
slim and straight. His conscience got into top gear.

'Go back, leave her alone, think of Helen.'

'Go on, it's no crime to want a woman.'

'Ah, but it is, you're only supposed to want one woman.'

'Go on'—'Go back.' She walked on, temptation in every
step. He heard nothing but the sound of her steps, no one
existed in the whole world but this woman, he could smell
her scent, cheap and tawdry but more enticing than all the
perfumes of the East. She stopped again and turned to face
him and as she did so the moon broke through the clouds and
dispelled the shadows like scurrying rats. With sobering
horror he saw her face, terribly scarred, twisted and puckered,
almost devoid of lips, with which she smiled, a pitiful attempt
at allure, a travesty of invitation. Gair turned and ran cruelly
down the road. Once he glanced back to where she stood,
branded and alone.

At dawn next morning he left Sorrento for the last time,
not able to say good-bye to Paddy, who was still unconscious
in bed. A few early risers were going to bathe in the green
waters opposite Capri. He did not think of the future.

Ten days later he got down into mud stiff and cold from a
cattle truck at a town called Arezzo. It was midnight, it was
raining and he could hear the guns.

A week in a waterlogged transit camp, dodging the drips
from the leaking tent, and then he drove via Florence over a
long mountain-pass where the truck boiled and big American
lorries rushed in endless convoy round the hairpin bends,
negro drivers grinning. They seemed to meet many ambulances, and it was bitterly cold compared to Naples. At the
summit of the pass sprawled an untidy, shell-scarred village
and there he found the company resting. They had just come
out of a battle and were rolled asleep in the draughty billets.

187

Many familiar faces were missing. He found twenty letters from Helen.

"Had a good time, sir?" McPhee was setting up the camp bed, sweeping the rubble into a corner.

"You didn't miss much by being away, this last one was a real sod. Monte Cattillo they called it, and they can keep it. Some of the boys are saying that Major Hardy's in for something—will you change for the M. & V., sir?—he deserves it, without him none of us would have got out."

David was in Florence for a few days, and Gair looked after the company as they rested and cleaned up. A few of them were very shaken. Rex had been away on a course and the officer in his place had been killed during the first German counter-attack. He had only known about war for five minutes. The company sergeant-major was dead. Mooney, whom he had known and liked for so long. Gair visited the cemetery by the town and wandered among the neat white crosses. Mooney, Sergeant Nisbett, Forsythe, Bryan, McLeod '08—so that was the end of Laurel and Hardy—McLeod '66, the large soft-spoken stalker from Lewis. All men he had first met years before, with whom he had shared a lot of laughter, and now they lay useless and stinking beneath the hard cold earth.

"God—if there is a God—tell me why they should have to die like this?" The grief was bitter within him but no tears came and he returned to nurse the survivors into shape.

# Chapter 13

BETWEEN the cities of Florence and Bologna lie the Apennines, the shoulders of a backbone that runs through the length of Italy. They have the same gigantic solitude of all mountains and are, as most mountains, very beautiful. Without the snow they are green with oaks and chestnuts and bushes and speckled grey with rocks. Many of the peaks are steep and desolate, and the roads from Tuscany to Lombardy twist and wind among them. Mountain dwellers of every land are a hardy breed, and the inhabitants of the lonely little farms and villages tucked in the valleys and ravines were no exception. The views were magnificent. From the crest of Pass 65 anyone desirous of loitering could see on fine days for fifteen miles down the long valley of Setta to the grim shapes of even higher mountains, the last remaining barrier before the Promised Land of Lombardy. What discouraged prolonged loitering on the open white roads was the fact that Germans looked over the valley from innumerable desolate peaks and in the clear autumn air could see every movement.

'I have seldom witnessed', wrote an enthusiastic nineteenth-century traveller, 'a grander panorama of Italian scenery, than from the top of the pass on a sunlit October evening.' An English milord, elegant in skirted coat and top-hat, coaching at leisurely pace among the rugged scenery, the brigand-infested hills, the rough peasants. Guardsman Sievwright jeeping rapidly among the rugged scenery, the German-infested hills, the rough shell-bursts, did not survey the scene with such a cultured intelligent eye. His reactions were perhaps different.

"I 'ope to flickin' 'ell I never sees another flickin' mountain in me flickin' life. Flick it!"

Another old-world voyager tells of the Apennines rising a bold and precipitous barrier between the Valleys of the Arno and the Po. Picturesquely she continues:

189

'These are Nature's own boundaries and to the aborigines of the plain they must have seemed well-nigh insurmountable. The enterprise of civilisation ever surpasses the force of savage life; and the refined youth of the nineteenth century—the expectancy and rose of each fair State—daily encounter dangers and vanquish difficulties before which the wild son of the forest would have shrunk in despair.'

The refined youth of the twentieth century daily encountered many and varied dangers as they clawed their way from peak to peak, the roses of a good many fair States vanquished a good many difficulties and many expectancies were bloodily cut short. The aborigines climbed painfully from the plains and died on the crests of Nature's boundaries. The rattle of the diligence was replaced by the roar of the bulldozer, the quizzing-glass by Zeiss magnification twenty, the rough peasants lay rotting into their meagre fields.

'These mountains, noble though they are in shape and height have not the grandeur of the Alps.' True, true. But they gave a remarkable impression of grandeur with stubborn men entrenched high among the bare crags, concreted in and impervious to anything but hunger. Through this wild country the Allies edged forward foot by foot, and then often only by courtesy of Messrs Wehrmacht.

It was a strange, lonely warfare waged often in the clouds, once off the roads there were nothing but rock-strewn tracks upon which only animal legs could move. The armies lived, when they were lucky, in farm-houses on which, if they were really lucky, remained some form of roof. By day little happened, the roads were shelled, mortar bombs fell with no warning on the tracks or on the occupied buildings to kill a man, maim another, frighten a lot more who were enjoying the autumn sunshine. Frequently single rifle shots echoed in the valleys; it was a sniper's paradise. And, of course, the patrolling, the continual nerve-racking expeditions over the darkened mountains, horrible and deadly, for the mines were scattered thickly and if a man was to lose a foot high up in the misty blackness it was an unamusing job to get him down.

'On the Italian front activity was limited to patrolling.'

Good heavens, old boy, don't they ever do any fighting out there?

The attacks grew less and less frequent, finally petered out and the war bogged down. It was not a general's war, there was no scope for pincer movements, enveloping left hooks, armoured thrusts. The armour was unable to thrust anywhere, the tank crews became infantry. It was the infantryman's war, he carried, he climbed, he fought, then he climbed and carried again. A war of small groups, of the individual, of stealth and cunning and sharp eyesight. When the S.S. took over opposite the battalion it became the war of total extermination, but that was not till the snow.

Gradually it became live and let live, with both sides springing treacherous little surprises. A war of echoes. The fall of a stone or the 'clink' of a pick was audible for hundreds of yards, the crash of a shell was stupendous. At night when the mist lay dense and heavy or the mountains stood revealed by the moon in all their cold desolation it became a live war, and a strange unearthly one. Short bursts of Spandau, single shots, Very lights soaring and the comforting thump of the old Bren. Perhaps a muffled shout. Then the mists rolled into the ensuing silence.

Gair enjoyed it for there was scope for long solitary expeditions, long periods of observation across the valleys watching, sniping, stalking. He loved the mountains; that many of them were hostile did not worry him, for there is an excitement in the hunting of armed men which is to be found in nothing else.

David was beginning to feel the strain. He had not been away from the company for more than a few days, his stomach was unfaithful after every meal, his face, always thin, was drawn and grey; on his jacket was the ribbon of the D.S.O. won immediately at Monte Cattillo.

"We banged away at some Germans for an hour or two and for some reason I was handed this." For two days and a night the Germans had tried to dislodge them from that vital hill.

"All covered in camouflage, green stripes across their faces and yelling like madmen. They were bloody good, we couldn't see them for long enough to shoot until they were

right in among us. An officer—long-nosed brute—went creep-
in about in the rocks and sniping the guardsmen with a Luger,
as cool as ice."

Sixty camouflaged corpses with stripes on their clay faces
were counted round the position.

For two months they pottered about in the same area,
doing the same uncomfortable, unrewarding routine varied
by brief spells in Florence. A fortnight in the line, two days
in civilisation and then back to ever-colder, ever-wetter
mountains, the trucks sliding and grinding up the hairpin
passes, occupants gloomy and silently remembering that there
were such things as women and real beds to share with them.
Casualties were few, but the drain was constant.

Then during a two-day orgy they heard in the Florentine
bars that an attack had been launched, and in those same bars
they heard for the first time the name Monte Colle, and hearing it ordered stiffer drinks. As mountains go Colle was not
so high, four to five thousand feet, compared with Jungfrau
or McKinley it was midget. It was exposed, rocky and un-
interesting and it swarmed with Germans, who would have
to be prised out of their emplacements with tin-openers—or
bayonets.

"Winkle 'em out, men! The Boche hates cold steel, always
did, and he's still the same old Boche." Monte Colle loomed,
ugly and menacing at the very tip of the long valley of the
Setta. The road seemed to end at Colle, all roads ended at
Colle.

When they went back it was to the village of La Garda,
tucked away in a ravine beneath a high red-stone railway via-
duct and out of sight of the cold, ever-watchful eye of the
mountain, where they were snugly quartered in buildings
with roofs and windows. But always it was there, looming
and dominating their waking thoughts, their conversation,
and if they stirred more than a few yards from the shelter of
the ravine, at once it reared hideous and deadly over their
prickling necks.

"That d-damned great heap breathing down our b-backs."

A breath which became colder every day. Plans for a possible attack were laid and passed on to the unenthusiastic companies. The honour of storming Colle itself did not fall upon the battalion, which was reserved for Mabelle, the ugly sister that lay beyond. Any time within the next two weeks. The magical words flitted from man to man as the first tentative flakes of snow settled on the brown-tiled roofs of La Garda. One company practised cliff scaling, another walking with sacking round their boots.

"Our job is quite simple really, just go forward, find and neutralise the minefields, nothing to it." David did not smile so much any more.

The doctor sorted his bandages and organised his dressing station, the padre asked the pioneers to run up a supply of crosses, the commanding officer made plan after plan, tore them to shreds and was in a vile temper. The guns stepped up their nightly chorus, the shell-bursts winking on the upper slopes, and the Germans, those unsporting figures who insisted on continuing when everyone knew they had lost the game years before, retired behind their concrete and ate what few rations they had and wondered perhaps if ever in their lives they would hear any sound but that of high explosive.

David and Gair sat in the solid farm-house and played picquet for millions of lire in front of a high-piled fire in which roasting chestnuts popped and sizzled. Next door Company Headquarters slept and swore and laughed, played poker or crown and anchor. There was a permanent feel of sleepy warmth and safety once inside the blanketed doorway. They lay snug in their sleeping-bags as the fire died down, sipping tea or wine, peeling the hot succulent chestnuts, pretending they would never have to leave that room. Men who entered had pinched faces and the breath was cloudy round their lips.

On the hill position above the village, where they went in turn for weekly spells, the men huddled in the draughty dugouts or peered upwards towards the dark outline of the mountain clear-cut sometimes against the frosty stars. Mortar bombs fell on them. Shush-shush-shush-crrrumph! Germans crept down to raid or fired attractive threads of tracer which went bouncing off the rocks. Sometimes they tired of passive inaction and crawled upwards to find their enemies, and the wind which caressed their listening ears was colder than ever before. It was a nervy business, especially when the mists were low, and the security of La Garda was welcome.

Good news was brought, and the most hardened veteran—could there be such a one?—gave a sigh of unrestrained relief. It came as all news, good or bad, via the latrine, thence to the cookhouse, to Corporal Tope the medical man and then outwards, snowballing as it went.

"Attack's off, sir." McPhee put down the shaving-water.

"Will you be getting up before lunch, or after?"

"Nothing to g-get up for, is there, McPhee."

"Nothing. Major Hardy's asleep still."

"Bring me a m-mug of tea at eleven, oh, and Jeeves."

"Sir?"

"You might remove s-some of the coal d-dust off your face, we aren't actually in a b-battle."

"Yessir."

The attack was not off, it was merely postponed. Gloom resettled like a great vampire. It was on. Off again. Within two days, within a week. A senior officer came finally to the village, and they were reprieved. Five months later an attack was launched up the bare face against starving beaten troops and the casualties were heavy.

To make up for the bitter disappointment a platoon was sent to occupy a farm thrust on its lonely own into no-man's-land and reached by one narrow track under enemy observation. In an access of low cunning it was sent under cover of darkness and with them it was deemed essential to despatch two jeeps loaded with Engineer Officers, a mule train and many Italians carrying bags of stones; also five extra officers and a posse of N.C.O.s to make up weight. The platoon reached its destination, having firmly travelled alone, but the hangers-on were ambushed and forced to retire in some confusion, the mules at full gallop, the Italians whooping and yelling, the jeeps roaring through the startled village under full throttle. A strange, ill-conceived idea, gestated in the brain of someone who, charitably one must suppose, was suffering from strain. Like that other remarkable manœuvre of storing ammunition in a derelict building also far into the eeriness of unoccupied ground. The Germans watched patiently as the cases of bombs were laboriously manhandled into tall tiers and then, when they judged the building could hold no more, came and blew it up in a glorious display of pyrotechnics.

"No wonder we're taking so long to win this infernal war."

Life was full of incident, and though in comparison with other fronts the tempo was subdued, the days were lightened by the little alarms and excursions of campaigning. Colin blown rudely from the seat where he sat immersed in an old copy of the *New Statesman* by the only shell which ever managed to reach the seclusion of La Garda; Guardsman Doppett, a huge, ungainly creature, running from the listening post, the breath rattling in his throat.

"They're coming! Stand to! 'Undreds of 'em." The officers' mess staff prepared to meet the onslaught with soup ladles, as out of the mist appeared very slowly, very gingerly two small Germans; cartoon soldiers with helmets too large, greatcoats sweeping the mud, their little frozen hands clutching their worldly possessions.

"*Kaput!*" they chanted in terrified unison.

"*Alles kaput!* Gif up we do!" They had even brought greenish bread for the starving Tommies.

Two men developed a disagreeable complaint, and, as there was not a woman alive within some miles, comment was both loud and coarse. Two mules were cited. It was a rough and ready existence with not overmuch danger and plenty of time to read and sleep and write long letters to Helen.

Hauptmann Von Reichenau came down from his particular mountain a little way to the East of Monte Colle. He was bearded, his uniform was ragged and lice-ridden, his fair hair matted and moulting under the battered cap, and he was almost starving, his body in the grip of a numbing weariness, for he had not slept for many days. The wound received at the Castle of Brolio hurt abominably when he breathed.

So he decided to give himself up. Not so long ago he would have shot himself rather than surrender, but now, deserted by his men, he was totally alone and finished. Men! Could such creatures be qualified as men? Snotty-nosed youths, whining for food and snivelling to go home, the scrapings of the barrel whimpering at the cold, the danger, the half-cooked chestnuts which were their staple diet. Gradually, by twos and threes they had slunk away in the darkness, in the mist. Two he had shot, but it made no difference, nothing could hold them, untrained, apathetic, the scum of the Ukraine, of Poland, Austria, traitors to their own lands and now to Germany. *Alles kaput!* Everything finished. The Army, the Reich, going down in flaming ruins. He stumbled over the sharp rocks, weaving like a drunkard. 'A promising fellow this Von Reichenau, should go far, a real officer of the old school, the old Imperial school.' And this was as far as he had got. A chestful of ribbons, six wounds and a year in Russia, fighting without pause except for hospitals. If his own boys had been with him the story would have been different but they, those who were left, had gone to defend the crumbling frontiers of the Reich and he, that promising fellow, was sent back, his latest wound still discharging, to lead a rabble which defiled the Wehrmacht uniform. There was a hazy roaring in his ears and hunger pains in his belly. He sat on a rock, his head in his hands, and wept silently. Then he heard the noise of boots scrabbling on rock, a voice shouted in English. Summoning what little dignity remains to an exhausted filthy scarecrow, he rose to his feet.

"Cor, stone the crows," shouted Guardsman Finch. "A flicking Jerry officer!"

"Watch out, lads, there may be more of them." Corporal Ridley stepped forward. But there was only this strange gaunt creature with his scarred and bearded face.

"Hauptmann Von Reichenau of the parachute army, to you I give myself up."

"Cor," muttered Finch.

"Picked him up on the San Martino track, sir, all by hisself."

"Entertain our guest, I've got to go to Brigade." David went out. They gave the German some tea and a piece of meat roll. He tore at the food bestially. There hung round him the foul odour of unwashed flesh and pus.

"When d-did you last eat?"

"Four days—ten days, I do not know. Chestnuts I have eaten, sometimes roots, no proper rations have reached us for many weeks."

"Why d-did you stick it for so long?"

"Please?"

"What made you go on like this?"

"I had my orders. I am—I was a soldier, and I was to remain on that mountain, just remain, nothing more for there is no longer a plan, the generals look over their shoulders to the Reich where the madman still sits in power. Ach, but I am tired, perhaps as a prisoner I can sleep."

He drank more tea, it spilled into his beard rousing the lice to busy activity. They talked of many things, but the German was rambling with exhaustion, his eyes heavy-lidded and dull. His English was good.

"Were you in Russia?"

"*Ja*, I was in Russia, for one year." He stared into the fire. "Here it is not so hard, uncomfortable, yes, but not so terrible. In the East it is the fighting of savage beasts—and the cold, oh, *mein Gott*, that cold. In Poland I have fought, in France and Crete and at Cassino but nowhere is it like Russia, nowhere is there the wind that howls across the snows; how can I describe to you the loneliness of that wind, that alien wind, that Russian winter wind. And the shells, *Kapitan*, many, many shells always falling. But still our soldiers, half dead on their feet, are forced to lie in the snow and wait for another attack and then another. And as they lie they chew the leather of their equipment, I saw a man, a friend of mine whose fingers were frost-bitten, I saw him gnaw those fingers to the bone to still his hunger, *ja*, *Kapitan*, here against you it is an easier war, men do not eat their own flesh. Still they come, the Russians, in the moonlight across the frozen plains and our dead outnumber the living and yet sometimes our men drag themselves up and go forward to meet the

197

hordes. It is hard to put out the spark of life even in men reduced to animals." His head nodded forward, he mumbled:

"Take care, my friend, you do not fight in Russia." He snored by the fire till they came to take him away. He tried to tear off his faded ribbons.

"For me they are no use, I have dishonoured them, keep them please as a memory of the German officer who had not the—as you say—the guts to continue." He saluted and held out a hand that shook.

"*Auf wiedersehen,* and thank you for your humanity and hospitality."

Later when Gair went outside it was snowing, small flakes which would lie, already the mountains were invisible and the roofs of the village were white; a thin wind stirred from the north and feathered the snow against his face.

". . . the lonely wind of Russia . . ." Gair shivered and returned to the warm firelit room and sat listening to the comfortable purr of the lamp. Soon there would be supper and a tot of rum.

## Chapter 14

With the snow there came new troops to oppose them, troops who did not desert, did not let live, but who struck swiftly and usually successfully out of the black-and-white darkness, travelling like wraiths on their skis, skilful, ruthless soldiers who did not consider defeat. The S.S. fanatical *élite* of a stricken army, the Old Guard flung in to stem the tide. A different atmosphere entered into the war, and it did not seem so nearly over, naughty boys had come to spoil the party, the sound of shooting was frequent, the bubble of security rudely pricked.

One night an earnest gawky major arrived in a rumbling half-track vehicle that awoke the echoes. He pushed his way through the blankets and stood blinking.

"Good-evening," he said, "I'm from Psychological Warfare. I went to your Headquarters, and the C.O. sent me across to see a—er Major Hardy—as—"

"Yes, that's me." David lay on his camp-bed. "Excuse me if I don't get up, but my doctor has recommended rest." He had hardly eaten for three days, was sick every hour.

"I have come to broadcast."

"Broadcast?"

"Yes, yes, propaganda, just over from the west coast. Unqualified success, two hundred prisoners in one day."

"Oh."

"Your company, I believe, is occupying the forward positions tomorrow night." He spoke with a slight north-country accent and did not wait for an answer.

"So I'll come up with you and broadcast in the small hours, human vitality is at its lowest ebb in the small hours, incidentally my loudspeaker has a range of five miles on a clear night."

"G-good God!" Gair looked up from his book.

"So that's arranged then, I'll be back in the afternoon and bring the equipment. How far can I get in the half-track?"

"To this village."

"Oh, I see, makes it awkward, still we'll manage somehow. You'll be surprised by the noise it makes."

"I'm sure I shall." The psychological major allowed himself a little joke.

"So will Jerry, ha-ha." He stumped out, shouting forcefully for his driver to turn as they were going back to Division.

David turned to the wall.

"Tomorrow night holds promise of being most eventful."

"Christ, bed-time stories for the S.S.!" The signaller went back to his dance-music on the set.

The company filed drearily up to the dug-outs and trenches on the hill, and with them came the unbelievable major and two munchkins humping a huge loudspeaker and various accessories.

"I think we're ready to switch on." The broadcaster loomed bulky in a duffle coat. A guardsman made a rude noise from not far away. There was some preliminary atmospheric, and then suddenly, frighteningly, appallingly a monstrous voice boomed and rolled among the silent white peaks, calling on the German soldier to lay down his musket, to come in to kind treatment, good food, a reading-lamp by his bed. All is over, roared the monster in German tinged with North Country. Germany is in ruins. *Sauve qui peut.* Rats, leave the foundering vessel and let Democracy give you a new deal. And more—plenty more. The company cowered ever deeper into its dug-outs.

Along the front the Germans plotted the position, swivelled guns, loaded their Spandaus. The S.S. provided themselves with grenades and prepared to sally forth. Gigantic cannon in the back areas near Bologna raised their snouts and waited.

The voice bellowed on. Give up! Give up! GIVE UP!

It stopped and with a final deafening crackle switched off. The silence throbbed.

"Now for it," thought or said the guardsmen, bleakly cursing the unnecessary disturbance. The munchkins began to coil cables.

"That should bring them in." His heart aglow with the thought of a fine job well done, the major hummed as he dismantled the equipment. With a concerted whining howl—or howling whine—the answer arrived. Shells, mortar bombs, tracer, a batch of screeching rockets. After two minutes the disagreeable commotion ceased, and but for the sound of pattering earth and of three men running down a stony path the silence was again complete.

Below in the village a half-track roared into frenzied life and bumped and squeaked away to Division at speed.

David yawned.

"Not a hundred-per-cent successful, I fancy. Our friends across the way appear to hold decided views on democracy."

Some weeks later it was decided by a master mind to send a company to occupy a small isolated hill, a pimple of frozen earth a mile from the British lines, and command of the forlorn hope devolved upon Gair.

"It's got to be occupied for five days, God knows why, it's of no possible value to either side, still there it is, it's got to be done." The commanding officer spoke in a tone which was, if not mutinous, at least non-co-operative.

They set out on a night of wind and stinging snow, feeling the cold through the jerkins, greatcoats, gas-capes, sweaters and mufflers in which they were swaddled. As fighting soldiers they were useless, each man a slow-moving tent. In addition to their weapons they carried picks and shovels, some men had brew-cans. At the rear were two mules laden with five days' rations.

The serpent of figures wound its way below Monte Colle; the squeak of trodden snow, the rattle of the utensils and brew-cans hideously loud.

"Good luck." The commanding officer had looked sad, Gair thought he had been going to shake hands.

What to do if the hill was occupied? No one had thought of that. No wireless, no communication; go there, dig in and sit in full view of Colle for five days and then come home.

They trudged slowly through the storm, snow-powdered,

minds and bodies numb, not caring that they were treading strange soil. Gair supposed he should have some plan but could think of nothing but the snow in his eyes, of how conspicuous they would be should it cease to fall.

On the map Point 512 was a dot, on the ground a shapeless mass of rock and earth, a few skeleton trees, lurking close below the western face of Colle, and there they dug themselves into a bank and skulked for five long days and even longer nights. During daylight they could not show themselves, after dark it became too cold for sleep and they lay in the crumbling little caves cramped and frozen. They could light no fires, conversation was in whispers, cold tinned stew their food. Morale sank low. He issued whispered orders. No shaving, no washing, no smoking. No movement by day, and no talking by night. No stamping of frozen feet, no laughter, nothing to cheer and warm save a spoonful of rum with the bitter dawns. As the third coming of grey daylight revealed the drawn pinched faces, the listless limbs, he realised that their endurance was cracking. They had whispered to him as he went among them in the darkness.

"Why are we here? How long must we stay?"

"Five days. I cannot tell you why."

A pale sun edged between the snow clouds on the third day and tried to comfort them, but at dusk the cold clamped down again with the impact of physical pain. It was impossible to imagine worse cold and yet that German officer had found it not so hard. If only they could light a fire, even a very little fire of twigs whose puny flames would loosen their taut skins. They had almost forgotten what it felt like to be warm; their brains were stupefied by the cold and worked sluggishly. Icy blizzards, raging in wild buffeting fury down the valleys deadening sound and thought, tearing at the gas-capes, burrowed to the very bones. Men hardened to discomfort whimpered with the cold and thought of nothing but fire and steam, hot water, hot food, the glorious idea of a bath. And as dusk turned to darkness and filled with fresh snow, there was nothing to look forward to, no warm house with fug-covered windows and log-fires sputtering, but only congealed lumps of stew shovelled between split lips by fingers numbed and blue. Behind them and before them the armies sheltered in buildings or timbered dug-outs; roofs to catch the pitiless snow, walls to halt the wind, flames to beat back the cold. But they, to realise some madman's scheme, existed in the open.

That was the Winter Line in all its cruelty, a line of desolation through the Apennines where nothing lived between the armies. No birds sang, no peasants worked, no buildings stood intact but only burnt-out shells. An area of devastation and mines, of death and burning, ghastly in its stark simplicity, the simplicity of organised destruction, the war of the scorched earth, the broken trees, the rubble. Senseless, brutal. They had done their job well, those men of the Master Race, those S.S. Every creature lay dead, humans, dogs, cows, chickens and pigs slaughtered and left to rot. When the Allies come, let them find nothing, d'you understand, nothing. *Jawohl, Herr Leutnant.*

Within a few hundred yards of Point 512 there stood a building.

"I'm going to have a look at that house, Sergeant Thomas, there m-may be a bit of a roof left, shelter where we could light a fire and send a few men at a time, s-some of them look as though they'll pack up if we don't do something."

"Want me with you, sir?"

"No, thanks, you'll have to stay and keep an eye on things." There were no other officers. Gair went on his way. The wind was freshening and on its freezing breath there sped more snow, light feathery stuff, Christmas-tree snow. Colle was hidden, visibility cut to a hundred yards. He felt himself inside a glass snow-storm. As he drew near to the house he saw that there were others, the harsh outlines of shattered masonry softened by the snow. He investigated the village and every house told the same story of direct hits of fire. Not enough shelter for a mouse. Dead chickens were strewn about, feathers ruffling in the wind and loosening the snow. He tripped on a small mound, looked closely and saw the torn boot and blue flesh of a child, another lay beside it, and others, larger adult mounds. They were lying all around, the inhabitants of that small lonely village, hidden beneath the white mantle of their common shroud. He counted forty-

six and uncovered three to discover how they died. Shot in
the back of the head, massacred in neat rows by repre-
sentatives of a people renowned for their tidy habits. Gair
wanted to get away from the wilderness of lonely death, cut
off by a curtain of snow. Supposing they were to stand up,
his hair prickled and he turned to go: as he did so a sudden
sound carried on the wind made him reach for the tommy-
gun. There might be Germans, in the cellars, approaching
through the blizzard. He heard it again, a weird sound, a high
keening moan. The wind in the ruins, just the wind, could be
nothing else; they were all dead and silent. From beyond a
broken wall it came, continuous now. Steeling himself, finger
caressing the trigger he rounded the end of the wall. Pow-
dered snow obscured his vision and at first blotted out the
scene, macabre as from the brush of Goya in a setting of
whirling snowflakes. It had been a farm-yard once, the remains of a dung heap piled against one wall, in a corner two
wooden crosses stuck askew in the iron ground, Frozen
German caps hanging. The snow on the earth was grey and
murky as though unwilling to be there. All those little things
he noticed, his brain afraid to grasp what lay in the middle of
the picture, and as he stepped forward his boot jarred on a
stone and made him jump. He remembered that, for years
afterwards he remembered that sound.

The heap must have been seven feet high. Not of straw,
nor dung, nor wood, but bodies, human bodies. Partially
hidden, in fantastic frozen attitudes, stiffened fingers dripping
crimson icicles, men, women and children piled like carrion.
He was not alone, for the terrible wailing began again and it
came from the corpses, and he could see two creatures, which
were alive, barely human as they huddled among the dead.
An old man, head cushioned on a naked shoulder, his upper
clothes rust brown with stale blood, beside him a woman, on
her lap a frozen baby; she sat bolt upright, her hands
clutching the shrunken object that had been her child. Her
hair, powdered white, stuck out in frozen lumps, and snow
had gathered on her eyelashes; her lips drawn away from the
teeth in thin blue lines; her eyes large and staring were
shining. She was mad. The gay skirt, her Sunday best, was

in dreadful garish contrast. From her soul came the terrible cry. The cry of an animal tormented beyond belief, a prayer for death. Gair motioned to her.

"*Inglese*. Friend. *Amica*." She did not move nor cease to cry out, she did not see him, or if she did it was only another human with a gun. He did not know what to do. "*Mi non— non Tedeschi—mi Inglese*." It was useless, darkness was hovering near. What could they do with her even if he got her back, he could not risk that sound in the position.

He turned to go, and for a long time after the storm had hidden the village he heard the ghostly cry, reproaching him for not having fired one more shot. Next day he took some men to the spot but she was dead, her eyes open and snow-packed. Another village had become a memory.

Two days later the company filed back to La Garda, staggering with fatigue, shuddering from the cold which had penetrated to their innermost vitals, bearded, encrusted with snow, and Gair, light-headed after exactly six hours' sleep in five days, reported their return to the commanding officer. He could say nothing, he fell down, dead asleep after two minutes in the hot room. No one ever told them whether their journey had been necessary, probably no one knew. In some headquarters a map pin was moved about an inch.

"That company's been brought in off Point 512, sir."

"Company? What company?"

"The one sent to occupy the vital ground here, sir, west of Monte Colle."

"Ah, yes. Bit of a change for them, troops get stale in this position warfare. Variety's an excellent thing, remember well how damned bored we all got in the last show, sitting in the trenches for days on end."

"Yes, sir."


Guardsman McPhee divulged information to some of the boys in the canteen of the Florentine billet.

"I tell you, lads, the boss was as flicking mad over those five days as we were. McPhee, he said, in the next war I'm going to join the German Army, all steamed up he was."

Gair had not said anything of the sort, but he might well have done.

It added tone to a letter when it was possible and accurate to write: 'I've just been spending a few days in our villa near Florence.' It added tone to their lives to have a place in which they could sleep between sheets and should they feel so inclined remain between those sheets throughout the day. The Villa Medici, country residence of that fabulous family of glittering names, Giovanni, Cosimo and Lorenzo, born perhaps in the same house which seemed to grow from the hill-side at Fiesole, its very stones, battered and chipped by bullet and shell, alive with the hints of intrigue and power. From the windows you could look down upon the roofs of Florence, across the Arno and to the south from whence they had come. A tattered notice had once flapped in the wind:

'To all troops. Owing to age . . . historical value . . . Out of Bounds.' But the notice became unstuck and fluttered away among the broken statues, the scarred cypress-trees, and the officers of the battalion took over the villa, where to the best of their ability and with the assistance of old Cesare, the bent and crippled caretaker, they respected the antiquity and historical value.

Gair revelled in an orgy of reading and looking through the books in the library, a room of heavy soporific luxury, red and gold, the rich tones of aged leather. Painted ceiling of nymphs and satyrs, between the book-shelves strips of black panelling. At night the uncertain flicker of lamps and candles failed to explore the corners or to pierce the darkness hanging below the ceiling, the fire flaring fitfully would light momentarily the bouncing satyrs, strike a burnished glow from the crimson curtains. It was warm, the chairs were deep and comfortable and there was always wine, smooth and ageless, Medici wine, concealed by Cesare from the Germans. Sometimes there was feminine company, grand ladies from Florence, contessas, marchesas with blue-stained hair, clinging still to their grand pre-war ideas, who talked so charmingly of their villas at Positano, their palaces in Rome, of their glittering lives and of how it would all be the same again. Rather different from the woman of the Winter Line. Dinner-parties, the soft glow of the candles very flattering on their beautiful patrician faces, their slender delicate hands; glinting on the silver and the ruby goblets. The luxurious scene reflected, distorted in the priceless Venetian mirrors, each one starred and ruined by a bullet.

"A drunken German, signor, an officer of our noble ally."

Bully beef off silver dishes, battledress and the expensive clothes of the women, conversation turning most easily to food and fuel and black market and then towards flirtation.

There was a dance. Arthur played his saxophone, some faces were slapped half-heartedly by marchesas, and if it had not been so cold many couples would have walked on the cratered terrace and lain invisible in the shadows of the cypress-trees. Someone threatened to shoot out the candles with a Luger, and there was a minor fight over an arrogant beauty. McPhee was sick in the hall. The South African nurses looked daggers at the titled Italians, who stared back contemptuously at the colonials in their drab khaki. Hair-raising jeep-rides down the corkscrew icy road, returning the marchesas to their respective palaces, not quite so *svelte*, not quite so *soignée*.

Twenty-four hours later. Gair left his dug-out to go round the positions on the hill. The snow was deep, the cold more intense, a fading smell of smoke hung over the black pits where half a dozen mortar bombs had just landed. To encourage himself he tried to remember the little dark South African nurse with the soft skilful lips.


One of the tasks that fell to him as second-in-command, and the one he hated most, was the organisation of the nightly ration columns to the company when it was doing its turn in an outpost position far from La Garda. Those who have had dealings with mules will understand what it was like to sort out, load and lead fifteen of the headstrong brutes along narrow ice-sheeted tracks; past corners regularly mortared, and sniped, along the edges of precipices which fell away into bottomless darkness. As bad as the mules were the muleteers, Cypriots with weak nerves and weaker bladders, who became, at the slightest provocation, not only frightened but hysterical. Every evening the frightful routine took place. At dusk the jeep convoy arrived at the mule point, laden with sacks and boxes and bundles, tinned food, bread, potatoes, onions; socks, spare boots, blankets, perhaps mail, massive jars of rum, reinforcements, the padre. Somehow in the melancholy murk of approaching night the chaos had to be sorted out. Not infrequently there were two separate parties of mules, bound for different destinations, milling about at the loading point. That way madness lay.

"Hurry up, get a bloody move on! We haven't got the whole night here—you, tie these boots on properly." The Cypriots relieved themselves against the off-side hind legs of their mules. Invariably during a journey at least one sack burst open, scattering tins, onions, loaves of bread. On a very dark, wet night a forward platoon, hungry and short-tempered, got nothing to eat but a bundle of boots and some socks.

At length after continued cursing and exhortation the column was formed up ready to move; he took his place at the head and the cavalcade clattered on the first lap of a long climb. The mule has not the softest footfall, there is nothing slinky about his strong sensible feet as he plants them with unerring aim on every rock. Half-way the gradient became so steep that the Cypriots were obliged to pull and push the straining beasts, shouting as they did so: "Aaah! Eeeeh!" Aaah-eeeh came back the echoes. Usually at the steepest point a sack fell off and a ponderous load of tinned apricots or condensed milk went bounding down the mountain-side.

"Aaah-eeeh-aaah!"

"Shut up that bloody row!" In the track were shallow craters, it was an unhealthy spot. A mule stopped, waxed stubborn and tried to turn round, its Cypriot whacked away with a stick, the mule lashed out, a fellow mule bit him on the rump.

"Aah-eeeh-eeeh-aah!" urged those at the back. An inextricable mass of mules milled hugger-mugger on the path.

Not far away was a drop of some hundreds of feet. More sacks fell off and a rum-jar exploded, the noise was deafening.

In a neighbouring valley Hans said to Kurt :

"Listen." It came to them as the hum of a far-away football crowd.

"Tell the officer." The officer spoke on a field-telephone, a moment later three mortars fired. The bombs rushed past the confusion on the track with sibilant whistle to burst far below on the frozen river.

A wail of terror rose from the Cypriots.

'I'm off!' intimated the leading mule, boring frantically into the heaving lump of animals. More bombs whistled down, distinctly closer, a Spandau ripped a stream of bullets high above them. Gair pushed among the mules, punching and pummelling; miraculously when the mortaring stopped there were no casualties, but four muleteers had vanished, and in the silence after the last bombs all the remaining Cypriots appeared to be passing interminable water. An hour later they reached the company, weary, overheated and dreading the return.

"You're damned late tonight, it's nearly nine o'clock." David was peevish.

Gair did not trust himself to answer.


The railway linking Florence and Bologna runs through many tunnels on its devious route in the mountains. There had been a time when trains rattled merrily along, but now the permanent way was rotting, the lines rusted under the snow and the damp-streaked sides of the tunnels echoed to the roar of jeeps, the clip-clop of mules, the voices of men. Both sides used those tunnels as storehouses, shelter, for communications, as covered approaches and gun emplacements. A gun on wheels would skulk in the tunnel and every so often pop out and fire a few shells, retiring hastily. At the dangerous mouth of one tunnel was situated the small village of Gardaletta, and in that village with the romantic name was always a platoon, living a troglodyte existence in cellars emerging every ten days to file through the tunnel for rest. A favourite game played by the German gunners was undoubtedly labelled 'Plant a shell in the tunnel.' They played it a lot, and for those in Gardaletta it was a boring game as every day more houses collapsed in clouds of dust, more roofs fell in. Not long before Christmas, the Germans feeling festive, switched bigger and better guns on to the tunnel game and rockets as well for sound effect.

"I'll go along with the r-ration jeep and see how things are at G-gardaletta." As soon as he had spoken Gair wished he had kept quiet as the sound of the steady bombardment came to them muted by the intervening hills. David put down his cards.

"Might be a good idea, I'd go myself but there's some company-commanders' conference about Christmas leave, tell Mike I'll be up tomorrow night."

The jeep bumped slowly down the long tunnel towards the pin-point of daylight, along the damp shining walls were boxes of ammunition, straw and mules, smelly oil-lamps hung at intervals and groups of men in the shadows, Gurkhas waiting to go forward on some expedition. At the end of the rails the white hole grew larger.

"Stop about t-twenty yards short of the entrance, I'll walk from there." The jeep stopped and Gair got out.

"About how long'll you be, sir?"

"Oh, I dunno, an hour perhaps, but, anyway, I'll—"

A gun fired the shell that won the game.

When he reached the hospital after six hours in a bucketing ambulance he was soaked to the waist in blood and not more than half conscious. In a large marble-floored hall a young doctor gave him a transfusion, and he lay, weak as a kitten, watching the dark-brown liquid in the upturned bottle and wondering where it came from as it dribbled drop by drop into his veins. Dipsomaniac, murderer, corpse, a German, an Italian, an Anglican bishop. A pint of bottled blood, please, and mum says not the expensive sort! But, darling, he's quite changed since he came home, he won't look at a woman now. Drip, drip, gurgle. Part of another life dripped slowly along the rubber tube.

In error he was put into the head-ward where crazed men raved and howled throughout the blue-stained night. His face throbbed aflame, he did not know the true extent of the damage and he could only speak with difficulty.

A man shouted from a mask of bandages.

"Sister, sister, tell that German to go away, he's keeping me awake, look at the bastard bicycling round the ward, for God's sake, sister, tell him to stop, it's driving me mad, aah, get out of it you lousy sod!" The night-sister spoke briskly to empty air.

"Go on, out with you, I've told you before not to bicycle indoors. There, he's gone now, is that better?"

"Thanks, sister, he's been bothering me for hours." Next morning Gair was transferred to a general ward. In the neighbouring bed was a Pole, a gay fellow. A bullet had severed the tendons of his right hand, but with his other he drew pictures of angels and children with which to decorate the ward.

"In Warsaw I was to become an artist, but now," he shrugged, "now I must look to another trade."

On Christmas Day there was beer and plum pudding and whisky for the stronger patients, crackers and paper hats perched above the bandages. Snow fell lazily past the big windows, the commandant wished everyone luck.

Some days later a wizened Jewish surgeon came to see the wound.

"The scar will not show too much, I think. Now, captain, how would you like to go home? This is the third time, is it not? There is a scheme for repatriation, and you must surely be tired of hospitals, yes?" But such glorious ideas take time to bear fruit.


He went back to the company with the golden promise of home dangling before his eyes and the horrid feeling that his nerve might go. His ears were constantly alert for danger, every shell, every mortar bomb, every bullet was aimed at him personally. The fear must surely show in his eyes, but if any of the men noticed anything none gave any indication.

"The commanding officer wants to see you."

"You're going home, Gair, bit of a rush, I'm afraid, as you've got to be in Naples by the twelfth so as to get the ship."

He was glad there was no time for saying good-bye as he must leave before dawn. On that last night in the mountains it was quiet, but he could not sleep and stood by the doorway staring up towards Colle. And in the still cold moonlight with the stars like diamonds, the mountains rising magnificent and aloof, he forgot the horror and the cruelty and the pain and remembered only the excitement, the free-and-easy life, the comradeship, the laughter and the fantasy. For an hour or so he did not want to leave, there was sadness in his throat. Then he went in to pack his few possessions in a kitbag. David was asleep; McPhee was asleep. He did not wake them, nor Sergeant Thomas, for he knew he would never be able to say good-bye. But the truck would not start, and the whole company turned out in the misty dawn to see him go. All he could think of saying was:

"Keep your heads d-down and . . ." Quickly he got into the vehicle.

"Come on driver, let's get away." 'Before I forget the stiff upper lip and make an exhibition of myself.'

The Germans, as a final farewell, shelled the road, and the truck tore over the bad bits between the tall plumes of snow and earth. His last impression of war was, like the first, the rising screech of the shells, the whirr of splinters—then they were through and driving down from the mountains towards the peaceful plains. He never heard another gun fire in anger.

*　　*　　*

So that was the close of an episode, a time spent as it were, in parenthesis. He had achieved nothing spectacular, done no more than many thousands of others, his exploits had not been tinted with glamour, he had not descended dangling on a parachute through extraneous darkness, nor had he crept ashore on enemy coasts to spread alarm and destruction. His beret was of faded khaki, and he depended for life mostly on his own two feet. There had been no heroic wanderings behind the lines, and doubtless because his doings had been so humdrum few paeans were sung in his honour.

For a short while he had led the life of an ordinary infantryman in the line.

From the moment he stepped on board the ship at Naples off the same upturned keel where he had landed he looked only to the future, to the start of the next chapter, to Helen. Vesuvius, Sorrento where he had been so happy, Capri, he noticed none of them, consumed as he was by blazing impatience to reach home and see her smile, hear her quiet voice, hold her in his arms.

The ship ploughed home in a small convoy, unhurried and dawdling over the sombre sea. Two days at anchor within sight of a rain-swept Liverpool, his restless expectancy wellnigh unbearable. Ashore in soaking darkness, stevedores slouching on the dockside, yawning and grumbling, soldiers formed up in the rain waiting as always for someone to tell them something. Ring up Flaxman 6248, number engaged, no more coins. Hang about till breakfast-time in heavier rain; soldiers still waiting for orders, for food, for a train. Bundle into a dirty, cold carriage and shunt forlornly backwards and forwards, kit tumbling off the overcrowded racks. At last the train started and rumbled slowly towards London. The heroes were home.

"Flat 2A? Top floor, sir, turn right out of the lift, a red door." He paused for a moment outside the little red door to still the absurd flutterings of his heart. A milk bottle stood empty by the mat, a neatly folded paper stuck from the letterbox, an airmail letter lay on the floor. He picked it up and saw his own handwriting, then taking a deep breath he pushed the bell-button, it did not work. Then he saw the door was on the latch, he pushed and it opened into a minute hall that

213

seemed full of fur boots and coats hanging one on top of another. It was dark after the passage.

Suddenly, with a rustle of silk and the quick flash of white skin, she was in his arms, her hair pressing into his mouth, her body yielding to his, her lips kissing his neck.

And the moment was a hundred times better than the one for which he had yearned and hoped through so many dark hours.

# *HOME AGAIN*

## Chapter 15

FOR two days they did not leave the flat. They talked for hours, they lay in each others arm's for hours and then they talked again, of their son, of the future.

"You think it was right of me to send him to Scotland, away from all these ghastly doodle-bugs and things? If anything had happened to him I could never have faced you."

"But it was you I was thinking of, Helen."

"He's so awfully sweet and happy-looking."

"I'm sure he is, but I don't know him, I know you and I love you, if anything had happened —"

"Darling!"

"Darling, darling!" The darkness of the little room was vibrant.

On the third night Helen said a surprising thing.

"Gair," she whispered, twining her leg about his.

"Yes," he was half asleep. Her lips brushed his cheek.

"You know it'll mean getting to know each other all over again."

"What on earth d'you mean?"

"Well, darling, we've been apart for so long, so much has happened to both of us, we've led such different lives, we're— we're not the same people and . . ."

"But we love each other, Helen. Don't we?" She did not answer. He felt the touch of her lips and murmured.

"Stop talking nonsense and go to sleep."

That was the end of it. But in the tortuous labyrinths of his mind a tiny seed of doubt fell, and, against his will, it fell on rich soil where imperceptibly it began to grow and ripen. Subconsciously he was being prepared for disaster. Therefore he was not taken so completely unawares when gradually her rapturous welcome began to change to tantrums and cold bad temper. A dream is easily shattered.

\*     \*     \*

217

Invisible projectiles fell upon London from the stratosphere showing by the ugly roar of their impact that the war was dying hard and slowly. Great fleets of bombers flattened German cities already shaken by a fantastic tonnage of explosive. Armies struck at the Reich from every side, but still the stubborn, reeling soldiers would not give in. Soldiers who so nearly had conquered the world and now in those last months, battered and exhausted, were holding off the combined attacks of vastly superior numbers boasting vastly superior equipment and unlimited resources. But at last the pressure grew too overwhelming; with a rush the floodgates opened and the field-grey soldiers could fight no more.

Peace had come. Not the peace of 1918 when joy was unrestrained at the finish of Armageddon, but sober joy, almost a half-hearted rejoicing, for on that first night many thousands thought of men who might still so easily die.

VE night in London was like a rocket which, having gone streaking into the night has petered out and fallen just before the point of bursting into multi-coloured stars.

Helen and Gair joined friends and went to celebrate. In an old-fashioned hotel they sat and drank to the end of darkness; they drank a lot and made more noise than had ever been heard at one time in the heavily comfortable lounge. Surrounding them were numbers of women in black dresses and fur stoles; their hair was uniformly musty and mousy, their shoes narrow and pointed. Veins stood out on their thin hands, large handbags stood by their chairs and they looked through their reading-glasses with faded indignant eyes, the library books open on meagre thighs. In the dining-room they would sit, each at her own table, which would be littered with labelled pots of marmalade, sugar and a small square of butter. Sometimes red-faced men, in tweeds, with protuberant eyes which saw always the sun and the sands of never-forgotten corners of Empire would join those lonely black crows who sat so straight in their chairs, so tight-lipped, so inexpressibly forlorn, so unmoved by victory.

"Come on, Gair, wake up and have another drink." Johnnie was flushed and noisy, calling for the waiter, an elderly stooping man with a dent in his ivory scalp.

"Drink up, fill up." Johnnie began to hum. "Excuse me, sir, some of the residents . . ." A suave foreigner, manager, perhaps, bared his gold teeth in servile protest.

"Oh, let's get out of this morgue!" Along Berkeley Street, playing football with a tin, chipping the polish off gleaming shoes, sweating into the service dress.

"Really, Gair, you must put your cap on straight." Helen's voice was like a bradawl. He pushed the heavy cap, his comic-opera hat, well down over his eyes in the approved fashion and defiantly gave the tin a final kick. She was right, of course, officers in uniform do not kick tins along Berkeley Street. Behaviour unbecoming to an officer and, as such, a gentleman! A dirty little boy was holding the tin aloft. "'Ere you are, throw-in for the coloured 'ats." Gair noticed Helen standing apart, aloof from such incredible vulgarity. He smiled at his wife. She stared back coldly.

"Let's try and get something to eat," suggested an unidentified girl in W.R.N.S. uniform.

They linked arms and joined the jostling crowds moving along Piccadilly. In most crowds you get the feel of definite emotions, gaiety, grief, anger, excitement, but in that crowd there was none. It seemed to be composed of people who crowded the streets because they felt they ought to, and not for any specified cause.

In the restaurant it was the same.

"They might all be attending their own funerals." Johnnie ordered champagne, and it was brought by a waiter who looked as though he might burst into tears at any moment. Gair ate his way through the expensive concoctions, drank many glasses of champagne, danced once with Helen, but not again as she refused to speak, except to comment unfavourably on his style, then often with the girl in the W.R.N.S. He liked her pert attractive face. Helen, when she danced with others, had plenty to say. The evening marched forward much as almost every other evening since Gair had come home. He sat crumbling the remains of a tasteless roll, remembering an endless succession of similar parties . . . Dancing, or shuffling on the overcrowded floor, to the music of fat brown men in frilly blouses, or whey-skinned men with cynical eyes, in dinner jackets in an atmosphere stifling with smoke and overheated bodies. Night after night, eating the same food, hearing the same syrupy music, seeing the same faces, uttering the same inane small talk, spending the same amounts of non-existent money. In fact, having FUN.

"Yes, we can, darling, of course we can, you can cash a cheque at the Idiocy." Or the Pompadora, the Two Hundred, the Bughouse. For they always 'went on' to a night-club where in a plush and gilt hot-house they drank watered gin and watched people, who slept with each other, on a postage-stamp dance floor. Inevitable cheque forms were produced and signed with unthinking abandon and whisked away by ingratiating gentlemen in double-breasted tuxedos. On most of the plush corner seats couples were melting into each other's arms, if not already inextricably locked in gin-fanned embrace. Then when the band had ceased to wail and eyes were watering from the smoke, they would leave and drive through deserted streets to the flat where usually they had a row, or if sufficient liquor had been drunk perhaps a moment or so of animal passion. In a few hours it was time to stagger to the bathroom and unsteadily shave, make strong tea, search for the aspirin and, furry-mouthed, to catch a clattering, clanking train to Colony Camp.

Back in the evening, head splitting wide open and eyes that smarted with fatigue.

"*Who* d'you think rang up and suggested a party? Bill Aylesbury. So I said of course we'd love to—well, you don't look madly enthusiastic, I must say." She slammed at the dress on the ironing board, hair fell across her peerless green eyes and her lips were unpainted. Here was Nature in the raw indeed.

"He's a b-bloody fellow."

"I see, I'm not to be allowed my own friends now." The dress steamed under the fierce strokes. "You're too tired, we can't afford it, now it's you don't like my friends. All right then, skulk at home, see if I care. I've got plenty of people who want to take me out, plenty."

"I expect you have," he countered wearily. "Where are we going and when?" He would have slept for the inter-vening hour if Helen had not been so noisy on the telephone and if the arrival of a V-2 had not startled him into moist wakefulness.

So the days and nights moved hectically, hysterically almost, to the finish of the war in Europe. And now here it was, at an end. But there was no end to this hideous existence, this torrent of artificial fun which was engulfing him in a miasmic swamp of fatigue, hangovers and overdrafts. Tonight is Victory night! Drink-up, drink-up, like we've done on every other night for weeks, for months, maybe he had been born in a night-club. . . . He jerked himself into the present, the ruins of the tasteless roll scattered over the cloth, heard the wailing music, and looked for Helen. She was dancing again, laughter on her lips. Without a sound the sinister folded paper appeared before him; the amount was considerable. Between them Johnnie and he managed to scrape it together.

Hazily and in company with many thousands he found himself outside the Palace; a few voices were singing, but nothing spontaneous. People stood about in groups, silently and refusing to coalesce, the singing failed to spread. Many of the uniformed figures were waving bottles. A girl, laughing with scarlet mouth, tried to snatch his cap. The rest of the party were lost in the dark background of a vast motionless crowd. Here and there were pin-points of noise, little swirls of movement. Some Irish Guardsmen began to sing and he joined them, feeling among friends again.

"That's right, sir, got to stick together." Many of the little groups muttered angrily.

"It's shameful." "And the war not over yet." A rival band of sailors took up a different song, the infection began to spread, almost got a hold but, unsupported, flickered and went out. With dim memories of descriptions he had heard, Mafeking, Armistice Night, Gair was bewildered, cheated and angry. He had no relations fighting in the East. For a long time he wandered through the crowds in the Mall. Once he asked an old woman carrying a bottle of stout, if she had seen his wife.

"'Ave a drop o' this luv, it 'elps a bit." With dignity he up-ended an empty bottle and thanked her. He'd heard the last words somewhere before, not that it mattered. With spots of stout on his tunic he sat under a tree in St James's Park, till the dew penetrated to his bottom, then walked home to the flat. The stairs were too much for him, and he camped half-way up. When he woke he found a note in his cap.

"Thought the Guards could take their liquor." Gair did not even smile, nor shave, nor see Helen, but polished his cap star with newspaper and caught the first train for camp. Handing over his duties to an abstemious friend, he borrowed the padre's bed and slept throughout the first day of peace.

Not long afterwards a crumpled letter arrived from David, it had been on its way for many weeks that letter and dealt with matters which had already passed into history and which were as he read them, Gair realised, events of what was practically the last war.

'. . . for a few weeks after you had gone they left us in peace below Colle and then a cretinous creature drew attention to our masterly inactivity. From then on life became unbearable . . .' (description of ceaseless movements to and fro behind the front) ' . . . presumably to hoodwink the wily Boche, but by then the Boche was too damned hungry and exhausted to be wily any more, and we only succeeded in hoodwinking ourselves. The final offensive began—thank God, the first phase did not take us—and apparently the chaps who had to tackle Colle were knocked about quite badly by a demoralised enemy—imagine what it would have been like last winter! For you the honour of the follow up, they said, and follow up we did, among the canals and poplars of Lombardy, that Promised Land for so long. It was very different from anything you knew. Dead flat with endless banks and dikes, ditches and little rivers. A lot of sniping by Tiger tanks and little nests of unpleasant young fanatics. Sergeant Thomas did quite superbly and in fact is in for a D.C.M. Later we were sent on an ambitious flanking man-œuvre up into the Comacchio area—look it up on your map, if you don't know—where we mucked about with assault-boats and no one quite knew who was where or why. Rex distinguished himself by swimming across to reconnoitre an island and then taking most of the company back there with him to occupy it. If there are any medals left over from Normandy he should get something, I hope.

'But they all did well, bloody well. They were tired and stale and knew the war was as good as over, but I heard of no cases of heads being kept unduly down. By the time you get this the whole stinking business should be over and we can start to pick up the pieces. I am leaving the battalion and going to South Africa for a few months—to an ersatz Staff College—not as you can imagine because I have become suddenly enamoured of Army life and desperately keen to rise to the top, but for the sordid reason that my inside has finally rebelled and sprouted into great crops of ulcers. Change apparently is the thing.

'Write and let us know how peace-time soldiering appeals. How is that grimy object, McPhee? Incidentally he owes me two hundred lire. Wish you'd been with us in this last bit, we'd have had some good laughs and no doubt you would have collected yet another foreign body in your anatomy . . . See you some day.'

Gair read the letter after lunch in the ante-room and then went to give a lecture on 'Morale', dreaming of glory that might have been.

After VE night the situation in the flat deteriorated rapidly. A civil word was seldom spoken, and once or twice moveable objects were broken. Being at the time either so tired or so abysmally blind he did not fully realise what lay behind the tantrums and spells of cold silence, the short interludes of sunshine. She pleaded strain, undue tension caused by his return.

"We've got to get to know each other from the start. Give me time. I know I'm being horrible to you. . . ."

It is pointless to describe further the vicious circle of accusation, recrimination, reconciliation, accusation which spun ever faster in the confines of a small flat. Suffice to say that more and more often Gair found himself unavoidably detained in camp. . . . How pleasant it was to sit with his fellows, chatting and laughing, and then go early and quietly to bed where he could fall into deep sober sleep for more than the usual two or three hours, to be woken by McPhee with a mug of tea. Lie listening to various bugles and the sound of sparrows in the limes outside the window; early-rising officers hurrying over gravel, the heavy 'thrum' of a truck on the tarmac. Distant shouting. Ordinary sounds that he knew and found a comfort. Lie dozing, the tea untouched, till Tessa nuzzled the blankets and it was time to make a move.

"Shaving water, sir." Breakfast at a leisurely pace, the *Telegraph*—the *Mirror* if he could find one—propped against the milk-jug. Mess waiters in white bum-freezers gossiping to the cooks outside in the pantry, the mess sergeant, corpulent and well satisfied with his lot, the officer who kept his cap on for meals, black as thunder over something in *The Times*. A smell of bacon and Tessa sniffing her way to the kitchen. Another cup of coffee, this time mostly grounds, and as he picked them off his tongue a pride of young officers clattered out for parade, stamping to straighten the crease in their trousers, tucking away the curls and wisps of hair the girls had found so irresistible not many hours before. He felt immensely senior as he watched them hurrying across the road towards the horror of morning parade. No longer was the mess filled with those elderly subalterns and unbelievable captains, they had vanished and in their places were younger, more casual officers, who did not glare at the first suspicion of a chuckle. Decorated officers with much experience tucked away behind their school-boy faces. Major Herbert Finch had departed, no doubt, by Rolls, to different pastures, and not even the fragrance of cigar smoke lingered as reminder.

Major Pillowe, the man with the bristling moustache and little breeding, for whom there can have been no conceivable excuse, had also gone, allowing by his departure the sun to shine into the ante-room.

The one remaining survivor of the Old Guard wore his cap and glared at *The Times* while Tessa sat expectantly waiting for him to notice the old kipper she had brought from the kitchen. The tip of her tail wiggled, she barked her

intimate little bark of hopeful friendship and regarded the
suffused cheeks with her bright eyes. The kipper advertised
its own presence. Beneath the table, his own dog Grenade, a
pompous terrier which should always have sported a well-
set-up cap, raised its grizzled chin from a polished toe-cap
and foolishly growled. Tessa's eyes hardened. Gair watched
the scene from over his paper. Grenade growled again. His
owner kicked at him, muttering "Stop it, old man." Gair
could see the muscles preparing themselves for action under
the silky sheen of Tessa's coat.

"Tessa!" With a quick look at him—so, sorry, no can hear
—she sprang, her jaws meeting like a steel trap; fortunately
Grenade was not between them but heading for the kitchen.

"Call off your blasted dog, she's a perfect menace!"

Mess waiters appeared at the double, wiping egg off their
faces, as Grenade by dint of tighter turns escaped among the
legs of the cooks and his owner stormed and threatened. But
times had changed, he was in the minority, no longer could
he shout and, by so doing, reduce all and sundry to angry
nervous twitching and then retire in triumph to his cronies.

They were rather a pathetic pair, he and Grenade, as they
sat together in the ante-room or walked stiff-legged to the
dingy office from where the master transacted such business
as the issue of coal or the allotment of firing ranges to cadets
at week-ends. Hardly anyone ever spoke to him, he never
seemed to go away, or to smile, or to remove his cap.
Perhaps he missed his port-swilling comrades.

At a leisurely pace Gair wandered in the warmth of the
morning towards his office from where he issued instructions
and information about patrolling. He was responsible for
teaching the rudiments of patrol activity to every squad that
passed through the ten weeks of training at Colony Camp.
The job suited him, being independent; he was as keen on
playing soldiers in the dark as anywhere else, and it spared
him the boring duties of a company second-in-command.
Checking stores, inspecting urinals and so forth.

Patrols had returned to the status of jolly games amid
the Surrey pines. Many hours he spent hiding in bracken
or lay looking at the stars, the trees black and sinister against

8                              225

the sky, while small parties of enthusiastic young guardsmen crept about in the sandy valleys of the training area. He gave them all the trimmings, trip-flares, tracer-bullets, a Spandau for realism. Tessa sometimes came out. She set off the trip-flares, barked at the unseen patrols, chased the tracer and on one unforgettable occasion, carried a little bundle proudly and tenderly between her teeth all the way into camp, to lay it down in the barrack-room, revealing a sausage roll of explosive, fused and ready for the match.

March back with the patrol, moving pad-pad in their plimsolls, eyes showing white in the burnt-cork skins, usually they sang. Cocoa and currant cake in the barrack-room, the faces incredibly young, bulging round the food. Most of them were about nineteen. Only the N.C.O.s looked tired. Gair sat on a bed and drank the greasy cocoa and watched them. Tessa ran up and down receiving lumps of cake.

"More cocoa in the can!" A rush, bursts of talk.

"All right, all right, keep it quiet, there are others trying to sleep." They'd forgotten about sleep. Live ammunition had crackled over them, they had handled explosive in the dark, had started a forest fire and put it out and felt themselves men, and not even ordinary men but heroic veterans.

"Is it really like that, sir?" asked a chubby grimy infant.

"Yes, m-much the same." Who was he to disillusion them? They crowded round, and he smelt the grime and the sweat, an occasional whiff of feet and cheap tobacco, and he realised he had a deep affection for such low-class odours.

"I'll try and fit in another n-night out for you." "Just the job, sir." "Piece o' cake." "This is the life." Their enthusiasm was as infectious as mirth.

"Weapon inspection first thing, Sergeant Dixon."

"Good-night, sir," they chorused. He walked to his room, very tired, very content. Some would certainly label him crazy, but he really did prefer to sit under the stars than in the foetid jungle light of a night-club.

"What makes them so keen, now that the war's over? They must know there's no chance of them b-being sent to the Far East."

"I don't know, I suppose they've always got something

to look forward to whilst it's still going on," answered Johnnie.

"L-look forward to?"

"Well, you know what I mean, we felt the same once."

"Did we? Yes, I s-suppose perhaps we did. Inconceivable, isn't it?"


"Ah, Gair, come in, I'd like a word with you." The commanding officer looked up.

"These night schemes of yours." A squad jog-trotted past the window, beside them sprang a wasp-waisted P.T. instructor, screaming in falsetto.

"Poor fellows," commented the commanding officer.

"There've been complaints."

"W-what sort of complaints, sir?"

"Noise and that sort of thing, disturbing civilians, frightening children, even," he flipped over a sheet of paper, "even reports of broken windows."

"But, they've got to be trained, surely these p-people must understand—"

"I'm afraid they don't see it quite like that. Is all this explosive essential?"

"I s-suppose not really, sir. I've been using it chiefly to liven things up f-for the squads. The trainees seem to revel in it and if they enjoy something they'll learn more." He felt red in the face.

"Quite. An admirable theory, but one which it looks as though we shall have to curtail or at least modify."

Gair felt mutinous.

"However, to enable you to continue with your bangs and fireworks, I have decided to send you up to Lobs where, as far as I am concerned, you can shoot thousands of rounds into the night air and set fire to anything you like. There's unlimited space up there. What about a week's leave?"

"Thank you, sir."

A long, lanky figure entered whose look bore the stamp of a fanatic. He saluted and went to his table, burning up huge amounts of energy as he moved.

"I couldn't get past that dog of yours, kept sniffing at my trousers and rumbling." He brushed away flecks of spittle.

"I've just been talking to Gair about his patrolling, Pat." The chief instructor by way of reply pounded the table with extreme violence, bringing a clerk to the door, inquiry blinking behind his spectacles.

"Ah, now you're there, Ferrett, get me that file on my new grenade—tried it out last Sunday, sir, seems to work splendidly, one or two prematures and a blind which apparently went off next day, but, after all—teething troubles." His well-socketed eyes glowed with fervour. The commanding officer began to speak, but Pat forestalled him.

"What about a catapult? Modified, of course, and strengthened—yes, by God, yes, something on those lines." He began to sketch. A small frown appeared on his senior's brow. Gair smiled to himself. A good man the chief instructor, for all his unquenchable zeal, a sincere man, a man devoted—one might almost say married to his Regiment and to the furtherance of her prowess and reputation. A pity there were not more like him.

Pat leapt to his feet.

"There you are, sir, what about that, the Pane-Galloway patent grenade projector." He leant heavily across the other's desk and in a spasm of nervous energy upset an ink-pot. The frown deepened. Gair began to make for the door.

"I'm sorry about this sudden posting, as I know—"

"Pull back to point A—there, at the bottom of the paper, sir, and—"

"I know you've got a house—"

"Issue them four or five to a section, I thought."

"In London."

"Perhaps springs would be better than rubber, but then on the other hand—"

"See the adjutant about details of dates and so on.—Now, my dear Pat, what on earth *is* all this nonsense?"

Gair and Tessa went home to Scotland to see his son. At the end of the week he left more determined than ever that the child should not be embroiled in the troubled times which lay ahead.

## Chapter 16

THE hills of Southern Scotland are not spectacular like those of the Highlands; their beauty is softer, their colours more subdued, and they are dotted with little lochs and small square woods of firs that pigeons leave with a great clatter of wings and where rabbits sit browsing along the edges. The contours are less harsh, rounded like a woman, and sometimes at sunset the hills seem to glow, but palely. Sheep move across the long, open slopes where the wind hisses in the grass. There is nothing grim about those hills; the loneliness has not the streak of cruelty associated with wild and empty places. By the shores of the silver lochs and on the summit of the hills, listening to the wind in the grass, the sound of the swifts as they twisted and dived in the spring air, the incredibly stupid but peaceful bleating of distant sheep, it was possible to achieve moments of great tranquillity.

But only on Sundays. Throughout the daylight hours of every other day the quiet solemn beauty of the countryside was rent and torn by the beastly passage of bullets, the echoing 'crump' of mortar bombs, sometimes even the screech of shells. Very often the sounds would merge into one continuous racket—termed by the experts a 'symphony of fire'. Bullets went 'phlonph' into the placid steel surface of unsuspecting lochs; explosions rolled among the hills, sheep scampered helter-skelter or fell dead and branches were cut from under the feet of perching pigeons. Some of the small square woods were blasted to splintered stumps.

Man was practising his hideous worst.

Gair, by virtue of his position as training officer at Lobs Camp, spent his days in the thick of it.

"Put all the emphasis you can on warfare in close country," urged the detachment commander, an easy-going soldier, who did not worry, did not fuss and did not interfere, a live-and-let-live man. Gair looked out over the miles of grass and wondered how to simulate a jungle. The guardsmen were still refreshingly enthusiastic; their newly-joined officers were, to a man, equally enthusiastic over the taking of strong waters and deplorable in their lack of skill, initiative and understanding. They did not share the belief held by the men under their command that they would have a chance at the Jap; they were bored and thought only of finishing their service. Two at least of them were true democrats and got tight with the guardsmen at the local inn. A strange, unsteady crew.

"I think I'll go and have a look at one of your platoons tonight," said the brigadier. "What are they on?"

"One's patrolling, sir, and this one, in its final week, is practising digging into a defensive position after dark. Ah, Gair, good, come in. Now where exactly is Number Fifteen Platoon?"

"This area," he thumbed a map square.

"Got a vehicle handy?" asked the brigadier. "Good, I'll come along with you and see what's going on."

They drove through the dusk; sheep blundered into the headlight beams, once an owl flapped from a tree-stump in slow-motion, the brigadier sat hunched in his British warm. Gair drove slowly over the pock-marked road, revelling in the smell of the night air. Suddenly into that night air there crept the odour of smoke. The brigadier sniffed loudly.

"Some bloody fool's set fire to something and gone home leaving it burning. It's these mortar smoke bombs."

"This is as f-far as we can go in the jeep, sir."

They walked on up the rising slope, the brigadier hunched deeper in his coat, Gair wondering when the sentries would challenge and whether they would be alert. He hoped so. The brigadier was himself a man of above-average alertness who liked to notice the attribute in others. There should by now be some indications of men at work digging slit trenches, moving about, kicking tin things and then cursing loudly. Gair strained his ears and heard nothing but the heavy breathing of one who found the incline too steep, stared ahead and saw nothing on the skyline but what looked like rocks.

"Taking up their positions damned well, aren't they?"
The tone was spoilt by suspicion. God forbid it was the
wrong hill. Gair shuddered silently.

With a thudding patter and little snorts the rocks made
off into the darkness of the hill top.

"The Almighty's turned 'em into sheep!" Gair tittered
nervously in response.

"Well, where the hell are they?" The titter died.

"I—er . . ." His diaphragm, that untrustworthy unit,
tightened and seized up, leaving him speechless. He pretended to be searching, going a few steps this way, that way,
peering furtively right and left. The brigadier contained himself for a moment, then shouted :

"No use going on like that, we both know they're not here.
Good lord, what's that?" Down below them by the faint
glimmer of a loch a tall blast of flame shot up into the night,
to die down almost at once to the normal illumination of a
large bonfire. "Come on!" the brigadier made off downhill,
and Gair as he followed could hear the unmistakable sound of
singing.

'There were rats, rats, big as flickin' cats, In the store,
in the store . . .' How many times had he heard that romantic
refrain? But, never, he was certain, in circumstances so utterly
inauspicious as these.

The platoon was gathered Scout fashion round the camp-
fire, the brew-can was on, the flames lit upon the happy
young faces, the gaping pits of mouths opened, wide in song ;
fists banging on a petrol tin added a martial flavour to the
proceedings. The brigadier had halted in the darkness and
stood motionless, probably drinking in the scene. Gair, close
behind him, was torn between the desire to leap among them
with shouts of rage and that of giving way to prolonged and
hysterical laughter. Without a word the brigadier turned
and strode up the hill. Gair hovered, undecided. Erupt into
their midst. What the hell, who's in charge and all the rest of
it or sneak away undetected ?

They were happy, and something told him that none of
them were likely to be so happy again for many days. He
followed the brigadier, wafted up the slope on the wings of

'O'Reilly's Daughter'. The drive home was a hundred-per-cent silent.

In the Company Office, blinking furiously in the light the brigadier broke the silence, broke it into a million little pieces. What he had to say was neither original nor grammatical, but it was to the point.

"Get the detachment commander," he added. Gair scurried to the mess. A clerk entering the Company Office *en déshabille*, whistling between his teeth, received a blast that shook his teeth in their sockets.

"Flickin' ell, wot's bitten 'im?"

The detachment commander sent for the officer concerned, put aside his easy-going manner and was cruelly rude, dissolving the red-faced moron into sweaty terror.

That was but one of the incredible incidents which occurred through the idleness, laziness or bone-headed stupidity of that strange unsteady crew. One of them carried his democratic principles so far that, on entering the Company Office, he saluted its only occupant, a corporal clerk, and asked permission to use the telephone. On VJ night, celebrated throughout the camp by rockets, Very lights, parachute flares, gas rattles and what gave every indication of being occasional live rounds, the red-faced youth, presumably to avenge his discomfiture, suggested:

"Let's beat up Brigade Headquarters." Loading their stomachs with whisky, their persons with every variety of explodable object and smoke canister, they rushed away towards the stately castle that housed the seat of power, where they caused alarm, indignation, broken windows and many minor fires. The brigadier entertaining a few guests was forced to do so in a choking fog of coloured smoke. Nothing was said. As soon lecture a troop of chimpanzees.

Sundays were good days, for then Gair was free to wander in the hills, lie basking in undiluted sunshine, listening to the haunting cry of curlew, the noisy wings of green plover.

Tessa ran and barked for the sheer joy of life, lay panting in the grass or, true to her ancestry, made cunning efforts to chase the sheep. Taking sandwiches, Gair would walk and laze all day, only returning to camp as the daylight faded from the hills and dusk crept over the surface of the lochs.

After the horrific explosions that ended the Second World War no one quite knew what to do, for the last remnants of purpose had vanished from the training. No longer was the enemy represented by a swastika and now not even by a rising sun.

'The German's a cunning adversary, gentlemen.' Not any more, he wasn't.

'Right, men, round me in a half-circle—move! What we are going on with now is ju-jutsu, as taught in the Japanese Army'. Even that tit-bit they were now denied. No soldier will enthuse over learning to attack a mythical enemy.

'And over here is an enemy pill-box.' Substitute German, Russian, Afghan or Kurdish and there is some small chance of gaining attention.

But the war was over. The soldier for the moment was out of his main job. There was no one to kill, nothing to which he could look forward. Mankind was now free and so pack up, lads.

Roll on demob! was the cry in the NAAFI. For many the holiday was over, and reality grinning skull-like this side of the corner.

McPhee spoke of the garage he had always wanted to run, the wife he was now going to find. The unsteady crew cast aside all lingering inhibitions and talked of nothing but university life.

Gair walked over the friendly hills and tried in vain to sort out the problems revolving in an unending circle through his mind. In the solitude he sat against the rough comfort of a fir-tree and blurted out aloud :

"But what to do now, that's the question, stay on or get out as soon as possible?" Tessa wagged her tail and snapped at a fly. She had no problems.

"I know nothing else. This is my whole life. No, no, not for years and years—yessir, nossir, hold your coat for you, sir." Tessa cocked her head on one side and gave a short bark of encouragement. That was her chief attraction, not even that sort of nonsense bored her. She was in fact the perfect companion.

"Come on, home. Something will turn up, it'll sort itself out in time, I expect. Get your stick." He never stammered with animals, they in turn never smiled nor looked embarrassed.

In his corner of the Company Office, the training programmes and pamphlets, the talc-covered maps, the rough outline of the next two-day scheme, they all mocked him with their out-of-date futility. He sat drawing faces on a sheet of paper, unable to settle down or to concentrate. The wound in his face throbbed and stabbed. He felt washed-out and incapable of further effort, maddened by the military matters being discussed all round him. He added a drip to the end of a pencilled nose and went to see the doctor. An efficient, quiet man who said:

"Sit down, this may hurt a bit." Gair felt a thin furrow of pain slash across his face.

"Hold this below it." He held a white kidney bowl, the doctor pressed and pus drained out.

"Suture gone bad on you, the knot hadn't dissolved, shouldn't give any more trouble now, though." Clean blood trickled down his chin and almost at once Gair felt better.

For a few more weeks he played about with thunder-flashes and blank ammunition, striving to amuse the restive guardsmen, and then just as the training syllabus was turning to farce, he was posted to London. Tessa was sad to leave so many sheep.

Most of the London barracks had at that time certain things in common. They were filthy dirty and many, many years out of date. The barrack-rooms were in the winter as cold and cheerless as railway station lavatories, the washing facilities were abominable, the general state of repair indescribable. There was throughout not one trace of paint nor colour to enliven the surroundings. Perhaps the Crimean warriors for whom those mausoleums had been erected were more easily pleased. To house troops in such places was not only a disgrace, it was as McPhee tersely explained:

"A flickin' crime." The guardsmen took it well and kept themselves scrubbed and polished, but their quarters even they found impossible to keep properly clean.

A composite battalion inhabited that particular grimy rabbit warren with men from each of the five regiments, and Gair, as second-in-command to his own company, spent fruitless mornings tramping through the gloom of cavernous rooms, inspecting the correct folding of blankets, the application of polish to various items of kit that were surely never meant to shine.

"Tell me, sergeant-major," he said one morning at the conclusion of a gruelling trip, "shouldn't they p-polish the studs of their boots?" The sergeant-major raised one huge eyebrow.

"Never been done to my knowledge, sir."

"Oh, well, perhaps not, I only thought, lifting their feet so high, someone might see—no, better leave it."

"Sir."

In the afternoons they practised street-lining drill for the Victory Parade, stringing themselves out along the square at intervals and bawling orders.

Two days prior to the Parade a pompous figure in shiny field boots and spurs advanced upon Gair.

"The commanding officer and I have been discussing the advisability of allowing you to take part in the parade. This st— er—impediment, he thought it too great a risk to take, after all if you were to stick it'd be damned awkward. You can see yourself how damned awkward it'd be, I expect. I'm sorry, but there it is. However, he's agreed that you can take up a supernumerary role where you won't have to give any orders. Come and see me in my office and we'll go into it." He strode away, upright and clinking.

And sent two or three letters to the War Office, copies to Financial Adviser, confirming the inclusion of Captain Mainwaring in a purely supernumerary rôle!

Pompous Ass.

As the ducks in St James's were squinting from under their wings to see whether it was in fact daylight, the companies stubbed out cigarettes and fell in, and as dawn dispersed the crimson aura that hangs over London so they marched to their places, halting at intervals and standing easy. Behind them the crowds emerged from piles of rugs and newspapers and commented unfavourably on the sudden appearance of broad backs to impede their vision.

"'Enry, wake up, the Guards are 'ere, now we're all right."

"Bleeding shame, I calls it. Sleep 'ere all night and wake up to find an 'ulking great soldier plumb in the light. Why don't they stay at 'ome and polish 'emselves?"

Gair, in his purely supernumerary role, was free to walk about and talk to acquaintances, to glance haughtily at the crowds.

As the hours wore on the guardsmen, full of tea, began to show signs of restlessness and had to be marched away in little groups to the canvas-screened latrines.

That provoked much merriment and ribald encouragement.

Ambulance men scampered, giving succour to green-faced semi-corpses, rows of blanketed bundles were carted away. Guardsmen moved their feet about like surreptitious cart-horses, and no one seemed to feel particularly Victorious, least of all the serried ranks which marched and marked time, concertinaed and changed step to the music of so many different bands. To the men who stood at the salute or to attention for racking minutes and hours the procession was never-ending. White men, black men, little brown men, yellow men who laughed behind their inscrutable faces and went back to wage war against these people who cheered them so lustily.

And women, white and black, marching every bit as well, 'chests out' to them no mere turn of phrase. 'Bom-bom-bom! Thomp-thomp-thomp!' went the bands in varied tempo. Tanks and guns and lorries, fire-engines, bulldozers and NAAFI vans squeaked and rumbled by. Generals, admirals, air-marshals, foreign officers festooned with gold. Colours and banners and the smell of petrol fumes, until Gair was so exhausted by saluting, so bemused by the masses of men and material passing so close before him that he could barely differentiate between a bulldozer and a foreign general.

But at last with final braying of bassoons the rear-guards passed from view and stiffened joints were allowed to relax.

The crowds unleashed themselves between the soldiers and in dribs and drabs the guardsmen had to fight their way back to barracks, having stood rooted to the same patch of hard concrete for exactly eight hours.

It was grand to get a front-line view.

## Chapter 17

TAKE a few worm-eaten huts, instal them on sand dunes miles from anywhere on the coast of North Wales, and call the resulting squatter area by the stirring title of battle camp.

That was the next port of call for the trio—who in Victorian romances might be called our hero, his trusted manservant and faithful hound. The manservant flung his pack from the truck, for once beyond speech. Johnnie appeared through a miniature sand-storm.

"Timed your arrival perfectly, all the lights have gone out, somebody cut a power line with a Bren-gun and the countryside's in an uproar. You look a bit under the weather, McPhee."

"Well, sir, I ask you, what a place!"

The officers' mess was situated in a Nissen hut with warping cardboard partitions. A few lop-sided easy chairs huddled round the usual smelly stove. Two regimental prints hung crooked on rusty nails, and a fine layer of sand covered the old copies of *Country Life*. A subaltern sat at the only writing table, doing something to a dismembered shot-gun.

"'Ow do," he said, and went on screwing or unscrewing.

"Bill lives out," said Johnnie. Bill was in nominal command, but Johnnie had been doing the work. More subalterns appeared, and they all had glasses of nasty sherry, then sat down to supper. ''Ow do' wiped his hands on a handkerchief and tucked into the rissoles and welsh rarebit with gusto. The mustard-pots were empty and a hard brown substance coated the bottoms. The mess waiter was extremely smart but spilt the soup, adding a new continent to the map of different coloured stains on the table-cloth. Johnnie did not appear to notice. Gair remembered he had never been a great one for caring about such matters.

When they had settled down by the stove with glasses of

cooking brandy and cigars, and the subalterns, including ''Ow
do' had vanished into the sand-dunes, the waiter came in.

"Excuse me, sir there's a farmer outside, wants to speak
to an officer, says it's urgent. He seems rather excited, sir."

"Hell, oh, all right I'll go." Through the door Gair could
make out a sing-song Welsh voice, once he caught the sinister
word compensation. He grinned at the cooking brandy.
Johnnie came in, banging the door. Minute flakes of rust
floated down.

"Claims we killed one of his precious cows, wants compensation. What are we playing at, using live ammunition
and the war over, look you, bach? I see his point. Get the
compensation officer on to it in the morning, dreary little
sod, worked off his feet. God, this cigar stinks. Now that
you've arrived you can take on the permanent milling mass of
irate yokels clamouring for justice, boy. Heh, Tessa, want a
cigar?

"How's Helen?"

"Pretty well, I think," Johnnie, being sympathetic and
understanding, asked no more and went on to talk of Army
matters, from them to Old Thingumajig, and, when the
brandy was low in the bottle and the cigars but pulpy leaves,
to Italy and what already were becoming the good old days.

They sang 'Lili Marlene' once or twice, kicking their heels
on the cooling stove and shuffled to bed through the sand.
I'll see you home old man. No, certainly not, let me, it's on
my way.

Gair went to bed with in his ears a confused mixture of
sounds. Tessa squeaking in her sleep, Johnnie playing his
oboe beyond the plywood wall, the cry of oyster-catchers,
and over all the dull hiss and roar of the sea as it broke upon a
beach not more than fifty yards away.

A Boy Scout atmosphere prevailed in that camp during the
glorious summer days. Shirt-sleeve order, picnics in the
mountains, expeditions with the platoons to the summit of
Snowdon where they sat and drank fizzy lemonade and then
came down by different route, the guardsmen jumping and
playing like children. Or to bottomless slate quarries, where
midgets worked far below. Schemes in the wilderness of

rocks and scrubby trees reminiscent of Colle; bullets zipped and whined off the rough stone walls. Long breaks for discussion and sun-bathing. Everyone grew tremendously fit and brown. In the evenings the whole camp emptied itself into the sky-blue sea, and then those who wished packed into transport and drove to sample the tepid pleasures of Caernarvon or Bangor. There were the minimum number of regulations, polishing was reserved for walking out, and crimes were few and far between. The relations between officers and men were for those few joyous months as they had been in the war. As far as possible in an always changing community the guardsmen were known as individuals and not as army numbers.

Bill Stephens came in to settle punishments, to inspect the camp and to drink a few gins before returning to his wife and family. His garden kept him busy enough each afternoon. Rarely did he appear to watch training.

"To tell you the truth, Gair, I'm a bit nervous of meeting any of these farmers—another gin and lime, please, McClausky—they're making my life a perfect burden as it is, ringing up my house, and God knows what. This morning a policeman arrived on a scrap-iron bicycle, sweating like a pig and blethering on about the power-line—incidentally how on earth anyone came to be firing a Bren-gun in that direction beats me. I've read the riot act time and time again about safety precautions especially now the war's over—McClausky, there's too much lime in this. So for God's sake be careful, any moment I'm expecting to hear that an entire family has been wiped out on some farm. Time all this live ammunition nonsense was stopped, as soon as I get a moment I'm going to write a letter—that's better McClausky. My table's piled high with complaints, one from the Hikers' Union, a party of hikers got bullets between their legs near Gladstone's Rock, must have been young Pocock—don't know how a chap like him got into the Regiment." He drank deeply. "I'm not a snob, but after all."

Gair excused himself and went to superintend a demonstration of explosives. It was a successful half-hour, the bangs most satisfactory, plumes of sand rose high in the air and many of the spectators said "Flickin' 'ell!" and that was praise. In the office Bill was apoplectic.

"What in the name of heaven d'you mean by setting off those ghastly explosions? The telephone's never stopped ringing. Windows broken, old women with weak hearts fainting. . . . Hullo, yes, speaking—oh, it's you, Palethorpe—what? Hullo. No, I can't speak Welsh—ah, Palethorpe? This afternoon? No, I said it was *not* convenient. Imperative? Oh, right then I'll be here—no, my name is *not* Caerphilly-Jones—Hullo—Blast!" He slammed down the receiver. "Now I've got to stay in till four o'clock to see that wooden-headed compensation officer."

Captain Palethorpe was a sad little man with rabbit teeth, tottering beneath a huge ledger in which were registered the claims.

"Major Stephens, the situation is getting out of hand, I have here in this book over a hundred claims. . . ." The plaintive voice droned in the hot office. Gair scribbled on his blotter.

'Two hundred piglets run over by tanks. A train derailed by an Army boot. Thousands of trees cut down in ranks. A whole battalion made off with loot. Pay up, pay up and play the game! Tell me your number, rank and name.'

" . . . and so you see, Major Stephens, why it is of the utmost urgency to instil into *all* ranks the vital necessity for care and consideration towards the property of these long-suffering farmers." He refilled his lungs. Behind this monotonous recounting of incidents Gair could see the dark Celtic faces like angry gnomes, hear the undulating voices.

"Offeecial, offeecial, look, my sheep, look you, they have fallen over the cliff."

"My cow she is dead."

"My fences. My windows. Bullets all round me, boy." They must have made tidy sums out of the Army, those long-suffering farmers of Snowdonia.

Week-ends were days for long drives through the mountains, on Army petrol—reconnaissance is so essential—walking and climbing up the treacherous black face of Tryfan.

Or quiet evenings on the mudflats of the estuary watching

the little parties of duck, the waders on their twinkling legs. Sunset a golden bar on the rim of the sea, and Anglesey black-etched against a furnace. Long strolls along the darkening beach before bed, Tessa splashing in the tide-line, unseen birds calling, and the sand still warm from the hours of sunshine.

Gradually, in the camp between the mountains and the sea, he began to forget the sadness and the bitter incomprehension inseparable from the first months of a crumbling \ marriage. He wrote long letters describing the beauties of the place; he would find a house and, in the solitude, communing with Nature, they would come once more to know each other. Whisky sent his pen hot foot over the pages, built in his mind a picture he knew deep down could never be.

"Is it not better," she answered, "to stay apart for a little while longer, to give us a chance to settle down after that miserable time? For it was just as miserable for me, you know . . . perhaps next month. . . ."

Fate, that inexplicable creature, thought up a different idea. Gair came down from the mountains at the conclusion of a two-day exercise, with the sensation of having a cotton-wool head. A cold shower did not help, and by evening he knew he had a high temperature. McPhee brought steak-and-kidney pie on a tray, but he could not eat.

"Is it the leg again, sir?"

"Afraid so."

"Anything I can get you, mug of tea or—?"

"No, thank you, just k-keep people away, that's all, oh, and you might ask Captain Cairns if Tessa can sleep in his room." He knew it would be bad for three days, then the fever would abate, leaving him as weak as an empty sock. Germs had crept into the wound three years before and every so often they grew energetic and rushed along the bloodstream.

A patch on the leg no larger than a crown piece, purplish, shiny, and from that mark of plague there ran a thin red line of infection to the groin. The fever heightened rapidly, but at first he felt elated, everything was magnified, distorted. If he talked the conversation was wild, overloud. Then as his blood began to heat so the pain came, the gripping dried-up pain of high fever, gnawing at his stomach, his lungs, constricting his breathing; and in attendance the smaller, sharper pain of the wound itself. Alternate bouts of icy shivering and pouring sweat until suddenly the blessed relief of half coma. Fantastic dreams, lucid moments when he felt the sail-cloth sheet rucked and ridged below his back but was too weak and hazy to move.

On the third day he usually woke to find the pain was gone and the germs were in retreat until the next attack, but this time they proved more stubborn, until at the end of ten days a dark, stooping doctor advised hospital.

He left the sea and the mountains and the clean white sands and came to a London hospital where a specialist surgeon was sharpening his scalpels.

It was a magnificent hospital and, unlike those of Italy, gave the impression of luxurious suffering. Nothing rattled or banged, trolleys agleam with the familiar instruments moved softly on balloon tyres. The nursing sisters were of a different stamp, efficient and competent, but without the look of ceaseless strain. Stretchers were unknown, and Gair was wheeled to the operating-theatre on a sprung trolley. A shining lift with walls of ebony hummed him downwards, and instead of to a room with other tables and blood and scraps upon the floor, they wheeled him to a little cubicle where a man in white waited with rubber tubes.

"Have you ever had pentothal before?"

"Yes." . . . The little Gurkha in the corridor, Vesuvius smoking, a curved needle flashing. Shister Perry, you are very. . . . "Yes, I have."

Helen sitting by his bed, stroking his forehead.

"Drink of water, please, a drink of water." He swam away through the writhing shallows of half-consciousness. She sat there until dusk listening to the mutters and the little strangled sounds of anaesthetic wearing off, until the sister gently and firmly turned her out.

"By tomorrow he'll be himself, but it may be sore." She looked at the low-cut dress, the long crimson nails, the greenish almond-shaped eyes, the glistening hair, and did not approve of what she saw.

"He's got himself a handful there," she told her friend Eileen as they brewed coffee off-duty.

"Another of these war-time marriages, I suppose." Eileen read a great many women's magazines. "Still, dear, there's bound to be another side to the story."

Gair lay in the trim white bed in the trim white ward, with the tugging pain of the new stitches to keep him company, and watched the other occupants who were so different. They had things wrong with their stomachs, their livers, their bladders, mostly they were querulous and peevish; they complained more often and more loudly. Soon he grew bored with the monotonous discussions of their dreary symptoms and fell back into his own thoughts, letting his mind drift at will among the maze of memories . . . the march to the I.R.T.D. . . . Reed—what was it they'd called him?—the first to die on Natale . . . the lonely wind of Russia . . . Montepulciano and the three hanged men . . . pile of corpses in the snow . . . the tunnel of Gardaletta . . . Sartano . . . Helen. . . . Suddenly it came upon him that he was thinking about Helen and no longer caring. He savoured the idea. Yes, that was it, quite suddenly he did not care any more. The grief, the corroding jealousy, the anger—they had all evaporated into indifference. Not hatred, nor soured love, but merely supreme indifference. To what she did, whom she saw. It did not matter one little scrap, one iota. In his heart he was free and calling for champagne.

At first she came to see him every day and then every other day and then once in the week. He felt no stir of desire when she leant forward to kiss him. The smell of her body washed over him unnoticed. "Careful, darling, you'll ruin my make-up," no longer taunted him, for he did not even want to try.

During the long hours before dawn, when sleep was a mirage hovering below the blue-lit ceiling and as he lay listening to the throaty murmurs and mutterings of illness, a new spark was struck in his mind.

A spark that was to become a devouring flame, an urge that would never let him be at peace. The awful, pitiless urge to write. An hour to spare—write! You cannot relax in holiday sunshine, you must write! Write and go on writing, till the words straggle exhausted across the paper. Once, during the war, in some waterlogged camp he had written by candlelight a singularly pointless short story called 'Execution', all to do with a revolutionary, Velasquez, who lay bleeding in the sawdust, seeing his life in flash-back. Machine-guns had stuttered, limping officers had polished off patriots with pistols. Everyone was dreadfully mixed up and unhappy. He had showed it to Denise, whose reaction had been cruel but sensible.

"I think it's much too gloomy, and quite honestly I don't see the point." The answer that should be given to so very many authors of short stories. But now, at last, he had something to write about. In a fever of impatience he waited for dawn, dreaming rosily. Stories, taut and dynamic. Hemingway. Maugham. Maupassant. Chekov. Then a book. Packed with danger and sex, masterly characterisation, superb description. Best Seller, Novel of the Year. Book Society Choice ten times over. Film rights. Translated into Russian, Swahili, Esperanto. *They Came from the Mountains.* ' . . . Sergeant "Rikki" went on up the slope, among the rocks and the dusty scrub, up towards the burning blue of the sky, the bald crest where the enemy waited. Goldsmid, the quick-witted lad from Bowery Alley, gave a choking cough and, blood pumping from his mouth, fell across a rock. Somewhere from down the slope a man was screaming as Sergeant "Rikki" went on through the dusty scrub—and as he went he knew he would die before he reached the top . . . .' Exciting stuff.

' . . . and they knew nothing as they lay in the speckled shade of the vineyard, locked in the thrusting ecstasy that is human love, save that they were man and woman . . .' and much more.

"Not asleep yet, Captain Mainwaring? What's the matter?" No use answering:

'The Muse has got me, sister.'

"Bit hot, sister, that's all." In the morning he asked for pencil and paper and wrote about the Italians massacred in the snow. From that moment he wrote for hours on end and began to know the strange restless feeling which was never completely to leave him. Some of it he showed to Clarabelle, the V.A.D. who attended to the chores of the ward. She had been a model and looked it, and she raised morale more than all the doctors and medicines put together. Her eyelashes were like little silken blinds.

"Is this your first attempt at writing?"

"Yes, why, is it so obvious?"

"No, I like it, mind if I show it to Ronnie?"

"Do." Ronnie was an Australian nerve specialist whose ring she wore on her long slender finger.

"What's your real name? I mean it can't surely be Clarabelle?"

"Margaret." She dusted the locker. "Your wife's lovely, isn't she? You must be very proud of her."

"I—well, yes, I suppose I am." He had not thought of Helen since she had last been to see him.

Ronnie liked the story too, and so with praises in his ears he set out on the long uphill trail of authorship. He did not tell Helen.


Gair went through the same door into the same room hung with military prints and glass cases aglow with medals and stood before the same desk that was littered with silver inkstands. But this time there was a different colonel behind the desk who did not get up, nor offer a chair. His assistants were different, younger. They all wore blue pin-stripe suits, grey speckly ties, stiff collars, watch chains hung heavy across their stomachs. Three bowler hats hung in a row above three dark blue-black overcoats; three umbrellas stood to attention dripping into a stand. But for their faces the three men might well have been triplets.

"How's the leg?" Colonel Carrington spoke crisply from under his large tidy moustache; his eyes like little grey stones were set too close.

"Better, thank you, sir."

"Like to go on the Staff?" His tone implied you're-going-anyway-so-don't-argue. Gair looked out of the window through which so long ago he had seen a girl pushing a pram and saw another girl pushing a pram. Nothing intervening might ever have happened. Perhaps there might be an idea for a story . . .

"You'll take over from Reggie Fotheringham as Q3 Staff Captain, understand?"

"Yes, sir."

"Be a bit of a change for you. You've done a lot of training and besides it'll give that leg a chance to rest up. When's he due to take over, Barry?"

The fat assistant cleared his throat and looked shifty.

"Do you know, or don't you?"

"Well, sir, I . . ."

"Find out!"

"Yessir, at once." He leapt into a flurry of action, issuing a stream of high-powered orders to the lean assistant who in turn wrote madly on his blotter and then rang a bell. A man with the huge coat of arms on his sleeve appeared.

"Sir?" The colonel indicated fat assistant who indicated lean assistant. Coat-of-Arms shifted his piercing gaze.

"Sir?"

"Ah, there you are."

"Yessir."

"About Captain Mainwaring's posting to London District."

"Just a moment, sir." He went out and could be heard bellowing for Corporal Mayfly. Gair started to count the medals. Colonel Carrington spoke savagely to some junior officer on the telephone. The coal fire spat gently to itself. Coat-of-Arms reappeared.

"On the tenth of this month, sir."

"Got a house in London?" asked the colonel.

"N-no, sir."

"There'll be a lot of telephoning, y'know, think you can manage it?"

"I'll t-try."

"Good, well, that's all, I think." He nodded his iron-grey head in dismissal.

"Just a moment," hissed the fat assistant. "Those designations, they're improper, where did you get them?" Gair glanced at the titles on his shoulders, expecting to read rude words.

"The battalion tailor p-put them on."

"They're quite wrong, look at the word 'Guards', the thread's too thick." The stewed gooseberry eyes peered peevishly. "You must get them changed."

"I think, actually, that the whole battalion has them."

"Oh." He turned to the colonel.

"Excuse me, sir, don't you agree it's a matter of absolute top priority to look into this and get them changed before the major-general's inspection?"

"Yes, of course," said the colonel, who was reaching for his bowler hat. Bells pealed. The superintendent clerk appeared with crumbs round his mouth. Many voices spoke in unison about various types of thread. Policy was formed. Decisions made. People felt immensely important.

In the middle of it the colonel looked at his watch, said he'd got to be at the Club by one and left. Gair edged quietly out after him. In St James's Park he laughed aloud in the rain.

It was all so exactly the same. Such tradition would never change, would remain placid and unshaken by fire, pestilence or war, rolling forward—or marking time—in its own incomparable, unbeatable fashion.

The gilded staff officer went on his way.

## Chapter 18

IN a large airy room overlooking Horse Guards Parade five officers sat at desks busily getting through the piled contents of countless wire trays. Telephones rang ceaselessly and jargon, unintelligible to the layman, was shouted or furtively whispered. Every so often civilian clerks came in with fresh files and planted them firmly on the tables. Two or three flies buzzed energetically in the dusty sunbeams, and in the room next door the A.Q.M.G. discussed the issue of extra blankets in a piercing voice.

Gair looked up from a file all about condemned clothing and out of the window across the parade-ground where a posse of regimental sergeant-majors was marching about with pace-sticks and a paint-pot making preparations for Trooping the Colour. Pigeons hopped along behind them. With a jarring clatter his telephone rang. Wearily he took up the sweaty receiver.

"Hello, Staff Captain, Q3, here."

"Are you the feller who refuses to let me have extra petrol for getting to the drill hall?" The voice leapt out of the mica, choleric, belligerent.

"Who's s-speaking, please?"

"Colonel Bassett." Gair rummaged among the pending files.

"Hello—hello! Is there anyone on this blasted 'phone?"

"Yessir, I'm just l-looking for your file." The colonel growled in an unfriendly way.

Gair found a letter, scrawled over it was 'No petrol for Bassett under ANY circumstances', signed by the A.Q.M.G.

Gair took a deep breath.

"I'm sorry, sir, but I'm afraid its impossible to—"

"Impossible! What the devil d'you mean, impossible?"

"Well, sir, the A.Q.M.G.—er—suggested the journey

c-could be done by bus—n-number 13A, changing at—"
The silence vibrated down the wire. Then:

"Bus! Bah!" followed by a sort of roar.

"Perhaps you'd care to s-speak to A.Q.M.G., personally, sir?"

A further torrent of abuse, then the line went dead. That was Bassett shot down for a day or two. He went back to the sad task of finding out what the Financial Adviser had to say about condemned underwear. Gair imagined him to be a cross between a seedy solicitor and an even seedier undertaker, lurking in a dark grimy office lit by the glare of burning treasury notes, his sharp nose scurrying along the closely printed lines of books on Army Allowances, his vulture claws guiding the vitriol pen that wrote such scathing retorts on all the files.

'Why so much? . . . I fail to see why this officer should be allowed . . . Please go into this matter of overpayment.' Sometimes he spoke on the telephone, and his voice had the quality of a hacksaw. Just a super-bureaucratic spoilsport.

Gair grew bored with condemned pants and decided to send them up to Bogmyrtle in Ordnance. It was only after he had inserted I.O.M. 38—(Inter Office Minute)— on the file cover he noticed that number 37 was from Bogmyrtle. He scratched out his long explanation, inserted 'Back to you. Financial Adviser's having a baby' and threw the file into the 'out' tray. The next file dealt with Rodent Extermination in hutted camps. He passed it swiftly via an I.O.M. to G. Training. That ought to keep it out of his tray for at least a week!

The clock registered eleven. He leant back and picked his teeth. At the next table Brian spoke earnestly on the telephone about A.C.I., number 628, amended in para. 81. A good fellow, Brian, but deadly keen. Surely it was time for the tea! Yes. Private Atkinson of the A.T.S., a stout jolly party, appeared with a broken-spouted tea-pot. Pens were thrown down, drawers opened and mugs produced. A hum of conversation broke out. Any telephone that rang, rang unanswered.

She returned with the NAAFI cakes. After a quarter of an

hour mouths were wiped, pens regripped and the fascinating work went forward. Out on the square a guardsman arrived on a bicycle with another pot of paint. Gair ploughed his way through further mountains of paper till lunch-time, then strolled slowly to the Club with Brian, who talked about the advantages of Staff Training.

Every club, I suppose, is an institution; that one, deep in the heart of Mayfair, even more so. It contained as all its fellows: a room where papers rustled and no one spoke and corpses of older members lay long undiscovered, a bar where you could always be certain of finding old So-and-So, a card-room where retired and nearly retired officers of great age and seniority played bridge at all hours of every day. Full-length pictures of famous guardsmen covered the walls, disbelieving what they saw passing below them. Young officers in regimental plain clothes scurried nervously about the carpeted corridors. The atmosphere was not exactly conducive to laughter and badinage though excellent for those who prefer to take their pleasure seriously. Gair preferred a tray in the nearest Lyons.

They ate cold meat and pickles and drank gaseous lager beer. At the next table three impeccable men argued in languid tones about the merits of rival horses. There was hardly a uniform in the room.

"Why d'you always wear battledress?" asked Brian on their way down St James's Street, stabbing at a piece of newspaper with his umbrella.

"It seems better and more economical to wear out a battledress rather than an expensive suit. And, anyway, I don't really mind being dressed as a soldier, I m-mean it's nothing to be ashamed of, is it? You m-might just as well be in the City or something."

"Yes, quite, but it's a—well, I suppose it's a sort of tradition in the Brigade that in peace-time you wear civilian clothes whenever you possibly can."

"I'm afraid I shall have to be t-terribly disloyal and go on with this despised uniform."

In the afternoon a man from an R.A.S.C. depot rang up and asked if he could send a truck from Staines to Norfolk without special authority. Gair had no idea and said, "Of course." Then he picked his teeth again and wrote part of a short story. Bogmyrtle rang up.

"About your I.O.M.," he began.

"I'll c-come up and see you." Gair found him in his little room—small and pale and desperately intent on doing a good job. He had his name down for the Staff College and would one day organise the refitting of tanks on a colossal scale. Gair spent a happy hour drinking tea and teasing him, and got back to his own desk in time for more tea.

The R.A.S.C. man rang again and asked "was he certain about Norfolk, as it was over forty miles?"

"My dear fellow, think n-nothing of it."

A few more files and it was time to pack up.

But some days were more hectic. Days when even Private Atkinson carried files instead of tea; when the telephones screamed like dervishes; when Mr Clay the chief clerk was in and out of the large airy room giving advice and assistance to get at the core of some tape-ridden problem; when Mr Waller—Mr Sam Waller—his assistant, stayed moderately sober, anyway till lunch; when the A.Q.M.G. was in a filthy temper and shouting continually for staff captains: 'To get a bloody move on and come here!' The tables groaned under the vast tonnage of superfluous paper, fountain-pens emptied themselves into countless I.O.M.s, Bogmyrtle's voice, squeaky with excitement, crackled on every telephone.

"But, I say, the problem's very tricky, very tricky indeed." Usually, on such days, Colonel Bassett arrived in person to see about his petrol. Once, frustrated at every turn, he accosted Sam Waller in the corridor.

"Come this way, sir, I think I can help you." Colonel Bassett, a stringy, lined, North-West-Frontier type, followed the lurching figure. At his desk, Sam put his finger to his nose and mumbled.

"Got something 'ere that's better'n petrol." He gave a minute burp and produced a bottle of whisky.

"'Ave a nip, sir, cheer you up." Curtain.

To add the final note of Hellzapoppin, workmen began to erect scaffolding outside the window where smart people in top-hats or the very latest summer dresses would sit to watch the Trooping. Workmen stripped to the waist peered into the room and made jokes to their mates. Snack lunch in Trafalgar Square, and Brian eating sandwiches at his desk.

Sticky and worn, Gair was glad when the clock reached the hour of departure. Scribbling an answer to the adjutant of a mobile bath unit in Camberwell who had had the temerity to put in for an extra issue of Lifebuoy, he flung the file to Atkinson, shoved everything else into 'Pending', picked up the receiver: "No more calls to Q3," and got his cap from the wall. The others had departed, only Brian remained, faithful as always to the twin gods of Paper and Work-for-Work's-Sake.

"Come on, Brian, let's go and get a drink."

"Can't leave now, not till I've got this business tied up. Rather an unusual case really, R.E.M.E. passed it to me as I deal with all questions of artificers' allowances and—"

"I'm off."

"Oh, yes, right you are then."

"Captain Mainwaring!" The A.Q.M.G.'s voice was forceful. Gair fled on tip-toe. The evening was warm, and he walked the whole way home, partly because he enjoyed the exercise, but mainly because he had very little desire to reach the Chelsea love-nest, where Helen and he lived so cosily together.

She had always wanted a house with window-boxes, so he found one which they painted and distempered, carpeted and curtained and pictured. It was complete with a red door and dolphin door-knocker in a street of whimsy little houses with gaudy old Bentleys and converted taxis outside the black area railings.

But in that charming little place—'It's so *romantic*, my dear,'—life went wrong again and ever more wrong till finally it reached the stage of you go your way, I'll go mine and no questions asked, which was altogether more satisfactory and civilised than breaking china. So, on his return in the evenings, Gair would walk slower and slower as he turned into the street, hoping, praying that she was out. Then he could potter about, cook his meal when and how he liked, go to a cinema, listen to the wireless, have a bath, all in blissful peace. Sometimes he heard her come in, but did not wonder nor care where she had been.

He knew it could not continue indefinitely, that fantastic life of two people who felt for each other nothing but naked dislike, and yet were expected by law, convention, moral standards, call it what you like, to cling on till death did them part.

That evening the house was empty, emptier somehow than usual, but it did not worry him. He threw his cap on the sofa, unbuckled his belt, removed his tie, got a drink from the tray and sat back. Later, as he cooked eggs and bacon, he noticed the sink was empty of dirty dishes. She must have been out all day. There was nothing on the wireless, so he went slowly, contentedly up the narrow stairs to bed.

The emptiness was more pronounced upstairs. A tap dripped in the bathroom. Her door stood ajar, and he went in. The bed unmade and rumpled had a peculiarly unfriendly air; within the closed windows there lurked the smell of stale cosmetics. A stocking lay contorted on the carpet beside two pages of a newspaper, underclothes sprawled flaccid across a chair, the lid was off the clothes basket and a towel, lipstick smeared, hung over the edge. It was a very deserted room.

And on the glass-topped dressing-table among the empty jars, the scrunched tissue paper, pieces of ribbon, hairpins and thin layer of powder there sat, as in a film or an improbable novelette, a note. He read it slowly and then again.

'. . . we can't go on . . . separation . . . making me ill . . . our nerves . . . six months at least . . . meet again to talk it over . . . don't try to see me . . . no use . . .'

The face that looked back at him from the powder-dusted looking-glass was smiling. Humming gently he turned on his bath and fetched another whisky.

He rang up Denise.


Life was better in every way during those six months,

simpler and far less gruelling. Even the files became more
readable, and in addition there were the preparations and the
rehearsals for the Trooping, which he could see from his
desk without even craning his neck. The blobs of paint dotted
so laboriously over the square were now covered by pairs of
huge stationary boots; the summer air vibrated with the
crash of martial music and within the Headquarters few
people spoke of anything but the issue of and the preservation
of scarlet tunics—and bearskins, those shaggy reminders of
Inkerman. The stands were completed, Moss Bros.
approached for tons of grey top-hats and the troops taking
part were removed from the cocoons of cotton-wool in which
they had been wrapped for months on end lest they should in
any way be contaminated by unceremonial contacts. The
master tailors fitted and sewed and cut; officers inspected day
and night and the guardsmen themselves, those remarkable,
long-suffering men without whose perfect co-operation the
spectacle would be impossible, polished and scrubbed and
sweated, pressed their tunics and combed the bearskins.

At the rehearsals, minor faults are ironed out; after them
the pundits hold long indignant post-mortems, during which
all and sundry are pilloried for slovenly marching or rippling
ranks. Secondary royalty or a general takes the salute, unruly
horses show a tendency to bolt at the first sound of the pipes
and, if it's a hot day, one or two men usually faint, much to
the adolescent delight of the newspapers.

Finally the day dawned, the day-of-days about which
earnest officers had talked so continuously, for which so
many had planned for so long. The windows of the large airy
room were crowded with smart little hats, alive with women's
pretty laughter and the files sat forgotten, collecting dust.

For everyone but the silent ranks of guardsmen the atmosphere is holiday. They stand in the sunshine within the constricting scarlet and feel proud, nervous, self-conscious or
merely thirsty according to their natures. The senior officers
wonder if they'll be able to make themselves heard, some of
the junior ones why they drank so much the night before.

"Coo, mum, I'd like to join the Guards and march about
like that." The uninitiated talk about redcoats and busbies,

rich Americans point expensive cameras. "Gee, honey, they're sorta cute." Ex-Guardsmen watch sternly for faults and see them where others see perfection.

The massed bands move majestically up and down the parade-ground, sunlight glittering on the great brass instruments, the massive sound echoing and re-echoing from the buildings; pigeons fly above and in the sudden silence that follows the music you can hear the jingle of a horse's harness, the cry of a child, the distant roar of traffic.

Scarlet ranks march and counter-march with magnificent skill, the Colour—in days gone by, the rallying-point of battalions cut to pieces—is slowly trooped; the square of embroidered silk to which men remove their hats, which is guarded and honoured as a permanent reminder of the soldiers who died in the fear and squalor of the battles emblazoned upon it. Gair stood between two overdressed women and watched the Colour as it was escorted down the thin red lines and remembered the shells that had pounded Natale and Reed who had died in the slime to add something more to that embroidered silk.

They marched past in slow time and in quick time, then they marched away to Buckingham Palace, the throbbing sound of the bands growing ever fainter. The 'crunch-crunch' of the boots fading into distance.

"My dear," said one of the overdressed women, "that was fun."

"Aren't they *marvellous*?" Turning to Gair. "But, of course, that *is* your chief job really, isn't it? Pageantry and things like that. I mean it's when the Brigade really comes into its own."

'Oh, you brainless and altogether ghastly woman,' he thought.

"N-not entirely," he said. Beyond the crowds who hurried away across the square, the bronze figures on the Guards Division Memorial nodded their heads in silent agreement with him. The women departed with their scents and their witless chatter, and for a while he sat motionless at his desk. 'It's when the Brigade really comes into its own.' The moment of crowning glory, was that what it was? Many people probably thought so. Ignorant people, spiteful people, jealous people. No! No! No! He thumped the table in his agitation.

The moments of greatness were not those when they strutted in archaic uniforms, performing miracles of colourful precision for the benefit of gawping crowds.

Guardsman McIntyre who spat on his hands and said "Let's get going." Corporal Rowley who saluted with his remaining arm. Smith looking at his amputated legs and grinning. Those surely were the moments of greatness? The moments which lay beyond the discipline and the fantasy.

The telephone rang. Returning with a jump to reality he answered.

"That Q branch? Ah, good. Well, look here, old boy, it's about the issue of scarlet tunics to a company that's going up to Edinburgh for the—" With an oath Gair slammed down the receiver. One more mention of a scarlet tunic would send him over the edge.

He rang up Denise.

*Chapter 19*

Food comes to Britain in ships. If the ships remain in the great ports with the food rotting inside them because no one will unload it, then in time the inhabitants of Britain will go hungry. It is as simple as that.

Weapons and equipment leave Britain in ships to supply her armies in far-off corners of an uneasy world. If no one will load these tanks and guns and ammunition into the waiting ships, it is likely that British soldiers and prestige will suffer. It is as simple as that.

Many things are made in Britain and sent in ships to foreign lands. If . . . then British trade and prestige will suffer. It is as simple as that.

But the dockers and the stevedores and the crane operators who left the food to rot, the equipment to pile up on the silent wharves, did not apparently think of those things as they stood in little groups along the Commercial Road and watched the troops go by. The troop-carriers whined over the cobblestones and inside them the soldiers and sailors and airmen sat packed like fish in a barrel, silently staring at the strikers. No one shouted nor booed nor catcalled. It was all quiet and boring as a stranger's funeral.

They turned off towards the docks, towards the gaunt cranes and the rows of patient ships, drove past the strike pickets and men in caps and mufflers, who turned away and in many cases spat, through the tall wire gates and into another world.

Bales and crates and sacks piled high in the warehouses; scummy water, gulls preening on the rigging of ships that had come from Spain, from Panama, from Australia; ships low in the water and storm-scarred. From beyond the ships there came the faint definable smell of the sea, for many the first smell of the sea. A few men in nondescript hats and Burberrys stood about with sheaves of paper in their hands, and policemen walked ponderously through the warehouses. There were a great many cats; Lascars crowded the rail of a merchantman, jabbering and grinning at the uniforms.

The guardsmen, excited as schoolboys, were told off into working parties and stood waiting, shapeless in their denims, whilst such beings as company sergeant-majors strode up and down between the great splay legs of the cranes, smart as you please. Sailors climbed up to the cabins and experimented with the levers, swinging the monstrous erections this way and that across the wispy blue sky. Officers conferred with the men in nondescript hats, and the Lascars, weary of the spectacle, lay down to sleep on the warm deck.

By the time that Gair had finally escaped from his desk on some flimsy pretext of checking conditions at the docks, and had bowled swiftly down the Commercial Road he had not seen since the noisy nights of 1941, operations were in full swing. A steady stream of guardsmen issued from one warehouse, pushing porters' trolleys piled with ammunition for Malaya, each man going at a jog-trot. A similar procession trundled gauze-covered sides of beef from a rakish Argentinian vessel. Coats were off, sweat was running free, the heavy loads were plummeting earthwards, a moment later the empty hook was soaring to the sky. Voices shouted, pencils ticked off load after load. Everyone, except the ponderous policemen, seemed to be immensely happy.

"Hullo, sir, thought you'd deserted us for the staff." Company Sergeant-Major Thomas paused with his trolley and mopped his face. He looked exactly the same.

"The boys are enjoying themselves a treat, feel they're doing a job of work." They sat on bales of hemp and talked.

"Not like the men we knew, sir." Thomas nodded at the young guardsmen who lay in the sun drinking their tea and chaffing the NAAFI girls.

"Good lads, some of 'em, but not the same, not the same heads on 'em." Gair threw a piece of cake to a gull. It flew away, mobbed by a score of screaming companions. A ship's siren blared.

"Are you g-going to stay on?"

"Stay on? What, in the Army, d'you mean? Yes, till I've done me time. It's a good life. And you, sir?"

"Suppose so, nothing else to d-do. But it's changed such a lot, so many of the old f-faces have gone—d'you ever see any of them, any of the original platoon?"

"Not since the end of the war. Higgins, sir, remember him, who was killed on those cross-roads, the bolshie one?"

"Yes, I remember Higgins."

"His mother, she lives near us, in the same street as a matter of fact, see her sometimes—oh, yes, and I met Wakefield—what was it we called him in the platoon?"

"Dopey." He remembered a dark square man.

"Yes, that was it—Dopey Wakefield—got an M.M. beyond Colle, after you'd left us. Scruffiest soldier I've ever seen. Saw him the other day, bus conductor on a 22. 'Improperly shaved, Dopey!' I shouted at him. See him jump!" Thomas stubbed out his cigarette. "Got a card from Major Hardy last Christmas, from somewhere in Yorkshire."

"He's farming." A whistle blew, dregs of cold tea sprayed into the scummy water and belts were hitched up.

"Be seeing you sometime, sir. They say the battalion's for Malaya before long. How can you build a square in the middle of the jungle? So long, sir."

The large figure disappeared with its trolley to push more meat. Gair found a small electric truck and drove sides of beef from the crane to the warehouse, pinging a bell and enjoying himself—in Runyonese, more than somewhat. Then ate an excellent meal on board the Argentinian ship.

By evening she was appreciably higher in the water, and a tally clerk was saying in tones of awe: "Your men are unskilled workers and yet they've shifted a remarkable tonnage, quite remarkable." The policemen had perforce to stride up and down outside warehouses filled to bursting with great mountains of meat.

"Do the same tomorrow and we'll think of hiring you permanently," said the clerk facetiously.

"All done by kindness—and bags of bull!" answered the guardsmen, equally facetious. "Find us some proper work next time." They left the faint smell of the sea and drove back between the groups of sullen strikers who were not facetious.

For many days they returned to the wharves and it was a pleasant break from London duties. No one suggested paying them for the heavy labour, none of them grumbled and they worked as hard as ever day after day till at length in some small back room in Bermondsey or Stepney a group of men decided that the strike, having doubtless achieved its object, could be called off and the troops returned to the dreary routine of barracks.

From the Headquarters orders and disorders had now to be sent in an unbroken flood, dispatching units home to such God-forsaken spots as Larkhill, Catterick and unpronounceable places in Wales. Blankets had to be collected in unbelievable numbers, petrol authorised and issued, surplus food disposed of. And the Financial Adviser tore at his few remaining hairs.

"Who's to pay? By whose authority? Why, who, under what? . . . Pay, pay, pay." He barked or bleated on the telephone. Officers worked under ice-packs, Sam Waller wrote memos in a whisky-coloured coma, Private Atkinson lost pounds and Brian revelled in the confusion, tying up problem after problem with yards and yards of rich red tape in his own quiet humourless way.

The Backroom Boys of Bermondsey had every cause for satisfaction. In stationery, telephone calls and general human wear and tear alone the strike must have cost the Army thousands.

Very often as an antidote to the days of exciting tedium he craved for nights of exciting relaxation and would ring up Denise, whom he found always to be an unfailing comfort.


Beside him he could hear the soft sound of her breathing, could feel the soft curve of her shoulder. The bell on the taxi rank rang and rang, light from the street lamp opposite lanced between the curtains and on to the ceiling, some of it that was spare trickled on to her face. On one elbow he looked

9*                                    261

down at the parted lips, the shadowed column of neck, the hair lying dark across the pillow. He kissed her.

"Mmm," murmured Denise in half sleep, moving lazily beside him. She opened her eyes, gleaming black in the pale darkness.

"How long have we known each other, darling?"

"Must be—oh, twelve years now."

"And it's still—no ties?"

"No ties, if that's how you want it, Denise." Her arm encircled his neck and pulled him slowly down.

"It's best for us, that way. Haven't we always agreed on it?"

"Yes, darling we have." Love with no ties, no fetters that might one day break or corrode.

"One day you'll meet the man of your dreams and marry him."

"One day, Gair."

"And you won't regret any of—well . . . ?"

"Us, you mean? No, darling, I won't, why should I? We are neither of us children, we know what we are doing. When we meet we are in love with each other, when we are apart we forget, no not completely, but we don't go about broken-hearted and inconsolable. No ties. Remember?"

When her lips were free again she said: "Talking of ties, what's happening about Helen?"

"Oh, I don't know, she's still with her parents, I suppose, in fact the last I heard was that she was in—good God, if s-someone doesn't answer that damned bell I'll—" She tweaked his ear.

"Yes, she was in the South of France somewhere, getting over the nervous breakdown she was always threatening, I expect."

"And when she comes back, what then?"

"We'll meet, I imagine to talk things over. How to make a go of it in one easy lesson."

"Don't be so bitter, Gair, it only makes things worse."

"I know, I know, but it's just that I don't think I can face that life any more, the ghastly scenes and rows all the t-time, on and on. I'm sure she can't either."

"Funny, really, isn't it, me of all people trying to drive you back to the arms of a loving wife, but I think she'll want to try again and I—"

"Let's not talk about my matrimonial difficulties any more, they're d-deadly boring and besides it's nearly three o'clock."

A passing cat peered through the chink in the curtains and, being a prudish animal, went quickly on her silent lonely way.


Life pottered along in a paper-lined rut, nothing of note happened in the large airy room. Sometimes to break the monotonous passage of days, Gair would insert a bogus file among the genuine ones, complete with I.O.M.s and carefully copied signatures. One, which had outstanding success, travelling from department to department, concerned the issue of a newly invented rat-trap to units in brick-built barracks.

Another, dealing with the disposal of used contraceptives, reached the very top-ranking trays.

To while away odd moments he would arrange things so that two officers in the same office were engaged in heated argument with each other by telephone. Brian, he found, was especially susceptible to this innocent deception.

One evening, however, the even tempo of his ink-stained life was rudely interrupted by the sight of a letter from Helen on his desk.

". . . six months now at an end . . . suggest we meet on Thursday and talk things over. . . ."


So they met and talked for long hours and in the small deserted restaurant, watched by a tired and impatient waiter and a sleepy tabby cat, the last dying moments of another marriage flickered and then—pouf!—went out.

Later, as he walked alone along the cold wet streets, it did not seem in any way strange that he had kissed her for the last time; that now she was a stranger to him, complete, as the old woman who hurried past to work through the deserted dawn; and that in time she would cease to bear his name.

*    *    *

In the Brigade of Guards there are two types of commanding officer. One is good, the other is bad, and the old saying applies: 'If 'e's good, 'e's bloody good, but if 'e's bad 'e's rotten.' There is no room, thank the Lord, for dull mediocrity.

Colonel David belonged to the former category. In stature he was small and with his little Kaiser moustache, his sleek brown hair and his miniature field-boots he was at first glance a burnished cock sparrow. He possessed, however, the ability, valuable anywhere, but priceless in war, to inspire great confidence and loyalty among those he led.

When Gair first entered the room to pay his respects his heart sank. The little colonel rose to his feet and shook hands, the ribbons of the D.S.O. and M.C. half hidden by the gleaming cross-strap. They talked of Gair's new job and of the changes at Colony Camp.

"At present we have a training company from each of the five regiments, formed of men who come here from Caterham and do ten weeks with us before posting to their various battalions. Your population will fluctuate, sometimes you will have to cope with six or seven platoons, at other times there may only be one or two. Officers are a headache, very few are coming from Sandhurst, and you will have to rely mainly on National Service ones, most of whom are good, but they remain here for too short a time, being always required abroad. Your regiment has a battalion in Malaya, so has mine, and we must see to it that every scrap of time is utilised. You are not entirely unfamiliar with the training of soldiers I believe." He smiled.

"You have come here with an excellent war record and a reputation of being able to teach things to guardsmen, but—" here he looked hard at Gair, "—I am told you are by no means a smart officer. That is a pity, for you will have under you very young men and very young officers who will in most things follow your example, and if there is one thing I will not tolerate it is an officer, N.C.O. or guardsman who dresses slovenly. The cap you are wearing, for instance. I am sure you are most attached to it—I myself have a cap at home which one day will repose in a glass case—and I am equally sure that you have a new one on order." Gair did not feel his usual blaze of insubordinate rage, he felt merely beetle-like.

"That your dog I saw trotting across the square?"

"Yes, sir."

"Had her long?"

"N-nearly ten years, she's getting rather b-blind."

"Wonderful friend, a dog. Don't forget the new cap—oh and you might suggest to your servant he gives those trousers a press." An odd, very likeable man.

Gair knew none of the N.C.O.s except the company sergeant-major, a craggy-faced individual still shaking the desert sand from his battered ears. What brain he had was concentrated in his boots; he was a wizard with the leather ball and thought of nothing but the formation of a super side. To that purpose he placed every man who could score a goal into jobs on the permanent staff.

"Ow, now, sir, carn't send McGubbin to Malaya, 'e's got chronic chilblains."

"Jamieson, sir? 'E's not fit for platoon training."

"I wonder, sir, could you speak to the adjutant about Corporal Tiptowe, 'e's surplus to establishment in 'Eadquarter Company and 'e'd do us fine as company clerk. Corse, 'e's crippled with arthritis in 'is 'ips. . . ."

Come Wednesday afternoon and those interested in football were treated to the surprising spectacle of McGubbin leaping like a hairy ballet-dancer, Jamieson shooting goals in triplicate and Corporal Tiptowe flashing about the field like a crazy thing. The camp was a hot-bed of subterfuge and deception. "What's the total strength of the company, sergeant-major, at this very m-moment?"

"On paper, sir, one hundred and thirty-six, and yourself, sir."

"And off paper, on training for example?"

"Ar, well, on training, well, there'd be Number Eighteen platoon, let's see—" His intellect creaked heavily. "That's thirty-one not counting Sergeant Lowther, oo's on compassionate leave. Then in Nineteen Platoon there's twenty-four, no, twenty-three, Plumtree's in the sick bunk with scabies."

"Yes, that's about sixty all told, including the company-office staff and the storemen. Now, if it's not asking too m-much, where are the other seventy-six?"

"There's Sergeant Foxglove, 'e's recruiting sergeant in 'Uddersfield, you remember Foxglove, sir, 'im wot brewed up a Jerry tank outside Tobruk with—"

"I was unlucky enough to miss the desert. But, good lor', am I really commanding a sergeant at Huddersfield?"

"Two guardsmen grooms in London, sir, on our strength." And so it went on. Men by the score, dotted all over the country. Clerks and messengers, storemen, dug away in London, and all for some extraordinary reason came under his command. Many more erupted or crept from under stones on pay-day, rubbing the scales from their eyes and blinking in the strong daylight. They were the messmen and cooks, boilermen, tailors' assistants, armourers' mates and officers' mess waiters without whose moral and invisible support the Army would surely crumble.

## Chapter 20

AT first when he became a major Gair could not walk more than a few steps at a time without glancing surreptitiously at the crowns on his shoulders. Financially it was a long stride forward, and the crowning joy was to be addressed as 'sir' by the Personnel Selection Officer, a uniformed psychiatrist who bustled from company to company ramming with unerring aim square pegs into round holes. He interviewed every man who came to the camp, asked lots of personal questions, frequently caused dissatisfaction and then arrived full of suggestions to Gair as how best to run the company. But now at least he had to salute and stand to attention, which was a step in the right direction.

"Good-morning, sir, it's about Rodgers, the man with a squint."

"Why, what's he done now?"

"No, that's where you're wrong, sir. I've gone into his background history and I find he is definitely maladjusted."

"Is that why he g-got tight and urinated into the corporal's boots?"

"A symptom, yes."

Or perhaps it was to suggest that Figleaf, old soldier and ex-booth boxer, should be allowed out of the Army on compassionate grounds. "He tells me he is too sensitive for the rough and tumble of service life." Gair sat open-mouthed.

No longer could the night air be rent by explosive; the training Spandau rusted on a scrap-heap, and the feeble pop of blanks was about the only warlike noise allowed except on the proper ranges where the ripple of musketry continued intermittently from dawn to dusk. Each platoon sported itself on the field-firing range for one day during the ten weeks. A narrow sand and heather strip down the length of which lethal weapons could be genuinely fired. The bullets had to travel between the limits indicated by two huge painted

267

boards; but bullets are often erratic little things and then as in Wales the telephones would ring. There were occasions when Gair, bored with the set-piece attack, unrealistic and farcical, would take a Bren-gun and fire at the overheated guardsmen. Above their heads; whipping the sand between them into violent spurts of dust, whining into the distance, the copper-covered bullets crack-crack-cracking with dreadful urgency.

Crack-crack-crack—Thud-thud-thud of the gun. "Where's it coming from?" shouted the rasping voices of the sergeants. "You, Smithers, lying there like a great sweaty whore—where's the gun, man? Christ, you'd be dead by now. Get yer face out of the sand, Roberts. Well, come on, come on, where is it?" A short burst cut through a clump of heather to their left, instinctively some of them reached closer for the earth.

"Don't just lie there to be shot at!"

"Sergeant, I've spotted it, by that dark patch— there it is, see the smoke." Thud-thud!

"What are you going to do about it? Tell the section commander, get moving—get forward! Go on, you're soldiers now, not flickin' little boys! Oh, suffering Christ, get a bloody move on!" Afternoons of sweating, cursing movement, through the hot dust of the range, followed everywhere by the pitiless bullets, the cruel tongues of the instructors. Those afternoons were few, for mostly the training was of a more refined type, more suitable for peace-time.

"You got angry—most of you felt bolshie. Ah, shut up, you w-wanted to shout at the instructors, 'Shut up and leave us alone, give us chance to think.'" The circle of resting men, grimy and flushed, murmured agreement.

"But in war you are not left alone, you are not given a chance to think, you have no idea what's going on, you are very scared and very tired, but there is no one to give you a b-break. In the n-noise and the smoke and the utter confusion you d-damned well have to go on. And you haven't even got the voices of your own instructors to drive you, there's usually nothing but the sight of your friends on either s-side, and when they've gone then there's absolutely nothing to keep you going, except yourself. That's why we try to give you some small idea of what a complete b-bloody chaos it can be, it's why you've got to learn to keep your heads whatever is happening round you. Right, break for ten m-minutes and then we'll discuss the attack." He lay in the heather and watched the vapour trails of invisible aircraft.

When it was all over and they were marching back for tea, they marched with a new swagger, a new assurance, for had not death been all around them in the spurting sand? Now they were men indeed.

'Am I a reactionary, a fascist beast, to continue with these methods in a new enlightened age?' he sometimes asked himself.

If there should be an accident one day and a bullet goes off-course, then, quite rightly, I suppose, it would be a court martial. The high jump, he told himself in mournful slang.

Naturally in time it reached the ears of Higher Authority. Naturally he was forbidden to point a gun anywhere near his trainees.

From then on he became just that much more bored, the trainees—who knows?—just that much more unprepared.

\*　　　\*　　　\*

"Looks like the train now, sir." McPhee stood awkward in the blue demob suit; on his head was a grey felt hat, by his feet two battered suitcases. A party of guardsmen on week-end leave clustered round a slot machine. Tessa pulled at her lead. She was too blind for public freedom.

"Don't forget her milk, sir, the cook always keeps it for her after tea." The train drew in. Gair looked at the thin ugly face under the preposterous hat, the unfamiliar suit, the cheap cases. His eyes began to prick. McPhee held out his hand.

"It's been a long time, sir." He blinked and bent to pat the patient Tessa, who licked his hand, looking up with her blue blind eyes. "Well, good-bye, lass," he murmured. Doors were banging, steam blew out in a deafening roar. There were so many things Gair wanted to say and all he managed was:

"I don't know what I'll do when the p-polish is off these shoes." The train began to move.

"Good-bye, sir—good luck to you both." Steam swirled between them. Gair waved and stared at the blurred carriages as they rumbled past, then the rumble ceased and there was nothing but pieces of paper blowing about. He walked slowly along the platform with Tessa. He was very sad, and if it had not been for her he would have felt suddenly very lonely. Ten years is a long time; the parting on a station platform very sudden.

\*      \*      \*

Many of the officers who arrived at Colony Camp were awaiting demobilisation and therefore cared little for discipline or regulations. The nights were lively with shouts and songs and sundry small explosions.

Other officers, if they were prudent, locked their doors on retirement, so as to avoid the fate of the assistant-adjutant, who was dragged from his bed and thrown kicking and struggling into the local canal.

The high-spirited fellows then drove to London and into one of the barracks where they hauled another unpopular and unfortunate subaltern from his bed and drove to St James's Park lake, into which they deposited him, leaving the weed-covered figure to return pyjamaed and dripping to the barracks.

"'Ere, 'old on, what the flickin' 'ell are you on, lad?"

"I'm Mr Braithwaite," shivering and soaked.

"Oh, I'm sorry, sir, didn't recognise you. Up, sentry!" Crash of the salute, the sentry goggle-eyed, the sergeant impassive.

His persecutors meanwhile had taken themselves to a famous night-club where they ordered bottles of champagne and set up a bar outside for the painted ladies of the town and any homeless waif who might be passing.

Until the arrival of policemen, fire engines and ambulances the affair was a staggering success.

Many high-ranking officers spoke to them, individually and *en masse*, and they were confined to camp for three months.

Finally the shindy every night grew to such a pitch that the guardsmen, who had to leave their beds at an early hour, were driven to voice complaints, and so the gay young blades roared away in their cars to make a noise elsewhere.

The regiments concerned lost excellent officers when at last the gang broke up and went their different ways to new and drearier pastures.

On the other hand, some of those who took their places were no more capable, physically and morally, of throwing anyone into a canal than they were of dealing with the men under their command.

They arrived in gangling groups, heads stuffed with education and knowledge of higher tactics, but put them in front of a platoon, tell them to get on with it and the results if they had not been pathetic would have been remarkably funny.

Many were, in their own opinions, highly intellectual and thus far above the childish pursuit of arms; they had large cars and liked their week-ends from Thursday to Tuesday.

"There's another lot on its way over to you now, two or three real shockers this time." The adjutant rang off and Gair prepared to meet the next batch, wondering how soon they could be shipped away on courses.

Gair found it irritating, pedalling about on the old company bicycle, to be splashed or enveloped in dust by his subordinates as they shot past in their expensive cars. They lounged about the company office, chatting of parties and girl friends until in desperation Gair sent them packing to the ranges where at least there was a remote chance of casualties.

In all fairness an equal number were keen, efficient and pleasant.

The platoons came and went, arriving like stiffened dummies from Caterham and departing, usually to Malaya, not quite such robots, walking with an easier gait.

'Teach them this, teach them that.' Letters, official and otherwise, came from the Far East. But gradually, inexorably it was becoming ever more difficult to teach them anything but ceremonial drill.

"You've got to realise, Gair, that our main function is to provide men properly trained and groomed for Public Duties,

271

for the Trooping and Guards of Honour." Almost daily someone told him that over the pre-lunch pink gin.

"N-not if we've got battalions in Malaya. It's appalling to send men to fight untrained. What the hell's the use of knowing how to stamp your feet if you can't shoot straight enough to save your l-life?" Often he grew so heated that he could say nothing and had to sit at bursting point listening to streams of fatuous drivel.

"We simply haven't got the men for both."

"What do you s-suggest then, go on sending out men who can't even handle their weapons properly or—"

"My dear fellow, they can perfectly well be trained out there in proper jungle-warfare schools. Anyway, to my mind, all this training business is overdone. What difference does it make once you get into action? Absolutely none."

"Except to save quite unnecessary c-casualties."

"Ah, balls!" He found few supporters and angrily waged a losing battle. More letters came pouring in. 'Why weren't the men being taught to shoot better?' Why this, why that. Why, indeed.

He wore a path in the concrete of the square, stamping angrily to and fro between his office and the orderly room. Colonel David was sympathetic, but his hands were tied.

"We've got to find the men for these duties from somewhere and we're down to the bottom of the barrel as it is. I know how you feel, and I'll do all I can to spare you the men marked down for Malaya."

Those were days of frustration and disillusionment when Gair had to sit helpless at his table and watch the platoons parading on the square for yet another rehearsal, the rifles with which they should have been learning how to shoot, agleam with polish.

Every day he asked the sergeant-major :

"Where is everybody?"

"Tunic fitting, sir."

"Guard-mounting practice, sir."

"Dock strike, sir." Meat strike. Undertakers' strike. Take them out of uniform and cease calling them by the name of soldier.

Gair could stand it no longer and applied to go abroad.

"Sorry, no one to replace you at the moment, besides, your leg would never stand up to tropical conditions." Back to the mess. In place of people like David, Rex, Johnnie and Anthony a different type was creeping into power. A type more at home in scarlet tunics, whose motto was Leisure and more Leisure, who drew their quite considerable pay under what might almost be termed false pretences and whose imaginations were in some cases no more than pin-head size. They busied themselves in returning as rapidly as possible to peace-time routine. Fairly fatuous men. Often, listening to their invigorating conversation, Gair remembered Anthony, who had stuck it for a year and then departed.

"I'll give you a year, two at the most and then you'll be on your way."

And yet in a battalion abroad he knew he would be happy. In the jungle he would find Rex and Pat and Company Sergeant-Major Thomas and feel at home again. That evening he found a fat letter from Denise. He kept it until after dinner, savouring the bulk in his pocket. Stretched on his bed he opened it, enjoying the tear of the paper, the feel of its fatness as an antidote to the futility of the day. But undoubtedly it was a bad day, for, on the first of the many pages, she wrote that she was going to be married.

He lay staring at a pattern of flaking plaster above his head. In the next room a man and a woman were being funny on the wireless. Tessa snored on her rug, and rain dripped from a choked gutter. He noticed all these things very clearly, thought more about them than the words on the thin blue paper. Budgett, in place of McPhee, blundered in.

"Same time in the morning, sir?"

"Yes, please."

"Battledress as usual?"

"Yes."

"Shoes or boots, sir?"

"Shoes." Shoes or boots, of what possible importance could it be? So she was going to be married. The end of a perfect relationship. Love with no ties.

"Tessa's snoring a bit."

273

"Yes, Budgett." What sort of a man had she chosen? If he finished the letter, very likely he would find out.

"Raining hard, sir."

"Yes, isn't it?"

"That all, sir?"

"Yes, thanks."

"Good-night, sir."

"Good-night, Budgett."

A sexually ambiguous voice moaned a song about 'you came along, the clouds rolled away.' He dressed and went out to walk in the rain, returning in the small hours, soaked and weary and with the first signs of a cold in the head.

In a moment of mental aberration Gair put his name down for the Staff College, that Mecca of budding baton-carriers, and started to study for the examination. First he gathered together every known pamphlet on staff affairs, a suitcase full of charts, diagrams and tables showing the formation and scale of such improbable things as Field Incinerating Units and Delousing Centres. Secondly, he threw away eighty per cent. of the pamphlets. Then, for an hour or so every evening, he settled down to cram his head with miscellaneous military knowledge. Soon his brain began to spin with extraordinary esoteric facts and figures. He found himself muttering as he walked about camp, and stopping to count on his fingers.

'There are ten tanks in the Headquarter squadron of an R.A.S.C. depot.' No, steady, that doesn't sound right.

'Then below the A.Q.M.G. comes the D.A.Q.M.G., followed closely by the C.R.E.M.E.—after the coffee or before —damn, C.R.E.M.E. deals in oily waste and carburettors.'

'The main duty of a staff officer at war is to transmit and receive information with intelligence and accuracy,' he read. 'Often he must employ great tact in dealings with commanders in the field.' He remembered vividly overhearing conversations on many a field telephone, many a wireless, when tact was more than conspicuous by its absence.

He read about bath units and bakeries; the characteristics

and capabilities of every known and unknown unit; the use of simple codes and how to speak on a wireless; the relationship between the staff and services—most of that he disbelieved; maintenance of everything from a tank transporter to a corps commander's hot-water bottle. And much more. Military law offences various, duties in aid of civil power, unlawful assemblies, the dispersing of. And much more. Current affairs. Morale and welfare. Unit amenities committees. He read till his eyes were pink-lined and there was a queer buzzing in his head. But it kept his mind off private perplexities.

They sat for the examination, scores of them in a large institute building. Invigilators strolled ferret-eyed between the tables and a man said:

"You can start—NOW." Gair felt about twelve. Officers round him wrote and wrote. He read the narrative of the tactics problem.

'After a successful initial advance the forces of Blue land ran into heavy opposition in the area High Wycombe–Pangbourne . . .' He drew a picture of a German soldier peering from a trench. Wrote a few lines and scored them out. Scratch, scratch went a hundred and fifty-nine pens, tick-tick went one hundred and fifty-eight brains. His own was comatose.

". . . the time of year is summer, the weather clement." How nice. He set about organising his paper formations for attack. For three days they scribbled away and then dispersed far and wide to await the results. Four months later Gair received a buff envelope containing a sheet of paper which stated that he had failed in the Administration paper and had thus not qualified for entry into the Staff College.

It did not worry him unduly, nothing worried him unduly, for by then he had met Georgina.


They tell us, the poets and such, that love brings a song to every heart, a smile to the dourest of mouths and they tell us quite correctly. Nothing is so invigorating, such a certain cure for all ills, both bodily and mental, as a happy and successful love affair. It is ten times better than a whole cartload of Harley Street specialists and psychiatrists for alleviating nervous tensions. However, enough of the obvious.

He met Georgina unromantically at a cocktail party. She entered his life with a plate of olives and saved him from a meandering conversation about married-quarters carried on with the intensely gushing wife of a naval officer who had the good fortune to be safely in Singapore.

"C-could I take an olive on the way?" She was small and dark, her smile was vivacious.

". . . and so you see, it really is almost as cheap in the end to take a house of one's own."

"I—er, yes—I suppose it probably is." He watched the neat little head as it moved among the milling, jabbering crush. The raven hair caught glints of light, and once he heard her laugh.

"Ooh, look out!" shrilled Gusher.

He found he was spilling his drink on the carpet and pulled himself together.

"Very n-noisy, isn't it?"

"I love it. So friendly, I always think."

"Oh." He could no longer see the hair nor hear her laugh.

Her voice had been small and like a child's. Her nose short and upturned, the eyes of a blue, dark as the summer sea. He thought there had been a minute mole on her cheek.

"Ooh, you've done it again." The glass had emptied itself on to the floor. Round him the noise reached a peak of parrot chatter.

"Ah, there's Lavinia Lightbody, I simply *must* speak to her." Gusher moved off. Gair stood in a coma, the noise battering at his ears surging over him.

"Have another olive," said the little childish voice.

Gair returned to camp by train, overshot his station and spent the greater part of the night shunting to and fro across Southern England. But those hours of cold empty compartments meant nothing to him. He changed when told to, otherwise he sat like Toad, in a sort of happy trance, careless of what went on around him.

Within the space of a few minutes, in the smoky hurly-burly of a cocktail party, he had fallen more hopelessly, more helplessly in love than ever before in his life. And all he knew about her was that her name was Georgina.

Inspection time was drawing near and putting Colony Camp into an absolute furore. The smallest suspicion of any useful occupation was suspended for an orgy of polishing, whitewashing and painting. Everything was painted, in every direction the eye was blinded by a sea of Brigade colours, red and blue, in stripes, in roundels, in blobs and splashes.

The little patches of lawn outside the Company Offices were rolled and trimmed and shaved. Where there wasn't paint there was whitewash, if no whitewash then polish. Men rushed hither and thither with mops and rags and scrubbers, barrack-room. Fill the fire buckets with burnished grains of sand! The Great Panjandrum's on his way.

The battalion on parade. Large cars drew up and disgorged a scintillating throng. A scarlet cap band brilliant in the warm sunshine. Each company inspected, the general, affable and sharp-eyed, walking steadily up and down the ranks, speaking to a man here and there. A band playing selections of light music: 'Oom pa-pa, oom pa-pa.'

"Why has that man got no magazine in his rifle?" Gair was thinking of Georgina and how the curls of hair showed so black against the whiteness of her neck. Jerking himself from heaven he almost said: 'Why don't you ask him?'

"Where's your m-magazine?" The guardsman, a cherub-faced lad stared owlishly, a droplet of sweat ran down his nose.

"Ah doan't know, sir, it must 'ave fallen out."

"Sergeant-Major, put him in the report, m-magazine deficient."

"Yeher!" The entourage which wound like a glittering snake behind the general wrote in note-books with small fountain-pens. A man in the rear platoon fainted.

"Quite a good turn-out, Major Mainwaring, a few hairs need cutting but the boots were excellent." Gair saluted. Anyway he had at least achieved 'excellent boots.' Fame at last! His day was made! With perseverance he might make the peace-time grade. That, however, was not the opinion of those who ruled.

"Major Mainwaring, your hair's a disgrace."

"Your brasses, Major Mainwaring."

"Wound stripes will no longer be worn, Major Mainwaring." The mark of the leper, perhaps. But these pinpricks, so necessary for the maintenance of discipline, no longer worried him. Whatever he was doing, whoever was nagging, he had his small private joy which made him want to smile, to burst suddenly into uncontrolled song.

Cheerfully he listened to the many and varied complaints, about his dress, his marching on the square, his carefree attitude, heard with but a fraction of an ear the profound inanities uttered from the mess armchairs, bore patiently with a myriad unamusing jokes, retiring when hard-pressed into the secret shell of his new-found love.

The months of high summer were filled for Gair with such supreme happiness that at times he felt suddenly afraid, as if a chill had entered into the hot sunshine; afraid that such perfection could not last, was not meant to last.

In Georgina, he found everything for which he had been searching. Sympathy, understanding and love. When he was with her he felt at peace and no longer at loggerheads with the world, with himself. From her love he drew strength and encouragement to continue in what had become a pointless drudgery. He even tried to be smart.

No longer did he rail and bite his nails in paroxysms of frustration when he saw the hours wasted, the company parading in the roadway with tunics over their arms, spare boots beside them, for yet another inspection.

Life was fragrant, a thing of blossom and beauty. Every day feather-light, filled with sunbeams and at the end of every day throughout three glorious months was the radiant, enchanting Georgina.

Nothing previous to those months had ever really happened. Like the uncertain figures of an already fading dream, ghosts from another life passed briefly through his mind. Sergeant Garner, Sheffield with the spats, Trained Soldier Russell; Anthony loaded with marching order on the day he left the Tower. Colonel Andy, Herbert Finch and his cigars. Johnnie. Helen, Denise, but no clearer than the others. The Mother Superior in Capri. Reed dying on Natale, funny, he could never forget that death. David; the German officer near Colle. Rows of half-remembered faces. Men he knew and liked. Nisbett, Simpson, Forsythe, Corporal Rowley. Luchino, the guide at Brolio. McPhee, the patient, loyal McPhee. And all the other guardsmen, patient and loyal, whom at one time or another he had been privileged to lead. Tessa. She was the only one who still remained, a link between the past that had contained so much pain, so much sorrow and yet so much laughter, and a future which stretched, a golden road into the distance.

Gair patted her head, she snuffled her nose into the palm of his hand. Her muzzle was very grey.

He began to change. Georgina was waiting.

"Same time in the morning, McPhee."

"Beg pardon, sir."

"Oh, sorry, Budgett, I was m-miles away."

"Shoes or boots, sir?"

"Shoes, I think." A bugle sounded. Tessa grunted and sighed.

"Good-night, sir."

"Good-night, Budgett."

It was a warm still evening, the smell of the limes hung heavy in the air, white-flannelled officers were playing tennis and guardsmen strolled in gym shoes to the NAAFI. Gair waited for the taxi to the station. So this is the end of the journey, in this peaceful backwater, pattering along, playing at soldiers. Well, at last I'm quite content. I'm in a rut and do not want to leave it. He wondered what Georgina would be wearing.

Two days later he was warned for Malaya.